The Green Ghost
and other stories

The Green Ghost
and other stories

Edited by Mary Danby

ARMADA

The Green Ghost and other stories
was first published in Armada in 1989

Armada is an imprint of the Children's Division,
part of the Collins Publishing Group,
8 Grafton Street, London W1X 3LA

Printed and bound in Great Britain by
William Collins Sons & Co. Ltd, Glasgow

CONTENTS

ACKNOWLEDGEMENTS

The following are the copyright owners of the stories used in this book:

Terry Tapp: *The Green Ghost* (© 1979), *The Junk Room* (© 1982), *The Doll* ((© 1978), and *The Day I Died* ((© 1981).

Rita Morris: *Hallowe'en* © 1983).

Rosemary Timperley: *The Sinister Schoolmaster* ((© 1978), *The Murderous Ghosts* ((© 1977), *Stella* ((© 1979), and *The Thing That Went Bump in the Night* ((© 1981).

Sydney J. Bounds: *Spirit of the Trail* ((© 1983), *Hunters' Hill* ((© 1978), *The Train Watchers* ((© 1982), and *The Haunted Circus* ((© 1977).

Alison Prince: *The Baby-Sitter* ((©1981), *The Servant* (© 1983), and *Can't Help Laughing* ((© 1982).

Tony Richards: *The Sound of Sirens* ((© 1983), *The Girl in the Cellar* ((© 1981), and *Someone Drowned* ((© 1980).

Ken Burke: *Dance of Death* (© 1981), and *The Return of the Lorelei* ((© 1981).

Catherine Gleason: *The Woodseaves Ghosts* ((© 1976), *The Longest Journey* ((© 1982), *House of Glass* ((© 1976), and *The Post Room* ((© 1978)

Mary Danby: *The Grey Lady* ((© 1978), and *The Ghost Writer* ((© 1982).

Joyce Marsh: *The Shepherd's Dog* ((© 1975), *Sir Harry Mortlake's Clock* ((© 1976), and *The Warning* ((© 1978).

Daphne Froome: *This Book Belongs To . . .* ((© 1979), and *Lisa* ((© 1977).

Roger Malisson: *Sarah* ((© 1976).

Ruth Cameron: *A Red, Red Rose* ((© 1976), and *The Ghostly Gardeners* ((© 1979).

Alan W. Lear: *Whoever Heard of a Haunted Lift?* ((© 1983).

John Duncan: *Child of the Future* ((© 1977).

Ann Pilling: *Gibson's* ((© 1982).

9

R. Chetwynd-Hayes: *The Third Eye* (© 1982).

THE GREEN GHOST

by Terry Tapp

Of one thing Emma Finch was absolutely certain: there is a life after death. She knew this as surely as she knew that night followed day, and she was quietly happy with her knowledge. Furthermore, Emma believed in ghosts. She believed in good ghosts and bad ghosts, and she most certainly believed in the Green Ghost that haunted Brampton Hall. What Emma did not know – and she intended to rectify that within the next few minutes – was whether Brampton Hall was *still* haunted by the Green Ghost of her childhood memories. After all, a lot can happen in eighty years.

Trudging up the steep, gravel drive to Brampton Hall, Emma was pleasantly surprised to note that the immense Victorian house had lost much of its bleak, forbidding appearance over the years. The bright blue curtains at each window were such a contrast to the deep brown curtains of her own era. And the garden was friendly too; a child's swing, a bicycle and a brightly coloured beach ball persuaded her that Brampton Hall was now a happy family home.

Now Emma stood before the massive oak door of Brampton Hall, her jaw set resolutely as she gripped the lion-head doorknocker and clamped it hard against the iron spike. Still holding the doorknocker, reluctant to let go of it, her mind spanned the years back to the time when people came to Brampton Hall on horseback, or in fine coaches. How many hands, she wondered, have gripped this very doorknocker?

Emma was about to knock again when she noticed a new bell-push set into the door jamb; she pressed it once. The resulting pandemonium caused her to jump back from the door in alarm. Two gigantic, hairy, barking, bounding, rollicking, shapeless dogs skidded joyfully around the house to greet her.

"Oh!" Emma cried. "Down, boys. You'll get my coat dirty."

She pressed the bell again, twice this time, her eyes fixed on the dogs as they barked and scampered around her, darting in at her legs, then turning away at the very last moment.

With some relief she heard the door bolt slide back and she smiled at the little girl who stood there, thumb in mouth, a scowl upon her pretty young face.

"Hello," said Emma. "Is your daddy or mummy at home?"

The child stared vacantly at her.

"Well?" Emma gave the girl an encouraging smile. "Are they?"

The child considered the question awhile, appeared to make some decision, and slammed the door hard in Emma's face, causing the two dogs, who had been watching events with pricked ears, to jump to their feet and set up a terrible row. After what seemed like a lifetime all over again, the door opened and the girl reappeared, thumb still wedged in her mouth.

"Yes," she said. "Mummy is here."

"I wonder if I might have a word with her."

Thumbsucker considered that question, too, as if everything Emma said demanded the utmost thought. Suddenly, without warning, she removed her thumb from her mouth and shouted at the top of her voice: "Mummy! There's an old lady here and she wants to talk to you!"

"An old lady?" That was a boy's voice.

"What – a witch?" A younger boy shouted that.

"No," said Thumbsucker. "She isn't a witch. She's just very, very old."

By now the two boys had clattered down the stairs and were standing before Emma, inspecting her with the unashamed curiosity children sometimes display.

"What does she want?" asked the smaller boy.

"Dunno," said Thumbsucker.

Then the dogs started barking again, bored with listening to human conversation. The two boys let out earpiercing whoops and shot from the doorway like arrows, chasing the delighted dogs back around the house where they had come from.

As Emma turned back to face Thumbsucker, she saw a young woman hurrying towards the door, wiping her hands on her apron.

"What is it?" she asked.

"This old woman," said Thumbsucker. "She wants you for something."

"Really!" The child's mother made an exasperated face. Then smiled at Emma. "Sorry to have kept you waiting – I didn't know if there was really someone at the door, or if she was playing a trick."

"Lovely children," Emma said.

"Lovely, *rude* children," was the reply. "I do apologize for their bad manners."

"Please, don't apologize," said Emma. "They are right, you know – I *am* an old lady. Sometimes I have to be reminded of the fact."

They both laughed at that, and then Emma explained the reason for her visit. "I would, very much, like to look over Brampton Hall again."

"Again?"

"Yes, I used to live here."

"Oh, really?"

"My entire childhood was spent in this very house, and it would be nice to view it."

The young woman looked puzzled. "View? Brampton Hall is not for sale, you know."

"I realize that," Emma said. "Anyway, I couldn't afford it even if it *was* for sale. What would I do with a large place like this to keep up?"

"Well, perhaps you had better come inside," said the woman. "My name is Jean Williams, by the way."

"I'm Miss Finch," Emma said. "Miss Emma Finch."

She stepped into the hallway and stared around her. The place had hardly changed at all over the years; it was uncanny. She breathed in the rich, lingering woody smell as she surveyed the carved wall panels. Suddenly, she was a child again, as she relived the memories so vividly. She could hear the laughter and the household noises of her childhood as plainly as if they were happening that very moment. Games of tag along the corridors, the sweet, enticing aroma of spiced cooking. It was all returning, unharmed by the voyage of years. Now she could see the rosy-faced cook, wide-eyed and smiling with pride as she carried the platter of Christmas meats, the pert faces of the two young housemaids watching the proceedings, yet struggling to keep hidden. Emma had adored the maids.

Now there was the smell of apples and woodsmoke, evoking autumn and shortening days. When Emma looked at the parlour door, she could almost hear the low, grumbling conversation of her father. What a serious man he was.

"Miss Finch?"

Emma looked at the young woman in mild surprise.

"You may have a look around if you wish," said Mrs Williams with a smile. "I've been talking to you – but you were miles away."

"Was I?" Then Emma realized that she had been so

14

absorbed in her memories, she had lost track of the present. "Yes, I suppose I was. It really is quite an exhilarating experience returning to Brampton Hall. I had such a happy childhood here."

Mrs Williams smiled. "Is this the first time you have seen Brampton Hall since your childhood?"

"The first time I have been inside," said Emma. "I have, on many occasions, passed by and glanced up the driveway, not daring to knock at the door."

"Well, you feel free to walk around as you please. You must forgive the children's bedrooms. I have told them that they must keep their own rooms tidy and, I'm afraid, they aren't very good at it yet. I'm determined to let the rooms go until they learn their lesson."

"I'm sorry if I have called at an inconvenient time," Emma said.

"It's no trouble."

"You are very kind."

"If you will excuse me, then . . ." said Mrs Williams, making for the stairs. "I really do have a lot of work to get through." Emma nodded absently, already absorbed in memories.

"I'll be in the kitchen," Mrs Williams told her. "And if the children start to make nuisances of themselves, send them to me."

"I will," Emma promised. "Thank you."

Standing on the bottom tread of the wide, twisting staircase, Emma looked up at the stained-glass windows, recalling how, on a bright summer day, the sun would tumble through the coloured glass and light up the whole hall like a carnival. She smiled, happy that the memories had not faded with the years; in fact, if anything, the memories had been enhanced by the passing of time. Once again she placed her gloved hand on the polished balustrade and then, on impulse, removed the glove so that she could feel the hard, enduring wood.

Slowly, savouring every step like a fine meal, Emma walked up the staircase, memories flooding in on her so fast that she had, at times, to stop and wait until the kaleidoscope of faces and events had settled in her mind. Each step disturbed the dusts of forgetfulness, and she was amazed at the things which she was able to remember, amazed and delighted.

There had been no major structural changes in the old house, and Emma was able to locate the rooms confidently. She turned at the top of the stairs, walked along to the far end of the narrow corridor which led to the servants' annexe and decided to explore the east wing first. The door of the master bedroom was ajar. Emma tapped gently, waited for a reply and, when there was none, she stepped into the room, her heart pounding against her ribs.

Full circle, Emma thought. Return to the birthplace.

The room was bathed in mellow, yellow sunlight which splashed the walls and furniture like butter. It was, Emma considered, miraculous how little the room had changed in appearance. The Italian marble fireplace still looked new, and the ornate ceiling was as perfect now as it was in her memory. Apart from the addition of some rather bright wallpaper and several pictures, the room was timeless and unchanged.

"What are you looking for?"

Emma wheeled around, startled at the unexpected intrusion of the child's voice. Thumbsucker was standing in the doorway, her thumb still lodged in her mouth.

"I'm not looking *for* anything," said Emma. "I'm looking *at* things."

"What are you looking at?"

"Everything," Emma replied. "I just want to look at

16

everything and remember how the house used to be. You know, apart from the fact that we had oil lighting, then gaslight, the house is much the same as when I was your age."

"Gaslight?"

"Yes," said Emma. "We used to have a centre light in this room and wall brackets over there." She indicated the far wall.

"Do you want to see my room?" Thumbsucker asked.

Emma smiled at her; she was a pretty child, about seven years old, with small, rather pert features.

"I would love to see your room," she said. "Lead the way."

The little girl removed her thumb from her mouth and offered her hand to Emma, who pretended not to notice; she certainly did not want to hold that sticky, wet little hand. From the master bedroom, they went out to the corridor, along the landing above the stairs until they reached the four smaller bedrooms. "This is mine," said Thumbsucker, kicking the door open with her foot.

"How lovely!" Emma cried, thinking exactly the opposite. The room was a jumble of toys, books, dolls and clothes. "My, this is a bright little room." She had to tread most carefully in order to avoid treading on the toys which were strewn across the floor.

"I fink it's awful," Thumbsucker said. "Mummy says she won't tidy it up for me."

"Quite right, too."

"But it's in such a mess."

"And who made it into such a mess?" Emma asked, trying to keep a straight face.

"It jus' happened," Thumbsucker replied. "Do you like my wallpaper?"

Following the young girl's gaze, Emma surveyed the psychedelic paper which covered the chimney breast. It was a brightly coloured paper, screaming, sickening, gaudy and busy-looking. "It is very – unusual," Emma said, feeling almost giddy as she groped for the edge of the bed. "Yes, very unusual indeed."

"Robin chose it for himself," Thumbsucker said. "He got Daddy to buy the paper."

"Did Robin used to sleep here?"

"Only for a while," said Thumbsucker. "Then he got scared, and I had to sleep here."

"Scared?"

Thumbsucker nodded vigorously.

"What was he scared of?"

"Ghosts," the child replied. "Robin is scared of ghosts."

"And he thought there were ghosts in this room?"

"There *was* a ghost here," Thumbsucker said. "Robin saw it and he cried."

"Have you seen it?" Emma asked, trying to keep her voice as calm as possible.

"I saw it – once."

"Were you frightened?" Now Emma was excited. Was it possible that Thumbsucker had seen the ghost of her childhood? It was very important to Emma to know the answer. But the child was engrossed in rummaging through her toys, apparently having lost all interest in the conversation. Determined to get an answer, Emma reached down and lifted the child on to her lap.

"You went a funny colour when you lifted me," Thumbsucker observed seriously.

"I expect I did," Emma said. "Sometimes I forget myself and do things which I ought not to do."

"So do I," Thumbsucker said confidently. "Yesterday I made a cake in the kitchen and Mummy told me off for making a mess."

"How long ago did you see the ghost?" Emma asked.

"Last year."

18

"I would be most interested to hear all about it," Emma said, trying very hard to conceal her impatience. "Would you like to tell me the story, starting from the very beginning?"

Thumbsucker gazed up at the ceiling as if searching for inspiration, her face creased in concentration. Sucking hard on her thumb, the girl started to speak. Emma gently took her wrist and pulled the thumb from the girl's mouth so she could hear what she was saying.

"You got bony knees," Thumbsucker told her, with the candid truthfulness of the very young.

"Yes, I know," Emma said. "But you must tell me about the ghost. It is very important to me."

"Well, it all started when Robin asked Daddy for this wallpaper," Thumbsucker said. Emma listened as the child related the tale, interrupting now and then to make quite sure that she had heard correctly, for Thumbsucker kept pushing her thumb back into her mouth out of habit.

It seemed that Robin had set his heart on the bedroom as soon as they had moved in, because he wanted to make it into his private den. Against his own better judgement, Mr Williams had promised Robin that he might choose his own decorations, and the result of that had been the psychedelic wallpaper. But, within a few days of moving into the room, Robin had started to complain of funny noises and voices which kept him awake at nights.

"The room is haunted," Robin told his father.

Mr Williams would not hear of such a thing. "Nonsense," he had told Robin sternly. "There are no such things as ghosts."

Thumbsucker had, of course, been enchanted by tales of hauntings and she had begged Robin to exchange rooms with her.

"But didn't the thought of seeing a ghost frighten you?" Emma asked.

"I *wanted* to see him," said Thumbsucker.

"So you exchanged rooms with Robin. What happened next?"

Thumbsucker began to tell the story of her first night in the room, and Emma listened eagerly, remembering the nights that she had spent in that very room. It was uncanny how very similar the stories were.

"After I had kissed Mummy goodnight, I tried to go to sleep right away," said Thumbsucker, her face rumpled with deep frowns as she concentrated. "It was hard getting to sleep in a new room, and I kept waking up because there were funny noises going on. I had to sleep in Robin's old bed and it's got all lumps in it and his pillow is harder than mine. I stayed awake for hours. I even heard Daddy and Mummy come up to bed."

"My!" said Emma. "That must have been very late indeed."

"It was," said Thumbsucker. "Anyway, that's when the green smoke came."

"Green smoke?" Emma asked, her voice trembling with excitement.

"Yes, green smoke. I was looking over at Bunnylite when I suddenly saw green smoke drifting up from my bed."

"Good gracious!" Emma said. "What did you do?"

"I was frightened at first. I thought my bed was on fire. Then the smoke sort of hung in the air and I could see a green light in the very centre of it."

"Luminous," said Emma.

"The green light got brighter and brighter, lighting up the room until it was brighter than Bunnylite. Through the mistiness, I thought I could see a face. Then, after a while, the face became clearer and I could see that it was an old, old man. He was even older than you."

"Then he must have been very ancient," Emma said without a trace of a smile.

"The old man had a green face and it was covered with warts," Thumbsucker said, her eyes wide open as she recalled the horrible apparition. "He was screaming at me, his eyes alight like fire."

"The Green Ghost of Brampton Hall," Emma whispered, but Thumbsucker was too immersed in her story to hear.

"It was cold, even in my bed, and I could see that the ghost was coming for me. I wanted to hide my head under the bedclothes, but I was too scared. He laughed, showing all his bad teeth, and when his mouth was opened wide I could see that, instead of a tongue, he had a snake!"

"A snake?" cried Emma, holding Thumbsucker close for comfort as if she were a doll. How many times had she seen that precise nightmarish face?

"It was a snake, coiling in the ghost's mouth, hissing at me. The ghost came nearer until his face was almost touching mine and then he opened his mouth again and the snake slid out, over his chin, and dangled in front of my face. I cried."

"I know," said Emma, rocking the child. "I know. It is a truly dreadful thing to see."

"Then he started to grow bigger, laughing all the time. It was as if he had taken a deep breath and his whole body swelled up. He filled up the room with his body and his laughing. His hands were near my face, and his fingers were long and knobbly, with nails like claws. The nails were bright red."

But Emma wasn't even listening now; she had become absorbed in her own memories of the evil ghost. She, too, felt the chill and the dank, cold clamminess as she recalled those terrible nights when the Green Ghost had haunted Brampton Hall.

"Then his talons touched my face," Emma said, completely oblivious of the fact that she had interrupted Thumbsucker. "His talons bore down on me, burning and scratching. And his eyes! They were bright, like emeralds, and so very, very evil." Emma was living her childhood again. She could see the malevolent, fluorescent face as it leered at her; she could feel those burning claws and smell the cold, dank smell of decaying food. "So he is still here," she said, realizing that she was frightening Thumbsucker.

"No."

"What do you mean?"

"He frightened me, so I sent him packing."

"How did you manage to do that?"

"Well, I thought it was very clever the way he kept changing shape, but I didn't like the funder."

"Funder?"

"Yes, it was loud funder and there wasn't any lightning."

"Ah – thunder," Emma said.

"It was very loud – much louder than his laughing. The noise was making my room shake, and I got scared in case Daddy thought it was me making all the noise. I get blamed for everything around here."

Emma smiled. "Do you, indeed?"

"That's when I told him to buzz off."

"You told the Green Ghost of Brampton Hall to buzz off?"

"Yes," said Thumbsucker. "I told him that he was making too much noise. So he went."

"What? You mean he just disappeared?"

"He sort of melted," said Thumbsucker thoughtfully. "It was like butter on toast. His green face seemed to melt and the smoke became thinner until he was all gone."

"How very brave of you," Emma said.

"I still don't understand why he just went when I told him to."

"You probably shamed him into it," said Emma. "Hurt his professional pride, no doubt. Nothing could be more demoralizing for a ghost than to be told to buzz off. Now, think very, very carefully. Have you ever seen him since?"

"No. He hasn't been back."

"How about other ghosts?"

"Other ghosts?"

"Ys. Have you ever seen a different ghost to the Green Ghost of Brampton Hall?"

"No," Thumbsucker said. "Do you think there will be one?"

"I shouldn't be surprised at all," Emma said. "Usually a house is visited by just one ghost, but if he disappears another ghost may sometimes take his place."

"I haven't seen one," Thumbsucker said.

"You are sure?"

"Yes. I would know if I had."

"Of course you would," said Emma. "Of course."

She got up from the bed, a smile upon her face, her eyes alight with happiness. "So the Green Ghost has gone at last."

"Come on," said Thumbsucker. "I'll show you the rest of the house. Would you like to see Robin's room?"

"Yes, that would be nice."

"After that we can see Philip's room, and then I can show you Daddy's study."

Emma followed the child, drinking in the memories as she entered each room. Everything – everything that mattered – was substantially the same. The house was still alive with people, and the bricks and slates were still there. The floors were the same floors which she, as a child, had scampered across. Even the fifth stair from the top still creaked loudly when trodden on. Somehow Emma had the feeling that Brampton Hall was indestructible; built before she was born, it would still be there, strong and immovable, long after she was dead and forgotten. It was a monument, in brick and stone, to Emma's happy childhood. Yes, Brampton Hall would endure to see many generations come and go.

It was a satisfying thought.

"I hope she isn't bothering you," said Mrs Williams, appearing suddenly at the foot of the stairs. "I could hear her chattering away all the time."

"On the contrary," said Emma. "We have had a most interesting discussion."

"And I haven't been naughty," Thumbsucker added.

Emma started down the stairs, smiling as her foot touched the fifth one from the top. "You have been most kind to allow me this visit. I have enjoyed it so much."

"You are welcome," Mrs Williams replied. "Now you must come into the kitchen and have a cup of tea. I've just made a fresh pot."

So they went into the big, warm kitchen, and Emma was delighted to see that the old kitchen range was still in use, sparkling as brightly as ever it did when she was young. The thick, crackling logs burned red and cosy, sending busy flames up to the massive iron kettle which sang and sighed in ecstasy. The whole house breathed contentment.

"Well?" asked Mrs Williams. "Do you still like your old home?"

"I love it," Emma said fervently. "It will do very nicely indeed, I am sure of that."

"Do?" asked Mrs Williams.

"Oh, yes. Very nicely indeed," Emma replied absently. "Especially now that the Green Ghost is gone."

"Green Ghost? Ah, you've been listening to make-believe stories," said Mrs Williams as she poured out a cup of tea and offered Emma a plate of home-made cakes.

They talked for nearly an hour, Emma delighting Mrs Williams with her reminiscences. When it was time for Emma to leave, she insisted on giving Thumbsucker fifty pence for telling her about the Green Ghost. "I am so glad he has gone," she said.

"Please come again," Mrs Williams said as she saw Emma to the door. "I enjoyed hearing about Brampton Hall as it was all those years ago."

"I will," Emma promised. "I'd love to come again."

But Emma never did return to Brampton Hall to delight Mrs Williams with more stories of her childhood. She waved goodbye and trudged back down the crunchy gravel drive, her heart beating excitedly. She smiled, turned and waved and was gone.

Some months later, as Thumbsucker lay upon her bed, in the throes of sticking Christmas cards into her scrap book, Emma came to her and sat on the edge of the bed.

"Where did you come from?" asked Thumbsucker.

"I just came," Emma said happily.

"Do you want to see around the house again?"

"No, thank you," Emma replied. "I've come to stay, this time. I'm going to stay here for ever and ever."

"Until you die?" asked Thumbsucker.

"Until I get told to buzz off," Emma replied with a twinkle in her eye.

"I wouldn't ever tell you to buzz off," Thumbsucker said. "I like having you here."

"That is nice to hear," Emma replied. "I'll try very hard not to make a nuisance of myself." Then she rose from the bed, crossed the room and floated straight through the bedroom door.

HALLOWE'EN

by Rita Morris

Alan was alone in the graveyard.

He was skulking just inside the gates, behind a wire rubbish pin piled high with withered wreaths. Their brown leaves rustled in the bitter wind. He was waiting for his friend Tommo to join him for their annual Hallowe'en tour of the graveyard, and he had every intention of jumping out from behind the heap to frighten Tommo as he came through the gates. It was traditional. He did it every year.

But minutes passed, and Tommo did not come. Slowly the red sky faded behind the old church. The air was noisy with the twittering of birds settling for the night in the bell tower. Darkness collected on the uneven grass and among the tilted gravestones, while a steady, piercing wind blew dust towards him up the hill and along the tarmac path. Alan wished it wasn't so perishing cold, and that Tommo would turn up soon. He must have been waiting here for *hours*.

In the black tower overhead the heavy bells chimed five: a mournful sound. There was a sinister rattle near his feet as the wind flipped a wreath off the heap and sent it skittering along the path.

"Come *on*, Tommo!"

Alan cursed quietly to himself and jogged up to the church porch, noiseless as a ghost in his sneakers. His toes were numb. He had never been so cold in his life. Whose daft idea had it been to come here every Hallowe'en anyway, his or Tommo's? He couldn't remember.

He only knew they'd been daring each other to come here every year since they were seven. Other kids dressed up and traipsed round from house to house, knocking on the doors for sweets; Alan and Tommo braved the churchyard. It was known to be haunted – well the church was, anyway – and Alan's own granny had told him of the time she'd been woken in the middle of the night by the sound of the church bell, tolling steadily. That was how they rang the bell for deaths. But whose hand had rung it in the hours of darkness, when every living soul was asleep? No, the churchyard was haunted all right, and every kid with a grain of sense steered well clear of it on Hallowe'en. Except Alan and Tommo of course, who weren't scared of anything.

"Waitin' for someone?"

The sound of that hoarse voice coming so unexpectedly from the deep shadows of the porch made Alan's heart jump into his mouth. He stood poised, ready to run, as a hump-shouldered figure shuffled awkwardly towards him and into the dim light of the overhead lamp.

Alan let out his breath in a sigh of relief. Only old Alice the tramp. Suppose he'd run yelling like a scared little kid from smelly Alice, and Tommo had copped him doing it? Tommo would never have let him live it down.

"Frightened you, did I?" The old woman chuckled richly to herself, fat shoulders heaving under her grubby mac. Beneath the frayed and fluttering headscarf her face was invisible in shadow.

"No."

Alan spoke loudly but she went on chuckling anyway, coughing to a stop at last. She came stooping across to one of the larger graves, a flat stone the size of a table, and sank down on it, hauling the two plastic carrier bags she trailed everywhere with her up on to the grave beside her. The lamp was now shining on her face. It was a soft,

27

withered old face with tiny sharp eyes, like the face of a fat schoolgirl who had somehow grown old without growing up.

"That's right," she said. "Nothing to be afraid of, is there? For all it's a graveyard on Hallowe'en. You're not scared of ghosts, though?"

"Not me." boasted Alan, shoving his cold hands deep in his jacket pockets. "I've lived here all my life."

"In a graveyard?" she cried, eyes widening.

Alan gave her a look; you could do that with Old Alice, you didn't have to be as careful with her as you did with ordinary adults.

"Where?" she asked, persistent. "Where d'you live now?"

"Up there." He jerked his head to where a row of orange street lamps showed beyond the graveyard wall. "Church Road."

"Ah." She nodded wisely to herself for a minute, tapping the back of one fat hand with the other. "Ah."

You ought to know, thought Alan rudely to himself; you've seen me often enough. And it was true, for Old Alice seemed to have a fondness for the graveyard, and she frequently hung around there – when she wasn't rummaging through the rubbish bins in the supermarket car park down town. It was even rumoured she slept there on fine summer nights. Alan had often seen her as he cut through the churchyard to get to the shops at the bottom of the hill, but she had never spoken to him before. Alice was a crazy woman – not simple, like the children at the special school near the hospital, but *crazy* – and she only ever talked to herself. She was a harmless old soul, said Alan's mum; not that she looked harmless now. A witch she looked, with her dirty face creased in wrinkles and her small, cruel, curious eyes.

"I'm waiting for a mate," said Alan, and turned his

back on her to check the gates again. "Tommo, come *on!*"

"Well he won't come looking for you here."

"He will," Alan answered with perfect certainty. "We do it every year. We always meet up for a game on Hallowe'en."

"He'll be afraid."

Her mouth fell open and she laughed again, showing one yellow tooth poking up out of a shiny gum. Alan turned away quickly, sickened.

"He won't be scared," he muttered. "Not Tommo. Me and him are best mates."

And it was true, though they were not much alike – Tommo was quiet and rather clever, and Alan good at games. But they were always together, closer than brothers, and had been since primary school when they had sat in the same class, Alan Chantler in the front row and Neil Tomlinson right behind. It had been Alan and Tommo ever since.

A great stillness was dropping over the churchyard now as the sky lost its final blue and became black. Despite the nearness of Old Alice, Alan felt with a shiver how lonely it could be up here. The square bulk of the unlit church loomed behind them like a beached ship; clustering trees at the graveyard's edge stood out against the orange gloom of the street beyond. Alan had a sudden weird feeling that every object in the churchyard was playing a Hallowe'en game of its own, a sort of Grandmother's Footsteps with him – that if he turned his back the trees and gravestones might shiver into life of a sort and creep up over the dead ground towards him . . .

He began hopping from one foot to the other, whistling soundlessly through his teeth, banging his fists against his ribs. The stars were coming out, bright and frosty overhead; it would be a bitter night.

"Cold, are you?" said Old Alice comfortably. "I don't feel the cold any more, me."

She shifted her large bottom on its stone seat and began tracing the letters cut into the sooty surface of the grave. Nearly all the stones in the churchyard were old, and covered with a kind of furry grime.

"There's eleven of them in here," she said thoughtfully. "All one family. Big families in those days."

Alan ignored her and trotted up the path to the iron gates to peer out anxiously, but Church Road was empty. There was no sign of Tommo.

In the front room of his own house the light came on, and his sister Debbie sat herself down at the table near the window, homework spread in front of her, chin on hand. Little swot . . . Of course! thought Alan, *that* would be what was keeping Tommo! As a friend he had only one fault, which was that he always did his homework before coming out in the evening. Alan, on the other hand, never did; he copied his from Tommo every morning on the bus.

"Makes you wonder how they'll sort themselves out on Judgement Day, doesn't it?"

"What?" Alan scowled back, irritated. He had almost forgotten Alice was there. He wished she'd shove off.

"On Judgement Day," she answered patiently, smiling at him and patting the stone. "You know – when the dead people rise from their graves."

Was she trying to throw a scare into him? Alan would show her it wouldn't work.

"Yeah, very tricky," he said. "Be like trying to resurrect a tin of sardines."

And then, to show her how boring her conversation was, he turned his back again.

"Hear about the accident?" she asked suddenly. Alan slouched slowly back, unwilling to show he was interested;

30

but he liked accidents. He had once had the great pleasure of seeing a goods train derailed.

"Somebody got run over," Alice said. She leaned towards him a little, her old face crafty. *I know something you don't know*, it said. *Ask me*.

"Where?" He made the question a yawn.

"Supermarket. Car Park. Young lad, it was."

She sat back looking pleased with herself, and more cunning than ever; whatever it was she was so proud of knowing, she hadn't told all of it yet.

"Who?" asked Alan, really intrigued now.

She almost giggled.

"Don't know his name. He lived up there, though." She nodded towards Church Road.

For a second Alan stood bewildered, and then he felt the hair on his scalp prickle and the blood draw slowly out of his cheeks. Tommo lived on Church Road, three doors down from him. They were the only boys on the street.

He whirled and ran towards the gates, and at the very moment he started to run through them he saw with inexpressible relief the bedroom light go on in Tommo's house, and Tommo himself come across to the window and draw the curtains shut. He looked preoccupied, almost sad, but very much alive. A wave of thankfulness swept over Alan; and then he became aware by a chuckle behind him that Old Alice was watching him closely, as if enjoying the effect of her Hallowe'en joke.

For a minute Alan stood without knowing what to say, and then he burst out with appalling and unusual rudeness:

"You toothless old bag! You don't know anything – you just make things up! You're crazy, you are. Everybody knows that. You walk around talking to people who aren't there. And you *stink*!"

31

For a second she sat facing him, rigid with shock, and then she got to her feet and, without a word, walked away from him down the hill, her two plastic shopping bags slurring and bumping along the ground as she went. Alan stared after her, alarmed by his own rudeness, but secretly comforted to think that being cheeky to Old Alice wasn't as risky as being cheeky to another adult. He could hardly imagine her knocking at his father's door to complain. Anyway – she had no right to go making up that lie about Tommo.

"You're just a smelly old liar!" he shouted after her for good measure. "Crazy Alice, Crazy Alice!"

"And you're a fool!" She turned her face back over her shoulder, twisting to snarl at him. "You didn't ask *when* it happened, did you? Two months ago it was!"

Alan laughed aloud.

"You're stupid," he said. "You're crazy! I've just seen him!"

Just as he thought she had really gone her voice floated up to him from the shadows at the foot of the hill.

"I shan't speak to you again, young man."

"Who wants you to?" yelled Alan rudely, and giggled with nerves.

There was a baleful pause.

"You'll be glad of me to talk to, soon enough."

He heard her slithering footsteps near the far gate and then a moment later saw her slow, bent old figure under the lights of the main road, heading for the town centre, creeping away like a fat old snail.

"Stupid old witch!" called Alan – but not too loudly, in case his father over the road heard him.

It was fully dark now; the last glow had gone from the sky. The birds had fallen quiet. Alan waited shivering under the porch light, wondering what to do. Maybe Tommo wasn't coming; maybe he'd got stuck with his homework. Perhaps they were getting too old for this game, anyway. Maybe it was time to go home.

At the thought of home Alan suddenly felt frozen stiff, lonely and tired. He started up the churchyard path again, towards the lights of his own front room where his sister was turning the page of her exercise book, flattening it down with her thumbnail . . . Coming here on Hallowe'en had been a silly idea. Tommo was right not to bother. He would tell him so in the morning.

The windblown wreath was lying on the path in front of his feet as he came to the gates and he stooped to throw it in the bin with the rest. There was a label attached to the dead flowers, the writing nearly washed away by the rain, but somehow it seemed familiar. Was that Tommo's writing? Alan screwed up his eyes and stared, but it took him a minute to puzzle out what it said.

To Alan, it said, *from Tommo. Best mates.*

THE SINISTER SCHOOLMASTER

by Rosemary Timperley

Peter wanted to go to the Comprehensive School because most of his friends in the area were going there. His mother, however, wanted him to go to a small, private school, where he'd get "individual attention". His father kept quiet and left mother and son to fight it out.

"I don't want 'individual attention'," Peter said. "I'd rather be one of the mob. I don't mind a bit of roughness, if that's what you're afraid of. If I'm bashed, I can bash back."

"That," said his mother, "is the very attitude I want you to discard. You tend to turn life into a battlefield. This nice little school should make you more gentlemanly."

Peter gave a voiced imitation of someone being violently sick.

"Don't be disgusting!" she snapped. "It's time you were taught some manners."

"They say on the telly that it's parents that's responsible for their children's manners," said Peter, "so if I'm awful it's because of the way I've been upbrung."

"Brought up," she corrected him automatically.

"Why?" said Peter. "You cling, you clung; you ring, you rung; you bring, you brung – "

"You ring, you rang, or you have rung," she corrected him.

"You ding, you dung," he muttered.

"*What* did you say?"

"Nothing."

"I should think so. You start at St Edmund's tomorrow, Peter, and nothing you can say will make me change my mind."

"*Saint* Edmund's," he moaned. "I expect the Head has long white hair with a halo balanced on top." But he knew that the battle was lost. His mother was only a woman, but she was tough as old rope when she set her mind on anything, and she wanted her son to be a "gentleman". It made you sick. He thought longingly of the state school, where his mates were going, and where some of the teachers even looked like human beings. He was full of gloom when he set out next morning for the first day of term.

He got on the bus, wearing his prissy uniform and carrying a small case with pencils, pens, rubber, compasses and similar daft things. The bus-ride took about fifteen minutes, then, "Church Road," the conductor said, and Peter knew that was where he must get off. He alighted, and the friendly old bus trundled away, leaving him alone on the edge of a new world . . .

It was then that the fog descended. It came down suddenly, cold and grey and blanketing, sending a shiver through him. He had been told which way to walk and now began to plod along a road with tall trees on either side. They were menacing, like sentinels. They watched and whispered. Peter was usually quick enough to be brave and defiant when there was something to defy, but in this blind-making fog all he could do was put one foot in front of the other and grow more and more uneasy.

He suddenly felt *afraid* of this new school.

All the same, he was grateful to see a light at last, though it must be a light from the hated school. Yes, there was a driveway, and a building crouching farther on, with one single golden eye glaring at him. It struck him as odd that there was only one light on in the building.

He knew it was a small school, but surely there should be more than one lighted classroom. For the window was that of a classroom, and class had started, so he realized with dismay that he must be late. He could say he was "delayed by the fog", of course, although he hadn't got lost or anything – had he?

He went closer to the window and looked in.

About a dozen boys sat there, in similar uniforms to his own. That meant he'd found the right school, anyway. The boys sat very attentively. They were pale of face and their eyes were scared. The teacher was at the desk in front of them. He was a short, bull-shouldered man with a red face, white hair, which was long at the sides but left a pink "halo" of baldness, top-back of his head. He was gesticulating with his right hand and carried something tucked under his left arm, ready for use.

It was a cane.

He asked a boy a question. The boy answered. Peter couldn't hear what was said, but the teacher gave a wolfish smile and beckoned to the boy, who came out to the front and bent over.

The schoolmaster seized the cane in his right hand, raised it, and brought it down crackingly hard on the boy's bottom. He hit him again, and again, and again, and his expression was joyful.

"Stop that!" shouted Peter.

The class froze. The teacher turned towards the window. Pale grey eyes peered into dark grey fog. Then the man marched across and flung open the window. "Who is that? You – boy – out there – what did you say?"

"I said 'Stop that'," Peter answered.

Thick arms, like a couple of little tree-trunks, shot out of the window and grabbed him by the shoulders. He dropped his case on the grass. He struggled. Useless. He was lugged inside. The window was closed again. Peter was dumped on the classroom floor, the man with the cane looming over him.

A terrible stillness seemed to have descended. The boys were quiet and motionless, seeming hardly to breathe. The man stood like a statue of wrath. Peter had to admit to himself that he was very frightened indeed.

Then the silence was broken. "And who," asked the sinister schoolmaster, "are you?"

"Peter Lorrimer."

"And what are you doing here?"

"I'm a pupil here. It's my first day."

"Your first day – what?"

"My first day being here."

"Your first day being here – what?"

"My first day being here at this school."

"Your first day being here at this school – what?"

"This school called St Edmund's," said Peter.

"This school called St Edmund's – what?"

"A rotten dump!" said Peter.

"Stand up!" Peter stood. "Bend over." Peter bent. Crack! The cane came down on his bottom.

"Did you enjoy that, Peter Lorrimer?"

"No."

"No – what?"

"No. I didn't enjoy it!"

Crack came the cane.

"No, you didn't enjoy it – WHAT?" screamed this maniac.

A whisper from the class: "Ssssay 'ssssir'."

Silence for a moment. The fog thickened outside. The oppressiveness of fear thickened too. Peter felt half-paralyzed in this nightmare. He was full of pain, yet it was a dead sort of pain, felt yet not felt. Weird.

Now the teacher spoke. "There is no pupil called Peter

37

Lorrimer in this school. You are an impostor. Why are you wearing our school uniform?"

"I am a pupil – my mother sent me – "

"Your mother sent you – WHAT?"

"SIR!"

Another swish from the cane.

"That's not fair," said Peter. "I said 'sir'."

"That was for being a liar."

Swish . . .

"And that was for arguing about it. Now go and sit at that desk." Peter obeyed. "Let's see how much you know, you impostor in the uniform of St Edmund's, of which I am proud to be headmaster. I go – I went. I come – " He stopped and waited.

He really is stark raving bonkers, thought Peter. But lunatics must be humoured, so he said hopefully, "You come, *sir*."

"The boy is a half-wit. A dunderhead. I come – " Again he waited.

"Thank you for coming," said Peter, adding a hasty "sir."

"Heaven grant me patience. Listen. I go – I went. I come – "

Light dawned. The silly clot wanted the past tense of "come".

"I came," said Peter.

"I bring."

"I brung."

"You WHAT?"

"I brung, SIR!"

"Brung, brung, brung? Anyone heard the word 'brung'?"

A titter of sycophantish laughter from the class.

Peter's conversation with his mother came blessedly back to him. "I brought," he said.

38

"I ring."

"I rung. No – take that back – I rang, or I have rung. Like you'd say 'I rang up' or 'I have rung up'."

"I wonder what strange country this boy comes from," mocked the teacher, "and what strange language they speak there. Rang up, rung up – what does it mean?"

"It means what it says, sir. Like when you ring someone up, on the telephone."

"The what?"

"The telephone. *Tele*. As in television, telegram, tele-communications – " His voice faded as the teacher's face turned a deeper shade of crimson.

"Thank you," said the man. "Thank you, Peter Lorrimer, for breaking into my class, disturbing my lesson, dressing up in our school uniform, pretending to be a pupil and then talking a lot of gibberish. If there are any words to be invented here, *I* will do the inventing."

"I'm not inventing anything!"

"You are not inventing anything – WHAT?"

"SIR!"

"Stand up! Bend over!" *Swish, swish, swish* went the cane. In Peter's ears, it seemed to turn into the sound of a raging wind, or a thundering waterfall. His ears would burst!

And it seemed suddenly as if they did. There was a sort of explosion in his head. Light blazed. He found himself lying on the pavement, and people were gathering round him. He supposed that the teacher had beaten him unconscious, then carried him here, bleeding and bruised, for he saw the tall trees which lined the road to the school. The fog had gone.

"He's coming round," a woman said. "It's all right, lovey. You're all right now." She helped him to his feet.

"What happened, old son?" a man asked.

"He was trying to beat me to death," said Peter. "He's mad."

"Kid's been dreaming," said another voice. "No signs of damage on him, are there?"

"No. Just a little faint, that's all it was," said the woman, brushing the pavement dust from his blazer. "Where do you live?"

Peter told her. One of the men offered to drive him home. He hardly spoke in the car. He felt exhausted. The driver dropped him at his own gate. "Shall I come in with you?" he offered. "Will anyone be there?"

"Yes, thank you. My mother's there. Thanks for the lift."

"You go in and have a good rest," said the man, and drove off.

Peter let himself into the house. His mother heard him and came into the hall, frowning. "Oh, Peter, how could you be so naughty?" she said. "The Headmaster has been on the phone to me – "

"I don't care what he said about me," Peter said. "He was horrible and cruel and mad. I'm never going back there. He tried to murder me!" And he poured out the whole story.

His mother listened. His tone was so convincing that she half-believed him. Then she said, "If you had such a beating, let's see how sore you are."

"I should think I'll be scarred for life," said Peter, pulling down his trousers and wondering, as he did so, why his bottom didn't hurt. His mother looked.

"There isn't a mark on you," she declared. "Not even the smallest bruise. You've been telling me lies – dangerous lies, too. If you were older, you could be had up for slander for making accusations like that against the Headmaster. And I know for a fact that you did *not* turn up at school at all this morning, because the Head rang up to

40

ask why you hadn't arrived. Oh, Peter, what am I going to do with you when you behave like this? I know you didn't want to go there, but to tell these wicked lies – "

"I wasn't telling lies!" cried Peter. "It happened! And all in that dreadful fog – "

"There has been no fog – none at all – except in your perverse mind," she said.

He went very cold. All the indignation died out of him. He whispered: "If it didn't happen – yet it did – *what* happened? Who was that man with the white hair and the red face, and thick arms and shoulders, and a beastly smile – and a voice which seemed to cut through you, just as the cane did? Who was he?"

"An invented character in your story," said his mother. "The Headmaster of St Edmund's is tall, dark, rather thin and has a very nice smile. I went to see him before I decided to send you there."

Peter felt dazed and ill. It had all been too much. You could go on fighting against circumstance for just so long, and then – he broke into tears.

As he melted, so did his mother. She took him in her arms. "Oh, darling, what is all this about?" she said. "Why did you make up that story? Did you really think I'd believe it?"

"It happened," wept Peter.

"Where have you really been all morning?"

"Where I said. Then I found myself lying in the street and a man drove me home."

"What man?"

"I don't know – a nice man – they were all very nice – the passers-by who stopped to pick me up – they were kind – people should always be kind – not like *him*! That – that sinister schoolmaster!"

Even if his home was sometimes a battlefield, his

mother now proved a gentle victor. She was so unaccustomed to seeing him cry that she realized something must be badly wrong. She took him up to bed, tucked him in with a hot-water-bottle, kissed him on the forehead and told him to go to sleep. He did sleep, too. Deeply, dreamlessly. It was evening when he woke, blinking contentedly in the safety of his own little room. Then his father came in.

"Your mother's been telling me – "

"It all happened, Dad. Honest!"

His father sat on the end of the bed. "We know now that you went to the school, Peter, although no one saw you there. Your case was found outside one of the classroom windows."

"That's right," said Peter. "I dropped it when that dreadful Headmaster dragged me inside."

"No one dragged you inside," said his father. "Your mother did wonder if there could be something in your story, as you were so upset, so she went to the school this afternoon. She thought maybe one of the teachers was like the man you'd described. No one there is even remotely like him. No one there *now*, that is."

"No one there *now*?" Peter echoed.

"The Head, Mr Rennick, has come to see you. He wants to talk to you about it." He went to fetch the other man, and Peter waited. If that villain with the cane walked in –

A tall, dark, anxious-faced man came in and closed the door behind him. He had a book under his arm, not a cane. "Hello, Peter. I'm Mr Rennick, the Headmaster of St Edmund's."

"Then who was the man with white hair?" Peter asked.

"Ever heard of John Bashman, nicknamed 'Old Basher'?" Mr Rennick asked him. Peter shook his head. "Here's a picture of him." Mr Rennick opened the book,

42

called "History of St Edmund's School", and displayed a full-page illustration. It was a reproduction of the portrait of a man, in colour. A white-haired, red-faced thick-bodied man. It was labelled: "John Bashman, the First Headmaster".

"That's him," said Peter. "That's the man who beat me."

"That man has been dead for a hundred years. He wasn't nicknamed 'Old Basher' for nothing. He caned the pupils for the smallest misdemeanour. He was a sadistic bully, to my mind, but in those days beatings in school were more common than they are now. It was an age of violence. Now your story is that you looked through the classroom window and saw him there; that he dragged you inside, and so on – "

"He did! In that awful fog!"

"There was no fog. It was a bright morning. The teacher who spent all morning in that classroom was taking physics. It's a lab. rather than an ordinary classroom. You realize now, don't you? You had some sort of dream-awake. A hallucination of some kind."

"You mean I saw ghosts of the past," Peter said calmly. "That would be why he'd never heard of the telephone or television. He said I was talking gibberish and that if anyone was going to invent words, he would do it."

"It was all a dream, Peter. You never wanted to come to my school. You were resentful about it. Your mother says you dashed out without any breakfast, so you were empty. You got to the school, couldn't face going in, dumped your case, fled back to the road – and then you fainted. Overwrought nerves. While unconscious, you had this dream. Does that make sense to you?"

"I suppose so. But it must have been more than an ordinary dream, as Old Basher really did exist."

"Yes. And I expect you'd read about him somewhere

and forgotten. What the conscious mind forgets, the unconscious retains. That's my explanation. It makes more sense than 'ghosts'. There are no such things." He spoke confidently, almost arrogantly.

He wouldn't be so cocky about it if *he'd* had Old Basher standing over him with that cane, Peter thought – and, suddenly, behind the Headmaster's shoulder, he saw a shadow forming –

The shadow gained colour and solidity. It seemed to have sprung in some curious way from the illustration in the open book, which Mr Rennick had placed on a shelf behind him. There was the white hair, the red face, the thick body – the raised arm with the cane in it – the curling smile – the pale eyes, glaring at the back of the Headmaster's head. "Impostor!" spat the lips – or that could have been the sound of rain falling on the leaves in the garden. The arm with the cane was raised higher –

"Look out!" screamed Peter. "Old Basher is just behind you! He's going to wallop you!"

As the cane descended, Mr Rennick gave a cry, and the light went out. Peter went right down under the bedclothes, in case Old Basher started on him next.

A few moments later, the bedclothes were pulled away from him. His mother was bending over him. The room was dimly lit by light from the passage. His father was outlined in the doorway. Mr Rennick was rubbing his head.

"It's all right, Peter," his mother was saying. "The electric bulb fell out of its socket and hit poor Mr Rennick on the head. That's why the light went out." She turned to the headmaster. "My fault, that. I couldn't have fixed it properly when I put it in the other day."

"I've always told you to leave that sort of job to me," Peter's father said irritably. "Sorry about this, Mr Rennick. Come downstairs and have a drink."

The two men departed, but before he left the room, Mr Rennick gave Peter a long, suspicious look.

Now his mother fussed over him a little and he lay down to sleep. Strangely, he no longer felt afraid of Old Basher, who had so obviously had it in for Mr Rennick rather than himself. Resented anyone else taking over the school, even a hundred years afterwards. That would be it. Peter did, however, feel a little afraid of the look Mr Rennick had given him. When he went to St Edmund's, there wouldn't be any beating or cruelty, but he wouldn't be popular. The Head definitely didn't like or trust him. Oh, life could be hell sometimes. It really could. He slept.

In the morning, his mother brought him breakfast in bed.

"You're going to stay at home today," she said, "then your father and I will arrange for you to go to the Comprehensive."

"Wow!" He nearly hit the ceiling with relieved delight.

"Peter, be careful, you'll spill your tea."

"What made you change your mind?" he asked her.

"I didn't," she said, rather grimly. "Mr Rennick changed his. He said he didn't want you at the school. He said some neurotic children cause outbreaks of poltergeist activity, and he didn't want the pleasant atmosphere of St Edmund's disturbed. He struck me as pretty neurotic himself," she added. "What a fuss to make over a falling light-bulb! As if *you* could possibly have been responsible for that."

It was Old Basher, thought Peter. Clever old ghost!

Then his father descended upon him. "Enjoying your breakfast and the 'good news'?" he said sardonically. "You cunning little devil! You were determined to get your own way, weren't you? Tell me – how did you wangle that poltergeist effect?"

"I didn't," Peter began. "It was Old – " Then he

stopped. It would be no use telling his father the truth. He had a sceptical nature, limited, lacking in imagination. Still, he wasn't a bad sort. Peter smiled. His father winked and departed.

In fact Peter felt friendly towards everyone this morning. Even Old Basher. Especially Old Basher! But for him, Peter would have had to go to St Edmund's . . .

"Thank you," he said, impulsively and aloud – and an echo in the air – or maybe it was only the gurgling of a water-pipe – said: 'Thank you – WHAT?" and Peter bellowed back: "SIR!"

HUNTERS' HILL

by Sydney J. Bounds

The village shop held the smell of bacon and apples and cheese. It was a small shop, with the counter and shelves crammed with tinned food and packets of crisps and chocolate bars. The floor space was a maze of sacks and cartons and bottles. At the back, behind a wire grille, was a counter that served as the local post office.

"We'll take a large tin of baked beans," Carol Clark said. "And a pound of sausages and . . . let me see – "

"Here, steady on," John interrupted in alarm. "Don't forget I'm the one who's got to carry this lot. And if we're going up the hill, I don't want any extra weight."

"That's understandable," Carol retorted.

For the first time, the old woman who ran the shop single-handed took an interest in them. Sharp, unblinking eyes stabbed first at Carol, a slim sixteen in jeans and hiking boots and checkered shirt, and then at her brother, a year younger, a head shorter and twice her size around the waist.

"The hill, you say?"

"Why, yes," John said. "There must be quite a view from the top. We're thinking of camping up there. We're on a hiking tour." He gestured with a pudgy hand at their rucksacks – "I suppose that's obvious!"

Carol and John had first seen the hill as they walked into the village through the valley, following the bends of the river. All morning they had seen little sign of life, and the village came as a pleasant surprise: lunch on the green and a chance to restock their dwindling supplies. The hill

47

towered above the village and, in the heat of August, promised a cool night's sleep. There'd be a fine view at dawn, too – if they could find a way up the thickly-wooded slopes.

The old woman seemed upset. "You'll do better to stay with the river – there's hills further along for easy climbing and a view. Hunters' Hill is best left alone. Aye, you'll find no local willing to tackle it."

"Oh, why's that?" Carol asked absently, picking up a tin of ham. "We'll take this as well."

"'Tis a legend in these parts. There's some say the hill's haunted by a great evil from the past. That's as may be . . .'Tis a fact a number of visitors have fallen over the drop. A dangerous place, and one to keep away from."

"I suppose any hill can be dangerous in that case," Carol said. "But I don't think we'll be falling over the edge." She paid for the food and put the change in her purse. "Good afternoon."

As they went out, the door-bell pinging, the old woman called after them: "G'day now, and mind what I say. You keep off Hunters' Hill."

Carol and John burst out laughing as they walked down the sunlit High Street.

"A legend! It's a sort of challenge – now we *have* to climb the hill."

"She never said where it gets its name."

"We never asked."

They left the village behind and struck across springy grass to the foot of the hill that reared high and dark above them. The summer air was hot and still, the sky a deep blue, and they strode along in carefree style.

The slope of the hill rose steeply before them as they climbed in single file with John leading. The trees grew close together, and the undergrowth was dense and tangled. Presently the track petered out, and they had to

48

force a way through dark green shrubbery. Thick foliage blotted out the view around them and, as the sun began to set, the temperature dropped sharply.

They stopped to put on thick sweaters, and Carol said, "Listen!"

John cocked his head. "I don't hear anything."

"Exactly. It's unnaturally quiet – no bird-song, no animals moving. I haven't even seen an insect on the way up."

They set off again, climbing into a silence that seemed to thicken about them. The tree-trunks appeared colourless in the twilight, and strange fungi clustered about their roots. The higher they climbed, the colder it became.

"This is ridiculous," John said crossly. "It's beginning to feel like winter, and we're nowhere near the top yet."

Carol shivered. "Perhaps the old woman was right after all. Perhaps the hill is haunted."

John's laugh did not sound very convincing. "You always were imaginative."

The setting sun vanished amongst a blanket of leaves. The last vestige of track disappeared, and they floundered on through brush that became more and more like a jungle.

Tangled brambles unravelled, lashing their faces like prickly whips. The ground became swampy, and they lost their footing and stumbled among tall stinging nettles.

"I see now why the locals keep away," John grumbled. "They're not so silly. And I'm getting hungry."

Suddenly he gave a cry of pain as a root tripped him and sent him sprawling on the ground. He sat up, massaging his ankle. "I think I've twisted it," he said gloomily.

"Perhaps we ought to go back," Carol said, peering into the darkness.

"I reckon we're nearly at the top anyway," John said, getting up and limping forward.

49

They went on slowly, pushing through the shadows, with Carol leading and John wincing with each step he took. Low branches slapped viciously at them . . . as if the hill was determined to stop them learning its secret, Carol thought uneasily.

"Look for an open space where we can camp," John called. "I can't go much further tonight."

They continued to climb, slowly and laboriously, through the dark wood. Higher up, the trees shrank back, leaving a circle of blackened earth where nothing grew. On the far side of the circle was a sheer drop to the valley below.

John sprawled on the ground. "Keep well away from that," he said. "But this is the only likely camping place."

Carol collected twigs and brushwood, and John built a fire. They made a hearty meal of soup and sausages and beans, with thick slices of bread and butter, followed by mugs of cocoa.

"Feels better," John said. "Any seconds?"

"Pig!"

Carol unrolled their sleeping bags and wriggled into hers, glad to be out of the cold. It really was unpleasantly cold for August. She lay under a cloud-darkened sky, counting the few stars that peeped through, and listened to her brother snoring . . .

Carol stirred in her sleep and wondered what had disturbed her. The hill seemed quiet enough, and now the stars gleamed cold and bright. She felt unusually alert, her nerves on edge, ears straining for the smallest sound. She scrambled upright, stared down the hillside and saw a row of bobbing lights.

She felt afraid. The hill appeared different somehow – but it would at night, she told herself. Fear turned to terror as a hound bayed. The lights flickered, like torch-brands in a breeze, and shadows flitted between the trees. There were people coming up the hill, a great number of people.

Carol panicked. They were coming for her. The hunters were coming.

She drew back into the shadow of a great oak, waiting, watching. The hunters ringed the hillside, men and women carrying lighted torches, with their dogs. There was no escape for her, except over the long drop. She tensed, legs trembling, a sick apprehension in her stomach.

She had thought she was safe here, that they would never dare to come up the hill after her. They never had before. She'd always felt safe on the hill.

The hunters chanted as they drew nearer; it was a monotonous chant, low-pitched, and she couldn't quite make out the words. The light of their torches grew brighter, pushing back the night.

Carol saw that they carried scythes and pitchforks, and she shuddered. She broke cover and ran; it was instinctive to run, but there was nowhere to run to. The hounds scented her and sprang forward in great bounding leaps, baying as they pursued her.

The hunters closed their ring, following the dogs as she slipped among the trees, keeping in shadow and forcing a way through the undergrowth. One dog snapped at her heels and she kicked it away. She threshed around in the brush like an animal in distress, her heart pounding wildly and her breathing ragged.

She tried to climb a tree, but a hand like an iron claw seized her ankle and jerked downwards; her hands slipped and slithered on bark and she fell in a heap on the ground. She lay there, panting.

A man's voice lifted in triumph. "Here she be – I got her!"

Carol was dragged into a clearing in the wood. Eager hands cut and trimmed a stout sapling and drove it into the earth. She was tied to the stake, and the men and women of the village collected brushwood and piled it around her legs. By the light of the torches she saw that they wore clothes of an earlier period and wondered if she were dreaming. It didn't feel like a dream.

They continued heaping brushwood till it reached to her waist. She was surrounded by a ring of hate. She stared into hostile and sweaty faces and sly eyes that would not meet her gaze.

Then a man with a cross hanging from a chain about his neck commanded: "Burn the witch!"

A smoking torch was thrust among the dry brush, setting it alight. The wood crackled as it burned. Pungent smoke rose, choking her. Fierce tongues of flame spread and, as the fire mounted, she felt searing heat and screamed. The blaze consumed her bonds and she broke free and stumbled away. The circle of hunters opened and reformed, driving her towards the edge . . .

John woke abruptly as a scream pierced his sleep. "Carol?" He turned his head; her sleeping bag was empty. "Carol, where are – "

In the starlight, he saw her slim figure moving towards the edge of the drop. "Carol," he shouted. "Stop!"

His sister did not seem to hear, but continued walking as if in her sleep. He wriggled out of his sleeping bag and ran after her. He forgot his ankle, not feeling the pain as he ran harder than he'd ever run before.

She was teetering on the brink of the long drop as he reached her, grasped one arm and jerked her back.

Carol woke up, staring blindly down at the silver ribbon

of river and the toy village far below. "Have they gone?" she whispered.

"Has who gone?" John demanded. "There's no one else here."

Carol looked fearfully around. There was no stake, no fire and no villagers; only the blackened circle of earth where nothing grew.

She felt suddenly cold, as though icy fingers stroked the back of her neck, and shivered. "The hunters, they were going to burn me at the stake. They believed I was a witch . . . it was so real."

"You were dreaming," John said insistently. "Sleep-walking."

"Was I?" Carol said, still doubting. "Yes, I suppose I must have been."

But as they walked back across the circle of barren earth, for a moment it felt as if they stepped into warm ashes.

THE BABY-SITTER

by Alison Prince

Nigel's mother came into his bedroom to kiss him good-night. She was wearing a long dress and smelt beautiful.

"You will be good, won't you?" she said. "Mr Pope is a dear old man – and it was so sweet of him to offer to baby-sit."

"I don't like him much" said Nigel. "He squashes caterpillars with his fingers."

Nigel's mother laughed. "You never know," she said, "it may be kinder than using these chemical sprays. And he is a wonderful gardener."

"Why couldn't Auntie Betty come?" asked Nigel, frowning.

"I told you," said his mother patiently. "Auntie Betty's ill. And Mr Pope has offered to baby-sit ever so many times – he really loves children, he says, and never had any of his own. And he does like a warm fire to sit by, poor old chap."

"Come on, Joyce!" shouted Nigel's father from the hall. "We'll be late!"

"Coming!" she called back. She bent and kissed Nigel again, then tucked him in and switched off the main light, leaving the bedside lamp. She touched the tip of his nose lightly with her forefinger and said, "Be good!" Then she went out.

"Tell him I want a story!" Nigel shouted after her.

Doors banged and Nigel heard the car start and drive away. Suddenly he felt very lonely. He pulled the bed-clothes up to his chin and stared out at the shadowed bedroom. He could imagine exactly what he looked like: the pitifully small face on the white pillow, the tousled fair hair and the blue eyes brimming with tears. And nobody had bothered to read him a story. Nigel was so carried away by the pathos of this picture that he did in fact begin to cry a little.

The sitting-room door opened. Mr Pope came out and started to climb the stairs, his footsteps as slow and measured as they were when he plodded down the garden path with a bundle of rose trimmings for the bonfire. Why did he never wear gloves? When he came in for his cup of tea his hands were often criss-crossed with bleeding scratches.

Mr Pope opened the bedroom door. Nigel rubbed his eyes on the sleeve of his pyjamas, but Mr Pope took no notice of the boy's pathetic state. "Your mother tells me you want a story," he announced. Then he closed the door behind him.

Nigel sniffed. "Yes, please," he said.

Mr Pope smiled slowly. Everything he did was very slow – stirring his tea, filling his pipe, pushing the lawn-mower. "I'm glad about that," he said. "Because I've been thinking for a long time about a story I'd like to tell you."

"You could have told me in the garden," said Nigel.

Mr Pope shook his head. "Oh, no," he said. "Oh dear, no. This is a bedtime story. I've had it saved up. Sooner or later, I thought, his Auntie Betty will be ill, then they'll ask me to baby-sit. I've offered enough times."

He brought a chair to Nigel's bedside and sat down, his scarred hands spread on his knees. Nigel stared up at him, fascinated and slightly afraid. Mr Pope's face never quite seemed to go with the big, rough hands. It was a hollow face, almost, Nigel thought, like Mr Punch from the Punch and Judy show at the seaside. The cheek bones stuck out boldly, but underneath them the cheeks fell away in deep hollows that ended in a craggy jaw and a thin, scrawny neck. When Mr Pope smiled his mouth was full of china-white teeth that seemed much too big – but the strangest thing about him was his eyes.

Mr Pope's eyes were very pale blue and he never seemed to blink. He gazed ahead of him with an unwavering, pink-rimmed stare which never quite fixed on the thing he was looking at. When he regarded Nigel his eyes seemed to be looking through him, so that Nigel sometimes glanced over his shoulder to see if the real object of Mr Pope's attention was somewhere behind him.

Tonight, Mr Pope's eyes were as unblinking as ever and as Nigel stared up at him he could see the tiny network of veins which threaded the whites of the eyes, surrounding the sky blue circles of the irises with wriggly red lines. Mr Pope seemed aware of this scrutiny for he said, looking through Nigel at the wall, "You've got blue eyes, boy. Like me."

"Yes," said Nigel huskily.

Mr Pope nodded. "That's good. Yes, that's all to the good."

"What about this story?" demanded Nigel.

"I'm coming to it," said Mr Pope, "as you'll see in a minute. Now, this is a true story, boy, every word of it. Afterwards, you must never think to yourself that I made it up. This is the first time I've ever told this story, and I shall never tell it again, not to a living soul. This is your story, boy, just for you."

"Thank you!" said Nigel.

"Yes," Mr Pope went on. "I've waited for years for this. To find the right person."

"And it's me?" asked Nigel, pleased.

"It's you," agreed Mr Pope.

"What's it called?" asked Nigel.

Mr Pope thought. "I never gave it a name," he said, "but I suppose I'd call it, 'Hacky Basham's Glass Eye'."

Nigel laughed delightedly and said, "What a funny name!"

Mr Pope didn't laugh. "Hacky Basham," he said, "got his name because he coughed. Terrible hacking cough it was. That's why we called him Hacky – you know how kids make up names for people."

"Oh, yes," said Nigel. "We call our teacher Bunny because her teeth stick out."

"Hacky seemed an old man to us kids," Mr Pope continued, "though I dare say he wasn't much above forty, not at first. He'd been gassed in the First World War, you see, boy, and that had ruined him. His hair turned white and he never hardly worked again through having such a cough. And he lost his eye."

"How awful!" said Nigel. "Did he just have a hole?"

"He did," said Mr Pope. "But he had a glass eye that fitted in it. Except that it didn't move, you'd never have known it wasn't real."

"What colour was it?" enquired Nigel.

"Blue," said Mr Pope. "The same as the other one. Just like mine. And yours, boy."

"Ugh!" said Nigel, fascinated.

"In those days," Mr Pope went on, "people didn't go in so much for baby-sitters, but my mum and dad were the careful sort, and if they went to the pictures they'd ask Hacky Basham to keep an eye on me. They were sorry for him, I think. 'He does like a warm fire to sit by,' they'd say. And they'd give him a bob or two for his trouble. But just *how* he kept an eye on me they never knew."

"How *did* he?" asked Nigel.

"When I was tucked up in bed," said Mr Pope, "like you are now, boy, Hacky would come upstairs, coughing

57

fit to bust because climbing put a strain on his lungs. And he'd come into the room and stand there, wheezing – and when he got his breath back, he'd say, 'I'm going to keep an eye on you, boy.' And he'd take out his glass eye and put it on the mantelpiece, right on the edge so it was looking at me. 'If you're naughty,' he'd say, 'my eye will tell me. It always does.' And he'd go off downstairs, laughing and coughing. And the eye would look at me. Even in the dark I could see it because there was a street lamp outside. The white part of the eye glowed, like a little moon."

"How *awful*!" said Nigel.

"But that was just the beginning," went on Mr Pope. "One night my cousin Jack had come to stay. He was sleeping in my room on a camp bed and I was glad of his company because my mum and dad were going out that night."

"Did Hacky Basham come?" asked Nigel.

"He did," said Mr Pope grimly. "And he put his eye on the mantelpiece and went downstairs, laughing and coughing like always. Now, Jack was older than me and he said, 'Here,' he said, 'we'll give the old boy a dose of his own medicine – and frighten *him* for a change. How long does he leave that thing here?' 'He comes to get it just before Mum and Dad come home,' I told him, 'so it's always back in his head when they come in.' And I knew, boy, because I could never go to sleep with that thing watching me. 'Right,' says Jack, 'we'll hide it.' And he made me put the bedclothes over my head so I wouldn't see where he put it, because he said I was a coward and I'd tell Hacky where it was. And I would have done, too!"

"What happened?" breathed Nigel.

"I lay there with the sheet over my head," said Mr Pope, "and I listened to Jack moving about, looking for a good hiding place. I heard him open drawers and shut them again, then he pulled the door of the wardrobe open – I know, because it squeaked. Then he shut that and I felt him stand on the end of the bed as if he was looking for a hiding place high up – and then he opened the window. And shut it again. 'You can come out now,' he said to me. And he was grinning all over his face. 'You haven't thrown it out in the street, have you?' I asked him – but I didn't think he had, or I'd have heard it smash on the pavement. He just laughed – and he wouldn't tell me.

"Anyway," Mr Pope went on, "Jack went to sleep. Snored like a pig, he did. I kept thinking about the eye, hidden somewhere and still looking at me from wherever it was, and I couldn't go to sleep. If I'd known where it was, I'd have put it back on the mantelpiece, and that's a fact. Then Hacky came upstairs. When he stopped coughing he looked on the mantelpiece, then he came over to my bed. 'Where is it?' he whispered. I told him I didn't know, and I felt as if we'd done a dreadful thing. He bent over my bed with his mouth right close to my ear. 'Whoever took it,' he said, 'will come to a bad end, very soon. But you, my boy – I'll keep an eye on you for ever.'"

"What did he mean?" asked Nigel.

"Don't rush me, boy," said Mr Pope deliberately. "I'm telling you, aren't I? Next morning, Jack looked outside for the eye. There was a window box on our sill – my mum was keen on flowers, see, but we didn't have a garden so she had to make do with window boxes. And Jack had put the eye in there, wedged in the earth among the petunias. But it had gone. It couldn't have slipped out, because the earth was lower than the edges of the box. And it was too big for a bird to pick up – but it wasn't there. We both looked."

"How odd!" said Nigel.

Mr Pope ignored him. "When my cousin Jack was going

home that morning," he went on, "he slipped on the wet road and fell under a truck. Killed him stone dead."

"No!" gasped Nigel.

"Yes," said Mr Pope. "And that night, when I went to bed, the eye was on my mantelpiece." He held up his hand as if to ward off any questions. "Hacky Basham hadn't been to the house. He never came again. An infection set in that very day in the eye socket, and went through to his brain and killed him."

"It's funny, isn't it?" said Nigel, trying to sound amused.

"Funny? Yes, I suppose you might call it funny." Mr Pope stared through Nigel again with his pale blue eyes. "I was *haunted*, boy. I've been haunted from that day to this."

"What d'you mean?" asked Nigel nervously.

"Hacky Basham's glass eye never left me from that day onwards," said Mr Pope. "It was always there, looking at me. I never knew where it would be. If I took out my sandwiches when I went fishing, there it was in the package, looking like a hard-boiled egg until it rolled over and stared up at me. It would be in my pencil case at school or in the toe of my football boot on a Saturday afternoon. If I got on a bus and felt in my pocket for the fare, the eye would be there among the pennies, waiting for me to put my hand on it."

"But how did it *get* there?" asked Nigel.

"I wish I knew," said Mr Pope. "It was no good hiding it. I put it in my drawer along with my socks once when I'd asked a girl to come to the pictures with me. I bought her a packet of peanuts in the interval, and when she opened them, there was the eye, staring up at her. She screamed the place down. She dropped the eye on the floor before she ran out of the cinema and I hoped that was the end of it. But, no. That night, it was back on my mantelpiece."

"I don't think it's a very nice story," said Nigel. "I'd rather you read me one. There's some lovely books on my shelf over there."

"But it's a special story, Nigel," said Mr Pope, gazing at him with the fish-cold blue eyes. It was the first time he had called Nigel by his name, and there was something oddly menacing in it.

"I don't like it," said Nigel.

"That doesn't matter," said Mr Pope. As if reminiscing to himself, he went on, "Yes, the eye ruined my life. I never married – it frightened off every girl I met. And it lost me job after job by turning up at the wrong moment."

"I'd have told my mother," said Nigel stoutly. "*She'd* know what to do."

"I tried that," said Mr Pope. "I held it out to her on the palm of my hand and said, 'Mum, this is Mr Basham's glass eye.' And she looked straight at it and said, 'Don't be silly, dear – there's nothing there.' Dad couldn't see it, either. They went to a doctor about me after a bit. Thought I was nuts. I had to pretend I couldn't see it any more or they'd have put me in the mad-house."

Nigel gulped. "What happened?" he asked. "In the end, I mean?"

"I don't know yet," said Mr Pope. "That's up to you."

He felt in his pocket and brought something out in his closed fist. Nigel looked at the scarred knuckles and knew what they hid. "Don't," he said.

Mr Pope turned his hand over and opened the fingers. There on the palm lay the glass eye, the pale blue iris pointing directly at Nigel, staring at him with a hard, wide-open, black-centred stare. Tiny veins of red threaded the china-white ball, exactly like those in Mr Pope's own eyes. Nigel could not look away.

"*You* can see it, can't you, boy?" said Mr Pope.

Nigel nodded, speechless.

Mr Pope got up slowly, and put the eye on the mantelpiece. "There," he said with a dry chuckle. "Now it will keep an eye on *you*." Then he sighed a small, happy sigh. "Peace at last," he said. "After a haunted lifetime. I'm grateful to you, boy. Grateful."

Suddenly a spasm of violent coughing shook him. Nigel had never heard Mr Pope cough like that before. He had never heard him cough at all. It sounded as if the man's lungs were being torn into shreds, so destructive was the fit, so racking – so hacking. Mr Pope's breath rattled in his gullet as he strained against the impossible attack, trying to drag some air into his lungs.

"Perhaps you'd better get a drink of water," said Nigel.

Unable to speak, Mr Pope nodded, his face scarlet and his blue eyes pouring tears. He lurched out of the room, and Nigel lay back in relief. He heard Mr Pope stagger down the stairs, still coughing; then the coughing gave way to a burst of wild, harsh laughter. After that there was a tumbling crash as though the man had fallen down the last few steps of the stairs. Then there was silence.

Nigel cowered in his bed, his whole body bathed in a cold sweat of terror. And the glass eye on the mantelpiece stared down at him with an implacable blue gaze.

It seemed a lifetime before Nigel heard the car come into the garage. A key scratched in the front door. Nigel's mother gave a shriek of horror as she came into the hall. Nigel heard his father say, "Oh, my God. Poor old boy." Then his mother came running up the stairs.

"Mummy!" screamed Nigel. "Mummy!"

His mother rushed in and hugged him in trembling arms. "Oh, darling," she said, "are you all right?"

"The eye, Mummy," begged Nigel. "Take the eye away."

Nigel's father came in, looking grave, and spoke to Nigel's mother quietly by the door. Nigel went on telling them about the eye but he could not get either of them to pay proper attention. Then his father went out again, saying something about ringing for an ambulance.

"Nigel, dear," said his mother, coming back to his bedside, "it's all right. Mr Pope's – well, he's had a little accident. But everything's all right now. No need to worry. Mummy's here."

Why were they telling lies, Nigel wondered without much interest. It was quite obvious that Mr Pope was dead. But that wasn't what mattered. He took a deep breath.

"Mummy," he said carefully. "Listen. Please take that eye away. Hacky Basham's glass eye. It's on the mantelpiece. Look."

Nigel's mother turned her head to follow the direction of his pointing hand. She got up and went to the mantelpiece and looked carefully along it. Then she came back and knelt down beside her son again, and took both his hands in hers, frowning a little as though she was worried. Nigel glanced again at the round white eye that stared at him with its blue, triumphant gaze from the mantelpiece and said irritably, "Why don't you take it *away*?"

"Nigel," said his mother gently, "darling – there's nothing there."

THE SOUND OF SIRENS

by Tony Richards

Late on the afternoon of October 19th, with the copper-coloured sun already drawing low over the skyline of Central London, the flood warning sirens were tested. Their noise was pale and eerie, like the wail of banshees on a starless night. And as it drifted across the tireless city, as it echoed back and forth across the murky waters of the Thames, many of the older people stopped what they were doing and looked up. They were remembering a time long past when they had heard a wailing just like that. It had been a dreadful time, and they had never once forgotten it.

Robin Cooper's grandfather was one of them, and had lived in this part of Vauxhall, just south of the river, all his life. He had just popped in for teatime from his own house round the corner, and, as the sound of sirens reached his ears, he stopped buttering his third scone of the afternoon and glanced out of the window.

"It's the flood-warning sirens, Dad," Robin's mother told him, reaching across the table for the teapot. "They're giving them a trial run, in case the Thames ever breaks its banks. It was in all the papers."

"Oh yes, I remember," he said quietly. He was a lively man for his age, given to long, vigorous walks. He was intelligent, too, and always kept up with the news. But as he listened to the sound of sirens, his grey eyes became old and distant, glazed. "It just gave me a turn, that's all," he said, "remembering the blitz."

"The *what*, Grandad?" asked Robin.

"The *blitz!* The Battle of Britain! World War II! The *Luftwaffe* used to fly over the Channel every night and drop their bombs on London like a rain from hell. The whole sky would be red with fire sometimes."

"It must have been exciting," Robin said.

His mother and his grandfather both laughed.

"No, Robin," said his grandfather, reaching out to ruffle the boy's hair. "It was frightening and terrible and stupid, just like all wars. I'm only glad *you* did't have to live through it." He looked at Robin's dubious expression and frowned. "Tell you what. I've got stacks of old newspapers from the time up in my attic. I'll show them to you some time, just to prove how bad it was."

Robin was puzzled – he could not imagine anything *that* terrible. But he said "thanks" politely to his grandfather before getting up.

"Is it all right if I go out now?" he asked his mother.

"You're going to that hideaway of yours, I suppose. Yes, all right – but don't get back too late or you'll be in trouble with your father."

"I won't," said Robin, snatching up his jacket and running for the front door.

The street outside was deserted. The shadows were growing long. Robin thrust his hands deep into his pockets and began walking southwards, towards his secret hideout at the back of the allotments a quarter of a mile away. His grandfather had helped him make it. They had tunnelled through the soft earth, made a cavern at one end, then propped the roof up carefully with planks. His parents, he remembered, had been worried it was dangerous. But his grandfather, an expert craftsman in his time, had talked them round.

Just imagine a man like that being afraid of a few bombs, Robin thought. *Why, he wasn't even scared when the scrap man's Alsatian broke loose!* He gazed up at the sky. *All red with fire*, his grandfather had said in a grave voice, as though it were not a thrilling, wonderful idea. There was no accounting for the working of the adult mind.

He was passing the derelict area now. On the three streets giving away to his left, there were no houses standing, only piles of blasted rubble. Weeds grew freely amongst the shattered bricks. The pavements were cracked and ruined, where there were pavements at all.

It had been like that for as long as Robin could remember, so desolate that it gave him a creepy feeling every time he passed. He hurried along, almost breaking into a jog, and was beyond the final of the three streets, Bursell Street, when he heard a noise behind him. He stopped and turned.

"Hello," said the boy who was stading on the corner of Bursell Street, though he had not been there a brief moment ago. "I've never seen you before. Are you new round here?"

He must have been hiding in the ruins, Robin told himself. "No," he said, "I've always lived here. And I've never seen *you*, either."

The boy was much shorter than Robin, with skinny arms and legs, and large blue eyes set in a thin, pasty face. He seemed to move almost nervously, as though expecting danger at any moment. But as he walked towards Robin his smile, his manner, seemed genuine enough.

He jerked a thumb towards himself. "I'm Joey Mullery." Then he halted and looked Robin up and down. "You're dressed rather funny, aren't you? Are you a foreigner, a refugee?"

"I'm English," Robin said, wondering what had made the boy ask that. And, thinking about it, Joey Mullery was dressed oddly himslf with his coarse grey shirt and baggy shorts, his thick shoes and his grey socks which came right up to the knee. One side of his face was smeared with soot. A striped school cap, set at an angle over his short-cropped reddish hair, completed the peculiar picture.

But the boy seemed to have forgotten the question of Robin's clothes.

"Are you going out to play?" he asked, rather hopefully.

"Yes," said Robin. "Why?"

"Well . . ." The boy shuffled his feet, embarrassed. "I was wondering if I could play with you. All my friends have been moved out to the countryside, you see."

"Er – yes, of course." He found himself, without knowing why, feeling sorry for this new boy, this Joey. So strange. So *out of place*. "I'll even take you to my hideout if you like."

"Your hideout?"

"It's a secret cave I dug at the back of the allotments. Don't worry, it's quite safe to go there."

Joey's face lit up like a beacon. "'Course it's safe," he said, "now that the All Clear's gone."

He pelted off down the street towards the allotments. Robin stared after him, bewildered, then started to trail behind, still wondering where the skinny boy had come from. Still wondering what he had meant by the "All Clear".

The allotments had always seemed strange and wild to Robin. Like an area of countryside walled completely in by tower blocks and terraced houses, an area of greenness under siege from the concrete city. The sheds were locked now; there was nobody about. The evening shadows were drawing together, overlapping, melding, like enormous pools of ink. Robin led the way through the nettles to the

67

entrance of his hideout and pulled away the boards which hid it. Then, glancing back at Joey, who was strangely pale against the dusk, he began to crawl inside.

It was as though an icy wind were chasing him down the tunnel. A sudden chill had settled over him, and Robin found his skin prickling, found himself growing nervous without knowing why. He crawled faster than normal, reached the opening and scrabbled frantically around until he found the torch, switching it on just in time to see Joey scramble out behind him.

The small boy cast no shadow. None at all.

Robin almost panicked, almost yelled, before his common sense took hold of him. It's a trick of the light, he told himself, that's all. His heart was thumping like a hammer, but he forced himself to stay calm, smile, act naturally.

"Cripes!" breathed Joey, staring about him. "This is smashing!"

It was not Aladdin's Cave, nor Ali-Baba's, nor the Tomb of Tutankhamen. It was not even high enough to stand up in. But to Robin it was a very special place, almost a magic place. He had kept it as tidy as he could, made sure each day that the walls were packed meticulously tight. Against the farthest wall he had arranged a half dozen old orange crates to act as shelves. They contained an assortment of toys and games, a pile of comics, going mouldy now, and a transistor radio.

Joey asked, "What time is it?"

"I'm not sure," said Robin. "Gone six, I should think."

"Could you switch on that little silver wireless?"

He means the radio, Robin told himself, switching it on. *What's wrong with him? Why does he talk so funnily?*

He had never had problems with the radio before, had always kept the batteries fresh. But when the pop music came floating out, it was overlaid with crackling noises.

Robin fiddled with the tuning knob but the interference would not go away. Joey was oblivious. He was leaning back against one packed-earth wall, completely relaxed, smiling. He was rocking his head from side to side in time with the music.

Or rather, Robin realized, in time with some *other* music, not that coming from the radio. And he was singing softly, under his breath.

"We're happy girls and boys," he sang, then stopped and looked at Robin. "That's a shame. It's finished."

"What's finished?" asked Robin. "What were you singing?"

Joey peered at him quizzically. "What do you mean, what was I singing? The song on the radio, of course. What else would I be singing?" He got to his knees, as though ready to leave. "You might as well switch it off now. Old Lord Haw-Haw will be transmitting in a minute."

"*Who?*" asked Robin, feeling cold and numb again and somehow . . . somehow lost, displaced.

"Haven't you ever listened to your wireless before?" the boy asked. Then he shrugged. "I'll meet you same time tomorrow at the corner of my street. I've got to go now, or else Mum and Dad'll go whacko."

And with that he turned and disappeared into the tunnel.

When Robin finally found the nerve to follow him out, when he merged above ground, there was no sigh whatsoever of the small, pale boy. Like a dream, Joey Mullery had suddenly appeared in his life – and, like a dream, he had vanished just as swiftly.

The sky was almost dark by now, and a few stars glimmered distantly. A cold wind was whispering across the allotment. Robin wrapped his arms around himself and stood there, shivering, listening to the noise of the radio emerging from the tunnel. There was no crackling at all, now that Joey Mullery was gone. Only modern music. And the voice of a modern disc jockey. And yet, the sense of being lost, of being displaced, still remained.

Today is Monday, October 19th, 1983, Robin told himself, shaking. *Today is Monday, October 19th, 1983*. It seemed to reassure him, although why, he did not have the first idea.

The following day, the 20th, was as dry and golden as the autumn leaves on the trees in Vauxhall Park. It was a day when Robin did not play much with his friends, when he coasted through the day at school as though lost in a dream. He did not hurry home for tea that evening. Instead, he dashed through the narrow, cluttered streets till he came to the door of his grandfather's ancient house. He rang the bell and waited on the porch impatiently till his grandfather answered.

"Robin, what are you doing here?" The old man had been redecorating the house. He was wiping paint from his hands with a turpentine-soaked rag. "Still, come on in. Excuse the mess."

The house smelled of more than fresh paint. There was history here, there was tradition, in the dozens of black-and-white photographs, the trophies and souvenirs which cluttered the shelves, the Spitfire propeller which hung on the living-room wall, the stacks of dusty books and magazines. Memorabilia, his grandfather called it. It smelled the way a small, friendly museum would smell.

"Now, young man," said his grandfather, putting the rag aside. "What can I do for you?"

"I just wanted to ask you a few questions."

"Ask away, then." His grandfather smiled.

Robin repeated the snatch of song he had heard Joey

Mullery singing the previous night. "What is it?" he asked.

His grandfather had an expression on his face almost as blissful as Joey Mullery's. "That? Why, that's the Oval-teenies song. The Ovalteenies was a children's show, with songs and stories. Your mother used to listen to it when she was a little girl."

"It's a very old song, then?"

"Yes, very old indeed."

"And how about Lord Haw-Haw? Who is he?"

"Who *was* he, you mean. Lord Haw-Haw was a great traitor, an Englishman who went over to the Germans' side during the war. He used to make what they called propaganda broadcasts every night, telling lies about how the British were losing, trying to upset us. Not that anyone took any notice of him." Grandfather's face became suddenly puzzled. "What's all this interest in the Second World War anyway? Oh, I remember! It was that conversation we had yesterday teatime, after the sirens. I promised to show you those old newspapers."

It was not, initially, why Robin had come. But, listening to his grandfather, things had begun connecting in his mind. There seemed to be a link between the war and Joey Mullery.

"I'd like that very much," he said.

"Well come on then," said his grandfather.

He led the way up the stairs into the attic. And there, amongst the cobwebs, he leafed his way through piles of flaking newspapers, handing the best to Robin. They were all in neat piles, month by month, year by year, from 1939 to 1945. HITLER INVADES POLAND! read one head-line. DUNKIRK – OUR FINEST HOUR, SAYS MR CHURCHILL! reported another. And then there were the pictures. Of vast black formations of bombers, of fighters duelling in the clouds, of the night sky above St

Paul's Cathedral, criss-crossed with spotlight beams. A city at war. A city in flames and yet still fighting. After they had looked at all the newspapers, they stayed there in the attic, and Robin's grandfather explained how all the street lights in the city had been turned out so that London could not be seen from the air, how most of the young children had been evacuated to the safety of the countryside, how all the metal railings in the parks had been torn down to make new tanks, how sugar and butter and meat had all been rationed. And then there were the sirens. The first siren meant that the enemy bombers were on their way. The second meant that they had gone, that it was safe to come out of hiding. It was called – the All Clear.

"'Course it's safe," Joey Mullery had said, "now that the All Clear's gone."

As Robin listened, silent, still, he felt a prickling sensation down his spine, felt a cold sweat beginning to form there. It could not be! It could not! And yet he had seen Joey Mullery with his own eyes, had spoken to him, taken him to the hideout. And, if the boy was true to his word, he was waiting on the corner of demolished Bursell Street right now.

Robin got abruptly to his feet. "I've got to go now, Grandad."

His grandfather looked almost startled. "Something urgent?"

"Yes, I think so. Thank you for your time." He was at the door before he stopped. "By the way, Grandad, have you ever heard of anyone called Joey Mullery?"

"The name rings a bell," said his grandfather. "Why do you ask?"

"I just wondered," Robin answered. And then something came to him. Joey had referred to Bursell Street as

72

his street, despite the fact that it lay in ruins. "I think he used to live in Bursell Street," he told his grandfather.

"That's *right*," his grandfather mused. "There *was* a family called the Mullerys there. Never knew them well. They must have been moved to another part of London after the big bombing."

"What?"

"Didn't you know? Those three streets were destroyed by German bombs. That's one night I'll *never* forget. Twenty-first of October, 1940."

He rummaged through the newspapers for that month until he found the relevant edition. Robin squinted to read the faded print.

22nd October, 1940, read the date at the top. *The Vauxhall area suffered its worst bombing in a month last night, with Dowham, Foxton and Bursell Streets being completely destroyed. Most of the inhabitants had already moved to safety, but amongst the casualties were Mr and Mrs Wilfred Crow and their daughters Maisie and Eileen, Mr Arthur Hunter, Mrs Sybil Clark, Mr and Mrs Ronald Mullery and their son Joseph . . .*

Like a small, deathly-pale doll against the evening gloom, Joey Mullery was standing on the corner gazing skywards as Robin approached. The sky seemed to engross him, though there was nothing up there except the evening-tinted clouds. Robin stopped a good distance away, in the shadow of a derelict building. What was he doing here? Why had he come? This thin boy he was staring at, this Joey Mullery, was – *had to be* – some kind of *ghost*. Forty-three years dead. Killed by a bomb. Any sensible person would turn and run.

And yet, some force, stronger than anything he had ever known before, had drawn him back. It was not curiosity, or pity. It was the feeling that he was now somehow – *involved*.

Joey spotted him and came running towards him. Robin stood frozen to the spot.

"You're late! Where have you been?"

Robin forced his jaw to move. "S-sorry. I was – kept in – after school."

"Teachers!" Joey snorted. "Are we going to your hideout?"

"Y-yes. Yes. I suppose we are."

They began walking along the street. Joey was staring at the sky again, and Robin was staring at Joey. The boy's skin seemed to have a faint, almost translucent look, as though it had been frozen to his bones. His blue eyes seemed to glow like small twin lights encased in ice. And all the while Robin looked at him, he wanted to run. And could not.

Joey noticed his insistent gaze and smiled, quite unaware that anything was wrong. He reached into his pocket and produced something which Robin found ridiculous – two carrots on ice lolly sticks.

"Want one?" he asked.

"Why – why are they on sticks?" was all Robin could manage.

"Can't get proper lollies any more. It's the rationing. No sugar."

He began to nibble one and, taking Robin's silence as a *no*, popped the other back into his pocket. The carrot crunched between his teeth. Juice dribbled down his chin. It was a fresh, new vegetable.

"Er – Joey," Robin asked, "where exactly did you get those carrots?"

"From the newsagent's on Foxton Street."

"And *when* did you get them?"

"Just before I met you, of course. Five minutes ago."

Robin glanced behind him at the piles of rubble. **Bursell** Street, Dowham Street . . . There was no newsagent any more. There was no Foxton Street any more. Nothing but blasted bricks.

As his mind worked furiously, as his legs carried him on and on, he realized that Joey Mullery was far more than a ghost, a boy from the past. He was a *link* with the past. He had been summoned by the sirens, by the All Clear, as he called it, into this modern world of 1983. And yet, though Robin could see and hear him clearly, he was not completely here. He inhabited a . . . a no man's land between the past and present, sleeping in a house which was not there, buying from a shop which had been demolished long ago. He was caught between two times – the time of rationing and war, and the time of disc jockeys and radios and Robin Cooper.

Robin decided to test his theory.

"Dark, isn't it," he commented as casually as he was able.

"'Course it's dark. It's blackout time. No lights."

Robin nodded, and then pointed down a side street towards the park. "We can always play in there instead. If we climb over the railings."

Joey stared at him. "What railings? They took those down months ago!"

"Oh, right," said Robin quickly. "I couldn't see properly. In the dark."

"Don't you know anything?" Joey said contemptuously.

They walked along in silence, Robin violently trembling now. For an instant, when he had pointed at the railings, they had seemed to blur and fade away before his eyes. And now, as he glanced up at the streetlamps, their light seemed to grow dim, almost non-existent. The air around, he noticed, was gradually becoming chill, as though with frost. He tucked his head down and marched swiftly on.

Today is Tuesday, October 20th, 1983. Today is Tuesday, October 20th, 1983. Today . . .

"Come on, let's run," said Joey. "I want to listen to the wireless."

They were out of breath by the time they reached the hideout. They scrambled deep beneath the soft, dry-smelling earth, Joey first, and Robin edged past him to switch on the radio. The modern music was still there, and the crackling was still there. But above both of these, Robin could hear faint voices from another time. The same voices which, he guessed, Joey could hear quite clearly.

He was very cold now, as though in that tiny enclosed space Joey Mullery were drawing all the warmth out of the air. He rubbed his arms, and listened.

There was a woman called Vera Lynn singing something about the cliffs of Dover. Then there was a comedian called Arthur Askey. Robin had heard both of them before, had seen them on TV, but now . . . they sounded much, much younger. He huddled close to the radio. Somebody was reading the news now. A King was mentioned. King George VI.

Now he knew why he had come back this evening! It hit him with a sickening shock.

He was being drawn into Joey's world! He was being, slowly and surely, absorbed into the world of the past!

All of a sudden, Robin wanted to get out of there. He lunged for the opening – and then drew back sharply, his entire body shaken to the bone. In his panic, he had *touched* Joey's elbow, and his hand had passed through. The ghostly flesh was so cold it left Robin's hand aching. But there was something else, something far worse.

Joey Mullery was now half-solid. Touching him had been like putting your hand into a pool of water almost turned to hard, unyielding ice. And if Joey Mullery was

76

becoming real, then maybe tomorrow, on the 21st, the bombs would become real as well.

Joey suddenly sat bolt upright.

"Crikey! It's the air-raid sirens!"

Distantly, as though in a dream, Robin could hear them too.

"Let's get out of here!" Joey shouted. "We don't want to be caught on open ground!"

"Wait a minute!" Robin blurted.

But Joey was already in the tunnel. His voice drifted back. "Same time tomorrow!" he shouted. Then he was gone.

Robin stared blankly after him. There *are* no sirens, he told himself. There *are* no bombers. *There is no war.*

Then the ground trembled beneath him. Loose earth fell from the ceiling, almost blinding him. He scrambled out of the hideout; terrified, and bolted for his home.

He hardly slept at all that night, and by the following afternoon he was finding it difficult to stay awake at school. He was practically dozing at his desk, exhausted, when the teacher asked him a question which he did not hear and he was kept in for detention. He was over an hour late as he pelted towards Bursell Street that evening of October 21st. It was already dark.

The street seemed somehow unfamiliar. Shadowy figures hurried past in hats and long flapping overcoats like actors out of an old film. The coldness he had experienced the night before settled round him once again, like a frozen cloak.

By now he knew what he was going to do. Joey Mullery was unaware that he had died, that more than forty years had passed, that anything was different. Perhaps, if Robin explained the truth to him, then all of this would end – the war, the bombs, the voices on the radio. Perhaps, if he explained the truth, then the ghost would be laid; Joey Mullery would rest in final peace.

If only there was time.

Joey Mullery was waiting impatiently on the corner of the street. He was twirling a conker round his finger, and did not look away from it when Robin spoke his name.

"You're late *again*," he said. His voice was sullen.

"I was kept in after school."

"That's what you said yesterday."

"But it's the *truth* this time," Robin protested. "You've got to listen to me."

Joey stopped twirling the conker. "I think you're a liar," he said. "I don't think you're my friend at all."

He turned away from Robin angrily and began walking down the street towards the park. Robin stared at him aghast, realizing that everything was going wrong. He hurried to catch up.

"Joey!"

He got no response.

"Joey, what year do you think it is?"

"1940, of course. Why ask such stupid questions?"

"And King George VI is on the throne? And Winston Churchill is Prime Minister?"

"Who else? I think you must be barmy."

"I'm not! You've got to lis – "

And he suddenly stopped dead. Without thinking about it, he had reached out and grabbed Joey Mullery's arm. His hand had closed on solid flesh.

Joey Mullery had become real. It was too late to do anything about it.

Robin glanced around him. The street lamps were out. The railings in the park had gone. Dowham, Foxton and Bursell Street were there, huge, threatening silhouettes. There was a newsagent's sign on the corner.

"Oh no!" Robin murmured to himself. He felt as though he were drowning. "Oh no!"

Pale and eerie, like the wail of banshees on a starless night, the sound of sirens reached his ears. That was all at first. Before he heard – it couldn't be! – the droning noise of hundreds of propeller-driven planes.

"Oh crikey!" Joey shouted. "Jerry's caught us on the hop!"

"*No, Joey,*" Robin said, making one last desperate attempt. '*This isn't happening.*"

The first bombs landed, a long distance away. They sounded like a giant's footsteps trampling the earth. As Robin listened, the first wave of panic spread through him.

"We don't have time to make it to the shelter," Joey gasped. People in 1940s clothes were dashing everywhere by now, gas-mask satchels swinging from round their necks. "Come on, we can hide in the cellar of my house."

"But – "

"Come *on!*"

And he grabbed Robin, and began hauling him towards Bursell Street.

The sound of explosions was drawing closer. The sky was turning red.

For all of Joey's leanness, he was frighteningly strong, tough as piano wire. Robin began to struggle against him, fighting to break free. It did no good. Joey Mullery gave him a solid yank, and they rounded the corner into Bursell Street.

"What's the *matter* with you?" he was shouting. "We've got to get under cover!"

He didn't realize at all. He obviously thought that Robin was panicking. His grip tightened, and he dragged Robin closer to the dark, doomed house.

The planes were almost above them. A bomb smashed

79

down into a street off to the east and exploded; flames and debris leapt against the sky.

And that was the final shock Robin needed. He was wild as a terrified, trapped animal by now, and he clawed his way out of Joey's grasp, shoved the boy away from him.

Joey Mullery stared at him bewildered, tears forming in his wide blue eyes. He opened his mouth as if to say something. And then his own survival instincts took over, honed sharp by month upon month of this war, and he forgot Robin, left him for dead, turned and ran towards the house.

Robin stood there shaking, watching Joey Mullery disappearing down the street.

"Joey!" he shouted hoarsely. "Come back! Come out of there!"

The noise of the planes and the bombs was deafening by now. Joey could not even hear. As Robin watched, the small boy rushed into a dark house on the left and slammed the door.

"*Joey!*"

There was a whistling noise, of something falling, directly above.

The bomb hit.

The sound of the explosion was so loud Robin thought his head would burst. He was lifted from his feet and flung backwards like a rag doll. And as he hit the pavement, everything went black.

"Robin?" said a voice above him. "Are you all right?"

There was a dull ache all over his body. He opened his eyes, squinting. The street lamps were back – he could see clearly by their light. There was only rubble around him, shattered buildings, weeds.

His grandfather, out for an evening stroll, was crouching over him. Robin got slowly and shakily to his feet.

"What were you doing down there?" his grandfather asked.

"Didn't you hear it? The planes? The bombs?"

"What bombs?" His grandfather looked puzzled, then amused. "Oh, I understand. You've been playing soldiers, haven't you. All that talk about the war."

And then his grandfather frowned, walked across to the street lamp on the corner, picked something up from under it and turned it around in his hands.

"That's odd. I haven't seen one of these for ages – not this colour anyway."

It must have got knocked off in the final struggle. It was a striped school cap. Joey Mullery's cap. Robin stared at it a long while, and then he tipped his face, damp now, towards the evening sky. He closed his eyes and, faintly, in his own head, he could hear the sound of sirens.

DANCE OF DEATH

by Ken Burke

It was already dusk when they found little Molly and took her back across the fields to the farmstead. The rain had been falling in torrents for more than an hour, whipped about by a strong wind. Overhead, the dark clouds rushed headlong over the mountains into black night.

Molly was delirious when they got her back and tucked her into bed, and she coughed occasionally, a dry, painful rasp which made her mother and father wince.

"Sure, 'tis pneumonia," said Great Grandma Shaughnessy, shaking her old, wise head. "The doctor'll have to be brought, or she'll die."

The day of the telephone had not yet arrived at the lonely farmstead, which lay at the bottom of a valley, with one or two fields wrested grudgingly from the harsh terrain. Nearby, the woods spread up towards the crooked outline of the Galway Mountains. The country was the wildest on the whole west coast of Ireland, and it was as bleak and pitiless as the edge of the world.

Molly's father took the car, and like a madman drove through the sheets of falling water, away over the treacherous mountain road. It was a drive of two hours at the best of times to the nearest town and back. This time, Molly's life depended on it.

While her mother and Grandma Shaughnessy busied themselves in the kitchen, Molly's fourteen-year-old brother Rory went out to get logs from the woodstore in the adjoining outhouse.

It was more than an hour, now, since Rory had seen

Molly's dun pony Jupiter trot back into the courtyard alone. At ten years old, his sister had taken to sneaking off on her pony without telling her parents, knowing that they would forbid it. By the time the pony had returned the rain was already falling hard, and Rory recalled how it had started – with a clap of thunder so loud it shook the very ground. It may have been the thunderclap which had startled the pony enough to throw Molly into a stagnant ditch, where she had remained unconscious for perhaps an hour before being found.

Now she lay pale and dangerously ill in her bed, while the women fussed anxiously around, building up the fire in her bedroom and filling hot water bottles. Rory came up the stairs into the low, oak-beamed room, lit only by the crackling logs on the fire. He was shocked to see how ill she looked. Her straggling black hair was more ruffled than ever, and still looked damp, although her mother had dried it as best she could. Molly's small face was pinched, and drops of perspiration stood out on her brow. Rory felt a surge of love for his little sister, and knew he would be heartbroken if she were taken from them. He choked back his emotion and went slowly and thoughtfully back down the stairs.

In the kitchen, he gathered his logs and stacked them in a corner on the tiled floor, away from the scrubbed farmhouse table and chairs. He hung up his anorak, then tilted his head to listen.

"Did you hear that, Ma?" he asked his mother, who was slowly stirring a pot of soup.

"Hear what, Rory?"

He frowned. "Outside, Ma. A sort of . . . wailing."

His mother tossed her head impatiently.

"Rory, the wind and rain are making so much noise I can't hear a thing. Like a dog, do you mean, or what?" She reached for her dishcloth.

"No, not a dog. More like a bird. More like a screeching."

"Faith, 'tis only the stable door that's blown open and creaking backwards and forwards."

"Maybe it is." Rory zipped up his anorak and opened the kitchen door. "I'll go and look, Ma, and make sure Jupiter's OK."

Once outside, he couldn't hear the strange sound, only the howl of the wind and the pattering of the rain. He ran across the farmyard to the shelter of their small barn. Inside the entrance where the hay was brought in and stored, the stable door was securely latched. Rory glanced in and saw that Jupiter was restless, pawing the ground every now and then and shaking his head about.

"There, there. Quiet, boy, 'tis only the storm." Rory patted the pony's head, and this seemed to calm him, although his eyes were wide, showing their whites.

Rory stiffened. The strange sound came again. He could hear it, far off in the mountains, a mournful cry, as of a lost soul. Jupiter began to stamp the ground, shaking his head again. He had heard it too.

"Quiet, boy." Rory stepped to the open barn entrance and peered out through the gusting rain.

At first he could see nothing in the darkness. Then he became aware of something green and shimmering in the distance, coming closer. It glided down across the meadow, towards the farmstead. As it approached, Rory heard the howling rise in pitch, then stop abruptly, as the figure halted at the far end of the farm buildings. The pony became very agitated, rearing up in his stall.

Rory couldn't see clearly through the rain, but he had an impression of a tall, crooked shape, and a billowing green cloak, *through* which he could see the outhouse walls. Then it glided silently across the yard to the farmhouse. A sudden gust of wind blew a curtain of rain into Rory's face, and when he looked again, the figure had gone.

Calming the pony down again, Rory crossed the farmyard at a sprint and threw open the kitchen door. His mother turned at the kitchen range, startled when she saw his face.

"Lord love you, Rory! Have you seen a ghost?" she said, coming over and fussing at his damp black locks with a towel.

"I'm OK," he said impatiently. "What about Molly?"

"She's about the same," his mother replied. "Your great-grandma's with her now, watching over the poor wee mite."

As she helped him out of his wet things, Rory told his mother of the strange, flickering shape he'd seen. She turned suddenly pale, put her hand to her mouth and sat down heavily at the kitchen table.

"Lord save us," she whispered. "A banshee, Rory. That's what you've seen. There's to be a death tonight."

She raised her eyes and looked up at the ceiling where, in the room above, little Molly lay in her bed, watched over by Grandma Shaughnessy.

Puzzled, Rory said, "A banshee, Ma?"

His mother looked up at him with anxious eyes. "We Shaughnessy's have lived in these parts for a long, long time, Rory. And this farmhouse has been the family home further back than living memory. Just before the death of a member of the family it's said that the cry of the banshee was always heard, back in the old days. The last time anyone heard it was when your great-grandfather was ill, many years ago. A dreadful wailing sound came in the night, and when they went into his room soon after, he was lying on the floor, dead. That was the odd thing, they said. Him being so ill, he could never have got out of bed on his own."

Rory's mouth had dropped open. "It – it happened in this house, Ma?"

There was a worried frown on his mother's face as she said, "In this same house, son. You ask your father. He was here himself, he says, and heard the banshee. I pray to heaven he won't be too late coming with the doctor." Her voice broke, and she began to sob.

Rory went to her and put his arm around her shoulders.

He said, "Don't cry, Ma. Molly won't die. You've got Great-Grandma and me here, and we love her more than our own selves. We'd rather die than lose Molly."

She gave Rory a kiss on the cheek and a brave smile. "You're a good boy, Rory. You're a great comfort to your mother, so you are." She dabbed the corner of her eye with her apron and rose from the chair to go to the kitchen range.

She said, "Take yourself up the stairs, now. See your Great-Grandma Shaughnessy drinks this broth. And make sure your wee sister's as well as she can be."

"OK, Ma." He saw that her mouth was trembling, but said no more and took the steaming bowl up the stairs.

As he approached the room where his sister lay, a peculiar feeling of unease crept up his spine. He stopped outside the door. There was the sound of someone singing inside the room.

"Round and round," went the voice. "Round and round."

The tonelessness of the voice chilled Rory to the bone. It was Molly's voice.

Rory put the soup down and slowly opened the door. Before the bed was his little sister, dancing in a tortured carousel upon the rug. With her danced a tall, elegant lady in a flowing black dress and lace shawl. Their faces were lit up by the flickering flames from the log fire, and their shadows capered madly on the wall.

In the corner between the bed and the fire, Great-Grandma Shaughnessy was sleeping through it all. Rory knew she would have braved Satan himself rather than let Molly get out of bed, yet here she was as though the final trumpet itself would never awaken her.

The lady in the long gown saw him and dropped her grasp on Molly's hands. Molly continued dancing round and round the rug, her eyes bright and staring. Rory saw then how desperately wan she was, and how her little face shone with fever.

The lady spoke.

"Dance on, little girl," she said in soft, deadly tones. "Soon you will be free."

At this Molly danced faster, singing, "Round and round. Round and round."

Involuntarily, Rory cried out, "You'll kill her! Make her stop!"

The lady turned her eyes upon Rory. He saw how beautiful she was, with her long, fine-spun hair, and her darkly glittering eyes which held the reflection of night.

"So, Rory."

He started when he heard his name. She threw back her head and gave a tinkling laugh. "Yes, I know you, Rory Shaughnessy, who would endure a thousand tortures to save his little sister. But it's already too late. See the whiteness of her face, and the fever that grips her body. Before morning she will breathe no more."

There was a hypnotic quality to her voice and her dark eyes. Rory looked at Molly as she danced, and saw the truth of what the lady said. Somehow the knowledge did not frighten him. He accepted it as inevitable that Molly was going to die.

He vaguely remembered something about his grand-father being found dead on the floor, and not in his bed.

Now here was Molly, dancing round the floor to the command of the dark-eyed lady.

"Who – who are you?" he stammered.

She did not appear to speak, but he heard her voice echoing in his mind.

"Some call me the *Bein si*, the woman of the fairies. Other times I am known as Nyx, daughter of the night. I call those to me who are about to die, and carry them softly into the next world. Accept it, Rory. It will happen. One day it will happen to you."

Rory took a step forward. He struggled to remember something he had said to his mother. He saw Great-Grandma Shaughnessy sleeping in her chair by the fire, and himself standing helplessly by as Molly danced herself to death.

Then he remembered what he had said. Something about loving his little sister more than his own self, and that he would rather die than lose her.

Suddenly he knew that it was not too late to save Molly, and that the beautiful lady had tried to trick him. He put out one arm to push her away from him. To his surprise, his hand passed right through her and struck the wall. Blind terror shot through him. She was no less than a wraith, a malevolent spirit of the mountains come to fasten on those who were sickly and carry them off before they were meant to die, into the world of darkness.

Filled with overwhelming fear for the life of his sister, Rory leaped forward and scooped Molly up. She seemed hardly any weight at all, slumping into his arms in a dead faint. Rory stood defiantly holding Molly and faced the tall lady.

"The Dance of Death is over, spirit woman!" he cried. "'Tis empty-handed you'll be this night. So go and haunt the dead, not the living!"

As he spoke, the shape of the beautiful lady began to

waver and dissolve. Her tall figure became somehow twisted, and the black dress became a swirling, greenish cloak. Her beautiful face seemed to fall in until it was merely a shadow under the green cowl.

It was the banshee.

A loathsome odour of decay oozed from it, filling the whole room. The right hand, now shrivelled into a bony claw, slowly rose and pointed at Rory. He heard a croaking voice which echoed as if from far away, shearing through his brain like the blade of a knife.

'*You have cheated me of this prize*,' it said. "*But remember that where the banshee walks, death always follows*."

The apparition receded across the room and faded away through the outside wall. As it went, Rory saw with horror that under the green cowl there was no face, only the shadow of a skull. And then he was looking at a blank wall once again. All he could hear was the pattering of the rain and the howl of the wind across the mountains.

He realized that he was shaking and covered with sweat. Molly lay unconscious in his arms. So shallow was her breath that she seemed hardly to be breathing at all. In her weakened state, the dancing had exhausted her to the very point of death. He bent down and laid her gently in the bed then pulled the coverlet over her.

The next hour passed in a haze. Rory vaguely remembered going out to the top of the stairs and calling his mother. Together they tried wakening Great-Grandma Shaughnessy, but she slept too deeply. All they could do was to watch helplessly over Molly's tiny form huddled in the bed, and wait for the doctor to arrive.

When at last Rory's father returned with the doctor Rory was hustled firmly out of the bedroom. He took a torch and went out to the barn. There was no sign of the banshee, and Jupiter was calm, now, dozing in his stable.

It was quite some time before Rory was allowed back in to Molly's room. He entered to hear the doctor say: "I've given her some medicine. Plenty of rest, and she'll be right as rain in a few days."

Everyone in the room sighed with relief.

"What about Great-Grandma?" asked Rory, suddenly aware that she was not in the room. Then he noticed how quiet his parents were, and how the doctor stood there in the firelight with the expression of a man who too often is the bearer of unhappy tidings.

The doctor smiled sadly and shook his head. "She was old, Rory. Her time had come."

"'Tis the will of God," said Rory's father, putting his hand on Rory's shoulder. "We must count our blessings."

And in his heart Rory knew that his Great-Grandma would have wanted it to happen this way, that she was happy to die, if her death meant that little Molly could live. The banshee never again returned to haunt the Shaughnessys, and Rory never told anyone of what he had seen that night. But sometimes in his bed, when the rainclouds were dark overhead, and the wind howled down the valley he imagined he could hear the banshee's long, mournful cry echoing in the mountains. Then he would shiver, and pull the bedclothes a little more firmly over himself, and hope morning would come quickly.

THE WOODSEAVES GHOSTS

by Catherine Gleason

"The only snag about staying at Woodseaves," said David Mitchell, "is the library."

"Yes," his sister Sally agreed. "Do you remember how frightened we were when we first saw it? We were sure there were ghosts about, hiding in the corners!"

"I'm not so sure that it isn't haunted," said David, with an air of mystery. Sally was two years younger than him and she usually believed every word he said.

Her eyes grew big as saucers. "You don't really think so, do you? What do you mean?"

"Well, you remember reading in that local history book about the boy and girl who were supposed to have disappeared in there? It was exactly a hundred and fifty years ago that they vanished. So they might turn up again." His voice dropped to a whisper. "One of these Fridays, when we're in the library doing our school work, the air will turn cold and the door will slowly start to open . . .creeeak . . ."

"Oh, stop it!" cried Sally. "You're making me shiver!"

"And then," continued David in a creepy voice, "something dressed in a long white gown will glide in . . . and – grab you!"

Sally gave a little shriek and covered her ears, while David burst out laughing. "Only teasing you, silly."

"You are horrid, David," said Sally, giggling in spite of herself. "You're just trying to scare me because we have to do some work in there tonight. Well, I'm not afraid!"

"Neither am I, really," said David. "Come on, slow-coach, we're going to be late for tea. Where's Max?"

The heavy golden labrador lumbered up to them and they made their way back through Woodseaves Park to the Hall.

Great-Uncle Timothy Mitchell owned the Hall, and lived there with his housekeeper Martha and, of course, Max. Like his house, Uncle Tim was rather Victorian and rambling, but David and Sally were very fond of him and loved spending their summer holidays at Woodseaves.

This was the first year their parents hadn't been with them, because their father had taken a job in America that summer and Mrs Mitchell had gone with him.

Martha was very neat and motherly and precise, and she had been Uncle Tim's housekeeper for donkeys' years. She was only ever strict about one thing, and that was their doing an hour or so's work in the library on the subjects they hadn't done very well in at school. This, as David said, was the one snag about staying there, but then it wasn't much of a disadvantage, considering all the other things that Woodseaves had to offer. Midway between the town and the country, everything was within easy reach, from riding stables to a cinema.

"What did you do with yourselves today, children?" Uncle Tim asked them over tea.

He and Martha had always called David and Sally "children", and David suspected that they always would, no matter how big they grew.

"We fed the goldfish in the pond, and then David climbed a tree and nearly fell in the stream, and then the Smithson twins took us over to South Meadow to see the lambs," said Sally. "They're getting quite big now."

"What, the Smithsons?" The old man looked startled.

"No, Uncle, the lambs," giggled Sally. Uncle Tim was so vague at times.

"I was reading about ghosts in a local history book," said David. "Do you know there are supposed to be two of them here at Woodseaves?"

"That's right." Uncle Tim chuckled. "A brother and his young sister, about the same ages as you two. They were said to have been murdered by their wicked stepmother, or some such nonsense."

"Why?" demanded Sally, who had more than her fair share of curiosity.

"The stepmother wanted Woodseaves for her own sons, and the other two were in the way, I suppose."

"Really, Mr Timothy, you shouldn't be filling the children's heads with such stories," said Martha reprovingly. "We've lived here more years than we care to remember, and we've never seen any ghosts."

"That's probably because there aren't any such things," suggested David.

"Exactly. Ghosts don't exist."

Sally wasn't so sure.

"There. Finished at last." David threw down his pen thankfully and stretched, pushing back his chair. It had taken him nearly an hour to plough through his French exercise.

"Well, hang on a minute," said Sally crossly. She was struggling with a maths problem.

"OK." Idly, David glanced around the library. All the other rooms at Woodseaves were light and modern-furnished, but even in the height of summer the library looked gloomy, damp and ancient. Hundreds of old books, some very valuable, were shut into dark, glass-fronted cases against the walls, and the firelight cast weird dancing reflections on to them.

"Nearly finished now," said Sally, one hand stroking Max, who shifted restlessly beside her. The big dog always seemed uneasy in the library. Suddenly he jumped up and ran over to the window, barking furiously.

"Max! Come and lie down," ordered David.

Max slunk reluctantly away from the window, tail down, to the opposite corner of the room. He made a funny sort of noise, half way between a whine and a howl, and scratched at the door, looking back at them with piteous eyes. David opened the door for him and the dog shot out of the room as if something was after him.

"That's strange," said Sally. "Maybe he saw a cat outside?"

"I don't think so." David peered out of the window at the dusky night. "Perhaps he – "

Suddenly all the lights went out, and, except for the glowing fire, the room was plunged into darkness. Sally gave a little scream.

"It's all right," said David calmly, sitting by the fire. "The lights have fused, that's all. I expect Uncle will have them on again in a minute."

"I hope so," said Sally. "It's rather scary in here with – oh!" She broke off with a cry of astonishment.

David swung round and followed her gaze to the window. His mouth dropped open in sheer amazement as he saw two strange figures, hand in hand, passing straight through the window into the library!

David and Sally clutched each other in terror. But the figures did not look terrifying; they were a boy and a girl, dressed in old-fashioned clothes.

"Do not be afraid. We are not come to harm you," said the boy.

"What . . . who are you?" asked David in a quavery voice.

"My name is Lucretia, and this is my brother, Comus," said the girl, with a slight bow.

"Er . . . how do you do," said Sally, a little unsteadily.

"May we sit down? We have been wandering for many years, and we are somewhat fatigued," the boy introduced as Comus said politely.

Sally rubbed her eyes and stared. The ghostly figures sat quite calmly in the two leather armchairs opposite and, through their outlines, she could see the chairs quite clearly.

"David," she whispered, "do you think we're dreaming?"

"No," said David excitedly. "I think they're the two who were murdered here – don't you remember Uncle Tim's story? – and they've come back to the – to the scene of the crime," he finished lamely.

"Indeed, you are right," said Lucretia in her sweet, light voice. "Our lives were cut short very much against our wills, one hundred and fifty years ago this very evening."

David nodded. "Uncle Tim told us about you."

Sally wriggled in her chair. Half of her was scared enough to dash straight out of the library, shrieking for Uncle Tim, but the other half was full of inquisitiveness. After a short struggle, curiosity won.

"How did it happen?" she asked finally. "Your being murdered, I mean."

"Yes, how?" David, too, was still a little frightened, and spoke rather more aggressively than he intended. "Our uncle said you were killed by a wicked stepmother, like people in a fairy tale, and it all sounds very fishy to me."

Comus and Lucretia looked at each other in a puzzled way.

"It had nothing to do with fish," said Comus. "It was poisoned veal, as I remember."

"That is right," said Lucretia. "You see, our mama died when we were a little younger than you are now, and

95

Papa married again, almost straight away. He was a very good man, and he wished to secure a second mother for us."

"But his second wife, our stepmother, was a most wicked woman," continued Comus. "She was widowed too, and she married Papa in order to provide for her own baby sons. Really, you know, she did not care a rap for him or for us. She only wanted her children to have Woodseaves, and we stood in the way, because Woodseaves would have been ours when we were old enough to inherit it."

"At first, we did not realize the extent of her malice," Lucretia resumed, "though we did consider it odd when she told us that deadly nightshade was good for us, and to eat as much as we could if ever we found it growing wild."

"And she was always suggesting that we go for a bathe in the deepest part of the river," added Comus. "After we told her repeatedly that we could not swim!"

"Yet she was always very pleasant to us," Lucretia sighed. "We hardly believed she could wish us any harm. Then, one evening, she served us a dish of veal here in the library where we were reading, and that was that."

"You were poisoned?" asked Sally, round-eyed.

"Yes – we fell asleep, and awoke like this." Comus held up a transparent hand.

"And what happened to your stepmother?" asked David.

"She died of the consumption shortly afterwards, and confessed on her deathbed to having poisoned us. Her sons did not long survive her, and so it was all a wasted effort, really." Lucretia looked sadly into the fire.

"What a shame!" cried the warm-hearted Sally indignantly. "I think it's terrible that you should have had such short, unhappy lives. Honestly, David, we don't know how lucky we are, do we?"

"You're right," agreed David seriously. "We do have marvellous parents, when you come to think about it. None of this wicked-stepmother stuff at all."

Comus and Lucretia exchanged glances of something like envy.

"Your parents, then, are very kind?" asked Comus wistfully.

"Oh, yes! They couldn't be nicer," said Sally eagerly. "I wish we could help you," she added to their phantom visitors.

"Perhaps you can," said Comus at once. "For we have come here tonight to offer you a proposition."

"What kind of proposition?" David asked suspiciously.

"We wish to change places with you," said Comus simply. "If you are agreeable to our suggestion, we would become you, and you would become – "

"Ghosts?" said Sally faintly.

"Er . . . I don't think we'd like that very much, thank you," said David. "Anyway, why us?"

"Why, because you are here at Woodseaves," said Lucretia. "And you are about the same ages as we are. Being a ghost can be great fun, you know," she added mischievously. "Watch me!"

And before their eyes, she vanished. David and Sally watched breathlessly as a heavy vase rose into the air, apparently by itself, and flew across the room. "Catch!" came a gleeful cry from nowhere, and David had to go into a quick rugby dive to save the vase before it hit the ground.

There was a tinkling laugh and Lucretia appeared again. "There! You see? Some very naughty ghosts do that sort of thing all the time."

"I don't think we'd want to drift about chucking vases around, actually," said Sally, as David rubbed his bruised elbows.

"Oh, dear!" sighed Lucretia.

"Perhaps you would prefer to reside in the celestial regions?" suggested Comus.

"What do you mean?" asked Sally. "You do talk oddly, you know!"

"Everybody talked like that a hundred and fifty years ago," David reminded her.

"Precisely. I beg your pardon," Comus apologized to Sally. "I meant to say, how about Heaven?"

And just then, the door opened.

"Are you still in here, children?" Martha fiddled with the light switch. "Have both of the light bulbs gone? What a nuisance!" She came into the firelit room, glancing straight at the ghostly figures in the armchairs.

"We were just talking, Martha," said Sally.

"Well, don't stay too long, dears. Bed in half an hour, you know."

"Why didn't Martha see you?" asked David, as soon as she had gone.

"We did not wish her to," said Comus.

"What was that you said about Heaven?" Sally demanded impatiently.

"My brother wondered if you would care to go there," said Lucretia carelessly.

"Have you really been to Heaven? I don't believe it!" said David.

"Indeed we have," said Lucretia, with indignation. "We might have stayed there, too, but that we kept on hankering after life on earth, and THEY do not like it if you are half-hearted about Heaven. And so we came back. Won't you change places with us, please?" she asked imploringly. "THEY wouldn't mind, you know."

David and Sally did not ask who THEY were; they rather thought they knew already.

"Well, really, I don't think . . ." began David doubt-fully, but Sally was overcome with curiosity and cut in with:

"What's it really like in Heaven? Do tell us all about it."

"Oh, it is a wonderful place, of course, but much depends on whereabouts you go. There are many different sections," explained Comus.

"How do you mean?" Sally was puzzled. Heaven was Heaven, wasn't it?

"Well," said Lucretia, "there is one part where all the soldiers go who have been killed in battle. They feast and drink all the time, and have their wounds bandaged. I found it monotonous – dull, you know," she added, wrinkling her nose and tossing back her light brown ringlets. "All of their conversation concerns war and battles. It is messy too, with all that blood and iodine."

"Valhalla!" cried David excitedly. "I've heard about that at school – it's the Heaven of the Vikings. Do all the Chinese Kung Fu fighters who get beaten go there as well?"

Comus looked puzzled. "I have never heard of this Kung Fu," he confessed. "The Eastern people generally seem to go to Nirvana, where they do nothing but sit and think all the time. They call it meditation. Now that really is dull."

"The Mount Olympus one is quite pleasant," said Lucretia doubtfully. "If you like hatching plots and chasing fauns through forests, that is. I believe they have a few unicorns and winged horses there, too."

"Really? Winged horses?" Sally was thrilled. She was pony-mad.

"Yes. And there is ordinary Heaven as well, where you walk on clouds and wear haloes," said Comus. "A great many Royal Air Force pilots seem to end up there. I think they really mean to go to Valhalla, but they cannot resist the wings, you see."

"It also helps if you play a musical instrument," added Lucretia. "Won't you change places with us? I am sure you would like it very much."

"How could you do that?" asked David curiously.

"Oh! That is very simple," said Comus. "We hold your hands for a second, and concentrate very hard, and our minds would change places with yours. You see? It is extremely easy."

"Well – I'm really very sorry," said David, "but I'm afraid we can't."

"No," said Sally regretfully. "It's our parents, you see. They would miss us terribly."

"Ah, but they would never know," argued Comus. "After all, we would look exactly the same as you. It's just that we should have swapped minds. Within a few weeks we could learn to talk as you do, and then nobody at all would be able to tell the difference."

"I'm afraid it's impossible," said David slowly.

There was a sad little pause. Comus looked very downcast, and Lucretia dabbed her eyes with a transparent lace handkerchief. Sally thought longingly about unicorns and winged horses, and David tried very hard not to think of Valhalla.

"Well!"Comus said finally. "Then there is nothing more to be said. We had better be going."

"I'm so sorry we couldn't help," said Sally, "and it's been simply marvellous talking to you."

"It has been our pleasure," said Comus and Lucretia politely. "We wish you goodnight." And they put out their hands in farewell.

"Goodbye," said Sally and David, and without thinking they shook hands with the ghostly pair.

* * *

"Now then, children!" Martha pushed open the library door. "It really is getting late. Oh, good, the lights are working again. I've cooked you some fish fingers for a suppertime snack – come along to the kitchen before they get cold." And she bustled out again.

They looked at each other and smiled.

"What on earth can fishes' fingers look like, Sister? Evidently a new variety of fish has been discovered."

"Indeed; when we were here last, fish did not even have hands, let alone fingers. Let us go and try them."

Hand in hand, they walked out of the library to find the kitchen.

LORIMER'S BRIDE

by Mary Danby

Elizabeth opened the shallow box on her dressing-table, unfolded the tissue paper and took out the stockings. Sheer silk. She had never worn any so fine before. Behind her, on her bed, lay the long white dress, trimmed at the neck and waist with tiny pink satin rosebuds. It had been specially made for her by her mother's dressmaker.

"White, I think, for her first ball," Elizabeth's mother had said.

"Silver sandals, with perhaps a hint of a heel." That was the lady in the shoe shop.

"A little extra height here . . . and here . . ." her mother's hairdresser had suggested, lifting strands of Elizabeth's thick, dark hair and twisting them into a shiny knot.

Elizabeth had felt like a thoroughbred being prepared for its first race – and the comparison was a good one, for behind all the fretting and fussing, the primping and grooming, the dancing classes and lessons in etiquette, was the unspoken desire of her parents that she should eventually catch the eye of a suitable husband. She was, in fact, about to enter the Marriage Stakes.

Every Easter, Colonel and Mrs Hope-Massie gave a large ball at their manor house in aid of a charity. This year, Elizabeth had been invited, and she and her parents were to attend Mrs Hope-Massie's dinner party beforehand.

"I believe Mrs Hope-Massie has found you a young man, poppet," said her mother. "You'll be sitting next to

102

him at dinner, and he'll be your partner at the ball, too, so you won't have to worry that nobody will ask you to dance." Elizabeth, filled with excitement, had hardly noticed the little insult.

Her own young man. It was all so thrilling. Perhaps he would be tall and handsome, and all eyes would be upon this elegant young couple as they waltzed around the ballroom. He would give her a rose, and say: "Its beauty is nothing compared to yours," and she would smile dreamily up at him as he escorted her to supper . . .

"Time you ran your bath, darling!" Her mother was calling from across the landing, where Elizabeth could see her sitting on her bed in a pink crepe de Chine dressing-gown, painting her toenails poppy red. Her mother was very pretty, with wavy blonde hair and blue eyes that seemed almost to give off sparks when she was at her lively best. She was always the centre of attention at parties, and Elizabeth suddenly wished that she could arrive at the ball alone, like Cinderella, anonymous and fascinating, with no one to say: "Ah, yes, Selina's daughter. Of course . . . The divine Selina . . . My dear, your mother is quite the most ravishing – " Or the wittiest. Or the most amusing, most glamorous. Elizabeth had heard it all so many times.

"Do my tie for me, will you, old thing?" Elizabeth's father emerged from his dressing room, stiff and remote in his high white collar and black tails. Her mother rose gracefully from the bed and began expertly to make a bow with his white tie. He jutted his chin forward while she was doing it, and Elizabeth thought he looked rather military, like Colonel Hope-Massie, only without the gingery moustache.

As she went along to the bathroom, she heard him say: "Don't be too long, Selina. I'll make us a cocktail before we go."

103

When Elizabeth was dressed, she went to look at herself in her mother's long cheval mirror. It was certainly a lovely dress, and Elizabeth couldn't help but smile at herself. She looked young, romantic – like a bride, almost.

"Sweetie, you're a picture!" her mother declared, advancing on her with a tiny pot of rouge. "We'll just dab on a teensy bit of this . . . and . . . there! Beautiful rosy cheeks!"

She herself was dressed in a cream-coloured lace gown with a choker and ear-rings made of agate and pearls. She was stunning. She smelt of lilac, and her skin was soft and clear. She put her head next to Elizabeth's, so that they were framed together in the mirror. "We could be sisters," she said.

They went down to the drawing-room, and Elizabeth's father said: "Damned if I haven't got the two finest women in the county!" Then he went over to Elizabeth, picked up her hand and kissed it. "Lovely, my dear," he said quietly. He turned to his wife. "I can see we'll have to treat her as a young lady, now. In fact, I think perhaps she might even be allowed a rather weak cocktail."

They drove to the Hope-Massies' in their silver-grey Lancia. The sun was slipping down behind the trees as they swept through the gates of Lake House and made their way up the long drive. To their right, the large lake reflected the last orange rays, and the dark surface of the water moved gently in tune with the evening breeze.

"Do people swim in the lake?" Elizabeth asked.

"They used to," replied her mother. "But not any more, I gather. There was an accident a couple of years ago. I dare say you were away at school at the time."

"What happened?" Elizabeth stared at the cold grey water. "Did somebody drown?"

"Very nearly, I believe. It was the Hope-Massies' daughter, Helen. But she's all right now. She married soon after and went to Canada."

They had drawn up in front of the house now, and someone was opening the car door for them. Inside, a parlourmaid took their wraps, and a butler ushered them into the drawing-room. Colonel and Mrs Hope-Massie stood ready to greet them, a matching pair of pouter pigeons – he, proud-chested in a stiff white shirtfront, she large and fluttery in turquoise chiffon. There were about a dozen people in the room already, and Elizabeth stood shyly to one side while her mother's admirers paid their usual homage.

"Now then, Elizabeth," said Mrs Hope-Massie with an encouraging smile, "there's someone who's just dying to meet you."

This was it. She was about to come face to face with the Romeo of her dreams.

"May I introduce Hubert Glossington? Hubert, this is Elizabeth Fletcher."

Her eyes were demurely cast down, so that all she saw at first were the three gold studs above his white waistcoat. As she held out her hand, she raised her glance, then immediately lowered it again. A cruel, mean disappointment. So this was to be her beau for the evening: a toothy, pop-eyed, apple-cheeked individual, who looked as if he would be happier mucking out a stable than tangoing till the small hours.

"How do you do?" she said unenthusiastically.

"Gosh. I say. How do you do? Gosh. Yes," he replied, waggling her arm like a pump handle. "Jolly good do, this, eh? I say, do you hunt?"

On the other side of the drawing-room her mother was entertaining a small crowd of laughing men. She was very animated, waving her hands about as she made her clever

105

remarks and smiled her dazzling smile. Elizabeth felt dumpy and dowdy, her beautiful dress no more than an old dishrag.

"No," she said dispiritedly, in answer to Hubert's question. "I haven't the stomach for it."

They sat next to each other at dinner, and Hubert told her, in great detail, the best way to gut a woodpigeon. Over the coffee, he confided: "I say, I think you look awfully super. I mean, your dress, and all that."

She wasn't bold enough to say thank you. Instead, she gave an embarrassed little smile and looked down at the table.

"Yes," he went on. Then he gave a chortle. "Actually, you remind me of a super horse I once had – all white and sort of leggy. Different coloured mane, of course. Hers was grey."

"How nice," said Elizabeth.

In the ballroom, he grasped her round the waist for a quickstep. His hands were warm and sweaty, and stuck to her. He was too busy talking to listen to the music, so his steps were very often out of time. Elizabeth had difficulty avoiding his large feet. Her parents danced by with great style. They made a very handsome couple. Her father winked at her, then they turned, and her mother gave her a questioning look. "Having fun?"

"Lost the fox down by the quarry," Hubert was saying. "Cast a shoe on the way home and didn't get back until half way through dinner. Mother thought it was a bit off." (He pronounced it "orf".) "She says it isn't fair on the servants, keeping them late. Not that they've got much else to do, what?" He stuck out his teeth in a grotesque smile.

Elizabeth gazed desperately around the ballroom, seeking some means of escape. But it wasn't until she had endured two more quicksteps and a slow foxtrot that her chance arrived.

"I say, fancy a little something?" asked Hubert. "Let's see if we can find the chappie with the drinks, what?"

"I think I'll just sit here for a moment," said Elizabeth, indicating one of the delicate gilt chairs that ringed the ballroom. "I'm feeling a little dizzy."

Hubert raised his eyebrows. "Poor old thing," he said, looking surprised, as if he'd had no previous experience of such fragility. "I'll see if I can find you a sausage roll or two." He clumped happily off towards the supper room, leaving Elizabeth staring dismally around, not at all cheered up by the jolly expressions on the faces of the other guests.

The band came to the end of a waltz. The dancers clapped, then Colonel Hope-Massie announced: "Take-er your partners, ladies and-er gentlemen, for the Gay-er Gordons!" Just before the familiar music began, and the pairs began to parade round the room, there was a brief moment when everything seemed suddenly to go silent, and in that moment Elizabeth heard a gentle tapping coming from somewhere behind her. She looked back at the thick velvet curtains that fell from ceiling to floor and thought they probably concealed the high windows that led on to the terrace. Standing up, she held aside the edge of one of the curtains.

The moon was bright, and she could see the wide grey terrace with its picturesque pots of flowering shrubs and solid stone balcony. She thought she could see someone standing there, for a moment, but then the moon was dimmed by a cloud, and the terrace appeared to be empty.

Mrs Hope-Massie came up behind her and took hold of her by the elbow.

"Come along, dear," she said brightly. "There's nothing interesting out there. What have you done with Hubert?"

"He's just coming," Elizabeth assured her. "Everything's fine, really."

"Good, good," said Mrs Hope-Massie. "So long as he's looking after you." She patted Elizabeth vaguely on the arm and sailed away.

Across the ballroom, emerging from the supper room with two glasses of champagne balanced on a plate of sandwiches, Elizabeth saw Hubert, a look of cheerful anticipation on his face. Suddenly panicking, she slipped behind the velvet curtains into the window recess. Her heart thudding, as if she were playing sardines, she waited. In a little while she heard Hubert ask some of the other guests: "I say, have you seen my partner? Dashed odd – she seems to have vanished. Ah well, more sandwiches for me, what?"

She gazed out at the terrace again. The moon slid from behind its cloud, and yes – yes – there *was* someone there – quite definitely, leaning back against the balcony and watching her with an amused grin on his face.

Was he one of the guests? Elizabeth didn't remember seeing him inside, but he was certainly dressed like the other men, in white tie and tails. Perhaps he was a would-be gatecrasher. He certainly looked the devil-may-care type, with his crinkly, laughing eyes and dashing moustache. Now, thought Elizabeth, if *this* man had been her partner, and not the galumphing Hubert . . .

The man was holding up his hand, beckoning her, as if wanting to share a secret. Elizabeth turned her face away, pretending not to notice. She felt a bit wicked standing here, watching a strange man. She had been brought up to ignore anyone she hadn't been formally introduced to. But she felt excited, too, and very feminine. The way the young man was staring at her made her feel attractive, desirable. He had that look that men had when they were with her mother. Captivated. He smiled at her invitingly, and she tried the handle of the French window.

It was locked. Disappointed, she shrugged her shoulders at the man and made helpless gestures with her hands. In reply, he pointed at the steps which led up to the terrace, indicating that she should leave the house by the front door and join him outside.

Elizabeth bit her bottom lip. Her parents would disapprove most strongly. Still, it would be an adventure, and she could do with some excitement after nearly four hours of Hubert. She smiled and nodded to the man, then slipped back into the ballroom.

Hubert was only a few yards away, chatting loudly to a plump girl in green shantung. Elizabeth would have to slide quietly past. She thought she had made it, when –

"Tally ho!" bellowed Hubert. "Thought you'd gone to ground, what? Care to trip the light fantastic?"

Elizabeth could think of no less suitable way for him to describe his way of dancing. "No . . . no thank you," she muttered, edging away backwards. "I'm just off to, er, powder my nose. Excuse me." And she turned and hurried away out of the ballroom.

In the hall, she was stopped by her mother, who was having a noisy, high-pitched conversation with Colonel Hope-Massie.

"Hello, sweetie, how's it going?" Her mother's eight-inch cigarette holder was lifted in a questioning pose.

"Fine. Lovely." Elizabeth tried to sound convincing. "But it's a bit hot in there. I'm going outside for a moment."

"All right, poppet," said her mother. "But don't stay out too long or you'll get a chill. Positively *frappé* for April, wouldn't you say, Geoffrey?" She turned her attention back to Colonel Hope-Massie as Elizabeth opened the heavy oak door.

She found herself running, lightly and softly, around the side of the house to where stone steps led up to the terrace. He was waiting for her, very starkly black and white in the moonlight, and she felt a shiver of nervousness – or was it cold? An icy breeze came from the lake, and Elizabeth wished she had brought her wrap. At the foot of the steps she paused, uncertain, but the man held out his hands to her, and there seemed to be a tenderness, a longing about him, a hypnotic passion in his dark brown eyes that drew her up the steps to him.

Without a word he took her in his arms. Through the ballroom windows they could hear the band beginning a waltz, and he swept her around the terrace, his right hand firm against the small of her back, the tails of his coat swinging out as they danced round and round. He was a wonderful dancer. He made her feel elegant and dainty, and she wished they were in the ballroom, with the eyes of the other guests all turned upon them. Look, Hubert – see what a difference a good partner makes . . . Look, Mother – I'm dancing with a dream.

He hadn't spoken to her yet, but she could feel his warm breath against her cheek. She twisted her head slightly to look at him, at his sharp, noble profile. His eyes were closed, as if he were intent on savouring all the pleasures of this dance.

After a while, she asked: "Who are you?" but he seemed not to hear her. She tried again. "Are you a friend of the Hope-Massies?"

Instead of answering her, he tightened his hold and began to dance faster and faster. "Hey!" said Elizabeth, as her feet started to falter. "Stop! Too fast!" He was lifting her off the ground in his mad whirling, which left the music far behind and made her gasp with fear. She could feel her heart juddering against her ribs, and she felt sick with giddiness. "Please . . . no more . . ." she pleaded. His eyes were still closed, and his face was a mask, white and still. His left hand, clasping hers, seemed suddenly thin and cold. "Please . . . Look, I don't think I . . ."

In the distance, she could hear voices. "Sweetie, where are you? Do come in, you'll catch your death out there." Then Mrs Hope-Massie, sounding agitated. "Elizabeth! Elizabeth!"

She tried to pull away, but the stranger held her hand in an iron grip. "Let me go!" she moaned. The band had stopped playing. People were clapping. "Let me go!" Something was happening to him, to her terrifying partner. Elizabeth, half-fainting in his arms, saw that his face seemed to be changing. His cheeks had become wide, dark hollows, and his eyes were receding into his head, leaving deep, ghastly holes. There was suddenly a strange, unpleasant smell about him, and his suit was not black but green, green and mouldy and tattered and . . . slimy. Water dripped from his clothes on to the stone floor of the terrace. As she felt the slime touch her skin, Elizabeth shrieked.

The high, piping notes of her screams climbed into the cool night air, and she heard Colonel Hope-Massie shouting: "Hurry, for God's sake!"

She was being pulled down the steps, now, her hand caught in a vice of bone as the creature – she could no longer think of it as a man – dragged her relentlessly after him. They reached the grass, and she was aware of people running around the corner of the house, seeing her, shouting. When they were at the edge of the lake, the creature waded straight in, his loathsome skull-face reflected in the moonlit water like a death's head. Elizabeth was stumbling forwards, splashing in the icy shallows as she tried to resist, and all the time she gasped and cried out in mindless terror.

111

The water was above her waist when she felt strong arms clasping her, and there was her father, and Colonel Hope-Massie, and they were fighting to wrench her away from her captor, who now was baring his rotted teeth in a fearsome snarl. There was no breath left in her, and she felt the water splash about her face. Some of it went into her mouth. It was brackish and foul.

At last, the battle was over. With a grimace that would haunt Elizabeth's dreams for the rest of her nights, the creature let go and plunged into the deeper waters. Soon he was lost from sight. Safe in the arms of her father, Elizabeth fainted.

"But, sweetie, *why*?" her mother was asking, ten minutes later, as Elizabeth lay on the sofa in Colonel Hope-Massie's study, wrapped in a towelling kimono. "Whatever possessed you?"

Elizabeth shivered, and gratefully accepted the warm drink which Mrs Hope-Massie offered her.

"Didn't you see?" she asked. "Didn't any of you see him pulling me? I couldn't get away." A tremble went through her as the horror came back to her, and her father, who was sitting on the arm of the sofa, stroked her shoulder.

"Who was pulling you?" he asked. "We thought you were just wading out into the lake. Thought you'd gone a bit loony."

"Oh, hush," said Elizabeth's mother. "Now, poppet, just tell us all about it."

At this point, Colonel Hope-Massie turned around from the window, where he had been standing in silence, the curtain held back so that he could stare out across the lake. He looked over to his wife, and something passed between them – a recognition of some secret knowledge.

'I think we can perhaps explain," he said slowly, and

he went over to the mantelpiece and took from it a framed photograph of a young girl in a white dress.

"Our daughter, Helen," he explained. "As you know, she's in Canada, now, married to a doctor."

The daughter, the daughter who was nearly drowned, thought Elizabeth.

The Colonel went on to tell how Helen had worn the white dress for a Hunt Ball at Lake House two years ago. She had seen a young man out on the terrace and had danced with him, only to find herself being dragged into the lake.

"She was saved by the gardener," he said. "And only just in time. He thought at first it was the weeds caught around her ankles. He had quite a struggle to get her out."

"The thing was," Mrs Hope-Massie added, "Helen would never tell us the whole story. All we could find out at first was that she'd had a very bad fright."

A brief, hazy image hung over Elizabeth's consciousness, almost out of reach, of flesh that had turned to bone, and the night air full of the smell of corruption. She knew that she, too, could never ever bring herself to remember with full clarity what she had really experienced.

"We thought at first she had somehow imagined the whole thing," Colonel Hope-Massie was saying, "that she'd just *felt* she was being pulled into the lake . . ."

"Yes," said his wife, "but then we were told something by the people who lived in this house before us."

Colonel Hope-Massie leant forward. "You see," he said slowly, "it appears that sometime in the last century – about 1860, perhaps – this house belonged to the young Lord Lorimer. When he got married, he brought his young bride back here and gave a ball to introduce her to all his friends. She was apparently very beautiful, and it

113

seems she spent rather too long in the company of a certain army officer. Lord Lorimer was furiously jealous. The next day he took his new bride rowing on the lake, but Lady Lorimer returned alone. She said he had fallen in and drowned. There were rumours, of course, of a quarrel, and some said she pushed him in. In any event, the body was never found. The lake is pretty deep in the middle, of course."

"How too, too ghastly," said Elizabeth's mother, giving a refined shudder.

"So how is this Lord Lorimer connected with what happened tonight?" asked Elizabeth's father. "Are you telling us he tried to drown Elizabeth? Seems a bit farfetched."

"Well, that's the story – make of it what you will. I can only say I'm most awfully sorry about all this. We had no idea it might happen again." Colonel Hope-Massie moved towards the door. "Now, I do hope you'll excuse us, but I think we ought to be getting back to our guests. Come along, my dear." He held out an arm for his wife.

Mrs Hope-Massie gave Elizabeth a kindly smile. "I'm so sorry," she said. "And you were having such a nice time with Hubert."

When they had gone, Elizabeth's father said: "Rather rum, eh? I think he's got the idea you were abducted by a ghost. Lord Lorimer, eh?"

Elizabeth, who had stayed silent up till now, looked up. "He wanted me," she said simply. "He wanted me for his bride. He wanted to take me with him, down to where – wherever he is." She saw her parents exchange a look which said: "It's her age. Too much imagination. She'll grow out of it," and suddenly she wanted to get away from this disturbing place, to return to ordinariness. She swung her legs briskly off the sofa and stood up. "Could we go, now? I'd like to go home."

114

"Poor sweet, of course we can. Daddy will fetch the car."

In the hallway, Elizabeth caught sight of Hubert whooping his way through a Scottish reel with the large girl in green. Still dressed in the kimono, and with her fur wrap pulled firmly over her shoulders, she hurried out into the night, clutching her mother's arm tightly and looking to neither left nor right as she walked down the steps to the car. He could be out there, watching her.

As the car slipped quietly down the drive, she glanced up, just once, at the dark waters of the lake. A sudden breeze stirred the surface, and she shivered.

"Cold, poppet?" asked her mother, putting an arm around her.

Elizabeth shook her head, but as she watched the surface of the lake settle into tranquillity, and thought of what lay beneath, she doubted if she would ever be warm again.

THE SHEPHERD'S DOG

by Joyce Marsh

Chauval lifted his head sharply; his sensitive, upstanding ears twitched as he listened intently. From outside the window a little twig scraped against the pane and the big white dog recognized it as the sound which had roused him from his uneasy sleep. His body relaxed as he allowed his shaggy head to drop down on to his forepaws.

He did not sleep again, however, as his olive-green eyes, lightly flecked with little pin-points of golden light, stared fixedly at the still form on the bed. For two long days he had watched that figure, waiting to see the tiniest movement of life, although by now his every sense told him that he hoped in vain.

On the first morning when the Master had not risen as he usually did at first light of day, Chauval had been impatient and slightly irritable. Even through the closed window his sensitive noise had picked up the exhilarating scent of the new day. His limbs had almost ached in their eagerness for that glorious, rushing scamper over the heather which began his every morning.

Restlessly he had padded around the room, scratched at the closed door and lifted his head to savour the fresh, clean smell of a new day. Then a long deep growl had begun low in his throat, but still the Master had not moved. The growl had become a whine, anxiety replaced impatience and Chauval had crept closer to the bed. He had thrust his nose beneath the Master's shoulder and nudged him violently. The man's head rolled on the pillow, but he had not opened his eyes nor made a sound.

116

One still hand dangled from the bed; Chauval licked it – it was so cold.

Then the big, shaggy white dog had jumped on to the bed, covering the man with his body, licking at his face and hands as he tried to drive out that dreadful cold with the warmth of his own body.

It was then that the vague anxiety had become a sickening fear, for the Master's well-known scent had gone and in its place was a smell that Chauval knew and dreaded.

So many times in his long working life the sheepdog had found a sheep which had wandered too near the edge and had fallen to its death on the rocky beach below, or a straying lamb which had become stranded on a ledge to die of fear and hunger. All these animals had the smell of death on them, and now that same hateful scent was upon the Master.

Chauval, in his panic, had leapt from the bed and rushed first to the door and then to the window, his head lifted in a long, despairing wail. Instinctively he knew that with his great strength and size he could, if he chose, break out of the room, but without direct orders from the Master, he dared not try.

All his life, ever since he had first come as a tiny puppy to the lonely cliff-top cottage, the Master had ordered and directed his every action. It was the Master who had taught him how to guard sheep, it was he who had told the dog what to do and when to do it. Even in those carefree, happy moments when work was done and the shepherd's dog was at liberty to rush pell-mell over the springy turf and wind-scorched heather, Chauval never forgot the law of instant obedience, for his playtime began on the Master's command and ended with his whistling call.

Chauval had been happy and secure in his trusting devotion, but now the Master's voice was still and the dog was alone and desolate. In his bewilderment and confusion there was only one thing of which he could be certain. When he was alone his duty was to stay on guard, so for two long days and nights he had been in his room. Even the gnawing hunger and thirst were forgotten as he crouched low, every muscle of his body tense and alert to protect his Master and his home.

Suddenly Chauval's head lifted again as another, much louder noise came from outside and the draught, blowing in through a broken pane, carried the scent of a human. Silently, but with his lip lifted in the beginnings of a snarl, Chauval moved to the window and raised himself on hind legs to look out.

On the path, a few yards from the cottage, stood a man. His head was thrown back as he shouted loudly:

"Are ye in there, Will? Are ye all right then, Will?"

Chauval looked back quickly towards the bed, half hoping that the sound of a voice might have called the Master back to life; but still there was no movement from the bed.

The dark-haired man, still calling the Master's name, had come very close to the cottage and was rapping on the door with his heavy stick. Chauval's snarl became more menacing and the hairs on his back stood up stiffly. He knew that man and he knew that stick. Once, a very long time ago, he had felt its weight upon his back; the man had come into the cottage whilst Chauval was alone and had walked into rooms and looked into places where only the Master was allowed to go. The dog had barked once in warning and the man had hit him with the stick. Now that man was an enemy – never to be allowed inside.

The knocking on the door had ceased as the man walked around the cottage, looking in at all the windows. He came to Chauval's window and stopped to peer inside. For a brief moment the man and the dog stared into each

118

other's eyes. The sound of the dog's angry barking echoed in the room and the man leapt back in startled fear.

But he realized that he was protected by the glass between them and he came forward again to look past the frantic dog into the room. He stared in for a moment and then, turning quickly, he ran off. Chauval fell silent. In the distance he could hear the soft, melancholy bleating of the sheep and, further away still, the wild rushing of the sea hurling itself against the barren, rocky beach.

Stiffly he dropped down from the window and crept back to resume his vigil by the bed, but, weakened by lack of food and little sleep, the spate of barking had exhausted him and his eyes closed again in slumber.

A long time must have passed, for the room was almost dark when Chauval was once more roused by the sound of footsteps and loud voices.

There was a violent banging on the cottage door and Chauval heard it fly open with a crash. Swiftly, he leapt on to the bed, crouching over the defenceless Master. He was sweating with fear and the perspiration ran off his tongue to hang in wet, sticky streams from his mouth.

The voices came nearer and nearer; the bedroom door flew open and in the opening was the Man with the Stick. The huge white dog remained motionless, hunched protectively and tense above his Master's body. His lip curled upward, showing long, yellow teeth, and the whites of his eyes gleamed through the dusk.

"The great ugly brute will ne'er let us come near. We'll have to shoot him first."

It was that harsh rough voice of the Man with the Stick. Chauval gathered himself to spring, but suddenly someone else spoke, softly and gently.

"Poor thing, he must have been locked in here for days. He's half starved. Maybe I can coax him out."

The cruel voice muttered and mumbled, but the man

stood aside and his place in the doorway was taken by a stranger.

"Good dog, come on then, we'll not hurt you, good boy, that's a good dog."

The stranger's voice was kind and reassuring. He held out the back of his hand with the fingers hanging limply down.

"Good dog, come here then."

With infinite slowness, Chauval eased himself off the bed. Never taking his eyes from the stranger's face, the dog crawled slowly across the floor. With all his heart he wanted to trust this man.

"For heaven's sake get on wi' it. We haven't got all night to mess around wi' yon vicious brute."

The harsh voice spat out the words, and out of the corner of his eye Chauval saw the stick raised above him. With a powerful spring he leapt up, and his teeth fastened in the hand holding the stick. He felt the warm taste of blood in his mouth as his body thudded into the man's chest and bore him backwards to the floor.

The room was full of noise and the smell of human fear. The stranger's voice, no longer gentle, was raised above the others and his was the hand which snatched up the stick and brought it down hard on the dog's back. With a yelp of pain and anger, Chauval turned to snarl a brief defiance at the stranger who was now another enemy and then he sprang past the men towards the open door. Frantic hands grabbed at his long fur but, snapping and snarling, the dog pulled himself free and leapt outside. With a few bounding strides he reached the cover of the bushes and threw himself down in the tangled bracken.

In an agony of confusion and fear he stared at the cottage. He wanted to go back inside to continue his guard over the Master, but he dared not. Lights had sprung up in the windows and the sound of voices drifted

120

out. The front door stood open and suddenly two men came out carrying something wrapped in white. Instinctively, Chauval knew that it was the Master.

The Man with the Stick had brought the strangers and Chauval had been driven out. They had forced him to abandon his post, and now his enemies were taking the Master away. The big dog raised himself up on to his haunches, his green eyes glittered in the twilight darkness and he began to whimper softly. Then he flung back his head, the long snout pointing directly upwards towards the pale moon, and the whimper became a long howl of desolation and despair.

"There he is, over there! Shoot him, someone, while ye've got the chance. He'll be no good now old Will's gone and if he turns rogue he'll be a menace to all of us."

It was the harsh, cruel voice, and close upon the words came a sharp crack and a singing bullet passed close to the dog's ear.

Chauval began to run as he had never run in his life before. Leaping, bounding, with lolling tongue and eyes bulging until they were nearly bursting from the sockets, he crashed through the bracken and undergrowth.

The lights in the cottage receded to pin points and the shouts of the men were borne away on the night breeze, and still Chauval ran. The scrubby trees and bushes thinned and the ground beneath his feet became more sharp and rocky as he fled up the steep, craggy hill which rose sharply from the cliff-top pasture. At last he could run no more and he flung himself down on to a flat rock.

His sides heaved and the breath rasped in his throat. The pounding of his heart quietened at last and he breathed more easily, but now he was tormented by thirst.

The big dog raised his head and the sensitive nostrils quivered as he explored the night wind for the longed-for scent of water. His senses told him that water was not far away, but he did not immediately go to find it. Instead he peered anxiously down the slope and listened intently. In his headlong flight he had taken no care to hide his trail and his enemies could easily track him down.

To his relief he could hear only the sound of rushing wind; for the moment he was safe. Gleaming wraith-like in the darkness, the dog weaved a cautious zig-zagging course towards the water. The clear mountain stream flowed abundantly. Bursting out from a fissure in the rock, it cascaded first into a deep pool before it ran off down the hillside. Chauval thrust his muzzle into the icy water and greedily drank his fill.

He was ravenously hungry, but the wild, rushing escape up the steep hill had drained the last of his strength and he was too exhausted to search for food. A flat, jutting shelf of rock offered him some shelter and he crept beneath it. Wearily he buried his nose into the long warm hairs on his flank and slept.

Chauval awoke at the first light of day and his first thought was the gnawing, agonizing hunger. He had never in his life needed to find his own food; no one had ever taught him how and now he had no idea where to begin. He whimpered and whined, calling for the Master. Even now he could still desperately hope to hear a whistle or the beloved voice calling his name, but all was silent except for the tinkling water and the lonely singing of the wind.

His green eyes flicked restlessly as he surveyed the barren hillside – there was no food here. There would be food in the cottage if only he dared go to find it. Hunger overcame fear at last and, moving carefully, with his body close to the ground, he crept down the hill.

The cottage was deserted: the strangers had gone and the Master had not returned. In the pale light of dawn the dog moved around the house, scratching at the closed doors, but there was no way to get in. The sheep, left unguarded, had strayed into the tangled undergrowth near the cottage, where they bleated dismally. Instinctively Chauval moved around them, expertly gathering them into a little flock and herding them back to the grazing land. Enviously he watched them eat their fill of the succulent grass.

Suddenly he heard the sound of a single sheep in distress and behind a large rock he found a young ewe with her lamb stretched out on the ground beside her. It had fallen from the top of the rock and its fleece was streaked with blood. The mother bleated pathetically, but the lamb was quite dead. With an expert little rush, Chauval drove the ewe away and nudged the lamb with his nose. It was still warm and the sickly sweet smell of the fresh blood made the juices flow in his mouth; but it was forbidden to eat the flesh of a dead sheep and Chauval would not disobey the Master's law – he would die first.

"Good dog, you may eat the lamb."

The well-known voice sounded loud and clear in his ear. With a little yelp of joyful surprise, Chauval looked round. The breeze blew in off the sea and the sheep called softly to each other, but there was neither scent nor sight of the Master. Yet his voice came again, urgently.

"Eat, Chauval – eat or you will die."

The pangs of desperate hunger gnawed agonizingly at his insides, but there was no need now to hesitate. Somehow and from somewhere far off the Master had spoken.

The long yellow teeth ripped and tore at the soft flesh as, with ravenous haste, the dog wolfed down the fresh meat. So intent was he upon satisfying his hunger that he did not immediately notice that he was no longer alone on the cliff top. A man, a woman and a boy were running towards him. They were shouting and waving their arms when Chauval heard them at last and looked up from his meal. He gave a quick, welcoming bark, for he knew them and they were his friends. Suddenly the youth bent down and picked something up from the ground. The next moment a sharp, hard rock flew through the air to hit the dog a stinging blow on the head. He yelped in pain and surprise; there was no doubting now the menace in their voices and gestures. Suddenly and inexplicably even these friends had become his enemies. Once more he fled upwards to safety. The full and satisfying meal had restored his strength and he moved swiftly.

The people stood by the bloody remnants of the lamb and watched him go.

"That were Will's old dog," the boy said.

"Aye an' I should've had my gun handy. He'll have to be shot now – he's turned sheep killer."

The woman answered her husband and there was pity in her voice. "Poor thing. 'Twill be a mercy to put him down or like as not he'll starve to death, for he'll not let us near him, that's for sure."

And so the barren rocky hill became Chauval's home and refuge. Water he had in abundance, but food was a constant, nagging problem. Once or twice he had managed to catch a young rabbit, but mostly he lived by what he could scrounge or steal from the scattered cottages on the cliff top. He had always to take care to search for his food when the people were asleep, for at the very sight of him they drove him off with sticks and stones and even guns.

At night or in the light of early dawn he slunk down the hill, moving cautiously with his body close to the ground. The Master's voice had never come again to give him leave, so he would not touch the sheep. In the pale light he moved like a great white shadow through the flock, and they, knowing him to be their friend, never ceased their constant nibbling at the grass as he passed.

While the cottagers slept, he padded silently around their homes, sniffing and searching for the scraps they had thrown away. Sometimes he ate the foul-smelling mash which the good wives had put out for their chickens. At other times he found a clutch of eggs laid in the undergrowth by a straying hen. Once in his maraudings he was attacked by a little half-wild cat; he had killed it and in his desperation had eaten even that.

In the weeks since the Master had gone the sheepdog had grown thin and gaunt. His long coat, wetted by the rain and dried by the sun and salt breezes, was filthy and matted. Twigs, thorns and brambles had become tangled in the long hairs where they fretted and scratched his skin when he lay down.

At night, especially when the moon rode high in the heavens, he yearned so desperately for the Master that he lifted his snout to the stars and let forth a long, desolate howl. Below, in the little hamlet, the people would hear his mournful wail and shudder in their warm, cosy beds.

One morning he had been particularly unsuccessful in his search for food; the sun had risen and the cottagers were stirring, yet his ravenous hunger would not allow him to abandon his scavenging. Suddenly he heard a door opening nearby and, in a quick, panicky scamper, he made for a clump of bracken, where he pressed his body close to the ground and trembled.

The cheerful sound of a woman's voice drifted out through the open door, and a few minutes later a tiny child, tottering on unsteady legs, came out into the garden. Chauval pressed down even further into the concealing bracken and his heart thudded painfully. The little boy was coming closer and the dog dared not move, for he could not escape without being seen.

With the casual curiosity of the very young, the child was peering into the bushes. Suddenly he saw the white dog and his eyes opened wide in surprise. For a moment he swayed uncertainly on chubby little legs and then plumped down in front of Chauval.

"Hello, doggy," he lisped. "Do you want thum buppy?"

With trusting friendliness he offered a thick crust of bread liberally spread with butter. Chauval took the food gently in his front teeth and wolfed it down. The boy gurgled his pleasure and stretched out his little hand to scratch and tickle at the sensitive spot behind the dog's ears. It was so long since Chauval had felt a loving, friendly touch. His delight in it now made him forget even his hunger. He crept forward and rested his head on the child's lap.

"Does doggy want thum more buppy?"

The little boy scrambled clumsily to his feet.

"Come on, doggy, let's get more buppy."

He set off towards his home, encouraging his new friend to follow. Longing to feel again that loving, friendly touch, Chauval crawled out of his hiding place. With tail tucked between his legs and head hanging low he slunk after the boy, but his progress was slow and the child grew impatient.

"Come on, silly doggy."

He grasped the dog's ears in both his little hands and tugged with all his strength. In an excess of grateful affection Chauval reached up and licked the baby's face, and it was at that moment that a piercing shriek rang out from the cottage doorway. A woman's voice shouted urgently:

"Husband, come quickly! The killer dog's got our Ian!"

Chauval leapt sideways and the child, startled by the note of fear in his mother's voice, ran to hide himself in her skirts. The woman was thrust aside and her place in the doorway was taken by a man. It was the Man with the Stick, only now it was not a stick but a gun that he held in his hand.

The terrified dog raced for the concealing cover of the undergrowth, but he was too late. The shot sounded almost in his ear and the searing bullet ran along his side, gouging a deep, bloody weal in its path.

For a moment or two Chauval ran on and felt no pain, but after a while his limbs stiffened and every thudding step was agony to him. He knew he could never reach the safety of his rocky retreat and he veered off towards the only other hiding place he knew – the tall rock on the cliff, behind which he had found and eaten the lamb.

He reached the rock and crept gratefully into its concealing shadow, pressing himself as close as he could to the cool, rough rock.

The bullet wound was painful, and for a long while he diligently licked at it until his rough tongue had cleaned it and soothed the pain. Weakened by the lack of food, and exhausted by the effort, he fell into a deep sleep.

When he awoke, the sun had long since reached its peak and had begun on its slow slide down towards the sea. Chauval was thirsty, his nose felt hot and dry and the inside of his mouth burned feverishly. He longed for the cool waters of his mountain stream and he peered cautiously out of his hiding place. The sound of human voices drifted over to him and the dog drew back in alarm.

Not far away, across the rich green pasture, a man, a woman and several children were playing with a ball. They laughed and shouted in their play, but their gaiety brought neither comfort nor reassurance to Chauval. He knew that he had but to show himself and their happy voices would become rough and harsh as they came at him with their sticks and their guns.

Behind him the cliff dropped down sheer to the sea.

There was no escape that way and the only way to safety was barred by the group on the cliff-top.

Patiently the big, white dog settled down to await his opportunity to slip past his enemies. As he watched, one of the children wandered away from the group and, unnoticed by the others, came towards Chauval and the cliff edge.

The breeze carried his scent to the dog's sensitive nose and he recognized the tiny boy who had befriended him that morning. The child tottered to the very edge and, with all the strength in his fat little arms, threw a pebble out over the cliff. He chuckled as it rattled and clattered on to the beach below.

So many times Chauval had seen the Master's sheep venture too near to the crumbling edge of the cliff, and he knew what should be done. Like the sheep, this human child should be herded back to safety. Yet, if he were to venture out, he would be seen and the man would attack.

The boy swayed dangerously on the very edge and Chauval could not decide what he must do. In his anxiety he whimpered softly.

As he watched the child with an ever-increasing confusion there came upon him an icy chill and he began to tremble violently. A small misty cloud had drifted in from the sea, enveloping him in its clammy touch. The hairs on his neck bristled and then, from somewhere in the vapour which hung over him, came the voice he had so longed to hear.

"Chauval, my good Chauval," it called. "Go then boy, fetch him back."

There was no hesitation now. The Master had spoken and Chauval leapt to obey.

"Steady boy, easy now," the voice called from behind, and the good sheepdog lay down in the grass. Then, quietly, so as not to startle the child, he moved forward in a series of little rushes. As soon as he was able, the dog placed himself between the boy and the cliff edge. The child, unafraid, lunged towards him, gurgling his pleasure, but with a warning snarl Chauval forced him back. Again the child came on and this time the dog herded him away from the edge with a little nip on the fatty part of his leg. More startled than hurt, the boy gave a loud indignant wail and ran at his protector with his clenched fists – but again Chauval urged him backwards from the cliffs.

The man and the woman had heard their son's cry and were hurrying to his rescue. Chauval paid them no heed as, with all the skill he had learned from guarding sheep, he forced the child to safety. It was the man who reached the child first and snatched him up in his arms.

"Get away, you evil brute."

He lashed out with his heavy boot. Chauval leapt back, but the blow caught him full in the chest, forcing him nearer to the edge. The man aimed yet another vicious kick and the dog felt his back legs slip away into space. The weight of his body dragged down and he clawed frantically at the soft turf with his front feet. For a brief moment he hung suspended, but his grip was too tenuous and he fell.

Tumbling and twisting, Chauval hurtled down. The seagulls got up from their rocky perches and their shrieks mingled with the screams of the doomed dog. His body smashed down on to the rocks and earth; sea and sky were blotted out in one final stab of pain.

The blood-streaked flanks heaved once, twice, and were still. The birds settled back on the rocky ledges and, from above, the man and the woman looked down on the still shape so far below them.

"Well, that's the last trouble we'll get from that vicious dog," the man said with cruel satisfaction.

"Aye," said his wife, "an' it might have been our Ian

lyin' doon there. We've only the dog to thank that it isn't."

The man looked askance.

"You're a fool, husband," she went on. "You've seen a dog work sheep often enough. Could ye no see that it weren't attacking our boy? He were herdin' him back from the edge – just like he would sheep."

The man hung his head. "Well, he's gone wild. He's better off this way, anyhow," he said sulkily.

"Aye," she said, and they moved off, while the child in his father's arms whined, "Nice doggy, where's 'at nice doggy gone?"

All was now very quiet upon the beach. The sun had dipped its rim into the sea and the shadows grew long and dark. A shrill whistle sounded in the breeze and a dark mist at the water's edge trembled like the heat haze of high summer. The misty cloud steadied and darkened and took shape. The whistle came again and a soft, white vapour hung over the body of the dead dog.

The cloud by the water's edge took on the shape of a man and he stretched forth his hand.

"Chauval."

The name was a soft sigh on the sea breeze. A great shaggy dog bounded forward, leaving behind the dead, blood-stained thing on the rocks.

The man moved off over the sands and the dog by his side leapt and danced in a transport of delight.

Few people now will venture down on to that part of the beach, for it is said that, in the late afternoon, just as the sun is about to slide into the sea, a man and his dog walk the sands. Those who have seen them say that the dog's olive-green eyes forever glow with a loving devotion, while the man smiles his contentment, and, as they pass, the air turns cold and is filled with soft sounds. Even the little waves breaking on the shore sing out the name . . . "Chauval, Chauval . . ."

THE JUNK ROOM

by Terry Tapp

On the outskirts of a tiny Devonshire village, surrounded by a wall of Dartmoor granite, a grey, forbidding house looks out over the rolling hills. Ivy trails over the blistered paint of a board which once offered the house for sale, and a couple of rusted iron gates hang crazily from granite pillars, groaning against the wind, crashing against the wall like cymbals.

Curving away from the frenzied, captive gates, the drive sweeps up towards Graston House, circling a raised bed of brambles and weeds. The drive is lined with cherry trees, regimentally spaced, yet bowed by the sharp winds of the moor. The studded door is locked and boarded now; the small-paned windows sightless with the growth of dust.

Inside the house time is frozen. Food has rotted in the refrigerator; clothes hang on wooden pegs in the hall. And, in the bedrooms, the sheets and blankets lie in disarray upon the beds, thrown aside carelessly – and left.

It is ten years since I put the "For Sale" sign in front of Graston House, and I have no hopes now of ever selling it again. Indeed, I shall do everything in my power to dissuade people from buying it – unlikely conduct for an estate agent, I admit, but I have good reason.

Although I have not set foot inside the house since I sold it to the Carter family, I know that the roof is in a bad state of repair and that the rain has penetrated. Left unrepaired, it is only a matter of time before the house will decay.

The story you are about to read has been assembled from the conversation I had with Mrs Carter, the present owner of Graston House, and the many letters she wrote to me. These are the facts of the matter, supported by my own personal knowledge, Mrs Carter's accounts and other reliable sources. So many stories are currently circulating about Graston House (stories of a light moving from window to window and of dreadful screamings and strange happenings) that I felt it my duty to set the records straight.

I well remember the look of surprise on Tom Carter's face when I immediately accepted his offer to buy the house. "But aren't you going to check with the owners?" he asked.

"No need," I assured him. "The owners have given me permission to accept the first reasonable offer for Graston House, and yours is not an unreasonable offer, Mr Carter."

The roof, being the most expensive item to repair, was patched temporarily whilst the Carter family set to work modernizing the inside of Graston House. It took two years of hard work to rewire the place and instal central heating, decorate the rooms and tile the kitchen. Ancient lead plumbing was replaced with copper pipes; green-painted walls were hung with bright, fresh wallpaper, and the blackened varnish which smothered the doors was burnt away, to be replaced with glistening white gloss paint. Now there was only one room left to decorate.

Tom Carter and his wife, Alice, had used this room to store funiture and toys, books, suitcases and decorating materials. Quite justifiably it had earned its name – the Junk Room.

Now that the end of the decorating was in sight, the Carter family set to work with renewed enthusiasm. Robin (a year older than his brother, Jason) worked with paintbrush and water, soaking the paper so that it would be easier to scrape from the walls. Their father tackled the paintwork with a roaring blowlamp, filling the air with the scent of burnt paint and wood. As they worked, the two boys chatted excitably above the roar of the blow-lamp, tackling the heavy wallpaper with vigour. Within the space of two hours, three of the walls were stripped clean, but the fourth, above the green marble fireplace, proved stubborn.

Mr Carter noticed a square-shaped bump under the wallpaper and advised the boys not to go near it with their scrapers. "It could be a gaslight outlet or, perhaps, and old electric socket," he said. "As soon as I've finished burning the paint off the door I'll have a look at it."

Later, armed with a screwdriver, Tom Carter gently levered away the layers of paper to expose a thin block of wood which had been screwed to the wall. The screws were rusty, but they eventually yielded to his largest screwdriver. Taking great care, Mr Carter levered the wooden block from the wall.

There were no wires or pipes behind the block, and the plaster (apart from the four screwholes) was intact. Tom Carter stared at the wall.

"What is it, Dad?" Jason asked, noticing the strange manner in which his father was regarding the wall. "What have you found?"

Robin paused from collecting up some of the wallpaper and glanced across the room at the two of them, a puzzled expression on his face. "What are you looking at?" he asked. "Come and help me with this paper."

When they did not reply, he went over to see what had taken their attention.

Painted on the wall, a few inches above the mantel-shelf of the fireplace, were two eyes, one slightly larger than the other.

The eyes glistened, fresh and dewy, as if they had been painted only seconds before. Surrounded by cream paint, they stared out from the wall, disembodied, complete in every detail. Rimmed with long black lashes, the blood-crazed whites of the eyes contrasted vividly with the bright blue irises. The pupils of the eyes were jet black, dilated and bright.

"They look so real," breathed Jason, his hand reaching out to touch the paintwork. "I wonder why someone took the trouble to paint them?" Suddenly, as if shocked by an invisible electric force, he withdrew his hand and looked away from the wall. "I don't like them, Dad. They're evil."

Tom Carter laughed at that. "How can you tell? You need more than just a pair of eyes to come to that conclusion."

"They do look real," Robin agreed. "If you walk around the room, the eyes seem to be following."

"An optical illusion," Mr Carter said. "It's all in the mind."

"Cover it over, Dad," Jason said, his eyes still averted from the penetrating gaze of the painted eyes. "Please – "

"Now don't be silly, Jason." A tone of impatience had crept into Tom Carter's voice. He was annoyed at his own reaction to the eyes and felt the need to dismiss the matter.

After lunch, when Mrs Carter had seen the paintings, she agreed with Jason. "I don't like them," she said, turning away. "Someone must have had a sick sense of humour to paint them on the wall."

"But why did someone take the trouble to screw a wooden block over them?" Robin asked. "Surely they could have scraped the wall, or simply papered over the eyes without going to all that trouble?"

"Which is precisely what we are going to do," said his

father cheerfully. "I'll burn the paint off the wall before we paper." He knelt down and turned the tap on the gas blowlamp, holding a lighted match near the outlet. Nothing happened. Puzzled, he shook the blowlamp against his ear. "Funny – " he mumbled. "Plenty of gas in it. The jet must be blocked up." Using the thin wire pricker he worked at the fine, pinprick jet, scraping away the film deposit. "There – that should do it." He turned the tap and smiled as the blowlamp gave out a healthy hissing sound. "Now, where are the matches? I had them a minute ago." He turned off the tap and looked around the room.

The search for the matches was interrupted by a loud knocking at the front door. "I expect that's the garden fertilizer I ordered yesterday," Mr Carter said. "Will you show them where to unload it, Robin?" Unable to find the matches, he put the blowlamp down by the door and followed the boys downstairs.

The unloading and stacking of the heavy sacks took quite a while, and when they had finished they decided to stop work for the day. After dinner Tom Carter wanted to spread some of the fertilizer on the garden, and Robin volunteered to help. Jason, protesting loudly, was sent to have a shower.

And that is when the first "accident" occurred.

As Jason started to undress, he heard a soft, swishing sound immediately behind him. Alarmed, he spun around. There was no one there, but he noticed the handle of the bathroom door slowly turning. A gentle clicking sounded from the lock, and Jason noticed that the key was missing. "Robin!" he cried. "Stop playing about!"

He waited, listening, blood pounding in his ears.

"Robin! You know I don't like being locked in!"

No reply.

Jason tried the door handle, rattled it, then shouted at the top of his voice. "If you don't let me out of here I'll kick the door down!"

A low, rumbling noise came from the landing; soft, filled with malice. Jason felt a cold draught of air around his shoulders. "Let me out! Let me out!"

Suddenly the lock gave out a sharp report, and the handle turned. Slowly, slowly the door opened, and Jason found himself staring into the eyes of his mother. "What on earth are you doing?" she demanded crossly.

"Robin locked me in!" Jason cried. "You wait – I'll get him for this!"

"He did not lock you in," said Mrs Carter. "Robin has been in the garden, with your father."

"Well, someone locked me in," Jason said. He looked up at his mother. "Was it you?"

Mrs Carter removed the key from the lock and replaced it on the inside of the door, her hand trembling slightly. "No," she said. "I didn't do it, Jason. Now hurry up and take your shower. Dad and Robin will be wanting to use it later." She turned away before Jason could see the worried expression on her face.

Later, after he had showered and changed into his nightclothes, Jason ran downstairs into the warm kitchen. Mrs Carter was applying glue to a broken vase. "I still think Robin locked me in," he told her.

"And I think you're pulling my leg," she said, not looking up from her task. "You must have removed the key from the door, otherwise how could you possibly get locked in when the key is always kept on the inside?"

Deciding to leave the incident for the time being, Jason went over to the vase. "What happened?" he asked. He knew that the vase was very expensive and that it had been a present from his father. "Does Dad know you've broken it?"

"I didn't break it," said his mother. "We heard a noise in the kitchen, and when we came in the vase was on the floor." She glanced up at the wall cabinet upon which the vase had rested for almost two years. "I can't understand why it fell."

Jason looked out of the kitchen window and noted that Robin was forking dead leaves on to a smouldering bonfire.

"Are you sure he didn't sneak indoors and lock me in the bathroom?" he asked.

"Positive," came the reply. "He's been out there with your father since before you went to get ready for bed." Mrs Carter checked her watch and tapped the glass with her forefinger significantly. "Which reminds me, young Jason. Time for you to go to bed."

"May I have a read first?" Jason asked.

"Ten minutes," agreed Mrs Carter.

"Twenty," Jason countered, knowing that a compromise would be reached at fifteen.

"All right," Mrs Carter said absently.

"Thanks, Mum!" Jason, surprised by the ease of his victory, dashed from the kitchen to take full advantage of the twenty minutes' reading time. Such was his haste that he pulled the kitchen door harder than he normally would have, and the sound of splintering glass stopped him in his tracks. He turned, then opened the door. "Sorry, Mum – " he started to say.

Mrs Carter was standing in front of the back door, which led into the garden. The eight small panes of glass in the door were broken, shards of glass lying on the kitchen tiles, glistening like frost. "It wasn't your fault, Jason," she said, her voice taut and strained. She spoke again, firmly this time. "Please go to bed."

Hearing the tone of her voice, Jason did as he was told carefully closing the door behind him.

Mrs Carter called out to her husband. "Tom, will you come in here for a minute?"

Leaving Robin to pile more leaves on the bonfire, Mr Carter hurried across the garden. As he approached the kitchen door, he shouted: "What is it? Are you hurt?"

"No," said Mrs Carter. "Just come into the kitchen. I want to talk to you."

"How did this happen?" her husband asked as he stepped over the broken glass.

Mrs Carter stared at him awhile before taking breath to reply, "You'll think I'm being silly – " she began.

He sat down at the kitchen table. "What's the matter?"

"Things seem to be happening," she said.

"Things?"

"First the vase – " She laughed, nervously, as if afraid to continue.

Tom Carter gave a grim smile. "These things come in threes," he said.

"I was going to show you this later, when the boys were in bed," she replied, opening the pantry door and reaching inside. She closed the door and turned to face him, revealing what it was she held in her hand.

"What is it?" he asked.

"What *was* it?" she said. "It *was* our electric kettle."

He took the twisted, crumpled metal from her. What had once been a shining copper kettle was now almost beyond recognition, screwed up like tinfoil, pressed tight and flat. "Good God," Mr Carter said as he examined it. "What on earth happened?"

"I don't know," she said, holding on to the table, her voice cracking as words spilled out. "Why should a vase just suddenly tumble like that? Why should the back door slam when there isn't a breath of wind?" She glanced at the kettle, then looked quickly away, as if afraid to gaze upon it too long. "And why . . ."

"How did it happen?"

Mrs Carter looked at her husband fearfully. "I heard a noise, and when I looked over at the kettle it was folding itself up – it – it was just folding itself up as if a hand had enclosed it, and. . ."

Mr Carter stared at the kettle, then tried to twist the flattened spout around. "Heat," he said. "You must have switched the kettle on without putting water in it. It's a wonder it didn't blow the fuse."

"It was not switched on," she said.

He smiled to comfort her. "Perhaps the socket is faulty. Heat must have caused this. Look, I can't move it." He made another attempt to twist the metal.

Mrs Carter nodded slowly. But she was not convinced.

By the time the glass had been swept away and the door had been boarded up to make the house safe and draught-free for the night it was ten o'clock. They decided to go to bed, then, and by eleven o'clock the family were all asleep.

The night was dark, low clouds snuffing out the stars so that the house lay sheathed in a black cloak. Nothing moved; it was as if the creatures of the night were afraid to show themselves. Even the leaves on the black-draped trees were still hanging limp and exhausted from frozen branches. Darkness closed in around the granite walls, stifling the building. And the Carter family slept on.

Jason was the first awake, his heart thudding in his chest. Something had caused him to sit bolt upright in his bed, and he stared into the blackness of his room, confused, unable to collect his senses. Suddenly his bed tilted from under him, and he rolled over, his hands reaching out for something to grasp. He lay where he had fallen, bewildered, too afraid to cry out. And the darkness closed in on him like a cold blanket, suffocating.

139

Mr and Mrs Carter, hearing the noise, were instantly awake.

"What is it, Tom?" Mrs Carter asked drowsily.

"Thought I heard something," he replied, cocking his head to one side. "Maybe it was a car backfiring."

He was about to lie down when he heard the scream.

Over the years Mr and Mrs Carter had become used to hearing one or the other of their children cry out during the night. But this scream was different. Chilling. It came without warning, wild and piercing, animal-like in its intensity, so that it caused the hairs on Mr Carter's neck to rise up as if a cold hand had brushed against him. Instantly he threw aside the bedclothes and put his feet upon the carpet. With a cry he withdrew them, his hand fumbling for the switch on the bedside light.

"What is it?" Mrs Carter cried, sensing his alarm.

"Don't know – " The room became bathed in a white, dazzling light for a moment, then the bulb cracked and glass splintered out from the shade, plunging them into a deeper darkness. "The floor," he said. "Something hot on the floor."

"Hot?"

Jason's next scream brought Mr Carter from the bed immediately. Without thought for his own safety he ran across the room and grasped the door handle, pulling it back hard.

The door was locked.

"Locked!" he cried. "The door's locked!"

"But it can't be," said Mrs Carter. "The lock doesn't work, Tom. Try again."

He tugged, harder this time, but the door refused to move. Jason was sobbing now and Mr Carter became desperate in his attempts to open the door. "It must be stuck, somehow," he grunted, his hands struggling to gain some movement from the door handle. Then he realized that something cold, something slippery, like a snake, was squeezing between his toes. He stepped back, only to find himself deeper in what appeared to be a pool of slime. "Find the torch!" he cried. "It's in the bedside cabinet!"

Before his wife could make a movement, Jason screamed again, and she cried out, "Tom!" in desperation.

Mr Carter stood back from the door and charged at it, his shoulder taking the full impact. The door did not move. Again he charged, catching his shoulder on the edge of the thick ornamental beading around the door panel. He recoiled, bruised and shaken. Switching off the socket, he pulled out the plug of the heavy electric bedside lamp and used it as a hammer, pounding the thinner door panels so that they splintered and cracked.

Robin awoke to hear the chaos – Jason screaming, his mother crying out, hammering and splintering. He reached for the light switch which dangled on a cord above his head, and when he pulled it hard the cord wriggled in his fingers, coiling down around his wrist, hissing and spitting viciously. He shook it off with a yell of terror, and, leaping from the bed, he ran across the room to the door. He was about to touch the handle when the room was suddenly lit by a flame. The door was burning! He touched the handle, but it was too hot to grasp. Feeling his way back to the bed, he reached for the blankets to insulate his hands against the heat and, as his fingers touched the bed, the thin, snaking cord was upon him.

By this time Jason had made his way across the landing towards his parents' bedroom, just in time to see the panels of the door split open under the frantic blows from the table lamp. He had never seen such a look of anger on his father's face, and he stood back as the door splintered like matchwood. Together they ran to Robin's room. This time, the door yielding instantly to Mr Carter's shoulder.

"Dad?" Robin's voice echoed in the darkness. "Dad – what's happening?" He was near to tears.

Mrs Carter pushed past them into the room, her arms outstretched to comfort Robin. And they stood together, frightened and puzzled.

"This has something to do with those eyes in the Junk Room" Jason said. "I wish we'd never started to strip the paper – "

"Tom? What do you think?" Mrs Carter's voice was almost a whisper.

"I think the boy is right," came the grim reply.

Suddenly books started to peel off the long shelf above Robin's bed, one by one, pages fluttering, then two by two, more, more, faster and faster, book after book. Ten, twenty, forty. The shelf bowed and twisted as if crushed in an invisible press that was snapping the wood, pulling out the thin steel brackets. Jason screamed.

The overhead light flashed on to reveal their ghastly white faces, then it went out, plunging them into greater darkness than before. A switch turned on the wall and fell to the floor, pulling out a length of fizzing, arcing cable. Water dripped from the ceiling, slowly at first, then faster . . . faster . . .

"Let's get out!" Robin shouted. "The house is falling apart!"

"Stay where you are!" Tom Carter's voice cut through the darkness. "Don't panic, now. I think this is all an hallucination. The answer lies with those eyes. I – I've got to get rid of them."

"Tom!" Mrs Carter's voice rang out.

Tom Carter paused. "Yes?"

"Be careful – " was all she could say.

"I've got to get rid of them," he repeated. "Take no

142

notice of what you see, or hear. It isn't really happening at all. This is an hallucination. Remember – this can't possibly be happening. Say it. Say it out loud. Repeat after me – this isn't happening. This isn't happening."

Mrs Carter started chanting. "This isn't happening."

"This isn't happening," Robin mumbled.

"Louder!" cried Mr Carter. "Shout it out! Louder!"

He turned, slowly making his way along the landing to the small room, his family following a few paces behind, chanting aloud.

The door was open, and a soft, luminous light flowed out on to the landing. It was cold. Tom Carter stood in the doorway and was about to step into the room when Jason screamed out. "Dad! Look! The floorboards have gone!"

Tom Carter turned to face them, the green light lending his face a sickly appearance. "This isn't happening," he said. "Whatever force this is – whatever evil is coming from those eyes – this is *not* happening to us. Now say it again."

Almost reluctantly they repeated his words and watched as he bent to pick up the blowlamp. This time the gas hissed out, and the flame leapt from the fine nozzle. Tom Carter looked across the room at the eyes.

Embedded in the wall, the eyes glared out balefully, the light of the flame reflected in them, so that they appeared to move. Tom Carter looked down at the floor, unable to meet that intense stare.

Between the doorway and the fireplace there was an open pit, the walls of which glowed green. He leaned forward, a grim smile briefly flickering across his face. Then he said: "The eyes are using these hallucinations to defend themselves."

"Drop something into the hole, Dad," said Robin. "That will tell you if it's real, or not."

143

"Whatever I drop will *appear* to fall into the hole," said Mr Carter. "No. There's only one way. I must have the courage to challenge!"

A low, menacing chuckle filled the air, and the eyes on the wall appeared to half close as if in ecstacy. Tom Carter took a pace forward, the blowlamp roaring vengeance.

At once there was a loud, anguished scream, and the eyes opened wide.

Tom Carter fell. Down into the pit. Down, his shrieks echoing insanely. Mrs Carter rushed forward, her mouth open in a frozen scream.

Down – down – down.

Falling endlessly.

Falling slowly.

Plunging, in slow, slow motion towards the eyes, which had disappeared from the wall and were now waiting . . .

The rest of the story is well documented. Naturally the police visited Graston House and searched for Tom Carter. Some villagers suspect that Mrs Carter murdered her husband and invented the story; others say that her husband left her. After all, when the police investigated the incident they found the floor of that room intact. There were no light switches broken away from the walls, no smashed doors. There was, however, a pair of eyes, freshly painted, staring down from the wall above the fireplace.

THIS BOOK BELONGS TO . . .

by Daphne Froome

"Isn't it a really splendid house?" said Jenny's grandfather proudly as he conducted her along the wide gravel path to the front door.

Jenny, instead of replying, gazed doubtfully at the large, rather tumbledown building with its untidy collection of added rooms, fussily arched windows, twisted wrought-iron balconies, and groups of chimneys leaning dangerously over the sagging slate roof. The whole effect was made even more grotesque by two incongruous turreted towers with battlements.

"It was built in the eighteen-thirties," her grandfather continued. "We're really quite proud of the place. The architecture's mock Gothic. There are any number of useful out-buildings, and sheds at the back as well, and a honeycomb of cellars underground. We haven't had time to explore those yet, but you can get a glimpse of them before going indoors by looking down the shute where they used to tip the coal."

Jenny followed him round the side of the house and watched while he lifted a manhole cover near one of the walls and revealed a large, damp, cobwebby cavity, disappearing into nothingness. Nodding without enthusiasm, she hoped that the exploration of the cellars would be left until after she had finished her holiday and returned home.

Her grandmother greeted her in the hall and led her upstairs and along a twisting corridor to a room at the end of the house.

"I've put you here because it has a lovely view out of both of the windows," she said. "You can see the river in one direction and look out over the old farm buildings in the other. I wish the room under this one was the sitting-room, and not the library, as the present sitting-room only faces the road – but the built-in bookcases would be very difficult to move."

Jenny felt obliged to admire the size of the rooms and their curious shapes.

"I never thought we'd be able to afford a grand home like this," her grandmother admitted, "but it's so dilapidated we were able to buy it very cheaply. The last owner went abroad many years ago and after some while decided not to come back here, so it's been left empty for ages. That's why it's so neglected. It'll be very pleasant, though, when we've got it nicely furnished." She paused. "We're very glad to see you, but I'm afraid you won't have much of a holiday this time."

"That's all right," Jenny replied. "It'll be interesting helping you move in."

It was rather like camping at first, Jenny decided, because the cooker hadn't arrived, and they had to manage on a couple of primus stoves, and necessary things like the tin-opener and the iron seemed to have been mislaid during the move; but the old house, with its twisting corridors and large overgrown garden (which, her grandfather said optimistically, would be marvellous once the weeds had been dealt with) proved far more fascinating than Jenny had first thought it would be, and she was quite happy helping her grandparents to arrange their furniture and hang up curtains.

One day, Jenny went into the library and found her grandfather standing at the top of a pair of very tall steps.

"I'm cleaning the shelves," he said, "getting ready to

arrange all my books. They'll look good here, won't they."

The top shelves were so high that they almost touched the ceiling, with its decoration of fat plaster cherubs that always made Jenny want to laugh. She ran to steady the steps, which had begun to sway dangerously as her grandfather suddenly stood on tiptoe and, scrabbling about in one corner, retrieved a dust-covered book.

He gave it to Jenny and climbed down the steps to the floor.

Jenny blew off the dust, sneezed, and read out: " 'The Knights of Hampden Castle,' by Richard Carter." Then she opened the book. Inside, on the endpaper, was a bookplate inscribed in rather flowery writing with the name Mabel Anne, and the date: 1839.

"I wish she'd written her surname," grumbled Jenny.

"Some people are never satisfied," her grandfather answered crustily. "I wonder if it's a good story."

Jenny handed him the book, and he glanced quickly down the first few pages. "Travel, adventure, brave knights, treasure – it looks like a marvellous yarn to me, a cross between 'Ivanhoe' and 'Robinson Crusoe' with a bit of 'Treasure Island' added for good measure. Though 'Treasure Island' was written much later than this, of course. Well, I can't stand here reading all day," he said as he handed the book back to Jenny. "I've work to do."

"It is a beautiful book," Jenny remarked, "but the edges of the paper are very uneven. And look – those at the end are still fastened together."

"Books are printed in sheets," her grandfather explained, "each of which contains quite a few pages. Then the sheets are folded into sections, and gathered together carefully in the right order and sewn up. So when the book is first put together many of the pages are still joined to each other at the edges. These days the pages are then cut by machinery, but it was not always so. Mabel Anne obviously had to get these cut by hand. By the look of the uneven way they've been separated she probably did it herself." He grunted. "You children don't realize how much is done for you these days."

Jenny hardly heard him. She was far too immersed in reading the first page of the book, then the second. This was no ordinary story – it gripped her from the very beginning, and went on to become more and more exciting with every enthralling line. She trundled a large leather armchair across to the window and, snuggling into it, began reading and reading . . .

Jenny's grandfather finished cleaning the shelves, then he folded the steps and put them away in a corner. "I'm going to have some tea now," he said, but Jenny neither heard him nor noticed when he went away.

Outside in the garden, the bright bare silhouettes of the winter trees gradually lost their sharpness as they began to merge into the darkening sky.

Jenny screwed up her eyes to try to focus on the print better. She thought she heard a faint sound in the room and looked round, expecting to see a grown-up about to say to her, as they so often did: "You'll ruin your eyes, reading in a bad light like that." But there was no one there. It was very cold and she thought that she had been foolish to sit there so long.

There seemed to be a draught blowing from somewhere behind her.

"Bother," she said, and went over and closed the door. "These old houses," she grumbled as she settled down again, and suddenly she wished she was back home with her parents in their small, comfortable flat.

The draught seemed to be stronger than ever. She looked round, wondering where it could possibly be coming from, and as she did so it caught the pages of the book, and flicked them over.

"Bother," said Jenny again. "Now I've lost my place. Oh, I'll go somewhere else."

She closed the book and stood up, but the draught caught at her hair, sending it across her eyes so that she blundered into the shelves, and at that moment the book was snatched from her hand and flung to the floor.

Instantly the draught died away. Jenny stared around her, and then, leaving the book where it had fallen, she rushed from the room in a panic.

"A haunted library!" exclaimed her grandfather, laughing. "I hardly think *that's* very likely. The library certainly *is* a draughty room – I must get something done about it – or else perhaps the book was so exciting it gave you the shivers."

"Well, it *is* exciting," replied Jenny grudgingly.

"Yes, I dare say," replied her grandfather. Then he changed the subject. "Your grandmother's tired, she's been shopping all day, so how about coming down to earth and giving her a hand with the supper?"

As the days of her visit went by without further incident, Jenny, who had not dared to venture into the library again, began to believe that perhaps after all she *had* only imagined the haunting. "It was all the effect of reading that exciting story on a gloomy winter's day," she decided.

Passing the library door one afternoon, she peered rather diffidently in. The room seemed perfectly ordinary; in fact it looked quite inviting with the winter sun streaming through the glass, picking out the gold letters and colourful spines of the books her grandfather had arranged on the shelves, the beautiful soft shades of the carpet he had laid, and the shiny surface of the round beaten brass table that her grandmother had spent so long cleaning up. Her grandfather had left his newspaper and reading glasses on the table and she noticed that he had hung his valuable collection of eighteenth-century prints over the fireplace. Obviously he didn't believe the room was haunted. She could quite distinctly see the exciting book, put back on one of the shelves.

Walking into the room, she took down the book, sat in the armchair and began to read where she had left off before. She had been reading for some time when a small, polite, but quite unmistakable cough made her jump.

A strange girl was standing in a corner of the room, her face in deep shadow, but Jenny could see that her long, dark hair was parted in the middle and tied back from her face with two neat ribbon bows, and she was so thin that her elaborate, high-necked, velvet dress, with its full skirt and white frilly apron, hung about her in deep folds.

Silently the girl began to move across the room. As she advanced into the fading light her shadowy figure became if anything less distinct.

The apparition wavered, then disappeared, only to appear once more, bending over the chair in which Jenny was sitting.

Jenny, shrinking back as far as she was able, caught a brief glimpse of a pair of wistful blue eyes as the girl gazed into her face before glancing downwards to the book. Then the figure turned away and was gone.

"A ghost!" exclaimed Jenny's grandfather. "You just imagined it, sitting there thinking about the girl who owned the book."

"I'm sure it *was* Mabel Anne," Jenny insisted, and she began to shiver violently.

"The child's had a shock; she'd be better off in bed," said Jenny's grandmother, and she hustled Jenny upstairs and insisted on tucking her in beneath a couple of extra blankets.

"You must keep warm, dear," she added. "I'd never forgive myself if you fell ill. Don't worry now. I was always imagining things when I was your age."

Jenny, left alone, dozed uncomfortably beneath the extra weight of the bedclothes, disturbed by strange dreams of Mabel Anne bending over her. They were very upsetting dreams, and she was glad when her grandmother woke her.

"I'm just on my way to bed," she explained. "I've brought you a hot drink and that book you were so interested in. If you find difficulty in getting back to sleep again you may like to read for a bit."

Jenny, propped up among the pillows, sipping the warm drink, felt slightly comforted. After all, the ghost – if there was one – lived in the library, not here in her bedroom. She took up the book and slowly turned the pages until she came to the place where she had left off reading before. It was certainly by far the most gripping tale she had ever come across, and, forgetting everything in the excitement of the story, she read on and on until she was almost at the end. Then, suddenly –

"Bother!" she exclaimed as she found she could not turn over the next page. She had come to the last section, where the edges still needed cutting.

She climbed out of bed and hunted in the pockets of her jeans until she found her penknife. Then she placed the book on her bedside table and began very carefully to separate the edges of the pages. It was a far more difficult task than she would have supposed, because the table was ricketty and the pages were made of very thick paper.

Once she was sure she heard a sound from the library below. She paused, listening anxiously, but the house was silent again. She must have been mistaken, she decided.

After quite a struggle she completed her task and was just climbing back into bed, holding the book, when she heard the library door rattle. There was a pause of a few seconds of complete silence, then the lampshade began to sway as a soft draught blew under the door. Jenny shivered, then sat rigid, clutching the book even tighter in her nervousness. Mabel Anne was slowly materializing. There was an anxious, almost yearning expression in her thin, pinched face.

The ghost glided, shimmering, across the room, and as Jenny drew back, fearful of being enveloped completely, she settled beside her on the bed and stared fixedly at the book. Shakily, Jenny thrust it towards her, then cringed as a strong current of air flung open the cover and ruffled the pages, turning them a dozen or so at a time. Jenny suddenly realized that the ghost of Mabel Anne barely possessed the skill to turn the pages individually, and certainly not to cut them. She looked so terribly ill. Perhaps she had died before finishing the story, and her poor ghost had hung around ever since, waiting to know how it ended.

Mabel Anne was quite unable to control the newly-cut pages, which were sticking together and turning over two at a time as the cold draught whipped them this way and that. Jenny cautiously put out her hand and steadied the book, then found her place again. Though her fingers were numb and frozen she managed to turn the pages, scanning the lines and trying to gauge the speed of the other girl's reading, but the ghost flickered impatiently long before Jenny finished each one. She decided Mabel Anne must be a much quicker reader than she was.

Eventually the last page was completed and the book closed. Then Mabel Anne seemed to drift away, turning towards her and bowing her head regally in thanks, and

Jenny found herself staring at nothing more interesting than the faded wallpaper beside her bed.

She replaced the book on the table, pulled the bed-clothes closely around her and tried unsuccessfully to go to sleep.

"You still look terribly tired," her grandmother said the next day.

"I stayed up late finishing that book," Jenny replied.

"Was it good?"

"Oh, yes. I've never read anything better."

"You can take it home if you like, as you seem to think it's so marvellous."

"No, thank you," Jenny answered very firmly. "I think it should be left here in the bookcase, where it belongs."

THE MURDEROUS GHOSTS

by Rosemary Timperley

It was his first Channel crossing. His first journey abroad, in fact. Abroad. Another world. And the sea had to be crossed before one got there. It was exciting. Strange, too. The rocking of the boat. Did he feel sea-sick? He'd been warned that he might. No, not sick exactly. Just dazed. A queer rhythm going on inside him, back and forth, back and forth. Or was it up and down, up and down? It was a weird, swooping mixture of the two. It made him feel different . . . unreal . . .

So he'd left his parents in the bar and come up on deck, even though all was grey and misty and there was a fleck of rain in the air. No one was about, at first.

He leaned on the rail and looked down into the water. Suddenly he thought of all that depth of sea beneath them. Suppose they sank! Nonsense. Channel steamers didn't sink –

"I hope she's sunk all right," said a voice behind him. A booming sort of voice, like a distant fog-horn.

Startled, he turned to see a tall man with a big black beard and moustache. "Seen my wife?" the man asked.

"Er – no – I haven't seen anyone," said Jack.

"Oh. Good. I expect she's sunk all right then. I was afraid she might have bobbed up, like a balloon." Blackbeard peered over the side, into the murky water. "No sign, thank goodness," he said. "Didn't really think there would be, but you never know with a persistent woman like Annabel."

"Annabel?" echoed Jack.

"My wife. Couldn't stand her any longer. Brought her on this boat for a trip to the other side. Pushed her overboard. Felt a bit sea-sick afterwards. Rested in the cabin. Then I was suddenly scared in case she'd bobbed up. No. No sign of her. Whew!"

He brought out a large grey handkerchief and mopped his brow, nose, cheeks, beard, moustache and eyes, then he smiled at Jack.

"Never get married, young man," he said.

"I don't think I ever would," Jack responded seriously. "I don't care much for females. They seem unnatural, somehow."

"Unnatural. Never said a truer word," agreed Blackbeard. "Their minds don't work, that's the trouble. They have feelings. All these emotions, perceptions, imaginings. Before I brought her on board, my wife said: 'You're going to try and get rid of me. I feel it in my bones.' Well, how could she know? Unnatural. But I did more than try. I *have* got rid of her. I hope." He looked over the side again. "Yes, she must have well and truly sunk by now. Fat woman. Do you know why wives are fat while girl friends are slim?"

Jack shook his head.

"Because wives relax, boy. They've got their man. They're secure for life. They have an income without work. Take Annabel. Beautiful girl when she was young. Loved her."

Tears suddenly filled his eyes and rolled down into his moustache and beard, so that his face in the greyness shone with mingled tears and rain. "Yes, loved her once. Really did!"

"Why?" asked Jack.

"Why? She was lively, affectionate, aimed to please. But once she had a ring on her finger and a house to sit in, she just sat. Sat and ate sweets and read novels and

155

watched telly. She sat and grew fat and she always wore black. Said she was 'in mourning for her life'. That's a quote from some Russian play she'd seen on telly. She said I had no soul. Well, I *had* to get rid of her."

"A man's gotta do what a man's gotta do," said Jack, quoting a recent telly advert.

"Exactly," said Blackbeard, with a sigh.

Jack said, "You are pulling my leg, aren't you? I mean – you didn't really push her overboard."

"Of course I did," fog-horned the man. "What else are we talking about? I wanted to be free!"

"I like to be free, too," agreed Jack, "but I wouldn't drown anyone to be it. It's not right to kill people, even if they're a nuisance. Suppose she comes back and haunts you."

"Annabel, a ghost? Ever heard of a *fat* ghost? No . . ." And at that moment a huge blackness seemed to form itself out of the nothingness of the mist, and a woman's voice said: "Is that you, Gregory?"

Blackbeard jumped so much that he nearly went over the side.

"Annabel!" he gasped. "But you're dead!"

"So are you," said the fat woman in black. She had a sweet, delicate voice. "I poisoned your drink before you drowned me. You're lying dead in our cabin at this moment, only you're so insensitive you don't realize it." She turned to Jack. "Hello, little boy. Can you see us?"

Jack nodded.

"Really? Dear child, you must be psychic. Gregory, it'll be interesting for us to wander around and find out who sees us and who doesn't. We can separate the sensitives from the clodhoppers."

"How did you get out of the water?" demanded her husband.

"I didn't. That is, my body didn't. But *I'm* here. You

really are dead, Gregory, otherwise you wouldn't be able to see me. *You're* not psychic. You have no more spirituality than a pudding. If you don't believe me, go along to the cabin and see for yourself."

"I did lie down in the cabin, feeling sick, after I'd drowned you," the man admitted. "It was a shock to my system. I remembered some of the old, happy times, before the rot set in. Then I pulled myself together and came up here."

"You pulled yourself together and came out of your body, dear, just as I did," said his wife. "Go down to the cabin and take a look at your old self."

"Oh, all right – just to prove you wrong." Blackbeard vanished.

The woman turned to Jack. "Are Gregory and I the first ghosts you've ever met?" she asked chattily.

"Guess so," muttered Jack – not that he believed for one minute that either of them was a ghost, but he thought it best to humour them. "What did you poison your husband with?" he asked, in the same chatty tone as the woman.

"Weed-killer," she answered with a chuckle. "Suitable, eh? He looks like an odd sort of weed, with all that hair. I knew he was going to drown me, you see. I'm a very sensitive creature and I felt it in my bones. It's because I always felt things so intensely in my bones that I let myself grow fat, to protect my bones. But I went on being sensitive. Anyway, I decided that if he could be so selfish and unfriendly as to murder me, I'd do the same to him. Tit for tat. Poor Gregory. Now he's lost his own life but he hasn't lost me. We'll be bound together for all eternity, the couple who murdered each other. What closer tie? But I will try to be nicer to him now. What do you think of it all?"

"You won't like it if I tell you what I honestly think," said Jack.

"Never mind, child. Out with it."

"I think," Jack said carefully, "that the rocking of the boat and maybe quite a lot of duty-free wallop at the bar has made you and your husband have delusions. You're having a sort of shared DT's. That," he explained patiently, "is *delirium tremens*. Alcoholics have it. They see things that aren't there, like green snakes and pink elephants and whatnot, and have other peculiar experiences. You may have wanted to do each other in, but you obviously didn't or you wouldn't be here. That's what I think."

He also thought she might be angered. Grown-ups usually resent very much being told that they're drunk, especially by a child, but she smiled at him affectionately.

"You dear little soul," she said. "Here you are, psychic as they make 'em, communing with ghosts, and you don't even realize it. I expect a lot of people you've talked to during your life have been ghosts, and you simply haven't known. You must take notice next time you bump into someone and feel nothing – or shake hands with someone, and find yourself grasping thin air."

She sighed, and a cool wind blew. "Do you know what I'm going to miss most now I'm a ghost?"

"The telly?"

'Oh, no. I can still watch that. I'll be invisible to most people, so I can walk into any living-room and join the family. Maybe the dog will growl or the cat's fur will stand on end or the room will turn chilly, but no one will know it's me. No, what I shall miss is eating. I've really enjoyed eating, since I was married and could let my looks go. Gregory likes his grub, too. He'll miss eating. We'll have that in common. A shared loss."

"But it'll be convenient," said Jack, joining in her

"game" again instead of being sceptical. "If you don't need food, you won't need money. Everything will be free."

"That's true. We shall be able to travel the world without needing any food to sustain us, and without paying any fares. Yes, it'll be lovely. We'll travel for the rest of our lives."

"Lives? If you're both dead?" said Jack sharply.

"Don't you try to catch me out, young man. The afterlife is as much a life as the one you've got. I don't know everything about it yet as I'm still a 'new girl', but I'm finding my way around."

Blackbeard appeared suddenly. He grinned. "Our cabin is empty," he said. "No body."

"That's nothing," said Annabel. "It only means that the steward found it while we were talking here and had you put wherever they do put dead bodies on board ship."

"Where would that be?" Jack asked, fascinated.

"I don't know," she said. "Gregory and I can go invisible walk-about later and find what they've done with him. In the old slave ships they used to put dead slaves in the cooking-pot to feed the crew. Perhaps the Captain will be having a fry-up of Gregory's kidneys for breakfast. I'd quite fancy that myself, with some bacon and a tomato – and butter and marmalade and toast – "

"Trust you to think of nothing but your stomach, even when you're dead!" blazed Gregory, then made a super-human effort to control his irritation. "Annabel, please understand that you *are* dead now – dead as mutton – dead as a door-nail – dead as the dodo – "

"Perhaps we'll meet a dodo on our travels," his wife said dreamily.

" – and therefore," Blackbeard continued, "you have no right to be here. It's not suitable. Dead people are supposed to lie down – "

"But you didn't, Gregory, and we're in the same boat. Where shall we go then?" She looked at Jack. "Any suggestions?"

"I suggest," said Jack, deciding at this moment that whatever work he took up in life he would not be a mental nurse or warden of a home for alcoholics, "that you go to the bar and have a cup of strong black coffee together – and make friends."

"Isn't he sweet?" said Annabel. "He still doesn't believe that we're ghosts."

"You've had a jolly good fight," said Jack, "drowning and poisoning each other, or pretending to, and now it's time to make up and be friends. Please! It would be – well – nice," he concluded feebly.

Husband and wife regarded each other.

"He's right," said Annabel. "It would be nice. We'll be together for ever now, Gregory, so let's be friends. I apologize for poisoning you with weed-killer."

"Now you apologize to her for whatever you did," said Jack.

"I apologize for drowning you," muttered Blackbeard. "I *was* sorry afterwards, actually."

"Now shake hands," said Jack.

They did, and Annabel said: "Place your hand on ours, to give us your blessing."

Jack tried to do so, but the boat lurched at that moment so he didn't actually touch the clasped hands.

"Oh, I do feel peculiar," said Blackbeard, in the tone of a bewildered fog-horn.

"So do I, love, but we'll soon get accustomed," said Annabel.

"I feel a bit sick, too. Excuse me," said Jack, and left them standing together at the rail. Cor! he thought. A right couple of loonies. But interesting. Leaves you with something to think about.

He walked on another part of the deck until his sickish feeling wore off, then began to make his way to the bar to rejoin his parents. As he passed a door marked MEDICAL ROOM, a man with a stethoscope round his neck – apparently a doctor – was just coming out and saying to another man: "It wasn't ordinary sea-sickness. People don't die of that, although they often feel as if they're dying. Food-poisoning, more like." And just for a second Jack wondered if Annabel's tale of poisoning was true, and those two had been ghosts, and he really was psychic. He tried bumping into a few people to see if he felt anything. He felt the bumps all right. So did his victims – "Look where you're going, lad! My corns are not for stamping on!"

At last he reached his parents at their table in the bar.

"Feeling seedy, darling? You're very pale," said his mother. "It is rather a rough crossing."

"You can say that again," said Jack.

His father brought him a glass of lemonade and he sat there sipping it. Everything settled back into a kind of normality. He even wondered if he'd dreamed those two people on deck. All this rocking and swaying did make one light-headed. Perhaps he'd imagined the whole incident –

Then the door of the bar swung open and the mysterious couple, Blackbeard and his wife, walked in, large as life and arm-in-arm. They didn't look at all drunk – and they'd made friends. Jack felt he'd had some share in that and, when they smiled and waved at him, he smiled and waved back. They went to sit at a table some distance away, but didn't order anything.

"Who were you waving to?" asked his mother.

"The couple that's just sat down over there. I met them on deck. They'd had a bit of a tiff but they're OK now."

He returned his empty lemonade glass to the counter

and, as he did so, heard one of the assistants say to the other: "Rough old crossing in more senses that one. A Mr Gregory Lake has died of food-poisoning, and his wife is missing, presumed drowned."

Can't be the same as my couple, thought Jack, giving another wave and smile to his friends. But they were absorbed in each other now, holding hands across the table – and she seemed to be slimmer than before, and prettier – and he looked younger and his beard was less aggressive –

His mother asked: "Jack, who do you keep waving to?"

"That couple – I told you – at that table." He pointed.

"But that table," said his mother, "is empty."

Jack went cold and whispered: "Are you sure?"

"Of course I'm sure. What's the matter with you?"

"I'm psychic," said Jack, with wonder and a touch of pride.

"Sea-sick, more like," said his father. "Never mind, Jack, boy. We'll soon be on the other side. It's like another world over there."

True enough, the ship was approaching the shore and the mist had cleared. They came out of it as if it had been a dream. They went to the rail to watch the land approach.

And suddenly Jack saw two figures who were going to reach the other side before the ship made port. They were walking, or floating, rather, ahead of the ship. They looked absurd, yet touching at the same time, the rather plump woman in black and the tall bearded man, hand-in-hand, skimming aross the water . . .

They're in love again, Jack thought proudly, and I "brought them together". But he was congratulating himself a bit too soon for, as he watched, the outline of the two figures became rather less lovey-dovey. Annabel looked as if she'd given Gregory a pretty sharp kick on

162

the ankle – and he'd kicked her back. The two heads turned towards each other, in obvious argument.

What were they saying?

A seagull shrilled across the sky. Through its cry, Jack heard Annabel's voice: "I am being nice – nice – nice – nice – "; and through the noise of a distant fog-horn came Gregory's angry: "Oh, you – you – you – you – YOU!"

SARAH

by Roger Malisson

Michael Dean was not impressed by his first view of
Lawnside House. His father echoed his feelings as they
got out of the car.

"Gloomy-looking old dump, isn't it."

"Never mind, John. You'll soon make it fit to live in,"
said Mrs Dean, opening the creaky garden gate. "Won't
he, Michael?"

"I suppose so," answered Michael doubtfully.

The house was a hundred-year-old mansion that his
father was buying. He was a builder and he renovated old
houses, converting the rooms into self-contained flats.
Michael knew that he was going to have quite a job with
this one, because Lawnside House had not been lived in
for forty-five years.

"Good heavens!" Mrs Dean stopped abruptly half way
down the path. "What was that?"

A white face had appeared fleetingly at one of the
curtained windows, then vanished.

"Oh, don't worry," Michael's father said. "That'll be
Miss Heseldine, the owner. I haven't met her yet, but she
told the solicitors that she would be here to meet us
today. She's very anxious to sell."

"That figures," remarked Michael. Who on earth would
want to live in a really tumbledown, decaying old building
like this?

The door was open and the Dean family walked straight
in. The house smelt musty and old. They found their way

164

to the drawing-room, where Miss Heseldine was waiting to greet them.

"Please sit down, Mr and Mrs Dean, and, er – "

"Michael," said Michael.

"Hm. I'm very pleased you have decided to buy," she said with a thin smile, turning straight back to his parents. "I have a private income, but with inflation and so forth I shall be glad of the extra money."

"Yes, of course," said Mr Dean politely. "I signed the final papers at the solicitors' this morning."

The talk turned to legal matters and Michael, bored, inspected the room. Like the hallway, it was furnished with old-fashioned pieces, and the faded flowered wallpaper was peeling. It was, however, spotlessly clean.

"May I take my wife to see the upstairs rooms, Miss Heseldine?" his father asked.

"Certainly," the old lady replied. "You will forgive me if I stay here. My doctor has advised me to climb as few stairs as possible."

His parents stood up. Michael cast an appealing glance at his mother, but she said:

"You stay here, Michael, and keep Miss Heseldine company. Plenty of time for you to explore later."

And so he was left alone in the chilly room with the chill old woman.

"You don't live here, then, Miss Heseldine?" he asked, when she showed no signs of speaking.

"No," she answered shortly, and that was the end of that little conversation.

From the start, he had not liked Miss Heseldine. She sat stiffly in her high-backed chair, plump and wrinkled, and looked at him with hard eyes. Very like a strict teacher he had once disliked in primary school, thought Michael. He tried to think of something to say.

"It's a very old house," he ventured at last. "Does it have any legends of ghosts?"

The effect on Miss Heseldine was startling.

"Of course not!" she snapped. "What a silly thing to say. What a foolish idea!" And she settled firmly back into her chair, turning towards the fireplace. Michael noticed that her spidery hands were suddenly fidgety, and she kept glancing nervously around the room. After that he gave up trying to talk to her and waited for his parents to come back.

"We shall be staying here on holiday for a few weeks while my husband starts work on the house, Miss Heseldine," Michael's mother told the old lady when they finally came downstairs.

"I am sure you will enjoy it. Raynforth is very popular in the summer," she replied.

"It has a smashing beach," Michael chimed in. "Do you live in the village, Miss Heseldine?"

Miss Heseldine gave him a frosty stare, and for a minute he thought she was going to say something corny, like "Children should be seen and not heard", but she merely said:

"No, I do not. I value my privacy, Mr Dean," she explained to his father, "and I trust you will contact me, if necessary, only through my solicitors."

"Very well. And now we must be going." Mr Dean stood up. "May we give you a lift anywhere?"

"Yes, please, as far as the village."

"By the way," said Mrs Dean warmly as the old woman was getting out of the car, "it was very good of you to have the house tidied and cleaned for us. You really shouldn't have bothered."

For some reason the remark seemed to startle and unnerve Miss Heseldine.

"It was no trouble, Mrs Dean," she answered shortly.

* * *

The Deans went home for three weeks, and during that time the builders painted the outside of the house and lit huge coal fires inside to drive out the damp. Lawnside House looked much more inviting the second time Michael saw it.

Their first few days were spent in organizing everything and making friends. Downstairs they only used the kitchen, and on the second floor they lived in three rooms: two bedrooms and one they used for a sitting-cum-dining room. In this way they were able to avoid most of the dust, hammering and debris when the builders, joiners and decorators arrived to convert the rest of the house into flats.

Michael helped his father to shift most of the furniture upstairs into the attics where, his father said, the servants of the house used to sleep in days gone by. He had been looking forward to exploring the attics, but there was nothing of interest. The little rooms were poky and cold with slanting ceilings, and he was glad to return to their cheerful sitting-room.

Michael soon made friends with a group of boys and girls from Raynforth, and began to enjoy his holiday. Raynforth, on the North Yorkshire coast, was partly a fishing village and partly a holiday resort. Michael went swimming or fishing every day, and sometimes walked over to the little town of Limeside with his friends for a game of football with the local team, or to go to the cinema. The weather was glorious that summer, and the five-mile walk took them over some wild and beautiful moorland.

It was one of the best holidays the family had ever had, though Mr Dean spent the mornings working on the house with the builders and Mrs Dean sometimes grumbled good-naturedly over having to do the cooking. The first few days flew by and it wasn't until the second week that Michael noticed that there was something extremely odd about Lawnside House.

At first it all seemed so silly and unimportant that he decided not to tell his parents about it, and they were too busy and happy to notice anything. In fact, Michael only realized what was happening because one day he lost his shoes.

He had been crab-hunting in the rock pools on the beach north of Raynforth with Rob and Janet from the village. They did not see any crabs, but the expedition was fun and they decided to go again the next day. But when Michael went to put on his beach sandals he could not find them, though he distinctly remembered having dropped them, sand-caked and stained, in the corner of his bedroom. After a search, he found them cleaned and polished and neatly placed in his wardrobe. Michael was puzzled. He asked his mother, then his father, if they had touched the shoes, but neither of them had.

After that, he began to notice odd little things. He happened to be an extremely untidy boy, but in the mornings his clothes were always folded away, and if he left books lying around they were always put back into the bookcase; in fact, his room was unusually tidy. Surely he wasn't sleepwalking, and tidying up as he went? That was a ridiculous idea.

One day he decided on an experiment. Rob and Janet came round for supper and a game of Monopoly afterwards. When Michael went to bed he purposely left the board, with its houses, counters, cards and money, scattered about the floor of his room. The next morning the whole game was tucked away into its box.

It was all very strange. He was quite sure that neither of his parents came into his room during the night, and there was no one else in the house. Or was there? He suddenly remembered how anxious and nervous Miss

Heseldine had looked when he had jokingly asked her if Lawnside House was haunted. Michael half-believed in ghosts, but he had always understood that they were meant to frighten. He had heard of some, what were they called? – poltergeists, that was it – which threw the furniture around and made houses tremble. On the other hand, he had never heard of ghosts going about tidying everything away. But what other explanation could there be?

Michael decided to find the answer once and for all. That evening he planned to stay awake all night to see what was going on.

Staying awake was going to be a big problem, of course. That afternoon he had been playing football and he was tired. He read adventure stories with great determination until half past eleven, when he found himself beginning to doze over the page. Midnight was supposed to be the hour that ghosts showed up, wasn't it? Very well, he could easily stay awake for another half hour. Switching off the light, he waited for his eyes to become used to the gloom. It was a fine, moonlit night, and he could make out all the furniture in his room quite well.

Michael straightened himself on the pillow. His head kept falling on to his chest and his eyelids drooped heavily. He tried pinching his fingers to stay awake, but his drowsiness increased. Glancing at the luminous dial of the travelling alarm beside his bed he saw that it was ten to twelve. Ten minutes to go, then. If nothing happened at midnight he would give up and go to sleep.

Two minutes to twelve. Was the room growing colder, or was he imagining that it was? Michael shivered and pulled his dressing-gown tighter round his shoulders. He yawned, and decided that nothing was going to appear. But just as he was snuggling down into bed the handle of

169

the door slowly began to turn. Something or someone was trying to get in . . .

Heart thumping, Michael drew the covers up to his chin, and the hair prickled at the back of his neck as the door opened, inch by inch, without a sound. When it was half open he was astonished to see, not some horrible shrouded creature, but his own football boots floating into the room. They stopped in mid-air and the door closed quietly. He watched breathlessly, his amazement nearly greater than his fright. The boots looked so funny, dangling there in a rather pathetic way, that he almost wanted to laugh. Almost, but not quite, for a frightening thought struck him. Was there some invisible thing in the room with him, holding the boots in its insubstantial hand?

"Who . . . who's there?" he called, trying to keep his voice steady.

He was answered by a despairing wail, and a girl's voice said indignantly, "Oh, it's too bad! You're awake! I simply can't go on – it's all too much!" And then came the sound of sobbing. With a thump, the boots fell to the floor.

Michael cleared his throat. "Er . . . please don't cry," he said awkwardly.

"It's all right for you," said the little voice. "I just can't cope any more, that's all. Painters and decorators! All the rubble! Every night it gets worse. I simply don't know what to tidy first! And the cleaning!"

The voice grumbled on in this strain for several minutes, and Michael grew more puzzled than afraid.

"But who are you?" he asked at last. "Can't I help?"

"Oh, I forgot, you can't see me. There!"

Before his astonished eyes a girl appeared. She was not much older than Michael, but very small and extremely thin. She was dressed in a long grey frock with a white

170

apron and cap. In one hand she held a large, old-fashioned dustpan and brush. For a moment they looked at each other, and then the girl began to laugh.

"Excuse me," she said, "but you looked so funny – so surprised. Your eyes nearly popping!"

"Well, I've never seen a ghost before," Michael pointed out, a little sulkily. He didn't feel afraid of this ghost any more, but he certainly didn't want it – her? – to laugh at him. "Anyhow, you're not my idea of a ghost at all. Shouldn't you be rattling chains and groaning a bit?"

"Oh, no. All I have to do is to tidy up and dust and clean – housework, you know. And as to my not looking like a ghost – feel my hand!"

Michael tried, but his hand closed on cold, empty air.

"Gosh," he said feebly. The experience shocked him rather.

"My name is Sarah," said the girl. "And yours is Michael, of course. I can't get on with my work until you're asleep. You're not supposed to see me, you know."

"But why do you have to do all this housework?" he asked curiously.

"I used to work for Miss Heseldine," explained Sarah, perching on the end of the bed. "I was never strong, and I couldn't do my work very fast. Miss Heseldine is a stickler, you know, and she insisted on having the house spotless all of the time. So I had to work very hard, even when I was ill. Drudge, drudge, all day from morning to night. She had never had a day's illness in her miserable life, so he didn't understand. Would you believe it," said Sarah, warming to her subject, "if she found one speck of dust anywhere she used to send me to bed without any supper. So, anyhow, I worked harder and harder and got weaker and weaker, and in the end I died."

"The inhuman old thing!" cried Michael indignantly.

171

"That's really shocking. You don't seem too upset about it, though," he added.

"Oh, it was nearly fifty years ago now," said Sarah, swinging her legs nonchalantly. "Forgive and forget. Do you happen to know where she's living now?" she enquired, a shade too carelessly.

"No, I'm afraid not – why?" asked Michael, suddenly suspicious.

"Well, I wouldn't mind seeing her again, that's all," said Sarah, and her eyes narrowed. "I have a score to settle with her, you see. Only she won't stay here because she knows that I'm around, and I can never find out where she's gone."

Perhaps that's just as well, thought Michael, startled at the crafty look which had crossed her face.

"I'm afraid I've no idea where she is," he told her. "At the seaside she said, but that could be anywhere."

"Never mind, I shall find her one day. Well, I can't stay here chatting all night, I really must get on. Goodnight!"

Sarah vanished, and seconds later Michael was asleep.

As usual, when Michael woke up the next morning, his room was spick and span. He set out for an early morning walk to think about his meeting with the strange little ghost. Glancing back to Lawnside House he shivered slightly. Sarah meant them no harm, he was sure, but it was no wonder that Miss Heseldine had seemed so ill at ease in the house. Once she had realized, more than forty years ago, that her stubborn little servant girl had come back to haunt her, she must have been terrified for her life.

She really ought to have told his father, though, before she had sold him the house. Michael wondered whether to tell his parents about Sarah. But what if the little housemaid hadn't been telling the truth? He remembered how sly she had looked when she spoke of her former

172

mistress. Supposing Miss Heseldine was entirely innocent, and had been driven out of her rightful home through Sarah's spite? Perhaps he had better investigate further before he said anything to his parents.

Michael returned to the house, and after breakfast he hung around the kitchen until Mr Crabtree came in for his morning coffee. Mr Crabtree was a professional gardener, and Michael's father had employed him to lick their garden into shape. Michael went to talk to him as he was drinking his coffee and puffing at his pipe.

"You've lived in Raynforth a long time, haven't you, Mr Crabtree?" he asked.

"All of my sixty-eight years, lad," replied the gardener.

"You would know Miss Heseldine, then?"

"Know her! Aye, everyone knew her. There weren't many liked her, though."

"She didn't seem very friendly when we met her," Michael said.

The old man removed his pipe before answering, deliberately, "She's a hard, cold, selfish, grasping woman. Always was. Vindictive, if you crossed her, and a tyrant as well."

"A tyrant?" asked Michael, hoping he was steering Mr Crabtree in the right direction.

"That's what I said," nodded the old man. "You ought to have seen the way she lorded it over her servants when she lived here. Not many would stay with her long. They couldn't put up with her finicky ways and endless nagging. Jobs were hard to find in those days, but even so, as I say, not many could stand her so long. It was over a servant that she left Raynforth, as it happens."

"Really? How was that?" said Michael encouragingly.

"Well, lad, there was one little girl came up from Wiltshire to be a housemaid. She wasn't more'n fifteen, and a frail, sickly little thing. Well, Miss Heseldine took advantage of her because she was young and had no experience – Sarah, I remember her name was. Miss Heseldine literally worked her to death, and though she could see the girl was wasting away she never saw that she had any medical treatment. It was a crying scandal, lad, and they remember it in these parts yet. Some of the neighbours and the servants talked of going to the police, but nothing ever came of it. A couple of days after Sarah died, Miss Heseldine moved out."

"What a terrible thing," said Michael automatically. He felt rather uneasy, not only because Sarah's story had been confirmed, but because the room had gone colder and he felt sure, though he could not tell why, that Sarah was somewhere about and listening to their conversation. It was an uncomfortable sensation, but he did not feel afraid.

"They were the bad old days, lad. We were all glad when Miss Heseldine took off. And I'll bet," he added, chuckling, "that she doesn't get half as much of her own way as she used to. I don't imagine that the staff of that posh Grand Hotel in Limeside like her any more than we – "

"Hush!" cried Michael. "You mustn't say that!"

"What's the matter, lad? I only said that where she's gone to live, at the Grand Hotel, the staff there . . ."

The old man talked on, but the damage was done. For Michael's quick ear had caught a faint, rather spiteful laugh, and the sound of a gleeful "Goodbye!"

The next morning Michael awoke and looked around his bedroom with a puzzled feeling. There was something unusual – ah! that was it! The room was untidy. Nothing had been put away. The little ghost had gone.

He got out of bed and began straightening the room before his mother saw it. In a way, he realized with a sigh, he was going to miss Sarah. And I bet I know where

174

she's gone, he thought uneasily. The Grand Hotel at Limeside. I hope she doesn't cause too much mischief there.

All that day, Michael tried not to think about what Sarah might be up to. But it wasn't till the following morning that the news broke.

Over breakfast, Mr Dean exclaimed, "Good heavens! Old Miss Heseldine's died. Look, it's here in the paper. 'Hotel Resident Plunges to her Death'."

"Let me see," said Mrs Dean, and Michael craned over her shoulder to read it too.

The local paper gave a full account of how Miss Heseldine had tripped over a large, old-fashioned dustpan on the stairs, and had died as a result of her fall. The Hotel Manager denied that the dustpan belonged to the hotel, and said that the accident was something of a mystery.

Sarah never returned to Lawnside House. Three weeks later the Deans left, and during the months that followed Michael often thought about the old mansion and the ghostly housemaid who had tended it for so many years. He wondered, too, what had become of her now that her mistress was dead, and a year later he thought he had the answer.

Driving through Raynforth one wet day on their way to Scotland, the Deans stopped to see Lawnside House, now converted into smart flats, and to have some lunch. Michael went to say hello to Mr Crabtree and some friends in the village, and on his way back he took a short cut through the local churchyard.

He knew that Miss Heseldine had been alone in the world, and so it came as rather a shock to see her grave, which should have been overgrown with weeds, neatly tended. The grass was trimmed, some flowers were blooming, and the headstone was polished: R.I.P., it said.

Walking back through the peaceful countryside in the quiet drizzle, Michael could not help shuddering as he wondered whether Miss Heseldine really was resting in peace, or whether her implacable little drudge was waiting upon her still, throughout all eternity.

A RED, RED ROSE

by Ruth Cameron

"My aunt Emily, your great -aunt, is a recluse," his father said, as they drove through the twisting Devonshire lanes. "That's why you've never met her. She lives all by herself in a caravan and doesn't welcome visitors."

"Then why are we visiting her?" Tom asked.

"Because she's over seventy now and she's had a spot of heart trouble, so I like to keep in touch in case she ever needs help. She'll probably send me away with a flea in my ear, but there it is. Well, we've arrived. This is Green Pool Wood."

"What a super name. Is there a green pool?"

"There is. Very pretty it is, too. You'll see it."

They left the car by the roadside and entered the wood. It was a windy summer day. The sun flickered in and out as clouds blew across its face. Birds sang and leaves rustled in the moving air. At first the path was narrow and overhung by trees, then they came to a clearing where a large pool stretched out before them. Because of the trees reflected in it, the water looked green.

"Green Pool!" said Tom. "It's fabulous!"

"It is rather out-of-this-world," his father agreed. "Now you'd better wait here, I'll go along to the caravan and see what sort of reception I get, then, if she'd like to see you, I'll come and collect you later. OK.?"

"Fine, I'd like to wait here." He was shy and had not been looking forward to meeting a strange old woman, even if she was a relative. So his father's footsteps retreated through the rustling leaves and Tom was left alone.

It was wonderfully peaceful after the long, hot journey by car, and he felt a touch of envy for his great-aunt Emily. He wouldn't mind living here in a woodland caravan himself, close to nature, unbothered by people and school and all the practical demands of everyday life. His eyes soaked up the greenness of the pool and the trees, and the wind became still so that everything fell silent. There was an eeriness about this sudden silence. He was aware of it. As if time had stood still . . . or ceased to exist . . .

Then the silence was broken by a laugh, a sweet, young, gay laugh, mocking, feminine, and he turned his head to see a girl running through the trees towards the pool, and being pursued by a young man. They were playing some sort of game, thought Tom, and they hadn't seen him, for when the young man overtook the girl, he seized her in his arms and kissed her.

Tom drew farther back under the willow tree which sheltered him. He felt rather embarrassed. Should he betray his presence or stay hidden? He took the line of least resistance, stayed hidden, and hoped they'd soon go away. But they didn't. They sat down on the bank.

"I've got something for you," said the young man. "I hope it isn't squashed. No – it's all right." From his pocket he had brought a red rose. Solemnly he presented it to her. "A symbol of my eternal love," he said. "In the words of Robert Burns, 'My love is like a red, red rose'."

She burst out laughing. "Martin, you *are* sentimental! Queen Victoria is dead, you know. You've been reading too many Jane Austen novels, with gallant men courting fair ladies. You're a sentimental silly." Her words were mocking, but she was beautiful, Tom thought, with her mass of black hair flowing over her shoulders, her tanned

178

skin, her big dark eyes, her long dress adding grace to her slender figure. There was mischief and wildness in her, too, a touch of the daredevil which appealed to him. It evidently appealed to this Martin person also, for he said:

"I may be sentimental, but I don't care. I really do love you. You only laugh when I tell you that. How can I make you believe me? Tell me what to do to prove my love and I'll do it. Anything!"

"All right." She stood up, the red rose in her hand. She tossed the flower right out into the middle of the pool. "Now bring the red, red rose back to me," she said, "and I'll believe you."

"Oh, you devil-girl!" But he was laughing now as he peeled off his shirt, waded into the pool, then swam towards the floating rose.

The events that followed this lovers' game were shocking and terrifying. For as Martin swam closer to the flower, something seemed to hold him back, to drag him down. He fought against some invisible undertow, gave a choked cry and sank, the green water covering his head.

The girl ran to the edge of the pool. "Martin! What's happened to Martin!"

His head came up once, only to sink again.

"Help!" screamed the girl. "Help! Help! Someone come! Help! Oh, God – I can't swim – I can't swim – Help! Help!"

Tom could swim, although he'd never done any lifesaving. He wanted to jump into the pool and try to rescue the drowning man, but paralysis seemed to be gripping his limbs. He literally couldn't move, although he struggled to do so. It was like a nightmare in which you're being pursued by wild beasts but can't run away. He struggled – struggled – and then felt someone shaking his shoulder, freeing his limbs by that touch . . .

"Wake up, Tom." His father was there.

A dream. It had only been a dream after all. There was, of course, no sign of the girl. The whole gruesome incident simply had not happened. Oh, the relief . . .

"We must drive into the village and fetch a doctor," his father was saying.

"Why? Is your Aunt Emily ill?" Tom asked dazedly, hurrying along beside his father.

"Yes. That is – she's dead, Tom. She must have had a heart attack. It looks to me as if she died in her sleep."

Tom said nothing. The news didn't mean much to him as he'd never even met Emily. He was more shaken by the effects of his recent dream than by the real event of the old woman's death. He told his father about the dream as they drove to the village, and when he'd finished the other said: "Tom, why are you pretending that was a dream?"

"Pretending? I'm not. When it was happening, I didn't know I was dreaming. One never does. Or almost never. I only knew it was a dream when you woke me up."

"You must have heard the story at some time, then, and it stuck in your mind. Did you mother tell you?"

"No, Dad. What story?"

"A tragedy in Aunt Emily's past. When she was seventeen she had a boy friend called Martin. He adored her, and she loved him too, in her own way, but she couldn't resist tormenting him sometimes. One summer afternoon she did throw a rose into Green Pool and tell him to fetch it for her, to prove his love. It was just a game, with a thread of feminine cruelty in it. But there are dangerous weeds in that pool which entangle swimmers' feet and pull them down. That's what happened to poor Martin. He was drowned."

"And it was her fault," murmured Tom. "She must have felt terrible. In fact, she did." He saw her anguished face again in his mind's eye.

"She did indeed," his father agreed. "She was overwhelmed by remorse. It affected her whole life. From being a flirtatious young woman, very much aware of her own attractiveness, she withdrew into herself, avoided men, never even married. She earned her living as a teacher at the village school and was respected, but was never really popular. It was as if she was afraid to give or receive affection. She often walked in the wood and sat by the pool. No one could stop her. She couldn't let him go, you see . . . or perhaps he couldn't let her go. Anyway, when she retired she went to live in that caravan near Green Pool. And now she's dead, poor old thing, and all that anguish seems to be so much waste. Did you really dream that incident, Tom? You're sure you hadn't heard the story from someone?"

"Quite sure, Dad. I swear it. I saw it happen, just as if it was really happening."

"Extraordinary," murmured his father. "How little we know about life, for all our science and our book-learning."

Tom thought deeply, then said: "Perhaps things that happen are always still there really – like turning on the telly. I mean, the programme's there all the time, but you have to turn the right knob to get it. So maybe when one's asleep, one sometimes sort of turns a knob on the past, and gets the – the programme, as if it were a recording. Perhaps there are recordings of past events all round us, only we don't know where the switch is to turn them on."

"Don't get too fanciful," his father said. "We've got to be very practical now. I'll have to return to the caravan with the doctor, so we must find someone to look after you till I get back."

"Oh, no – let me stay with you. I want to. I'm not frightened. I love Green Pool Wood, in spite of the dream."

His father gave in.

They found the doctor at his house and the three of them drove back to the wood. The place was bathed in moonlight by that time and so beautiful that it seemed enchanted. They walked along the same path until they reached the pool, then the doctor suggested: "If the boy would care to wait here . . ."

"Good idea," agreed Tom's father. "You'll be all right, won't you, Tom? Stay quietly here. We shan't be long. No falling asleep."

"No, Dad. As if I would!"

"Good boy." His father's comforting pressure on his shoulder. So real. So much more important than any dream. Then he and the doctor went on to the caravan.

Tom crossed to his special place under the willow tree and gazed at the water. Green Pool was not green now. It was silver and black. Silver for life, black for death, he thought. *Everything* is here. Past, present, future. Silver and black. And then – colour suddenly – a glow of red – for there, magically floating in the centre of the pool, was the red rose.

I'm not dreaming this time, thought Tom, although it was as if he had stepped back into his dream, picked up the thread of it from the moment of his previous waking. Yet the scene was different. No green and gold. All silver and black. The redness of the rose was the link between the dream scene and this one. The girl was standing on the shore, her face very sad. Now there was a movement in the water. The man's head appeared. He stretched out an arm and seized the rose. He set it between his teeth and swam towards the shore. When he landed, he tossed the rose to the girl, who caught it in both hands and pressed it to her heart. She was radiant now. He took her in his arms. They stood in close embrace, as if they would never let each other go again.

Tom stared and stared at these timeless lovers in the stillness and silence of this timeless time. The whole world of the night seemed to be standing still, as the lovers imprinted themselves on some eternal landscape . . .

A little wind blew up. Things began to move again. And Tom found that he was staring at the outlines of two little trees whose branches had intertwined . . .

A movement behind him. His father was there.

"We're going back now, Tom. The doctor's coming. He'll see to everything tomorrow. She died of a heart attack, as I guessed, poor Aunt Emily. However, there are worse ways to go. At least she went peacefully, in the place which she loved and where she felt at home."

"She's all right now," Tom said, and his father accepted the statement at its face value, saying. "Yes, she's all right. Death is nothing to be afraid of. It's part of nature." There was a little silence, and he added:"Something rather odd – " He stopped.

"What, Dad?"

"A little mystery. The doctor and I were both puzzled. Someone must have gone into the caravan while we were away. A passing gipsy, perhaps."

"Why? What had happened?"

"She was lying as I'd left her, except that her face was happier – although that could be an illusion on my part. But the odd thing was that someone had placed a flower on her breast. A rose. Fresh. Fragrant. A beautiful red rose. But who put it there, or why, no one will ever know."

Except me, thought Tom. *I* know.

WHOEVER HEARD OF A HAUNTED LIFT?

by Alan W. Lear

"Well, I hadn't for one. I thought you only got ghosts in crumbling old cobwebby mansions that had stood empty for centuries – nobody told me there was any chance of one turning up in the lift of a council tower-block that hadn't been built until the 1960s.

And I'd only ever heard of ghosts coming out at night. I mean, who'd expect to meet one at half-past two in the afternoon of a blazing hot summer's day? I bet you wouldn't.

Not – and let's get this straight from the beginning – that I believe in ghosts in any place, by night or day. Not me. Ghost stories are a load of tripe, and the kids that read them are a lot of twits – and if you don't like that, you can do the other thing.

But there was one time when I had my doubts . . .

This block of flats I live in is called Tompion Court, and it's in the middle of a crummy industrial estate on the edge of town. It couldn't have been up more than five years when Mum and Dad moved in, just before I was born. That means it's only seventeen years old now, but it's already falling to bits. You should see some of the enormous cracks in the concrete walls on the ground floor. Or the big glass door in the vestibule, which won't shut properly because the frame's warped. The part of the block I live in's not *too* bad, but I've heard of some people who've had to move out of their homes because of the condensation running down the walls.

Then of course there's the lifts.

There are two of them, and I reckon they spend more time out of order then working. That's no joke when you live eight storeys up.

And even when they *are* working – well, the one at the front of the building's dodgy enough, but the other one's never worked properly since I can remember. I know some old people who'd rather climb the stairs than use it. Maybe it doesn't fit the shaft exactly; at any rate, it shudders and rattles and groans all the time you're in it. Also it's got a really nasty pong, that clings to your clothes after you've got out again.

"It smells like something'd died in it," I said one day for no very good reason.

Uncle Derek looked up from the comic he was reading. "That's because something did, Colin," he replied. "Some *one*, that is."

Let me tell you about my Uncle Derek – he's the sort that laps up ghost stories. He's my mum's brother, and he's been living with us for the last three years, and he's a menace.

I've heard Dad telling Mum (when he thought I wasn't listening) that there's something wrong with Uncle Derek. He's sort of the black sheep of Mum's family. He must be pushing thirty, but he still dresses like he did when he was a teenager in the sixties – beard, shoulder-length hair, buckskin jacket and flared trousers. He doesn't actually wear beads and a Flower Power shirt – he wouldn't last long round our way if he did – but he keeps them in a drawer and prays for the day they'll come back in style.

What else? Oh yes: he keeps hogging the stereo with his corny old sixties LPs when I want to play my Heavy Metal singles. Like I say, he's a menace.

One of his favourite tricks is telling me all about the horror films he's always going to. Trying to scare me.

185

Like the one where this chap finds out that the Anti-christ has come to Earth. He gets into a lift to go and tell everybody about it; only the lift stops between floors, and then the cable breaks and comes whizzing down the shaft, slicing through the lift and cutting the man clean in two.

Uncle Derek told me that one hoping it'd give me nightmares. Pathetic, I call it.

So when he announced that someone had died in *our* lift, I just said, "Oh, come on!"

"No, really," Uncle Derek protested. "On my life. Ask your mum if you don't believe me. A little boy died in that lift the year before you came to live here."

"Had he found out about the Antichrist too?" I asked.

Uncle Derek shrugged. "OK, OK. Forget it. If you don't want to hear about it, I don't have to tell you."

He went back to his comic. That was supposed to be my cue to get all curious and beg him to go on. He must have thought I was a five-year-old. I just sat and waited.

Less than a minute later he started again. "His name was Billy Ross. He must have been about your age, Colin. He lived in this very flat, as it happens. His folks couldn't stand it here after the tragedy – that's why they moved out and let your Dad have it."

"Oh yes?" I said.

Uncle Derek leaned forward. "It was a summer's day in 1971. Billy was off school ill. He was ill a lot. He had asthma – you know, like your cousin Shirley. Had terrible trouble breathing sometimes, and he was very nervous and highly strung.

"Well, on this particular day he'd been out playing, and he got into that lift to come up to the flat, and just before he reached the eighth floor it stuck. You know how they do."

I knew. These lifts stick all the time. There's an alarm button you press if you get trapped, and everyone in the block's supposed to rally round and help get you free. Except of course nobody bothers. If they hear the alarm go off, they just shrug their shoulders and ignore it. They figure it's probably just kids having a lark; and if it isn't, well, there are people who get paid to do the job.

"So what happened?" I asked.

"Billy got stuck just below this floor. They think he pressed the alarm but no one came to help him. Then he got panicky from being cooped up, and the panic brought on an asthma attack, and he couldn't breathe . . . and so, when somebody finally did get the lift started again and the door opened, they found Billy lying on the floor, dead as a doornail. Terrible thing."

Uncle Derek didn't look like he thought it was terrible. I could see that big daft grin of his starting on his face.

"And he used to live in this very flat, Colin. He slept in your bedroom. Hey, I wonder if he ever comes back at night, and looks down at you sleeping in your bed, and thinks, 'How dare this smelly little animal invade my private room?' Maybe one night he'll get really annoyed, and then he'll stretch out his cold, bony hand and – "

"Derek Armstrong!" That was my mum's voice. She'd just come barging into the living-room with a basket full of washing, and she looked very red in the face. "Are you up to your tricks again, trying to frighten that boy? You should be ashamed of yourself, at your age . . . And turn that terrible row down! You'll have the neighbours complaining."

That 'terrible row' was Neil Diamond singing 'Cracklin' Rosie' on the stereo. One of Uncle Derek's favourites. I swear I knew it by heart, he'd played it so often. And I also knew songs by the Beatles, T. Rex, The Mammas and the Pappas, Manfred Mann and hundreds like them.

"Sorry, sis," Uncle Derek said, turning the volume down. Then Mum got going on me.

187

"What are you doing up, Colin? You know what the doctor said – get back to bed this instant!"

"Yes, Mum," I mumbled. There's no talking to her in one of those moods.

Now, I bet you're wondering why I should have been in bed, and what the doctor had to do with it. OK, I'll tell you. I'd just had mumps. Satisfied? The swelling was down, but I still had to wait another week before I went back to school. Well, I wasn't complaining about that, but it was beginning to get a bit boring lying in bed all day.

I think maybe it was the mumps that made things happen the way they did three days later, on the Friday. I mean, an illness can take it out of you. No matter how tough or how sensible you might be normally, it's easy to get funny notions in your head when you've been ill. Know what I mean?

Anyway, I must admit Uncle Derek's story preyed on my mind a bit. Not the idea of Billy coming into my bedroom at night – that was just plain goofy – but the thought of him stuck in that horrible, rickety lift, pressing and pressing on the alarm button and no one coming, while he got more and more terrified and fought for his breath. That gave me a couple of bad nights.

There's a glass window in the door of the lift, and when it's moving you can see the shaft go past through it. Just before you reach the eighth floor, there's a splash of paint on the wall. That's where I imagined it had happened.

As the week went past I got most of my strength back, and Mum stopped insisting on me staying in bed. By Friday I felt as large as life and twice as fit, and I could see she was getting sick of having me around the house.

"Oh, roll on Monday and getting you back at school!" she said. "Honestly, Colin, why must you be constantly under my feet?"

"Nothing to do, Mum," I replied.

She looked about her, searching for an idea. "Tell you what, nip down to the grocer's and get me a packet of detergent. It's not far for you to walk – you should be well enough to manage it."

"OK, Mum," I told her, pulling on my shoes, glad of the excuse to get out of the house. She handed me some money and I made for the door.

"Oh, you'll have to use the back lift!" she called just as I was leaving. "The other one's out of order!"

I don't know why it was, but the moment she said that I shivered. You know the expression, 'Someone walked over my grave'? Well, that's what it was like – and whoever it was, his feet weren't half cold.

I must have been thinking about that lift more than I'd realized. As I stood waiting for it to come, I kept remembering about little Billy Ross. About my age, Uncle Derek had said. I wondered: did he look like me? Probably not. He'd be all thin and pale from his asthma, like cousin Shirley. And now I was going to go down in the lift he'd died in – died wheezing and gasping, banging his fists against the walls, praying for someone to come and help . . .

The lift reached the eighth floor and stopped with a thud that made me jump. The door whirred open, and that nasty, fetid smell hit me in the face. Like something had died in there, I'd said – Whatever had put *that* thought into my head?

I looked into the lift, and the lift looked out at me. Its ribbed metal walls were soiled and covered in graffiti. Some dirty so-and-so had spat against one wall, and the spittle hung there glistening. The weak light in the ceiling was yellow and spotted with dead flies.

I forced myself to get in and press the ground floor button. The alarm was coloured red and was right at the top of the row of buttons, only just within my reach. If

Billy Ross was any shorter than me, he'd have had to stand on tiptoe to push it.

Forget about Billy Ross! I ordered myself as the door closed. I deliberately kept my eyes fixed on the muddy floor as the lift gave a thump and a shudder and began its descent. I knew the paint-splash would be going past the window, and I was determined not to see it.

Down we went together, the lift and I. It groaned and gibbered and shook and rattled, and the cable twanged in the shaft above me. I closed my eyes.

Then I opened them again, convinced there was somebody else standing in the lift with me. There wasn't, but anyway I pressed my back against the dirty walls so nobody could sneak up behind me. But what about hands coming *through* the walls and grabbing . . .

Shut up, you fool!

The rattle of the lift, the twang of the cable, the groan of metal under strain. And there was another noise as well, hiding behind the others. I couldn't make out what it was, but I forced myself not to listen to it anyway, just in case.

I knew I'd passed the seventh floor, and the sixth: the lift gave a specially heavy shudder every time it passed a floor. Now the fifth, and I told myself everything was all right; I was nearly half-way to the ground. Soon I could get out again and run away from the lift and never go near the flaming thing again . . .

The lift went *thud*! and stopped dead.

I think I moaned. "Oh no! Oh please, no!"

The door opened.

It was old Mrs Webb who lived on the fourth floor. She came bustling into the lift in a heavy woollen coat and headscarf, even though it was midsummer, dragging a shopping trolley. I could have hugged her.

190

"Hullo, there, Colin," she said. "Are you not at the school, then?"

She pressed the ground floor button. I explained about the mumps as the lift started off again. All my fear had vanished, like salt when you throw it in water.

"Oh, what a shame!" Mrs Webb exclaimed. "But you're better now, are you?"

"Fit as a fiddle. Back to school on Monday, worse luck."

"I bet you enjoy it really."

Why do grown-ups always say that? They all went to school themselves once. I couldn't think of any reply that wouldn't sound cheeky, so I said nothing.

Mrs W looked around her.

"Isn't this a terrible lift, Colin?" she commented.

"Rotten," I agreed.

"I hate going up and down in it. I'd walk if it wasn't for my sciatica." We were past the second floor now. "It's all these awful noises that scare me – the groans and rattles and all."

"I know what you mean, Mrs Webb."

"And there's one particular noise – there! did you hear it just then? It really gets on my nerves. You know what it sounds like?"

The first floor went past the window.

"No, Mrs Webb."

"It sounds exactly like a person wheezing. My Jim – God rest his soul – was bad with bronchitis, and he made just that noise when – "

The lift shook like a jelly and stopped. The door opened on the ground floor.

"See you, Mrs Webb!" I shouted, heading for the back door of the block. "Nice talking to you!"

Then I was out into the sunshine and running towards the grocer's as fast as my legs could carry me.

You know, there's nothing like a sunny day to make you laugh at yourself for having been scared. By the time I'd bought Mum's detergent and watched a couple of dogs fighting in the car park, I was calling myself all the twits that had ever lived. Fancy being frightened of a lift! I promised myself I'd never be so stupid again.

Mind you, when I walked through the back entrance of Tompion Court and saw it standing waiting for me, its door open like a gaping mouth . . .

I looked at the way to the stairs. For a moment I was tempted – but what was I, some sort of cissy? I reminded myself I hadn't been well. It might be bad for me to climb eight flights in my condition.

Besides, whoever heard of a haunted lift?

I marched myself in, took a deep breath – whew! that pong again! – and pressed button number eight.

Naturally it's more of a strain for a lift to go up than down. The motors in the roof have to fight against gravity; and in the case of *these* motors, it looked like the outcome of the fight was anybody's guess. The noises I'd heard while descending were twice as loud now. The groans were like Egyptian slaves dragging rocks for the pyramids. The rattles sounded loud enough to shake the whole block apart.

And the wheezes . . .

Wheeze . . . wheeze . . . wheeze. There was no mistaking it. A desperately ill little boy, fighting for his breath, running round and round the tiny floor, hammering on the metal walls, trying to call for help but not getting enough breath to shout with . . .

Why hadn't I taken the stairs?

By the third floor, all my fears had returned, and I was standing with my back to the wall again, clutching the cardboard box of Mum's detergent to my chest. The dim yellow light in the ceiling flickered. The fourth floor went past with a savage spasm, but Mrs Webb didn't come to save me this time. Then the fifth, then the sixth . . .

I began to dread passing the seventh floor. I knew what was going to happen. As soon as I reached the spot with the paint-splash on the wall – the spot where *it* happened – the lift was going to give one last shudder and stop. Because that spot, just a couple of feet below the eighth floor and safety, was where Billy Ross was waiting.

Now I was trembling, so badly that it made the lift shake all the worse. I wanted very badly to go to the lavatory, and I didn't think I could hold out much longer.

RATTLE! and the seventh floor went past. I tried to stop looking at the window, but I couldn't. The wheezing was getting louder and louder, closer and closer. A patch of red appeared on the wall of the shaft, slowly spreading as the lift slowly rose . . .

Red? Was it really paint?

Now it filled the window completely. I could hear my pulse banging in my head, but it didn't drown out the wheezing all around me. The cardboard packet crumpled in my arms . . .

And the lift, as unhurriedly as a dignified old lady getting on a bus, rose up past the paint-splash and headed for the eighth floor.

I thought I was going to fall over, or at least pee myself. The relief was amazing. I saw the bottom of the external door of my own floor appear in the top of the window. Now I could see daylight through the outer pane. Up, up I rose, until both windows were exactly opposite each other.

The lift didn't stop at my floor.

I began to jabber as the daylight disappeared beneath me. "It's all right. It's *all right*, Colin! You must have pressed the wrong button by mistake. It's happened before. Look, you're past the paint-splash now, past the danger zone. You've absolutely nothing to be afraid – "

The lift stopped dead. At the same moment the ceiling light went out, and I was plunged into total darkness.

And I heard Billy Ross say, "Hello, Colin."

I screamed. Oh yes, you'd better believe it. I screamed at the top of my lungs, and I pushed and pushed again and again at the alarm button.

But it didn't ring.

"That's right," said Billy Ross's voice. "You just keep pressing that button. That's what I did, twelve years ago. I pressed and screamed, but you know what? Nobody came. And nobody's going to come now either, Colin."

Where was the voice coming from? In my terror I couldn't tell. From the echoing depths of the lift-shaft? From inside my head? Or from the pale, stooping shape of a small boy that I could see forming in the inky blackness beside me?

"Did you really think you were safe?" the boy wheezed. "Just because you were past the spot where it happened? Silly Colin. I've had twelve whole years to make the shaft my own from top to bottom."

I found my own voice. "What do you want?" I yelled.

Billy Ross chuckled.

"They let me die, you know. They could have saved me, but they didn't. That means they owe me. An eye for an eye, a tooth for a tooth. You for me, Colin – you're the age I was, you sleep in the bedroom I slept in. You *belong* to me."

"No!" I screamed. "Leave me alone!"

"Twelve years I've had to plan my revenge. I've learned all sorts of tricks in that time. Don't you think it was clever of me to cut off the electricity from the lift? Don't you, Colin? And I'll tell you something else I've learned: I've found out how to unhook the cable. That means I can send the lift plummeting down the shaft to smash itself to pieces at the bottom. Pretty neat, don't you think, Colin?"

I sank to the filthy floor. Tears were streaming down my face. I started to babble, pleading with this ill, unseen, angry boy for my very life.

"Please!" I moaned. "I've done nothing to you, Billy. Why choose me? I wasn't even born when you died. My mum and dad didn't live here. *They'd* have come to help if they'd heard the alarm bell, you just bet they would. Listen, Billy, why can't we be friends? We're the same age, we probably enjoy the same things. I mean, I bet you like . . . I bet you like . . ."

Football, I was going to say, but then I thought, No! Billy was too ill for sports all his life. If I reminded him how much luckier I was, that'd be the last straw. Panic gripped me; I was on the point of blacking out, and then suddenly I knew the answer.

Uncle Derek's records!

"I bet you like pop music!" I yelled. "Don't you, Billy? Don't you? All those songs that were in the charts in 1970. Did you like this one, Billy? See if you can remember this one."

I began to sing. Looking back, it seems crazy – there I was, crouching on the floor of that stinking lift, staring death in the face, and I began to sing. Know what the song was? Uncle Derek's absolute favourite: 'Ride a White Swan', by T. Rex.

How I remembered the words, I don't know. How I managed to sing, when I was so scared I could hardly breathe – I don't know that either. But I did.

As I got to the second verse, I swear I heard a reedy, wheezy, wavering voice beginning to join in with me.

They fixed the power cut half an hour later. When they got the lift to the ninth floor and the door opened, they found me inside – hunched up in a corner, half out of my mind and two-thirds of the way through 'Sergeant Pepper's Lonely Hearts Club Band'.

The doctor gave me an extra fortnight off school to get over my ordeal. He reckoned the shock of being stuck in the darkness had been too much for me while I was still weak from the mumps.

I didn't tell anybody I'd met a ghost. In a lift. At half-past two on a summer's afternoon. They'd only have said that my disordered brain had imagined the whole thing. In particular I didn't tell Uncle Derek. I knew how he'd take the mickey if I told him I owe my life to the fact that a ghost enjoyed listening to pop music.

I only once referred to what had really happened, and that was the night before I was due back at school. Mum was doing the ironing, I remember.

"I suppose asthma's a rotten thing to have," I said.

"What's that, son?" Mum asked. "Yes. I'm sure it is. Were you thinking about your cousin Shirley?"

"No. I was thinking about Billy Ross – you know, the boy who died in the lift."

I saw Mum's face tighten with anger. She turned on Uncle Derek.

"Have you been filling this boy's head with your nonsense again?" she demanded. "I'm warning you, Derek – if you don't stop it, you can start looking for somewhere else to stay. After what he's been through. And who said you could fix your motorbike in here? Look at the mess you're making on the carpet!"

There was a lot more of the same. I picked up an old record sleeve and started reading about the Kinks. Billy Ross had gone right out of my head by the time Mum returned to her ironing and remembered me.

"Yes, Colin," she said, "from what I hear, he was a

pretty sad case. What with his asthma on top of everything else."

I wasn't paying much attention. "On top of what else?" I asked.

"Didn't you know? Billy Ross was stone deaf. Born that way. Deaf as a post."

It was a moment before that sank in. I looked up.

"You mean he couldn't listen to pop music?"

"Couldn't listen to anything, poor little mite. Now, Colin. Have you got your schoolbag packed for tomorrow? That's you all over – leaving everything till the last minute."

I didn't bother finishing the record sleeve.

Whoever heard of a haunted lift? Well, I haven't for one – and if anybody says I have, I'll punch him right on the nose.

THE GIRL IN THE CELLAR

By Tony Richards

"What a terrible night!" said Katy Brent.

She and Simon Murdoch were sitting by the window of the huge, well-furnished lounge, gazing out at the storm. It was the blackest, foulest of December nights. Torrential rain was pouring down. Great blasts of cold wind shook the trees into stark, leafless frenzies. There was no moon, no stars, not even lightning. Deadly dark outside. Simon turned to look at his cousin, saw how nervous she was, found himself wishing, not for the first time, that her visit would end and that she would go home to London, where she belonged. Katy was fourteen – and why was it, he asked himself, that anyone of that age or over seemed to hate storms? He was all right. His sister Daniella, eighteen months old this week, was fast asleep upstairs. But Katy was afraid, and from the noises in the hallway Simon could tell that his parents were ill at ease too. They were getting ready to leave.

"I don't fancy driving all the way to London in this." Mrs Murdoch was saying.

"I'm driving," her husband pointed out. "Besides, the Robinsons bought the tickets three months in advance. We can't back out now."

Mrs Murdoch sighed defeatedly. "All the same . . ." She left the rest of the sentence unsaid. Her fears did not stop with her own drive to town. She was worried about the house, and the three children. And the cellar. Especially the cellar.

"Katy! Simon!" she called. "We're going!"

Simon and his cousin trotted dutifully out. It was freezing in the hall, with the door wide open. Mrs Murdoch was huddling deep inside her new mink.

"You two will be all right, won't you?" she asked anxiously. She seemed on the point of deciding to stay, but her husband coughed loudly and glanced at his wristwatch. "We'll be back by twelve at the latest. Don't stay up too late, Simon. And don't give Katy any trouble. Bye-bye!"

The parents ducked their heads and ran the distance to the car. The door slammed shut behind them. There was the sound of a motor starting up, the crunch of tyres on gravel. Then the only noise which remained was the pounding of the rain.

The draught had left Katy shivering and pale, and Simon began to laugh. Katy tried to look stern.

"Well?" she asked sharply. "*Are* you going to give me any trouble?"

"I won't." Simon grinned. "But the ghost might."

"Oh, don't start that again!"

And, turning around quickly, she hurried upstairs to the guest room and left him alone.

It was a huge old country house, and in the eight months the Murdochs had lived there, Simon had come to love it. His father had bought it cheap – it had been all but abandoned since the turn of the century and was in a dilapidated state – and had spent the entire summer restoring it. Now, there was fresh ivy beginning its climb up the red brick walls, and there were roses round the porch. Inside were low, perfumed oak beams, and panels which might conceal secret doors. The whole place was a maze of corridors and sculleries and tiny pantries where a boy of ten might hide. And then there was the cellar, deep and fetid and dark, like some forbidden underworld.

It all gave one a sense of belonging to another time. With every creak of the floorboards, with every shiver of a window pane, Simon could imagine all the people who had lived there in the past. The house went back four centuries; it had *history*. And one part of that history was very grim indeed.

Katy walked into the lounge, carrying a book. Avoiding Simon's gaze, she settled herself in front of the fireplace and made a show of stretching out contentedly. She had obviously not wanted to remain alone upstairs. Slight colour began to return to her cheeks.

"Can I fetch you a cup of coffee?" Simon asked.

The girl glanced up at him, surprised. "What's this? You've finally decided to be nice to me for once?"

"Well, we humans have to stick together on a perfect December night like this."

Katy turned away again. She knew exactly what he meant by *perfect December night*. The first day she had arrived, Simon had explained to her the stories the villagers told, the weird, horrible tales which had been passed down through the generations. And now, here she was, alone in the house with a small boy and a helpless baby girl. And she was shivering, although she was no longer cold.

"I've heard it," Simon continued relentlessly. "Mum and Dad have, too, but grown ups won't admit that kind of thing. It started at the beginning of this month."

"Shut up, Simon," Katy said.

Simon pulled a face. "It waits until the dead of night, when everyone's asleep, and then it begins to howl. It rattles the door of the cellar, trying to get out. It screams. Just imagine, Katy, that poor mad girl trapped in a freezing cellar for two hundred years, crying and yelling and – "

"Will you shut *up*!" Katy shouted.

Her hands had dropped the book and were clenched into bloodless fists. Her expression was drawn between anger and tears, and her shoulders were quivering. Simon realized, half ashamed, that he had gone too far. He didn't know why he teased Katy, didn't know why he disliked her so. Probably because she was a girl, and older than him into the bargain. Probably because he saw her as an intruder into his mysterious, timeless world. He had used the ghost story to make her feel uncomfortable, perhaps shorten her stay. But there were limits; even he knew that.

"I'm sorry," he mumbled. "It's only a daft story after all."

"It's all right," Katy said. She was beginning to calm down.

"Shall I fetch you some coffee?"

"No, you'll only make a mess. I'll do it myself."

Later, when she had returned from the kitchen with her coffee and some biscuits and a glass of lemonade, they sat down by the fire with the Monopoly board. They played in virtual silence, whiling the time away. Around them, the windows rattled and the whole house shook and groaned. A carriage clock was ticking on the mantelpiece. The rain drummed against the wall like a thousand restless fingers.

At last, the fire dwindled and the room grew cold.

Simon glanced up at the clock. It was a quarter to twelve; his bedtime had passed several hours ago. Katy, he realized, was still very nervous, and wanted him to stay. He rubbed his chilled hands together. The girl did the same.

"Where's the coal?" she asked, glancing into the empty scuttle.

And, despite himself, Simon felt a trickle of fear on his spine. "It's in the cellar."

"Don't start that again." Katy walked to the window and stared outside. "Anyway, your parents will be home soon."

"They might have got stuck in the rain," Simon said. "They could be gone for hours. And I'm cold."

He stared at her unwaveringly, challenging her, defying her. She was older than him, and ought not to be afraid. A trust had grown between them in the last few hours. Turn back now, and she would never regain that trust.

Katy considered for a moment, then nodded solemnly.

"I'll come with you," Simon said. "After all, it *is* only a story."

But he was not so sure as he fetched the torch from the kitchen and went to the cellar door. He *had* heard moanings in the night. He *had* heard the latch rattling. Only the draught, his parents had told him in a less than certain tone. He tried repeating the words in his mind – only the draught, only the draught. Then why had his parents banned him from going down there? Why did his mother steer clear of the cellar, and his father only go there very quickly, in daytime, to fetch the coal? Only the draught, he told himself for the dozenth time . . . or a poor young mad girl, imprisoned and alone.

He led the way down the mildewed wooden stairs, the torch beam playing ahead of him like some spectral eye. The light made gross black shadows out of every tiny thing. Cobwebs became great wire snares. A scuttling mouse threw an image the size of a huge rat. Simon found himself praying that he would never be locked up in a place like this.

Jack, the ancient gardener from the village, had told him the full story one hot August afternoon. About the pretty fourteen-year-old girl who used to live in the house many years ago. About that girl's guardian, an ugly, cruel old aunt who hated anything beautiful or young. The girl was due to inherit the house when she reached adulthood, and that knowledge drove her guardian into a constant, malevolent rage. No friends or young people were allowed near the house. The girl was set to work from morning until night. And if she ever complained, or made the slightest mistake, her aunt would lock her in the cellar for hours.

And there the girl was locked one night in early December when her cruel aunt suddenly died. She was trapped in the darkness, in the crawling cold. From time to time people came to the front foor, found it locked and went away, and the girl, so it was thought, went slowly mad and starved to death. Months later, the house was broken into and the two bodies were found, and from that time on the house remained empty, a shrine to the legend of the mad ghost, sealed in its final prison, trapped in the cellar for all eternity.

On a summery afternoon, with the roses in bloom and the drone flies hovering amongst the tall grass, it had seemed like a story to frighten small children with. Nothing more. But now Simon was in that same cellar on a raging, terrible December night, and all at once the legend seemed uncomfortably real.

"The coal's over there," he said, rather loudly, pointing the torch at a dusty black mound.

Katy had brought the scuttle down with her. She went to fill it up, stumbling and slipping on the wet flagstones, while Simon held the light. Somehow, he could not keep the beam steady. He was more frightened than he thought he'd be and his hands were shaking. He kept losing sight of Katy altogether. Then, suddenly, there was a terrific crash. Simon yelled. The torch slipped out of his grasp and clattered to the floor.

It went out.

And Simon screamed out loud this time as impenetrable darkness swamped over him like a sable tide.

He was still scrabbling on his hands and knees when the torch came back on. Someone else had taken hold of it. The beam was pointed at his face, huge and glowing, blinding him. He squinted, but could not see anything beyond the glaring light.

"Katy?" he said. "Is that you?"

"Of course it is." Her face came into view, pale white in the surrounding gloom.

"What was that noise?"

"I tripped over something. Come on, let's get upstairs."

There was no need to tell him twice. Back in the lounge, Katy stoked the fire while Simon rubbed futilely at the slime embedded in his clothes. The chill of the cellar hung with him, that and the foul smell. And though the subject of the ghost had been a joke with him till now, he could no longer see the funny side.

His thoughts went back to the mad girl. She must have suffered terribly down in the dark. The cold, the stench of it, the utter loneliness of week after grim week. And, worst of all, she must have known that children of her own age were playing in the sun outside. All that time! All that misery! Five minutes had been long enough for Simon.

"Let's finish the Monopoly," he said.

He had hoped that the game would take his mind off things, but it was over much sooner than he thought. Katy had been well in the lead, but now, as she took each move, she fumbled with the pieces and seemed to forget the rules. She had lost within half an hour.

She slammed the board aside with the flat of her hand. Red hotels and bright green houses rolled across the carpet, and Simon stared at them blankly, quite amazed. "It was only a game," he murmured.

"It's a stupid game. I don't like games like that."

There was something wrong with Katy. Her face had lost all its colour again, and her eyes were glazed. She seemed freezing, even though the fire was now heating up the room. Either she had a chill, or the cellar had scared her far more than she would admit. Something in her eyes told Simon to keep quiet.

"Let's play something else," Katy snapped.

"I'm tired," Simon replied. "I'm going up to bed."

He was half way to his feet when the girl grabbed hold of his wrist. The pain shot through his upper arm. He yelled and struggled to get free.

"Let go!" He twisted helplessly. Katy's grip was as cold as ice. "You're *hurting* me!"

The realization that she was causing the boy pain gradually sank in. The anger died in Katy's eyes, and her fingers went slack. Simon backed away two steps, nursing his injured wrist. He glanced at the ticking clock. It was well past midnight now. He wished, desperately wished, his parents would come home.

"I'm sorry, Simon," Katy said. "It's just . . . I'm so afraid of being left alone again."

She spoke to him shyly, falteringly, as though she were a child herself. The Katy who had come up from the cellar was not the same Katy who had gone down. Something, Simon realized, had happened to her in the dark.

"I think you're sick," he said.

"I'm not. I want to play."

"I think you ought to lie down on the couch."

Katy grimaced frighteningly. "Leave me alone, you horrid boy."

And she turned her head from him and drew her knees up to her chest until she formed a tight, hard ball. She began to cry, rocking backwards and forwards, mumbling through her tears.

"No one ever plays with me . . . I'm all alone . . . all alone . . . I don't like it here . . . the rats . . . I don't like them . . . no friends . . . why can't I have any friends?"

Stopping suddenly, she gazed up at Simon and forced a smile. "Will you be my friend, Simon?"

Simon felt his marrow freeze. The yawning emptiness of the old house became a terrifying thing; its very size and solitude had imprisoned him. One mile to civilization, to the village, to human life. And he was trapped alone here with a girl who was quite mad. As mad as . . .

As the ghost girl in the cellar.

The clock abruptly stopped ticking. The fire guttered, died. Katy stood upright, her face contorted with rage.

"Why won't you answer me?" she screamed. "Why won't you be my friend? I need someone to play with! I've been so *lonely*!"

And she began to advance, her hands held out in front of her like claws. Simon turned and fled into the hallway. He ran for the front door, crashing against it in his flight, and grappled with the knob. The lock would not budge. It was new, it was regularly oiled, it opened with a whisper any other time. Simon pulled at the door with all his strength. It was stuck fast.

Katy appeared from the lounge, grinning horribly, beckoning. *Come be my friend. Come play with me forever.* Simon picked up a vase off the hallway mantel-piece and hurled it at her face. It missed her wildly, and the girl tipped back her head and laughed.

She was almost upon him by now. Lips drawn back, skin tight against her skull. She loomed over his cowering form, her shadow blocking out the light. Simon could

206

only wait for those final seconds to pass before he felt her cold, eternal grasp. And then there would be no escape.

Her fingernails touched his sleeve.

She stopped suddenly, a hairsbreadth from her goal. Coming from upstairs was a new noise, a thin, high, plaintive wailing. It was a baby crying. Daniella had woken up.

The thing that had been Katy cocked her pale head to one side. "The little girl! Of course!" she murmured. "So much better than a boy."

"Leave her alone," Simon said.

The girl took no notice of him. "Daniella," she mused. "What a lovely name!" And she walked up the stairs and turned the corner at the top, disappearing from sight.

Daniella stopped crying shortly after that.

Simon was still huddled in the hallway when his parents returned home. He scurried to them, burying himself in their arms. Mrs Murdoch stared at him, then at the broken vase by the lounge door.

"Simon, why are you still up? And what's been going on?"

"It's Katy," Simon blurted. "She's gone mad. She's upstairs with the baby."

"Gone *mad*?"

Right then, there was a loud thump from the cellar stairs. The door creaked open . . . and Katy stepped out. She was smothered in coal dust and spiderwebs, and there was a large purple bruise above her left eye. She blinked against the light. Simon's parents stared at her, dumbfounded.

"I bumped my head," she whispered painfully. "I must have been down there for hours."

Mr and Mrs Murdoch looked at each other. They could hardly dare to believe what was happening, could hardly find the words. *If Katy was downstairs, then who on earth was upstairs with Daniella?*

Mr Murdoch vaulted up the stairs two at a time while Simon and his mother followed on. The door to the nursery was locked from the inside. Mr Murdoch slammed his shoulder at it, once, twice. At the third attempt, it burst open on its hinges. The family rushed in.

Daniella was lying in her cot, laughing and waving her arms. Save for her, the room was empty.

"What happened?" Mrs Murdoch said, taking the baby in her arms.

Simon gazed blankly at the walls. "I don't know." He could feel the tears beginning to come. "I just don't understand."

The wind abated and the raindrops ceased to fall. Silence crept throughout the house. The stench of fear was there. And only Daniella seemed undisturbed by the fuss. She squealed, then chuckled loudly, and the noise of her childish laughter echoed down the corridors and out into the night . . .

The Murdochs moved out of their house the following morning. They stayed with friends for a while, until they found a new home in the London suburbs. None of them fancied living in the countryside ever again. The thought of all that solitude was more than they could bear.

It wasn't easy for Simon to adjust. He still had nightmares for a while and was afraid of being left alone. But gradually he began to forget the terror of that stormy night. One last thing nagged at him, however. What had happened to the ghost?

The mad girl could have taken Daniella easily. She wanted a friend so badly, and all the opportunity was there. Something had stopped her. Perhaps a flash of logic in her wild insanity. Maybe she realized she could leave the cellar and the house for good. Maybe, if she had changed places with Katy, she could take the place of other people, too?

No. It was a ghastly thought. Simon thrust it from his mind.

Daniella was two years old by now. She had learnt to walk in short, stumbling steps. She could speak a few simple words. Her affection for her brother knew no bounds; she would sit and sulk for hours when he was not there. One morning, Simon was helping her to build a doll's house out of plastic bricks, and was becoming bored. He wanted to go out and play with boys of his own age, but every time he made to leave the child started to cry.

He'd had enough of it. He hurried to the door.

It would not open. Just as in the old country house, it was stuck fast.

Daniella was sitting upright, looking at him with a strange expression on her face.

"I want to play," she said in a cold, lifeless voice. "I need someone to play with. Will you be my friend, Simon?"

And she began to laugh.

THE LONGEST JOURNEY

by Catherine Gleason

Only the clop of the ponies' hooves walking along the country road broke the quiet of the late summer afternoon. Both their riders, happy and tired after the gymkhana, were re-living the excitement of it. Jane Simpson, glancing down at Cameo's two blue rosettes, was sure the next ones they won would be red. Her handsome bay pony, with his creamy blaze and socks, had done so well in the jumping classes that he was almost certain to win a first when they went to Fourfields a week on Saturday. She turned to say as much to her friend Chris, and that was when it happened: round the corner roared a transit van, and Cameo took fright. There was a blurred and violent lurch, and a blow that knocked her breathless; then a hazy sensation of falling, weightless, drifting downwards through deep clouds, into developing darkness.

"I can't understand it. I really can't, can you, Jack?" said Mrs Simpson brightly, a little too brightly. "Who would have thought it? Chris said Cameo just shot across the road – and him so used to traffic! Whatever made him shy like that?"

Her husband put his arm round her shoulders and said soothingly: "Now calm down, Meg. Jane's a tough little lass – she's our daughter, isn't she? She'll be all right. They are doing their best for her in there." He gestured vaguely in the direction of the operating theatre.

Mrs Simpson took a deep breath and nodded bravely. It was only knowing her husband was even more frightened than she was that kept her from breaking down completely.

Gradually the blackness lifted, and Jane awoke. She raised herself on one elbow, blinking at the harsh, greyish light all around her. The ground was hard, shingle and shale. A pony (Cameo? – the light had washed out all his colour) was pawing the ground a few yards away, tossing his head towards a horizon lost in mist.

Jane pulled herself to her feet. Why did her head feel so heavy? With an effort she mounted the pony, obeying a nagging voice at the back of her mind which, confused with other noises that made no sense, was urging her to get home as quickly as she could, for she was terribly late. The pony began to walk, then to trot. Jane clutched tightly at his mane and trusted to his instinct.

A tall man in a white coat approached them.

"Mr and Mrs Simpson?"

"Yes, Doctor." Jack Simpson leapt to his feet.

"Your daughter is out of surgery now. She's been taken to Intensive Care. Sister will show you the way."

"How is she, Doctor?"

"The operation was successful," said the doctor, "but she has quite severe brain contusions, I'm afraid, and – "

A tiny machine in his pocket bleeped urgently.

"Excuse me. Sister will look after you," he repeated, and hurried off to the telephone.

Meg Simpson stared at her husband in bewilderment.

"What does he mean, brain contusions?"

"They're bruises to the brain, Mrs Simpson," said a quiet voice, and they turned to see a small, slim woman in uniform, with curly brown hair and kind blue eyes.

"When Jane fell and hit her head, the impact was such that her brain banged against the wall of her skull, and that caused the bruising. What the doctor was saying is that although Jane survived her operation, it's too soon for us to know what's going to happen."

Mrs Simpson steeled herself.

"You mean she could . . . she could die?"

"Not if we can help it," said Sister gently, "but I'm afraid we can't tell yet. We have to watch her continually. Would you like to see her now?"

They followed the neat, brisk figure down long white corridors, until she paused outside a door marked 'Intensive Care Unit'.

"I must warn you," she said, "that Jane looks like someone from outer space. We have to use lots of instruments to tell us exactly how she's progressing. They tell us about her breathing, her heartbeat, her brain and so on – but she'll look rather weird to you. Are you ready?"

They nodded wordlessly, and she pushed open the door.

On the bed lay Jane, but not the Jane they knew. This Jane was helpless and frail, her face white as her gown. From her head, her chest, her arms, proliferated tubes that were attached to the gleaming equipment around her bed. There were inverted plastic sacs of fluid in steel frames, a cylindrical respirator which thumped steadily, and bleeping monitors which registered, with undulating white lines, their daughter's feeble hold on life.

Mrs Simpson grasped her husband's arm for support, suddenly faint at the sight of the unconscious girl who seemed as remote from her as if she were, indeed, from another planet.

"Oh, Jane," she whispered, "Jane, where are you?"

Where was she? Jane only knew that they were alone, horse and rider, under a sky that had neither colour nor

212

cloud. The vast plain they were crossing seemed to stretch to infinity, stony, desolate, silent.

It troubled her; but the urgent desire to reach an unknown destination ahead overcame her unease and kept her clinging to Cameo's warm neck.

Although he was cantering steadily, no breeze touched her face.

Every half-hour Sister or one of the nurses came in to check Jane's condition and alter her position on the bed. It seemed wonderful to the Simpsons that they were so familiar with instruments which looked impossibly complicated. They were deft and quick, and always smiled reassuringly before they left.

"See how efficient they all are, Meg," said Jack Simpson. "They'll pull her through, you'll see."

"She looks so lost lying there, Jack," Mrs Simpson mourned. "So strange. Do you think she can hear us, somewhere in her mind? I've read that people in comas can, sometimes. Is she in a coma, do you think?"

"I don't know, love. What did Sister say? I couldn't take it in. I'll tell you what, I'll go and ask her again. And you could do with a cup of coffee – I'll get some on the way back."

The truth was that he was not sure he could bear the tension of waiting any longer, and the noise of the machines, unnaturally loud in the stillness of the room, clawed at his nerves. His wife understood, and pressed his hand. When he was gone she stood up shakily and walked over to the bed.

"Goodness me, Jane Simpson, what a fright you're giving us! You're so pale, and cold . . . I'll warm your hands for you. I used to do that when you were a little girl and came in from playing in the snow, do you remember . . .?"

* * *

Gentle fingers soothed the ache in Jane's mind, but it was getting colder and darker. The ground was sloping now, rising to a hilly ridge shrouded in mist, and Cameo was beginning to tire. Although he was still as eager, she could feel, her heart sinking, that he was losing strength. But they had to reach the hilltop. Not a blade of grass or a drop of water to be seen, and the air was so thin. Whatever happened, they must not stop on this dreary wasteland.

What were those shadowy horses ahead of them, swallowed into the swirling mist? She closed her eyes in fear and stroked Cameo's strong shoulder for comfort, silently coaxing and urging him as his feet stumbled on the flinty earth.

Then, from behind them, lumbered the grey shape of a riderless shire. It cantered clumsily past them, and its mane brushed Jane's arm with feathers of ice. She shivered all over, suddenly deadly cold.

Seconds before the machines told it, Mrs Simpson instinctively knew. Jane's life was ebbing away. Her mother withdrew her hand and stared in silent shock at the white mask of her daughter's face. She made blindly for the door to call for help as the noise of the machines grew ominously faint and the lines on the screens began to flatten, dispassionately recording the onset of death.

But the machines were also telling their tale on their twin monitors at the nursing station, and five men and women were instantly alert and moving. Before the distraught woman could reach the door they were running into the unit, almost knocking her off her feet. The surgeon took one brief look.

"Damn it, she's going! *Crash her, quick!*"

Skilled hands locked and pounded at Jane's chest, savagely hard, willing the failing heart to beat and lungs to breathe before the vital brain began to die. Five people

214

each with his task were a dedicated team pitted against a common enemy and working as one person to snatch back one life.

Jane's mother crouched against the wall, forgotten, her face twisted and streaming with tears, silently repeating a half-prayer: Don't go away from us, Jane. Please – let her come back.

There was no going back now. Cameo was faltering with weariness, every step laboured. He couldn't do it. Come on, Cameo, you must . . . you're the best, the bravest pony in the world. . . He tried hard to respond and then suddenly from all around out of the gloom appeared the threatening shapes of black horses, eyes gleaming in the half-light, making for them fast and silently.

Cameo stopped short, quivering.

Tall and menacing, the horses pressed in, surrounding them, nudging ever closer, until Cameo, snorting and plunging in terror, was in their midst.

They made no sound, and their touch was soft and cold.

When they began to move onwards, a tight and purposeful band, Cameo was drawn with them, swept along and spurred by panic, gathering speed till they were galloping at an impossible pace with the grim irresistible herd in its blind and timeless race. Jostled and shaken, Jane hung on, terrified of falling, of being crushed by those icy bodies and trampled beneath the sharp black hooves.

The ridge of the hill loomed nearer. As they approached it they slowed, the great black horses, veering away at a graceful canter into the shadows. Cameo, no longer pressured by their frozen, hectic urging, slackened also. He was barely trotting as they reached the edge of the ridge, glad to rest.

Jane looked up, and the sight of what lay below almost overwhelmed her.

A green valley stretched as far as the eye could see, bright with sun, threaded with streams of fresh water, studded with great friendly trees . . . and the horses! Horses without number, sleek and beautiful, a bewildering mixture of colours and breeds, sizes and ages, grazing, frisking, sleeping, ambling, in the endless summer valley.

Cameo swayed, almost fell, and stood with his head hanging in exhaustion. It was then Jane knew that he must not carry her further, that the time for parting had come – and that he, at least, must reach that healing valley.

The earth pulled at her, dragging her home. More lonely and more weary than she had ever been, Jane swung herself down, clasping his neck for support as her feet touched the barren ground. Velvet lips nuzzled her palm, and Cameo stood patiently, waiting for her. The last bond remained to be broken. With the dregs of her strength she raised her hand and slapped his flank as hard as she could. Startled, he jerked up his head and started forwards in a shambling trot. He cleared the rocky ridge. Jane could just see the lift of his head and the flick of his tail as his hooves touched the springy grass and he galloped free into the sunlight.

Longing only for sleep, Jane sank to the earth as the night gathered round her.

There were strange dreams. She was confused and unable to move. Weights in her head and body pinned her down. Ghostly-white strangers assembled and muttered and stared. Sinister horses bolted down twisting streets. From a distance she saw a girl, herself, lying on an unfamiliar bed. Why were her parents crying? She needed to tell them something very important. If only she could remember what it was . . . Cameo . . . there had been a fall, she remembered that – at the gymkhana? Oh, the gymkhana, that was it! Cameo, clever Cameo had come second in the jumping and next time he was going to win! At Fourfields he would prove to everyone how marvellous he was. That was the important thing she must tell them; they would be so thrilled.

It was like a miracle when Jane's eyes opened, the end of her parents' nightmare hours when they had thought that they would lose her for ever.

"Mummy," Jane said, and was vaguely surprised that her voice sounded so feeble and croaky.

"Everything's all right now, darling," her mother said softly. "You had a bad accident and you've been very ill, but you're going to get better."

Yes, the accident, she knew about that! But they must listen, Fourfields was so terribly important, and the red rosette . . .

"But it's Cameo, he . . ."

"Hush, Jane, please. You mustn't try to talk yet. Daddy and I knew Cameo would be on your mind when you came round. Poor Cameo, he died . . . But there was no suffering, so you mustn't fret about him, darling. He just couldn't make it."

A vision rose through the tears in Jane's eyes, of countless horses, of a lush valley filled with the living harmony of a perfect summer's day.

"But he did make it, Mummy," she whispered. "He did."

SPIRIT OF THE TRAIL

by Sydney J. Bounds

This is an account of a strange happening I met with on a trail drive from Texas to Dodge City in the year of '79, and written down by me, James Kelly. As the only education I got was at a cross-roads country school, I hope you will make allowances for the fact that I'm no great hand at letter-writing.

That year I was working as a fifty dollars a month cowhand for the Bar X ranch, and my bunkmate was 'Red' Peters. Red was a young hell-raiser and as full of himself as only a Texan can be. To hear him talk, he was the best with cows and guns and cards. His boast was that he'd never back down before any man. He had a temper to match his hair, which was as bright as a campfire and got him his nickname.

We were a week out from the home range, herding the cattle north, when we spotted an Indian camp on the horizon. 'Chuck' Wilson, our foreman and trail boss, warned us to keep away. With three thousand head of cattle to account for to the owner, he didn't want any trouble with Indians.

I was night-riding around the herd, singing softly to the cattle, when it came time for my relief. It was Red's turn, and he didn't show up. As I didn't want to make trouble for him, I kept quiet about it.

With the dawn I spotted him a-coming from the direction of the Indian camp. He sure seemed edgy and close-mouthed, and when I asked him what was going on, he just laughed and said, "Maybe I'll tell you about it one day, Jim."

That day came sooner than either of us expected, because bad luck began to dog Red. Other riders started to avoid him, saying he had the 'hoodoo' on him.

Trail driving is pretty tame most of the time, just drifting along fifteen or twenty miles a day. With the herd strung out for three-quarters of a mile from dawn to dusk, you're really only interested in getting through the day and getting your head down for a few hours.

Red and I were following behind, eating dust and watching out for strays, when Red's horse suddenly spooked – for no good reason that I could see – and threw him. As he lay sprawled on the ground, half-dazed, his horse reared up and tried to stamp him into the ground. It was mighty queer, a cow-puncher's bronc acting that way.

I got my lariat weaving and pulled that horse off him, and Chuck Wilson rode up and put a revolver to the brute's head and shot it dead. Wilson wasn't pleased about that because a good horse costs money.

Red swore it wasn't his fault, and said, "An Indian rose up out of the ground, right in front of me, and spooked the animal."

Wilson asked me if I'd seen any Indian, and I had to say, truthfully, "No, I didn't – but that doesn't mean there wasn't one."

Our trail boss scouted around but failed to find any sign.

Red got himself another mount from the horse-handler and we rode on together in silence. He was looking mighty peaked so I said, "Chuck'll forget it by the end of the drive."

Red murmured between barely parted lips, "But I

shan't. I didn't tell Wilson, but what I saw was the ghost of an Indian."

"Ghost?" I laughed. "Are you superstitious, then, Red?"

And that was when he told me what happened the night he went missing.

"I was just curious to see that Indian camp, Jim. I wasn't looking for trouble at all – and I didn't even get close. But this Indian came out of nowhere, it seemed – a full-grown buck, all of six feet and well-built. He was sure impressive, with some sign painted on his chest and a bow even taller than he was, and he had an arrow already loose-strung.

"He spoke clear enough for me to understand, said his tribe wanted nothing more to do with the White Man and ordered me to turn back. Waal, I reckon I don't take orders that easy. I made to go on, and he lifted his bow and pulled the rawhide back. He told me he was the tribe's medicine man and called 'He Who Strikes from a Distance'.

"I guess I must have laughed, 'cause I realized he was going to let fly at me. Waal, I lost my temper and drew my six-gun and shot him. I tell yuh, Jim, that gunshot sounded like a clap of thunder. I was imagining every redskin for miles heading my way in a hurry, so I turned my bronc around and high-tailed it. The funny thing is, no one followed me. No one a-tall."

I said, "The best thing is to forget it, Red. Just keep quiet."

Red still seemed to be brooding, so I added: "There's no such thing as a ghost anyway. It's just your imagination."

"Oh, no, it was him right enough, come back to haunt me. I saw him clear enough to avoid any mistake."

Things were quiet for a while after that, and Red

cheered up a bit. The herd moved on till we came to a river we had to ford.

We got the leading steers into the water and they were swimming strongly for the far side. It seemed like it would be an easy crossing. Then the cattle panicked, and Red was caught in the middle of them as they milled around.

Red's horse sank under him, and he was neck deep in fast-running water and bawling out that he couldn't swim. There was no chance for anyone to get near him in that crazy mixed-up knot of long-horned steers. He could have drowned as easy as roping a calf.

The only reason he didn't is because he had enough sense to hang on to the horns of one of the steers and get carried ashore.

He was out of breath and full of water and just about done in. Gasping like a fish, he said to me, real low: "Jim, 'twas the ghost of the medicine man again – I saw him clear as I see you now. He spooked them cattle deliberate, to get me."

I thought the near-drowning had upset him, and laughed. "Don't talk crazy, Red."

"I saw him, Jim – recognized that sign painted on his chest."

I had no answer to that, so I kept quiet. We moved on and reached Dodge City, and the boss sold the cattle and paid us off. Red and I went into town, bought a bath and haircut, and sat down to a meal of roast leg of lamb – you sure get tired of beef on a trail drive. Then we strolled along Main Street looking for a good time.

There were oil lamps burning in all the saloons, and plenty of cowboys on the boardwalks on both sides of the wide, dusty street. And the city's law officers were patrolling in force.

Suddenly a voice shouted, "I want you, Harvey!"

I turned towards the excitement and saw two men

facing each other. The lawman had his gun in his hand, pointing at the other. Harvey dropped into a gunman's crouch and made a lightning draw.

Then Red cried out, "The Indian! See him? *There!*"

"Where?" I asked, looking around.

Harvey's gun cracked, but his aim must have been badly off because he missed by a mile, and the bullet creased Red's scalp even as he ducked for cover. He staggered back, holding his hands to his head, and blood leaked between his fingers.

"How bad is it, Red?" I asked anxiously. "Heck, I never saw such wild shooting."

Red was shaking and his face had gone white. "Nearly got me that time," he mumbled. "That medicine man, he was right behind Harvey and jogged his gun-arm as he took aim."

I looked again, but still saw no Indian – only the marshal leading Harvey away to jail.

"Let's rustle up a doc," I said, "and get your wound seen to."

Red was so shaky he let me lead him to the doctor's surgery without a murmur. With his scalp cleaned and bandaged, it wasn't much of a wound after all. Just a graze that bled a lot.

Red was shivering when we left the surgery. "Jogged his arm," he mumbled. We found a hotel room for the night but he couldn't sleep. He sat on the edge of the bed and held his head in his hands.

"I ain't afraid of no man," he said in a despairing voice. "You know I ain't. But how can I fight a ghost?"

I didn't have any ready answer when I recalled that the name of the medicine man was He Who Strikes from a Distance.

Red took a deep breath. "I'm running, Jim. Soon as it's moonlight, I'm saddling my bronc and heading north, and

I ain't stopping till there's an almighty lot of distance 'tween me and him."

"All right. I'll ride along with yuh," I told him, not liking to leave my bunkmate alone in his state.

So when the moon came up full and bright, we walked to the livery stable and saddled our horses and rode out of Dodge. Red put on a spurt at first, as though the Devil were after him. Then I spoke up. "There's no sense in killing our mounts – we sure won't get far a-foot."

He finally saw the sense in that and eased the pace till we were jogging along smoothly, making ground all the while but saving our horses.

The Kansas plain was flat and featureless, and I could see for miles in the moonlight. There was not a soul in view; to left or right, before or behind. We might have been alone in the world, but Red was still uneasy. I hoped he'd get over his fear the further we got from Dodge.

Suddenly he screamed, "It's him, the Indian – drawing a bow on me!"

I darted a look all around and all I could see was a patch of mist that hadn't been there before. But I heard the twang of a ghostly bow-string and the swish of an invisible arrow.

Red fell from his saddle and sprawled still on the ground. His horse bolted across the prairie.

My horse reared in fright, eyes bulging and frothing at the mouth, and I had to fight to stay in the saddle. As I clung to the saddle-horn on that bucking bronc, I glimpsed the mist coiling and solidifying into a human figure, and I was touched by terror. I went cold all over and broke out in a sweat.

The figure was that of an Indian, so tall and impressive he seemed a giant to me. There was some sign painted on his chest, and I had no doubt this was the ghost of the medicine man called He Who Strikes from a Distance. He carried a mighty bow and a quiver of arrows.

Despite the fact that I could see through him, he looked as if he might have been carved from stone. His face held a terrible calmness and his eyes, like live coals, bored right through me.

I was paralysed; my skin crawled and my teeth rattled in my head. I blinked, and the figure faded and I got my horse under control.

I dismounted and knelt beside Red. He was a goner. The strangest thing of all was the gaping wound in his chest. I could see where an arrow had penetrated, but there was no shaft. I felt the wound and found a stone arrow-head embedded in his heart, and a sudden chill made me shiver.

I buried Red where he fell and made a cairn of stones as a marker and spoke a few words for my friend. Then I turned and rode south.

It was something more than curiosity that took me back to the Indian camp; I felt drawn there against my will. The tribe was just striking the teepees ready to move on.

It seemed they'd stayed till their medicine-man was fit to travel. I learnt that when his spirit returned to his body from the death-trance – after 'Fiery-hair' had paid the penalty – he made a truly astonishing recovery.

THE GREY LADY

by Mary Danby

"Peg-Doll? Buy a peg-doll, sir?"

Billy stood on the corner of Bond Street and Piccadilly, where he hoped to find customers among the rich, smartly-dressed shoppers. He was twelve years old, but very small for his age, and the tray of dolls hanging round his neck made him stoop slightly.

A man in a tall hat came by, and holding his arm was a pretty, elegant young girl. Billy stepped forward.

"Peg-doll for the lady, sir?"

The girl stopped and looked at him, at his pale, bony face and uncombed hair, the scraps of clothes that barely covered his skinny frame.

"Oh, dear," she said, putting up a tiny, gloved hand to stifle a giggle. "Look, John, he's wearing odd boots!"

"Dash me, so he is!" exclaimed the man. "What peculiar ideas of fashion some people have, eh?" He tweaked at the enormous floppy bow of orange silk which adorned his neck. "Would you like a peg-doll, precious creature?" he asked.

The girl turned on her heel and, with a dismissive wave of her hand, said: "Heavens, no! They're altogether the quaintest things I ever saw!"

Billy withdrew, as if to protect his dolls from her scorn. They were like people to him – his only friends. He liked to give them names: Princess Paula, Dancing Jenny, Wizard Wonderful, the Silver Prince . . .

A little girl came skipping towards him, followed by her mother. Both were wrapped in warm, woollen cloaks.

"Peg-doll, ma'am? Peg-doll for the little one?"

"Oh, Mama . . . here's a boy with pretty dollies. May I buy one? Please, Mama, oh, please!"

Billy smiled at her and tilted the tray so that she could inspect the dolls. He held them up for her to admire: the Fairy, the Bride, Cinderella, the Snow Queen . . . "Only twopence," he said. "Lovely peg-dolls. Only twopence."

The little girl bought the Cinderella doll, with its ragged skirt and dear little raffia broom. She skipped away down the pavement, and Billy clutched the two coins tightly in his thin and grimy hand.

"Peg-dolls! Buy a peg-doll, sir? Buy a peg-doll, missus?"

A sharp east wind blew down from Piccadilly Circus, and he moved round into Albemarle Street to escape its cold bite. He had no coat to keep him warm – just an old, frayed jacket with holes where the elbows had once been. The daylight was fading fast, and gentlemen were leaving their offices and making for the comfort of their clubs, or their firesides at home, where their lace-capped wives would pour tea for them and hand round plates of toasted muffins and seedcake.

A hansom cab drew up at the kerb and a man leant out. Billy hurried forward eagerly, thinking the man wished to buy a doll, but he was merely asking the whereabouts of the nearest flower-seller. Billy told him, then had to step back quickly to avoid being hit by the cab's wheel as the horse bounded forward, stung by the driver's whip. Billy's foot slipped in the gutter, and two of the dolls fell out of the tray. He picked them up and gave them a brief wipe on his sleeve.

"Peg-dolls! Peg-dolls!"

But though he waited until the street-lamps were lit and the home-going crowds all departed, he could sell no more that day. He packed the remaining dolls into a drawstring calico bag and lifted the strap of the tray over his head. Then, with the tray in one hand, the bag in the other, and six pennies – his day's takings – tied up in an old handkerchief, he trudged to a stall at Oxford Circus where he could get a cup of soup and a slice of pudding for twopence.

Mrs Gibbins was talking to her friend Mrs Fraser on the steps of number 42 as Billy edged past them, making for his room at the back of the house.

"'Evening, Mrs Gibbins," Billy greeted his landlady.

"'Evenin', Billy."

Mrs Fraser cast a knowing eye over the hunched, shuffling figure, the threadbare clothes. "'E's lookin' sorry for 'isself," she remarked.

Mrs Gibbins folded her arms and leant against the doorframe.

"Didn't you 'ear?"

"'Ear? 'Ear what?"

"'E's on 'is own, now, Billy is. 'Is sister went and died on 'im last week. Took very sudden. It were that cold spell, y'see. 'E comes 'ome one day and finds 'er gone. Well *gone*, I mean, she was *there*, but she weren't, if you understand my meaning, Mrs Fraser. They buried 'er Friday mornin'."

"There now." Mrs Fraser sucked at a gap in her teeth.

"She was a good girl, was Sarah. Paid me the rent regular and made no noise to speak of. But then, they came from a very respectable 'ome, y'know. Their father was a clerk or some such."

"Parents dead, eh?"

Mrs Gibbins nodded. "'S far as I know. Not that they ever used to talk much to me. Kept themselves very private. She used to sit in that back room all day, makin' 'er dolls, and 'e'd be out sellin' 'em . . ."

"What now, then? If she's gone, who's to make the dolls?"

"'Oo indeed?" said Mrs Gibbins, peering down the gaslit hallway to see if Billy might be listening. She turned back to Mrs Fraser and said under her breath: "And what bothers me is, no dolls to sell, no rent money, see? Unless 'e can get work somewhere, o' course, but e's none too strong in the body – nor the 'ead, for that matter."

"Weak in the 'ead?" asked Mrs Fraser.

Mrs Gibbins shrugged. "'Ee's not an idiot, I don't mean. Not *wanting*, you understand. But 'e can't read, nor write neither, even though 'is sister could, and she must 'ave tried teachin' 'im. And when I asked 'im what 'is plans was now 'e's on 'is own, 'e gave me this funny look, sort of blank, as if I'd gone and asked 'im the name of the man in the moon."

"You'll 'ave to turn 'im out, I s'pose," said Mrs Fraser. "That's a nice back room you've got. Someone would be glad to pay as much as two shillin's a week for that, I dare say."

"Do you think so?" asked Mrs Gibbins, brightening. "I only gets one and sixpence from '*im*.'"

"One and sixpence?" echoed Mrs Fraser. "My 'usband's young nephew 'Orace would pay much more than *that*. And it 'appens 'e's lookin' for a room this very moment . . ."

"Oh?" Mrs Gibbins sounded most interested. "Well . . . if you think 'e'd be comfortable . . . If you think it might suit . . . Of course," she continued, "I couldn't tell young Billy to go right away, not just like that. But if 'e's not able to pay . . . Mind you, I dare say it'd be the work'ouse for 'im, 'im being only twelve-ish and no parents."

"It'd keep 'im off the streets, though," said Mrs Fraser. "Otherwise 'e'd turn to thievin', like as not."

"Yes, that's the truth of it," agreed Mrs Gibbins. "I dare say it would be a kindness to the boy. Poor motherless lamb."

Billy tipped his four remaining pennies into the tobacco tin he kept under his pillow. There was a shilling in there already. Tomorrow was Friday, when he had to pay the rent money to Mrs Gibbins. That meant he would have to sell at least two dolls, if he was to eat as well. He opened the calico bag and laid the dolls out on the thin blanket that covered his bed. He should have had Sarah's blanket too, now that she was no longer in need of it, but Mrs Gibbins had removed both bed and blanket. There was, however, no reduction in the rent.

The Princess, the Wizard, Fairy Bluebell, Greta the Gypsy, the Snow Queen, the Dancer, the Peasant Girl, the Soldier, the Silver Prince, the Spanish Bride. Ten dolls left. If he sold them all, that would be ten times two pence, which was . . . Billy counted on his fingers, then rearranged the dolls into sets of three. "Three dolls is sixpence, Sarah said, and two sixpences is one shilling. One and sixpence . . . and a bit . . ." That was enough for the moment, but what would happen when all the dolls were sold? Perhaps he could get work in a factory. Jobs were difficult to find, but so long as he could earn enough to keep his room, he would be able to manage somehow. The main thing was to have somewhere to come home to at night.

He packed the dolls carefully away, then, without washing or removing his clothes, he climbed under the motheaten blanket and tried to sleep.

But sleep wasn't easy, when you were used to being lulled by the even breathing of someone in the next bed. To lie awake listening only to the sounds of Mrs Gibbins' husband cursing at someone or something in the front room made Billy feel very lonely. He thought of the kind, soft face of his sister, her gentle smile, the way she never complained, even when her hands were red-raw from the cold, and her fingers torn by sewing needles, and the cold had gnawed through to her bones, so that she used to press her hand to her back when she rose from her chair in the window. "But Billy," she would say to him, "we have each other, which is more than all the money in the Bank of England."

Now, though, he had no Sarah – and very little money either. Just a cold, damp room, a bed hard as the pavement outside, and one and fourpence in a tin beneath his ear. A tear slid from Billy's eye to wet the hard little pillow. From the next room came a bellow of laughter. Mrs Gibbons, at least, could find something to laugh at.

The next day it was raining, and no one wanted to stop and look at Billy's dolls as he sheltered beneath a shop blind. But, at last, just as he was about to turn and head for home, an old lady came and bought the Spanish Bride for her granddaughter.

"Who made these?" she enquired. "Not you, for sure," she added, inspecting his unwashed appearance.

"No, ma'am. My sister, ma'am. She's dead."

"Oh . . . indeed . . ." The old lady backed off, as if she thought he might have something catching. "What the Lord giveth, the Lord taketh away."

"Yes, ma'am," said Billy meekly.

He went straight home. There was enough for the rent, now, but nothing to spare for food. He would have to go hungry. Perhaps tomorrow the sun would shine and everyone would want peg-dolls; then he would have enough for a meat pie and perhaps a pickled onion as well.

Mrs Gibbins and Mrs Fraser were at their usual post

when he arrived home. They seemed to be looking at him with great interest as he went past them into the house.

"Rent day today, Billy," Mrs Gibbins called after him. She turned to her friend and said smugly: "Not that I think for a moment 'e can pay. Now now 'e's by 'isself, I mean. Well, Mrs Fraser, about your 'usband's nephew . . ."

Billy took the old lady's twopence out of his handkerchief, then felt under his pillow for the tobacco tin. One and fourpence, and twopence, that made . . . let's see now . . .

He picked up the pillow and shook it. His poor, pinched face, already pallid from lack of nourishing food, went as white as paper. The tin was not there.

Feverishly, he tore back the bedclothes, and, still not finding the tin, he searched the whole room. But he was sure he had left the money under the pillow, and it couldn't have just vanished. Had it been stolen? The only other person who ever went into his room was Mrs Gibbins, who occasionally waved her mop around the bare floorboards. And surely *she* wouldn't have taken the money. After all, it was her rent.

Gulping back his sobs, Billy ran out to her.

"I had it, Mrs Gibbins," he said tearfully. "I had the one and fourpence in a tin under my pillow. And, look, here's the other twopence." He held out the money.

Mrs Gibbins, smiling indulgently, took the coins and said: "Twopence rent, for a lovely room like yours? No, no, Billy. It's one shillin' and sixpence. And *that* hardly pays me for the trouble." She turned to Mrs Fraser and gave a coy little laugh. "Dear me!" she exclaimed. "Whatever next?"

"But I *did* have the money," Billy insisted. "It's been taken."

"Taken? Taken?" Mrs Gibbins said in a high affronted voice. "And who by, pray? I hope you're not goin' to suggest . . . No, you wouldn't be so evil, I dare say." She looked hard at him for a moment, then gave him what she meant to be a smile, but which was more of a leer. "Never mind," she said. "I'll tell you what we'll do. As one with a 'eart of gold, I'd never want it said that Mrs Gibbins turned anyone out on the cold streets. So you can have until Monday to find the money. All right?"

Billy, crestfallen, nodded and turned to go back inside.

"And if you can't pay," added Mrs Gibbins, "I'm sure I can find a nice kind constable to escort you to the work'ouse. We wouldn't want a young man like you to get lost on the way. Now then – " She addressed Mrs Fraser. "I think we could say Tuesday for the new lodger, don't you?"

Saturday was another wet day, and Billy's cry of "Peg-dolls!" went unheeded as people hurried through the rain. He did manage to sell one doll, though – the Snow Queen – to a young gentleman waiting for a cab.

By the evening, it was beginning to look a little brighter, and Billy decided to move to the Edgware Road, in the hope that he might be able to sell to people coming out of the music hall. There were puddles everywhere, and he had to jump over them, as his ill-matched, worn-out boots let in so much water. Yesterday's rain seemed to have seeped right through his skin, and he felt very shivery.

As he stood outside the music hall, a commissionaire came and waved him away. "Not there, boy. The customers don't want to be a-falling over you. Move along, now. Move on."

Billy retreated, but as soon as the show was over and the people came rolling happily out, singing snatches of the songs they had just been entertained with inside, he stepped boldly up to them.

"Peg-doll for your lady, sir?" he invited, interrupting himself with a fit of painful coughing. "Peg-doll for the lady? Twopence each . . . only twopence . . ."

The Gypsy and the Dancer were soon sold, and then the merry-makers were gone. Still, that was – Billy counted out the coins – sixpence in all, which was better than yesterday. He ached inside with hunger, not having eaten for forty-eight hours, and when a baker's man passed, with a tray of warm bread balanced on his head, Billy decided it would be all right to spend just one penny on a floury roll.

That night, he slept with his money clutched in his fist, and in the morning, when he awoke, he found his hand still tightly closed over the seven pennies.

Not being well versed in sums, he was not sure how much more he needed for the rent, but he thought it must be something under one shilling. Tomorrow, Sunday, should be a good day for him, if the weather was fine, for people would come with their children for walks in the parks, and young men would be out courting, and anxious to buy presents for their lady loves. "God's favourite day," Sarah used to call it, making Billy spruce himself up.

True to her, still, he went out to the yard at the back of the house and washed himself at the pump before setting off for Hyde Park, where the gentry rode in open carriages in the hope of being admired by their friends. It was not the gentry, however, that Billy was seeking, so much as the young working men – the tradesmen and suchlike – who were easily persuaded to part with a few pence if by so doing they could impress their lady friends.

As expected, it was a good day. Of the six remaining dolls on his tray, Billy sold five: the Soldier, the Peasant

Girl, the Fairy, the Princess and the Wizard. The Silver Prince was beginning to look a little grubby, having been held up for inspection by so many hands, and nobody seemed to want him. However, delighted by his success, Billy spent twopence on a hot potato and a cup of milk, then he bought a pennyworth of cough drops, which burnt his throat with their healing fire.

"One and sixpence by tomorrow," reminded Mrs Gibbins when he returned home.

She thinks I can't pay, thought Billy, counting coins on the floor. Fourteen pennies . . . twelve was one shilling . . . and two. That meant . . . he needed four more, which was two dolls.

Two dolls? But he only had one! And the Silver Prince was looking very shabby indeed. Billy sat on his bed with his head in his hands. "Sarah," he whispered. "Oh, Sarah, *help me*."

As if in some kind of answer, his eyes were directed to the wooden box in the corner of the room. Sarah's workbox. He had never looked inside it – at least, not since her death – feeling that he had no right to do so. After all, they were Sarah's things, not his . . . He walked over to it and undid the catch. Inside was a wonderful assortment of ribbons, and braid, and scraps of this and that – velvet, linen, satin, lace – little pots of paint, and brushes, and glue, scissors, pins and pegs.

Billy had often watched Sarah making her dolls. She would decide on a character, paint the face and hair on the round knob at the top of the peg, stuff tubes of pink ribbon for the arms, then glue and sew on the costume. The shoes would be painted on to the ends of the legs. It was surely not all that difficult. And if he could even make just one, he might manage to pay the rent tomorrow and avoid being marched to the workhouse. He was afraid of the workhouse. Boys were made to work terribly hard there, and were beaten if they were lazy – sometimes, even if they were not, he'd heard. The food was mostly a kind of thin porridge, and he believed the beds to be little more than wooden boxes. Worst of all, he would be a prisoner, unable to move freely around the city.

"I *won't* go to the workhouse," he said under his breath. "*No*." With his mouth set in a determined line, he began to sort through the workbox. He would make a Fine Lady, with rich red lips and light brown hair, just like Sarah.

Painting the face was not as easy as he had thought it would be. Sarah's touch had been so deft and delicate, and his was much too rough. He tried to wipe off the features with his sleeve, but he simply made a nasty blur around the eyes. Choosing a piece of grey silk for the dress, he wrapped this around the peg and fastened it at the back with large, clumsy stitches. Then he made a hooded cloak out of grey crêpe. He pulled the hood well down over the face, so that the smudged paint was less noticeable. That done, he painted grey splodges on her feet and hoped they looked like elegant boots.

The daylight was fading, and he lit a candle. By its shifting glow, he thought the doll looked quite attractive. Not as nice as any of Sarah's, of course, but he thought he would be able to sell it. That left just the Silver Prince. He found that by brightening up the crown here and there with silver paint, and dabbing at the clothes with a wet cloth, he could make it look a great deal better. Perhaps he would be able to sell both of them, then Mrs Gibbins would get her rent. Everything would be all right.

Poor Billy could not think further ahead than one day. That he would have to find another one and sixpence by the following Friday had not yet become clear in his mind. If it had, it is doubtful whether he would have spent that night in such calm and dreamless sleep.

* * *

It must have been some lucky star that guided Billy to Piccadilly the next day, for he was approached by the same little girl and her mother who had bought the Cinderella doll from him only four days earlier.

"Mama! Here is Cinderella's Prince Charming!" exclaimed the little girl, looking eagerly over the edge of the tray. "Oh, may we buy him? Cinderella *must* have her prince. Please, please Mama!"

The girl's mother smiled fondly down. "You are right," she said. "They would certainly make a most agreeable pair. Very well, then." She sniffed. "At least he's a better buy than this other doll, this strange-looking lady, here. Why, I do believe her clothes were stitched by someone with paws instead of hands!" With a tinkling laugh she handed Billy twopence, then the little girl took the Silver Prince and they were gone.

Billy was a little cast down by her remark. However, there were many hours left before he need return to his room with the rent money, and surely someone would take a fancy to his Fine Lady. No, 'Fine' was perhaps the wrong word. She would be the Grey Lady, instead.

He wandered down towards Hyde Park Corner, then up Park Lane. Nobody here wanted a peg-doll. Perhaps in Oxford Street, if he stood alongside some of the other pedlars there . . .

"Off with you!" said a man selling matches. "This ain't where you belong."

"Look at 'im," cried a girl with a basket of artificial flowers. "All 'e's got is one doll to sell, and that's not worth a halfpenny. See – 'er eyes is all funny!"

Billy ran from their laughter, and the running made him cough, so that he was forced to stop for a while. His chest ached, and he found himself blinking back tears. It was no good. No one would buy the doll. Mrs Gibbins would turn him out and he would have nowhere to go but the workhouse. He was glad Sarah was gone, and couldn't see him in his plight. She had once said to him: "I'd rather die than go to that place." He'd said: "Me, too," at the time, but now all he could think was that he would, at least, get something to eat there, even if it was just a bowl of gruel. He was so very hungry.

He was in one of the small streets to the north of Marble Arch, now, and a carriage was approaching over the cobbles. It was a smart, four-wheeled conveyance, drawn by a perfectly matched pair of dapple greys. Their oiled hooves clattered to a stop on the cobbles right by where Billy was standing, and he looked up at the black-liveried coachman, sitting stiffly upright on his seat at the front, his legs covered by a heavy-looking weather sheet.

The coachman kept his eyes straight ahead and moved not a muscle. He was thin and grey-faced, and he sat in his place as if he never left it.

After a moment, the door of the carriage opened, and a lady appeared. She was cloaked and hooded, and Billy couldn't see her face properly. He thought she must be visiting a nearby house, but she came straight over to him.

"P-peg-doll, ma'am? Will you buy a peg-doll?" he asked in a quivering voice.

When she answered, her voice was as sweet as sugar and as soft as swansdown.

"Is this the only one you have left, Billy?"

Billy took a step backwards. How did she know his name? He gulped anxiously and replied: "Yes, ma'am. It's twopence, ma'am."

The lady looked at it, at the smudged paint and the badly-stitched dress. "I'll have it," she said.

Billy gave a weak smile, then began again to cough. His thin shoulders shook with the effort.

"Please," said the lady, holding open the door of the carriage. "Won't you ride with me?"

Billy shook his head nervously. Sarah had said never to go with strangers, however nice they might seem.

"I have food inside," the lady went on. "Cheese patties and gammon rolls – oranges bigger than your fists . . ."

Billy bit his lip. He was so hungry that nothing else seemed to matter.

"Come along . . ." invited the lady.

Billy unhitched his now empty tray and climbed into the carriage.

The lady kept her hood up even in the carriage, and he still couldn't see her face properly. Perhaps she had some disfiguring skin disease which she didn't want him to see. Or perhaps she was someone famous. On the stage . . . or royalty, even.

"Help yourself, Billy."

She had pulled out a hamper from under the seat and was spreading out the contents. There was food such as Billy had never tasted before: partridge pie, apple turnovers, rich fruit cake, cold pork sausages. As he ate, they were both silent, and Billy, intent on eating all he could, scarcely noticed that the carriage was moving.

When he finally looked up, they were on the outskirts of London, and seemed to be heading east. The River Thames lay over to their right, and Billy could hear the hooting of the barges as they brought their wares up the river.

"How do you feel?" asked the lady, when Billy sat back, unable to eat another morsel.

Billy smiled. "Wonderful, thank you, ma'am."

"Good." She, too, sat back, and Billy felt the grey crêpe cloak brush against his arm. Grey crêpe. Like the peg-doll. The Grey Lady. Yes, of course, she was so like The Grey Lady. He began to feel a little frightened. Who *was* she and, even more important, where was she taking him? This wasn't the way to where Billy lived. The light was beginning to fade, and if he wasn't home with the rent money soon, Mrs Gibbins wouldn't let him keep his room.

"Excuse me," he said, "but could you tell me where we are going?"

The lady seemed not to hear.

"Excuse me." He tugged at her cloak. "Can we go back, now? I have to go home."

The Grey Lady turned, and he saw her face.

It wasn't the strange, crooked mouth, bright ruby red in a pale face, nor the flat, round nose . . . It was the eyes, blurred and expressionless, which really terrified him. The dreadful, painted face of the Grey Lady had come to life, to torment him with its horror.

He screamed and clutched at the door of the carriage. "Let me out!" he shrieked. "Oh, for love of pity, let me out!"

They were quite close to the river, now, and there was a thick mist which muffled the sound of the horses' hooves as they slowed to a walk. The door would not open. Billy pushed with all his meagre strength, but it would not move.

"Please!" he begged. But the Grey Lady only turned on him those smudgy eyes, with their horrible blankness.

"*Please* let me go home . . ." moaned Billy.

Then the red mouth smiled a crooked smile, and the sweet voice said: "But we are going home, Billy. That's what I've come for. To take you home."

They were going down a slope, now, and Billy saw to his horror that it was a slipway, and that nothing but the cold, black, churning river lay ahead. As the horses stepped silently into the water, they were swallowed by the haze, and Billy turned despairingly to the lady.

239

"Home, Billy, I'm taking you home . . ." echoed her voice. It seemed to be both inside and outside the carriage, carried here and there by the mist.

He huddled in his seat as the water began to seep under the carriage doors. "Sarah?" he asked pitifully. "Sarah, is it you? Please let it be you . . ."

The Grey Lady stretched out a hand to him. He took it. It was soft and pink, like the hand of a stuffed toy, but it comforted him on the short, dark journey home.

CHILD OF THE FUTURE

by John Duncan

Rebecca ran lightly up the wide staircase and looked out of the upper landing window into the garden below. "That will need a lot of work," she said aloud, smiling at the estate agent's description on the sheet of paper. "'Mature garden', indeed. 'Overgrown' would be a better description."

Rebecca glanced at her watch. Her parents would be arriving in about an hour, and that gave her plenty of time to look over the house.

How many houses had they viewed in the last few hectic days since they had decided to move to the West Country? She shook her head and smiled. House-hunting was fun, anyway.

This house was once the residence of the Duke of Knowle-Seymour, and it was built to his own design," the estate agents had written. "There are ten bedrooms, five reception rooms and a servants' annexe with three bedrooms, etc."

"This must be the master bedroom," Rebecca said to herself, pushing back the large double doors. She went into the room and opened the tall wooden shutters, allowing the dusty sunlight to tumble into the room. "Twenty-four feet by sixteen feet," she read aloud. "That's not right, surely."

She paced the room twice and arrived at the conclusion that the master bedroom must be elsewhere; yet the hanging wardrobe, the servant's bell sash and the Italian marble fireplace were all described accurately on the paper. Furrowing her brow, she went on to the landing and glanced at the other bedroom doors.

The landing was L-shaped, and she counted the doors, ticking off each room as she walked by. "It's no use," she sighed, after a frustrating ten minutes trying to work out the positioning of the rooms, "I'll have to get the tape measure from the car."

Frozen, stony faces stared at her as she ran down the stairs under the disapproving portraits of people in old-fashioned dress.

Reaching her small red car, parked under a mimosa tree, Rebecca collected her tape measure and returned to the house, noting that there were five chimney stacks on each branch of the building; ten altogether.

"What a swizzle," she said as she rechecked her measurement of the 'master bedroom'. "This room is only eighteen feet by sixteen." Upon checking the adjoining room, she found that there was just over six feet difference in the measurements the estate agents had recorded, and the actual measurements of the room.

"That's twelve feet," she calculated. "Where have I made the mistake? One can't mislay a room." She tapped the wall with her pencil and was surprised to hear the hollow, empty sound it made. "This is only a partition wall. But I wonder where the door to this extra room is?"

She leaned out of the window and tried to locate the window of the extra room, and she felt along the adjoining walls in both the bedrooms to see if there was a concealed opening. She hoped there was. How excited her mother and father would be if they were to find a house with a secret room.

Finally, Rebecca went out into the hall and examined the area of wall where she thought a door ought to be. There was a massive oil painting of a man in red clothing, and Rebecca pulled it away from the wall. But it was not until she had pulled it some distance that she realized the painting was, in fact, a door.

"A secret room!" she breathed, ducking her head through the dark doorway. Perhaps she would be allowed to have the room to study in if she passed the entrance examination to become a nurse.

"Close the door," a voice said imperiously.

"Mum?" Rebecca jumped at the sound. "What are you doing here? I thought you were coming on the bus with Dad, later on this afternoon."

The room appeared to light up, like a theatre when the performance is finished, and Rebecca saw that dozens of candles were flickering busily in a glass chandelier.

At the far end of the room stood a woman, her hair piled outrageously high on her head.

"Mum?" Rebecca approached the woman. "Is that you, Mum? Please don't play games with me. I'm a bit frightened."

A cold draught of air slithered down Rebecca's neck as the woman turned to face her.

"I asked you to close the door, child," she said severely. "Close the door, I say. You know how cold your poor mama becomes when the door is left ajar."

Still keeping her eyes on the woman, who resembled her own mother so much, Rebecca pulled the door shut and stepped into the room.

Books lined the walls, and there was an antique desk to the left of the fireplace. The woman was dressed in a long silk gown and her face was garishly rouged.

"Rebecca." She surveyed the girl with annoyance. "Whatever is the matter with you, child? It seems to me you have been acting very strangely of late. It's almost as if you weren't really with us half the time."

"Where did you get the costume?" Rebecca asked, venturing a pace or two nearer so that she could examine the woman more closely. Yet somehow she knew that the figure standing near the fireplace was not, in fact, her mother . . . although she looked so much like her, and the voice was the same. Rebecca put her hand to her head, wondering if it was a dream. Then she noticed that she was no longer wearing her watch. Not only that, but she seemed to be dressed in similar design and fashion to the other woman.

"My dress!" she gasped.

"And what is wrong with your dress?" the woman snapped as she delicately picked up a small log and placed it on the roaring fire.

"*I'm* the one who should be asking questions," Rebecca thought, panic-stricken. "This isn't happening to me. It can't be happening." She stared at the woman. "Who are you?" she asked.

"Who am I?" The woman laughed shrilly. "Who am I? Why, Rebecca my dear, you must have a fever. I am your mother."

"But your clothes, this house . . . How did you get here?"

"I think you ought to retire to your bedroom, child." The woman apparently tired of the conversation. "I will send a coach for Doctor Harris. He'll probably have to bleed you again."

"Bleed me?"

"Obviously you have some poison in your system, Rebecca, and the good doctor will know what to do."

Rebecca gaped and backed away. It was like 'Alice Through the Looking-Glass'. What was happening to her?

"Do you live here?" she asked, hastily adding: "I mean, do you only live in this one room?"

"My . . . Oh, my!" The woman came across the room and peered intently into Rebecca's face. "The poor girl is

244

losing her reason. Such silly questions. You know that your father had this room built especially for me because I feel the cold so much. You know that I am your mother." The woman examined Rebecca's face and put her hand out to feel her forehead.

"Don't touch me!" Rebecca cried, stepping back from the icy fingers. "You are not my mother!"

"Rebecca, *dear*," the woman coaxed, "you must not say such things or people will think that you are mad. Your father will never allow me to keep you in the house if he thinks you have lost your reason. He loathes illness of any kind – you would have to be sent to Bedlam."

"Bedlam?"

"The priory of Bethlehem at Bishopsgate, dear, where they keep people who are mad."

"Mad?" Rebecca asked weakly. She stared at the fire and felt the fierce heat of the flames as they devoured the tiny logs, and she put out a hand to touch the solid wall behind her back. "I am not mad," she said defiantly. "I came here to view this house, and my mother and father will be arriving shortly. They are looking at some properties in Newton Dyneswell first."

"Newton Dyneswell?" The woman laughed. "But there are only fields at Newton Dyneswell, child. Whatever made you say a thing like that?"

"The estate agent knows that I'm here." Rebecca slid along the wall, trying to place some distance between the woman and herself.

"Estate agent?" The woman shook her head slowly, so that the high confection of powdered hair would not be disarranged by the action.

"I know what you're doing," Rebecca said firmly. "You're trying to make me believe I'm mad. It's a joke, but you won't convince me." She rushed over to a chair, where she could see the corner of a newspaper protruding from behind a cushion. "Here," she cried, "now we shall see what the date is."

She stared at the single sheet of paper. There was a drawing on the page, and Rebecca read a passage aloud. She stood there, hypnotized by what she was saying.

"And it is further reported that Lord North has been taken ill with the shock of the news that General Burgoyne surrendered his men to General Gates . . ."

"That's enough, Rebecca," the woman snapped, taking the newspaper from her. "You know that your father would disapprove of you reading such things."

"The American War of Independence;" Rebecca cried. "But that was two hundred years ago."

"Seven weeks ago," the woman corrected.

Suddenly Rebecca broke down and began to sob. It was all too much.

"There, there, child." The woman was at her side instantly. "You must not distress yourself about the loss of one colony. The King will not allow such insubordination to continue for long."

"Please," Rebecca sobbed, "please stop it. Tell me the truth. Who are you?"

"Hush, child." The woman stroked Rebecca's forehead with icy fingers, and she shuddered at the touch.

"Listen." Rebecca shook the fingers from her head and stood up to face the woman. "It's not seventeen-seventy something. You can't fool me. I came here with a watch on my wrist. I drove a car. I. . ."

The woman rose from the chair, her eyes blazing angrily. "You are not to get yourself in a state, Rebecca," she admonished. "I will not hear this nonsense. You are talking gibberish."

"Then tell me you don't know what a radio is and a telephone and aeroplanes and television. Tell me that

246

men have not walked on the moon, that ships don't travel under the sea and that people don't. . ."

A stinging slap silenced her.

"Stop it!" the woman shouted. "You know what happened the last time you had one of your attacks."

The slap seemed to drain all the anger and energy out of Rebecca and she suddenly felt sorry for the woman, who seemed to be genuinely worried about her.

"Look," she said soberly. "I don't know what has happened, but something very strange is going on. I don't belong here. I live in a time that is two hundred years away. Men have progressed; they do things that you would not ever dream possible." She wanted to console the woman, but she could not bring herself to touch her.

"Men walking on the moon. . ." the woman said. "How is that possible, child? Oh, I know you have been right before, but the things you are saying are just too fantastic to be true."

"I was right before?" Rebecca asked. "What did I say? I don't even remember having talked to you before."

"Captain Cook," the woman replied. "You were right about this discovery of a new land. You were even right when you said it would be called New South Wales. However, it is ridiculous to – "

"But I didn't talk about Captain Cook!" Rebecca exploded. "He's just a figure in our history books at school."

"School?"

"Yes, school. I passed all my exams, and history was one of my best subjects, so I know what I'm talking about. Captain Cook was killed at Owhyhee on February 14th, 1779, and England went to war with Spain on June the 16th."

"But how can you know that?" the woman cried. "It's

1777 now. How can you know what is going to happen in the future?"

"I live in the future." Rebecca stared wildly around the room. "And I must get back. I don't belong here with you."

"Now, Rebecca." The woman's voice held a warning in it. "Don't you start off again. We don't want to have another of your tantrums, or I will have to strap you tightly so that you cannot harm yourself."

"I'm all right." Rebecca spoke evenly, trying to make her way to the door. "Please leave me alone. I'll be fine in a moment."

The woman appeared to relax, and Rebecca took advantage of the moment to rush for the door.

"Stop! Rebecca!"

Almost crying with the effort, Rebecca gripped the ornate brass door handle and wrenched the door open.

"Don't go!" The woman's voice sounded so pitiful that Rebecca hesitated for a brief moment.

"I must," she said, gritting her teeth to keep control of herself.

The woman was standing near the fire, and a log spat hot cinders out on to the carpet.

"There's ash on the carpet," said Rebecca, pointing. Then, as the woman looked down, she pulled the door shut and ran out on to the landing.

A blast of warm air seemed to slap her in the face, frightening her and making her break into a run.

"Rebecca . . . Rebecca!" the woman's voice came echoing after her.

"Go away!" Rebecca cried.

"Rebecca . . . Rebecca!"

Past the oil paintings, down the stairs . . .

"Rebecca, Rebecca!" There was an evil hint of laughter in the voice, and Rebecca tried to block out the sound as she fumbled with the handle of the front door.

"Rebecca!" The voice seemed nearer.

"Rebecca! Don't leave me, my darling!"

Fingers curled around the doorknob. Frozen fingers that seemed unable to turn it.

"Rebecca, come back to me! Come back to your mother, my child."

"You're not my mother!" Rebecca shrieked as the door swung suddenly open. And there, before her, stood her mother.

Rebecca screamed.

All the force she was able to muster went into that agonizing scream; a scream that drove all the breath from her lungs and all the energy from her limbs. She collapsed, grateful and spent, into the blackness of her mother's arms.

"She's coming round," the voice said above the hum of the car engine. "Silly girl." It was her father's voice. "I told her not to view houses on her own. She's far too imaginative and easily frightened."

"All the same," said Rebecca's mother, wiping her daughter's face with a cool flannel, "I didn't like the place very much. It was spooky and I – well, I had the strange feeling that I had been there before."

"Stuff and nonsense!" Rebecca's father replied, pulling the car over sharply to avoid an oncoming fire engine. "Dammit," he said, watching the engine career around the corner, "that was close. We could have been killed."

Rebecca sat up and stared through the back window. "It's going to that house," she said dumbly. "A log fell out of the fire."

"Fire, darling?" Rebecca's mother asked. "Why should there be a fire in an empty house?"

"There was," Rebecca replied. "Look! Stop the car, Daddy!"

Far below them in the valley, under a pall of grey

smoke, the house was burning. "It was an evil place," Rebecca said as she watched the flames leap high.

Then, as they watched the firemen rush around the house like busy ants, Rebecca told them of her experience. As she was about to finish, she saw that her father was staring at her.

"You must have been dreaming, Rebecca," he said. "Maybe you're ill." He started the car. "Look, I'm going to take you to the hospital. There's something wrong with you."

"No," her mother said firmly. "I think we had all better go home and try to forget about this."

"But . . . Aren't you worried about her?"

"We are going home," Rebecca's mother insisted. "And we will throw this away." She opened the window and, taking the crumpled sheet of paper from Rebecca's hand, she tossed it out. "Drive us home, please," she said. "There's something evil about this place."

Rebecca snuggled against her mother, the way she used to when she was a child, and the car sped away as the flames devoured the house in the valley below.

The wind snatched the sheet of paper and tossed it high in the air, playing with it noisily for a while, then tiring of the game. Exhausted, the paper fell on to the grass, rolled and rustled and anchored itself to a granite cross.

The wind crept over the hedge and whistled casually through the gravestones, lifting the edge of the sheet of paper to read the inscription that was carved on the tombstone.

Here lies poor Rebecca,
Sweet Peace at last.
Child of the Future,
Gone home to rest.

Then the wind tore angrily at the sheet of paper and threw it down into the valley, where the flames of the house devoured it.

LISA

by Daphne Froome

It was the half term holiday, and Lisa felt so happy she fairly skipped up the two flights of stone steps to ring the bell of Miss Fraser's flat.

"I've been sent to tell Miss Fraser we've sorted out all the jumble ready for the sale," she said brightly to the strange lady who opened the door.

The lady gazed down at her blankly.

"The jumble sale for the stray animals' charity that she runs," explained Lisa patiently. "It's to be held at the scout hut at three o'clock this afternoon, and as it's one o'clock already everyone's wondering why she hasn't arrived yet."

"Oh, but Miss Fraser has suddenly gone down with 'flu. I'm waiting for the doctor now," said the strange woman. "She's quite bad, so I'm sure she wouldn't want to be bothered with jumble sales today. *I* think she does far too much charity work and tires herself out."

"I'm sorry," Lisa answered. "Is there anything I can do to hep?"

"Not really," replied the woman. "She just needs to keep warm and rest."

Lisa hesitated. "She has some raffle tickets I'm supposed to collect. We're going to raffle some of the better things . . ."

"Yes, yes, I dare say." The woman looked worried. "I don't know where they are. I'm only her next-door neighbour. But you can come in and look for them if you like, only don't make a noise, Miss Fraser is asleep.

251

There's a great pile of letters that came this morning, too – they were still on the mat when I arrived. I've put them on the desk. If any of them are to do with this charity of yours, perhaps you could deal with them."

Lisa tiptoed into Miss Fraser's study. She knew all the charity things were kept in there. Yes, here were the raffle tickets on the desk, with the morning's post beside them. There were a good many letters, Lisa looked through them and found two or three addressed to the animals' charity. She supposed she *ought* to open them in case they contained something urgent, about the jumble sale, for instance, and she *had* often gone through the post with Miss Fraser before.

She took up the paper knife, which was plastic and in the shape of a London sparrow, the emblem of their charity, and, feeling quite important, she began to slit open the envelopes.

The contents seemed to be very disappointing: just advertisements, or bills. But what was this last one, that bulged so very interestingly? It was a letter on blue notepaper and, as Lisa unfolded it, a key dropped out.

"Dear Dolly," it read. (Lisa stifled a giggle; she could never have imagined anyone addressing Miss Fraser, who was tall and angular and had a habit of looking at you severely through large spectacles, as 'Dolly'.) "We left in such a hurry for our tour of the Lake District that I quite neglected to answer your request for something for your sale. I haven't any jumble, but there are four quite valuable plates, worth at least five pounds each, which I would be happy for you to collect from 3, Regency Grove. You will find them in the box-room on the second floor, between the two bedrooms. They are in a large brown paper carrier-bag, so you can't fail to see them. Back in two weeks, key enclosed. Jane Benson."

Lisa knew 3, Regency Grove. She had been there to

collect jumble before. It was right in the centre of the City, not far from Bow Church, but quite a short journey by bus from Miss Fraser's flat. If she went at once she could collect the plates and be back easily before the beginning of the sale, and how pleased everyone would be if she turned up with four plates worth five pounds each. Twenty pounds! That would push the takings up.

"Are you all right, dear?" asked Miss Fraser's neighbour, behind her.

"Yes, thank you," answered Lisa. "I've found the raffle tickets and opened the charity letters – "

"Ah, that sounds like the doctor now; you'd better go."

Lisa found herself outside the flat.

Feeling quite excited, she hurried along the road and caught the bus into the City. This jumble sale was proving far more interesting than she had imagined; in fact, the stray animals' charity work seemed to get more and more interesting all the time, and next week the helpers were actually to take part in the procession at the Lord Mayor's Show. Miss Fraser kept on about what a wonderful advertisement it would be for the charity, and, though Lisa had to agree, she could not help also thinking, secretly to herself, how thrilling it would be to travel along on the float behind the fine carriages of the Lord Mayor and all the important London people, with the crowds cheering.

As she walked along Cheapside towards Bow Church, the clock was just striking two and a slight November mist was making everything look smudgy and nicer than it really was. Not that Lisa did not like London. She had been born in the city and could not imagine living anywhere else. She liked it when it was noisy and bustling, and now, when it was sleeping in its Saturday afternoon quiet.

She made her way along the side streets that led to

Regency Grove. It was a small, out of the way cul-de-sac set in among tall new buildings, like a bit of the past that had somehow been forgotten. In fact, Lisa noticed that all the other houses in Regency Grove seemed to be offices now. It must have been much nicer when they were first built in Regency days and all occupied by grand families, she thought. Not that the Bensons' house did not still look prosperous, even with the windows all firmly closed, the brass knocker and letterbox dull and the short path leading in through the wrought iron gate from the pavement dusty and unswept. Perhaps it had something to do with the two supercilious and dignified looking gargoyles, one each side, scowling down from the tops of the gate-posts. They seemed to be regarding her very suspiciously, so she ran past them quickly and put the key in the lock of the heavy front door. She suddenly felt very grand, walking in. "Just as if I was very wealthy and lived here," she thought, and she was sorry there was no one about to watch her go in and close the heavy door behind her.

The house had a slightly frightening, shut up, deserted feeling, but, making her way up the wide, curving stair-case, Lisa soon found the box-room. The door was open, revealing a small room of little use for anything, since the window had been bricked up in the days of the window tax, and very different from all the other beautifully furnished rooms in the house. Lisa switched on the light, went in and automatically pushed the door shut behind her. Yes, there was the carrier-bag. She looked inside, and there were the plates. She lifted them out and laid them on the floor. They were fine china and very, very pretty, with an intricate pattern in gold around the edges. She put them carefully back in the bag and turned to go.

She had forgotten she had shut the door. She looked for the handle. Bother, she thought, it seemed to be missing. She began to hunt round for it. It was not lying about anywhere, and there were no cupboards it could be in. In fact, the room was quite bare except for a rickety-looking wooden chair and a couple of cardboard boxes, one containing an old straw hat and the other a few outdated and uninteresting looking magazines.

"Bother!" she exclaimed, aloud this time. She put down the plates and hammered on the door. It was a very solid door, smooth and well-fitting, so there was no way of getting a grip on it from the inside. It refused to budge. Lisa wished the light was brighter so she could see better. Even though it had no shade it was very dim. The walls, with their faded, floral-pattered paper, looked as solid as the door, the ceiling was of heavy plaster, and the floor was thick boarding.

She was a prisoner; there was no way out unless she could batter down the door.

She took up the rickety chair, held it firmly by the back and swung it sideways at the door. The back broke off and the rest of the chair fell with a crash to the floor, but, except for a few faint marks, the door remained unscathed.

Lisa began to shout and scream. She went on screaming until her voice was hoarse, but no one answered. Indeed, who was to come to her rescue, she thought, as she collapsed on to the remains of the chair, on a Saturday afternoon in the deserted City, where she was surrounded by empty offices that would remain unoccupied until Monday? "And even on Monday, if there did happen to be anyone passing, who could possibly hear me," she wondered, "in a room without a window, so well shut up, at the back of the house?"

"Don't lose your head, Lisa," she instructed herself as bravely as she could. "Someone's bound to find you sooner or later." But no one knew where she was, and the Bensons would be away for ages. "Back in two weeks," they had said in their letter. What a fix to get herself into! And only a little while ago she had been so very happy. This time yesterday she had been in the car with Mum and Dad, driving round the route of the Lord Mayor's Show.

"This is where you'll be riding," her father had said, "with Mum and me cheering you on."

They had finished the outing by going up on to Hampstead Heath, and Lisa remembered asking how long there had been Lord Mayors in London.

Dad, who, being a Cockney, seemed to know everything about London, had answered: "Since the Middle Ages – there were Lord Mayors long before the time of Richard Whittington. It's nearly six hundred years, you know, since he sat over there on Highgate Hill and heard Bow bells pealing, calling him back to London."

"Dick Whittington and his cat? I didn't know they lived as long ago as that," she had answered.

"Bless me, what do they teach you at that smart school of yours? As Lord Mayor he served three kings – Richard II, Henry IV and Henry V. Difficult times they were, what with the fighting and feuding – they say pirates, too, often came up the Thames in those days."

Difficult times! She reckoned Sir Richard Whittington had never got himself into a situation as difficult as this.

She fumbled in her pocket and found the Bensons' letter and key, a handkerchief, the raffle tickets, some money and half a bar of chocolate.

"That won't last long," she thought. "I'd better keep it for a bit. Oh, what *am* I to do?"

Her shoulders drooped dejectedly. "Perhaps I could pass the time by counting," she thought. "When they find me I can say how many I've got up to, and if it's millions it'll sound terribly impressive. But if it was millions, that would mean I had been here for days and days!" She decided it was better not to count after all.

In the end she just stared at nothing, and, as the minutes dragged into hours, she even gave up glancing at her watch. The jumble sale must have ended ages ago, she thought, and everyone would be wondering whatever had become of her, and why she had not returned after collecting the raffle tickets.

The house was terribly silent except for occasional strange creaking sounds, which made it rather creepy. Then, suddenly, Lisa thought she heard bells ringing. At first they began quietly, and she thought it must be some trick played by her overwrought senses, but as the sound grew louder and louder they seemed to be ringing from everywhere in the room, from the walls, from the floor, from the ceiling, jangling through her head until Lisa felt she could bear the terrible sound no longer.

"The place must be haunted," she thought. "I can't stand it!" she cried out loud.

As if in answer to her cry, the noise gradually subsided, as though all the bells had been loaded on to a giant truck and slowly driven away. Then she heard the sound of midnight striking. She was trembling, shivering . . .

Lisa spent several minutes trying to focus her eyes on the cat which seemed to be crouched in the far corner of the room. She found it almost impossible to tell where his black fur ended and the shadows began.

They gazed at each other for a very long time. His eyes seemed to gather up the faint light from the bare electric light bulb, dye it green, and send it on to Lisa in a long, leisurely stare. She noticed he had one white whisker. He busied himself licking each paw in turn, stopping to eye her inquisitively from time to time.

After a while he stood up on all fours, stretched, and

suddenly, without any warning, sidled very deliberately across the room, leapt lightly towards the wall, and disappeared.

Lisa rubbed her eyes. Had he gone through the wall – or simply vanished? "He can't have gone through the wall . . . it's solid," she told herself.

She was quite baffled, and still very shaken, too, after the deafening clamour of the bells. She staggered to her feet, went over to the wall, and looked at the place where he had disappeared. Then she searched carefully around the room. Except for the bricked-up window it was ordinary enough. "I must be going mad," she thought. "It's the shock of all this. I must try to keep calm."

In spite of all her brave intentions, she decided that she must have started to cry at this stage, because when she caught sight of the cat again, edging slowly along the same bit of the wall as before, his shape looked more blurred and uncertain than ever.

He did not hesitate this time, but bounded straight across the floor, travelling purposefully towards her. He glanced at her once before vanishing through the wall again.

She waited a while but he did not return.

Lisa suddenly felt terribly lonely. She began to examine much more thoroughly the area where he had disappeared. When she tapped it, it made a curious sound, wooden and hollow, different from the dull thud of the surrounding brick.

"Perhaps it's not as solid as I thought," she said to herself, and, seizing the remains of the chair, she struck with all her might. Nothing happened at first, but then suddenly, with a dull, muffled, splintering noise, the chair crashed through. She peered into the opening, attacked it again with the by now very battered chair, and peered again. It was a chimney! She was at first pleased and then

258

bitterly disappointed, but she went on tearing away the wallpaper, breaking down the thin boarding, until the remains of a fireplace appeared. It was better than doing nothing.

And then, to her surprise, she noticed the cat again. He leapt, almost flew, she thought, across the few feet between them, landed beside her, and began to scrabble over the broken bricks and soot that had fallen down over the years, and the bits of wood and paper that Lisa had torn away, into the chimney itself. She peered up after him. It was very dark and he was little more than an indistinct blur anyway, but she was just in time to notice his dim shape disappearing up the narrow chimney.

"Oh, puss," she called, "I wish I knew what you were up to."

To her surprise, the cat suddenly came back down again and sat for for a moment looking almost solid, eyeing her with just the kind of stare – reproachful with a peppering of impatient sterness – that Lisa remembered seeing on Miss Fraser's face when one of the charity helpers was being particularly stupid.

Then he began his upward journey again.

Lisa wondered whether to try to follow him. "Supposing I get stuck?" she thought. "It does look so terribly narrow. Oh, anything's better than staying in this awful room," she decided, and she shovelled away the debris in the fireplace as quickly as she could and scrambled in after him. It really was very dark, and at that moment she could think of nothing more difficult than trying to follow the progress of the ghost of a black cat up a soot-grimed chimney in the dark. She squeezed further in. There seemed to be a bend about five feet from the ground, which curved backwards into a kind of platform. Lisa twisted round with considerable difficulty, and, pushing with her feet, hauled herself up on to the ledge. The cat was obviously some way ahead of her. "Which is just as well," she mused, "for there would never be room for us both."

She felt around in the darkness. The chimney seemed to go off to the side now, and she crawled along, blinking the dust out of her eyes. The passage turned to the left, and suddenly became very wide and spacious as a number of other chimneys joined it. Looking up towards the top, which now seemed not much more than a few feet away, she could see quite clearly the outline of the stack against the open sky. A little way above her, the cat, which had been sitting perched on a kind of foothold, jumped easily on to another, then another, until, when he had almost reached the top, he stopped and waited. Lisa could almost feel him willing her upwards. "They're steps!" she shouted. "Steps!" But then she hesitated. Supposing some should be broken? ("You can always go back, silly," she chided herself.) Or that they should give way beneath her weight? ("Well, I'll just have to test each one.") The sides of the chimney were sharp to her hands and sometimes crumbled at her touch, but the old brick steps, which, she thought, must once have been used by chimney-sweeps, held.

She looked up once. Yes, the cat was still there. "All right, mog. I'm doing my best," she called breathlessly. "I might not be as light and wispy as you, but if you can do it, so can I."

Lisa needed all her strength to finish her climb and clamber out on to the roof. Once there, she stood still for a very long time. She had never before felt so grateful to be breathing fresh air, and the space between her and the hazy moon seemed endless.

The cat waited, rather impatiently, she thought, at the edge of the gutter.

Lisa tried the slates cautiously, then she went slowly

down them towards the place where the cat was waiting. There, zig-zagging down from the roof, was a fire-escape leading to the ground. Lisa's legs felt very shaky beneath her as she climbed down the iron steps, but eventually she reached the gate and went through on to the pavement.

She leant against the railings and closed her eyes.

When she opened them again she could just make out the shadowy figure of a horseman cantering towards her through the mist; and, as he approached, she heard the bells begin to peal again, the sound seeming to gather in the little cul-de-sac, echoing around her, growing louder and louder. But she hardly felt frightened any more.

The man reined in his horse opposite Lisa, turned and bowed gently towards her, and as he did so she caught a glimpse of the great gold chain of the Lord Mayor of London; then he extended his arm to the cat, which jumped up in front of him, and horse, rider and cat seemed gradually to become part of the mist. By the time they had disappeared altogether, it was silent again in the street.

"And after all that I didn't remember the plates," thought Lisa.

She was travelling along in the procession on the stray animals' charity float, which really did look splendidly gay. It was a wonderful pageant: there were the Lord Mayor and the aldermen in splendid coaches, the horses, the people. Lisa caught a glimpse of her parents. They had somehow managed at the last minute to find special places next to Miss Fraser, who looked pale but recovered, on the Mansion House balcony. They waved enthusiastically; she waved back. The band was playing a stirring march. Then the rain, slight at first, turned into a sudden downpour. It gathered on the rim of Lisa's new hat, bought specially for the occasion, and then, spilling off, ran down between her neck and the collar of her new, matching coat. Her skirt began to cling, sodden, to her legs, her feet slopped about in her shoes as she moved. She waved to the girl opposite, whose hair was flattened wetly to her head. The girl grinned back. The band was playing even louder now, the people cheering them on. Lisa had never felt so exhilarated in her life.

Her father stood watching her from the balcony. He was very pleased to see Lisa looking so fit. When she had returned from her adventure she had been delirious with fright, insisting that she had heard Bow bells pealing in the middle of the night, and had been saved by Dick Whittington's cat. He had doubted very much if she would be well enough to join in today's festivities. But there she was, seemingly without any after-effects at all. He really felt very proud that she had kept her head and reasoned out the only possible way of escape so cleverly . . .

Suddenly he saw a black cat standing proudly beside Lisa, right on the front of the float. A black cat with one white whisker, and, in spite of the rain, very fluffy and quite, quite, dry. The cat caught his eye and winked knowingly before fading slowly into nothingness.

THE TRAIN WATCHERS

by Sydney J. Bounds

Brian Lester sat on the grass at the top of a high embankment, looking down into the cutting. Polished railway lines reflected the dazzle of bright summer sunlight. The grass was a withered brown, the patches of bare earth dry and crumbly. Rain was long overdue, and even the blackberry brambles had wilted.

Twelve-year-old Brian wore jeans and an open-necked shirt with sneakers, and had a spiral-bound notebook in his lap. He chewed on a ball-point while he waited. Since his parents had moved to the country, he'd learnt that train-spotting here was very diferent from the crowded platform of a London terminus. There might be one train in two hours, and he was on his own.

He looked up at the blue bowl of sky; there was not a cloud in sight. He'd heard of sudden summer storms, but it didn't look as if there'd be one this year. A pity . . . it would have been interesting to test the village rumour for himself. Not that he believed in ghosts, of course.

Far below, the tracks vibrated. Brian concentrated his attention. There came a roar of sound, a thunderous chatter of goods wagons as the train passed below him like an immensely long mechanical caterpillar. Then the noise receded into the distance.

He jotted down his notes and looked around. In the distance, he saw the bowed figure of old Mr Kemp leaning on a fork in his vegetable patch. Perhaps I can scrounge a cup of tea, he thought, and pocketed his train spotter's guide and strolled that way.

Evidently Mr Kemp saw him coming, for he stuck his fork into the ground and vanished into his caravan. Brewing up, Brian decided; good!

As he approached the caravan, Mr Kemp appeared briefly in the doorway and called: "Sit you down, lad. I've just put the kettle on – tea won't be but a moment."

Mr Kemp had a head of snow-white hair and a deeply furrowed face browned by working outdoors. His clothes were old-fashioned and baggy, as if he'd lost a lot of weight. And he always had a friendly wave for Brian when he was train-spotting above the cutting.

Brian squatted on the grass, and broke off and chewed a stem while he waited, imagining how long school holidays would seem if he didn't have such an absorbing hobby.

Mr Kemp reappeared with two mugs of dark tea, scalding hot and sweetened with condensed milk. It tasted very different from the tea Brian got at home.

"I don't mind taking a break myself," he said. "I'm glad of a bit of company – not many folk get up this way. You picked a good place for train watching. My grandson, Davy, used to be up by the cutting all day long – you'd have made a pair."

Brian sipped his tea slowly. "I heard a story in the village, about a boy who was killed trying to prevent a train crash. Apparently the cutting collapsed in a storm and blocked the track."

"Oh, aye," Mr Kemp said after a pause. "Likely you did. It's true enough – getting on for six – seven years back. He was too late, and the express crashed. Three killed, a lot more injured."

He stared into the distance as if he could see it again and refresh his memory.

"The story I heard," Brian persisted, "is that the boy appears – as a ghost – every time there's a bad storm. It seems he's down in the cutting, waving his lamp, trying to stop the train."

Mr Kemp snorted. "A ghost now, is it? And you'll be telling me who it is fool enough to be out in a storm to see?"

He pulled a large shiny watch from his pocket and studied it. "Drink up, lad. The Inter-City's due, and you won't want to miss that."

As Brian walked slowly away, he wondered why neither of them openly admitted that they both knew the dead boy was Mr Kemp's grandson, Davy . . .

One evening, a week later, Brian was again on the embankment when the sky clouded over, turning from blue to grey to black with no warning. This must be what they call a freak summer storm, he thought. A wind blew, so strong he could hardly stand. Lightning zig-zagged across the sky, starkly illuminating the landscape so it appeared like an old black and white film on the television. Raindrops, fat and warm, fell like stones.

He looked longingly at Mr Kemp's caravan – the only nearby shelter – but the windows were closed and the door locked. He supposed the old man had gone into town on one of his rare shopping expeditions.

Within minutes the rain pelted down, and Brian was soaked to the skin and imagining he had been suddenly transported to the bottom of Niagara Falls. He'd never seen such heavy rain before. He began to run for home, and then wondered why he was running. It was certain he couldn't get any wetter than he already was.

Through the steady hiss of driving rain he heard a drumroll of thunder. At least, he thought at first it was thunder, but the long, low rumble of sound seemed never-ending, and there had been no lightning preceding it. And there was a swishing sound of shifting gravel and the definite clink of stone on metal.

Brian stopped and looked back, incredulous. A landslide? He recalled it had happened once before. If the cutting was blocked, with an Inter-City due . . .

He ran back towards the embankment. The worst of the rain eased off to a steady downpour, and the sky lightened enough so that he could see.

When he reached the top of the high embankment and looked down, he knew the worst. Tons of earth had been washed down by the deluge, and the line was completely covered. So he had to try – like Davy all those years before – to save the train. He ran along the top of the embankment, towards the end of the slide. He had to get down on the track . . .

Ahead of him, a lamp bobbed in the rain. So someone else was investigating; but Brian was surprised that there should be anybody else up here in the storm. The figure was that of a boy, about his own age. Brian called to him, to let him know he was not alone, but there was no answer.

He ran faster but could not catch up. Then the boy started to move down the embankment, towards the track, and Brian stopped. The figure was not that of a real boy at all.

Brian could see muddy earth and tufts of grass glistening with beads of rain, *through* the figure carrying the lamp. It was Davy's ghost!

His skin prickled, and he shivered in fear. He had an overpowering reluctance to take another step forward. An icy hand clutched his heart and squeezed.

Then, in the distance, he heard the faint scream of the engine as it rushed to disaster. He forced his legs to move, and scrambled down the bank. A ghost couldn't hurt him, he told himself – and he had to try to stop the train.

266

He slid on mud, almost falling, regained his balance and arrived at the bottom of the cutting breathless. He ran along the side of the track, waving his arms and shouting. The sound of the approaching train was much louder now.

Davy was still ahead of him, in the dead centre of the rails, moving with a strange, gliding motion, his lamp swinging from side to side.

The noise of the oncoming train became a deafening roar, magnified by the walls of the cutting. The metal rails vibrated. Brian cringed as the monster hurled itself headlong towards him, the light in the driver's cab like a great staring eye rushing at him. He wanted to run away, but didn't dare.

He was hoarse from shouting, and his arms, signalling like semaphore flags, ached as he stumbled on. Davy's lamp appeared as a brilliant spotlight, Davy himself fading to a shadow, as if all his spectral energy was now concentrated in the signal lamp.

The diesel-electric began to slow with a screech of brakes, sparks shooting from its wheels. It ground to a halt yards from him, and Brian felt weak with relief.

The driver opened his cab door and jumped down. "What the devil's going on here?"

Brian gulped in air to steady his voice. "A landslide – the line's blocked."

The driver went striding along the track, stared ahead through the rain, then came back.

"It was lucky we saw your light in time," he said. "I reckon the papers will turn you into a hero, son. There's no doubt you saved our lives."

"Not me," Brian protested. "I didn't have a lamp. It was – "

But when he turned to look for the boy with the ghost lamp, there was nobody there. Davy had vanished.

* * *

After the newspapers stopped pestering him, and his parents suggested it might be better if he forgot his story about a ghost, Brian Lester climbed up the hill to Mr Kemp's caravan.

The old man gave him a searching look. "I was hoping you'd come, lad. Just let me pour the tea and you can tell me about it."

So Brian sat on the grass, and presently Mr Kemp pressed a mug of tea into his hand.

"There was a ghost," Brian burst out. "There was!"

"Oh, aye, I'm not doubting you. It's a pity I was away that day."

Brian slowly sipped the hot tea and told about the ghost boy with the lamp. "You do believe me, don't you?"

"I believe you – it was Davy, right enough."

Mr Kemp looked off into the distance. His eyes were shining and he looked years younger.

"Aye, Davy wasn't too late this time, and now he can rest. And so can I . . . You see, lad, I was driving the train that ran him down."

THE WARNING

by Joyce Marsh

Philip stepped out briskly through the gathering dusk; if he was to be back at his hotel in time for dinner he would have to hurry. He shivered. The day had been overcast and chilly, and now, with the night coming on, it had turned quite cold – more like November than September, Philip thought gloomily.

For the first few days of his holiday the weather had not been kind, which was a pity, for this was a very special holiday. At eighteen, this was the first time that Philip had been away alone without either his parents or a school party. He had chosen to come to Devon because he had already spent many childhood holidays here, when the sun had always seemed to shine on blue seas and pale, white-gold sands.

But this was not the weather for lounging on the beach. Fortunately, however, this remote corner of Devon could offer a happy alternative in the lonely wilderness of its moors. Philip had already walked for miles, exploring the many little tracks and lanes which led off from the main road to meander through the wild heather before dropping down to the sea.

He zipped up his anorak against the night wind, which stung his cheeks as it whistled through the stiff gorse and mingled with the plaintive call of distant night birds. Before him, the road stretched blankly for miles, and Philip knew that he must walk at least as far as he could see before the welcoming lights of his hotel would come into sight.

A little way in the distance he could see the white gleam of a signpost pointing with one rigidly outstretched arm. Philip was immediately interested; here was yet another lane to explore – tomorrow, perhaps. He came up to the signpost and stopped to read its directions.

"Pant . . ." The rest of the name had long since been worn away by wind and weather, and it was hardly surprising that no one had bothered to re-paint it, for the lane to "Pant . . . something-or-other" was rough and so overgrown that it was almost non-existent. It seemed that few people these days travelled that way.

Philip was so intent upon his speculations as to the possible ending to a place name beginning "Pant . . ." that the ferocious snarling of a dog somewhere behind him came as a sudden shock. Even as he spun round, Philip had a second to notice that the wind had dropped and, except for the snarling growls, an eerie hush had descended on the moor.

The dog was standing squarely in the middle of the road, barring his way. It was a spaniel – not a large dog, but, like all its breed, sturdily strong and muscular. It was staring at Philip with evil, white-ringed eyes, whilst its lips were lifted to show wicked, snarling teeth. Deep, rattling growls began in its throat and rose to a crescendo ending in a menacing bark.

Philip scowled. An evil-tempered brute like this should never be allowed out alone. He advanced on the dog, shouting and flapping his arms.

"Go-orn . . . get-out-of-it!"

The dog was not to be threatened off; it became even more menacing. Philip retreated slightly and looked around. There was no one in sight, and there was no house or village for miles. It was odd that such a beautiful little animal should be out on the moors alone, for it looked well cared for. The light rippled and gleamed on its long, silky ears and rich, golden-brown coat, whilst its domed, intelligent-looking head was highlighted by a flash of soft, pale blond hair.

Suddenly, with a little chill, Philip realized that he ought not to be able to see so much detail in this dusky light – but he could. It was almost as if the dog was . . . well, lit up from within. There was something uncanny about this dog, and Philip became anxious to slip past and be on his way as quickly as possible. He took a step first to one side and then the other, but the dog was not deceived by this manoeuvre. It moved with him. Then Philip saw the powerful muscles tense for a spring, and instinctively he braced himself to ward off the fearsome, snapping jaws. The dog was frighteningly quiet now, the light flickering along its rippling muscles as, with a powerful lunge, it launched itself at Philip. The dog sprang high. It was close enough for him to see the slimy strings of saliva drooling from its open jaws. He flung up an arm to protect his face . . . Then, suddenly, in mid-leap, it . . . vanished.

In all the stories Philip had read about people who encounter ghosts, they are described as searching for a natural explanation when their apparition disappears, but he knew at once that no normal body movement had carried the dog away. One second it was there, then . . . poof! . . . it was gone.

He was quite gratified to find that he was not in the least afraid. On the contrary, he was relieved. A real dog might have given him a nasty bite, but common sense told him that a ghost dog could do him no real harm.

Nevertheless, this was an eerie spot, and he had no mind to linger, so he set off again at a brisk jog-trot. As he ran, a smug little smile played about his lips. He was quite pleased to have joined the ranks of those who have actually seen a ghost. He imagined himself relating his experience and creating quite a stir in the office where he worked. However, if the story was to have its full impact it needed a bit of background. He promised himself that he would make a few local enquiries about that fierce little cocker spaniel.

The pleasant, purplish-grey dusk had darkened into gloomy night and, as he ran, Philip's light-hearted acceptance of his ghostly vision began to fade. He became increasingly nervous and oppressed by the eerie quietness of the moor. He could just make out the clumps of heather and gorse growing close to the roadside, but beyond that the moor seemed to drop away into black emptiness. He had the nerve-racking impression that he and the road along which he ran were silently suspended in a vast nothingness.

To add to his nervousness, he realized that he was not completely alone. Once or twice he glimpsed a vague shape moving through the bushes by the roadside, and keeping pace with him as he ran. Instinctively, Philip knew that it was the dog. He slowed his pace and took several breaths; he was surprised to find himself trembling, and he had to fight against an unreasoning urge to turn around and flee along the way he had come.

Anxiously he peered ahead into the distance and, to his relief, he could just make out the tiny little pin pricks of light which must be the village and the safe comfort of his hotel. Eager to be home, he went on again, but he had moved only a few paces when he was puzzled to see a faintly glowing shape lying in the roadway some little distance ahead.

His heart thumped with an inexplicable fear as he forced himself to walk towards the unknown thing which lay between him and safety. He came very close and was within a foot of it before he could recognize the box-like shape for what it was. Then he stopped dead, and a shuddering thrill of cold horror ran through him, for he found himself staring down at a gleaming, brand-new coffin.

Horribly abandoned, it lay there on the road with an unnatural radiance coming from the highly polished wood and finely wrought metal handles. A brass nameplate, ominously blank, was set into the lid, and carefully arranged along the top was a single, pure white lily. It was so close that, despite his horrified revulsion, Philip bent forward to touch it. The wood was curiously unresisting, and so cold that Philip felt as if his fingers were sinking into slime. He tried to draw back, but his hand was suddenly seized from inside and tightly held by icy fingers.

For one horrifying minute the boy felt as if some awful dead thing was trying to use him to drag itself free of its grave. With a shuddering effort he freed his hand and leapt back. Then, with horrified fascination, he watched as the coffin began to disappear. It did not vanish instantly, as the dog had done, but slowly. With a kind of lingering reluctance it sank into the road. The last thing Philip saw was the flower, the fat, white lily, and then the surface closed over it.

Philip examined the roadway. There was no mark to show where the coffin had stood. A trembling fear began in the boy's knees and flooded through his body, then he began to run, and he did not stop until he could see the comforting welcome of the light flooding out through the open door of the hotel.

The next day Philip made a few tentative enquiries, but he could find no one who had heard of a dog haunting the main road over the moor. He discovered that the lane near the spot where he had seen the dog led to a place known locally as Pantacombe Bay, but his description of the ghostly spaniel was greeted with such amused disbelief that he could not bring himself to mention the second and more horrifying apparition. He pretended to accept that the vanishing dog had been no more than a trick of the light, nevertheless he brooded on his experience. Fearfully, he told himself that the dog must have appeared as a kind of warning, and the coffin was the forecast of some frightful tragedy to come if he did not heed that warning. One thing was for sure, he decided, nothing was going to tempt him to walk along that particular road again.

However, as his holiday neared its end, he found that he had explored as much of the district as he could without travelling on the main road. The weather was still too chilly for sporting on the beach, and he was beginning to feel bored. So when he heard of an old fishing village whose inhabitants had long ago been driven away by the erosion of the sea, he could not resist going to explore, even though it meant walking over the haunted road. In the crowded comfort of the hotel lounge he made his plans and confidently told himself that his chances of being haunted for the second time were very slight.

Nevertheless, he set off early, promising himself that he would be sure to start for home in good time to be safely back before dusk. But, as the poet tells us, even the best laid plans "gang oft agley". The village was a long way off, and it was difficult to find; he did not arrive until well into the afternoon, and by the time he had explored the ruined, tide-washed cottages, the bright glitter of the sun had darkened to a glowing orange. Even as he started out for home, he knew that he could not possibly pass the lane to Pantacombe Bay before dusk. Nevertheless, he hurried, in a desperate bid to beat the sun as it fell down towards the edge of the moor. It was a hopeless race and one that he could not win; his eyes were already straining through the purple-grey dusk as he saw the signpost pointing to Pantacombe Bay.

With sinking dread he felt once again that hushed stillness descend about him. Then he saw the dog. It was in the middle of the road, not snarling or growling yet – just waiting! By its weird, inner light he could see the rich golden coat and the deep brown eyes gazing fixedly towards him. The dog lifted its snout to the sky and sent out a low, whining wail. Philip felt the hairs prickle on his scalp, and his hands became moist with the sweat of his fear. Instinctively, he knew that if the dog was there it was a warning that the other thing would be there, too – lying in the road waiting to deliver its horrible prophecy of some mysterious doom.

He walked on – there was nothing else to do; somehow he had to find the courage to pass the dog and then the dreadful, abandoned coffin. As he drew nearer, the spaniel lifted its lips in a snarl and the growling began deep in its throat. Philip's little store of courage deserted him. He sprang back, looking wildly around. Surely other people used this road; there had been cars enough this morning – why could not one come along now? But the moor was deserted and eerily quiet. Then his eye fell upon the lane to Pantacombe – of course, why had he not thought of it before? The lane was rough, and heaven knew where it led, but it was a means of escape. He darted down it, running as fast as he could over the rutted surface. Once he looked behind, and the dog was following, gliding smoothly and silently, yet warily, as if challenging him to turn back.

About fifty yards down the lane he glimpsed the thatched roof of a cottage nestling amidst a solitary clump of trees, and to his enormous relief there were cheerful lights blazing out of the windows. He ran towards it, but as his hand reached for the gate he saw the dog bound forward. Its stumpy little tail was vibrating merrily, and it bounced slightly, as dogs do when they are pleased. The spaniel was no more than a foot or two away when, just as it had done before, the little dog abruptly vanished.

At once, all the little night sounds vanished; the evening breeze carried the faint tang of the sea as it rustled pleasantly through the trees. Everything now seemed so normal that Philip was suddenly ashamed of his previous panic. He took his hand away from the gate and decided to go on, not back to the road – his newly returned courage was not quite equal to that – but on down the lane to Pantacombe.

The rough track narrowed and became even more overgrown as it dropped steeply down towards the sea. If the village of Pantacombe had ever existed, there was no stick or stone left of it now. The road eventually led on to the cliff edge, where it curved around, following the line of the bay, before it turned back across the moor to rejoin the main road a hundred yards or so beyond Philip's hotel.

It was more than three years before Philip returned to Devon. He was that much older, and the pressures of business did not allow him so much time for walking. Therefore, the next time he took that familiar road across the moor, he was driving – and in some haste, for he had a dinner appointment. With a twinge of apprehension he realized that it was dusk, and fading into night when he saw, once again, the tall signpost still rigidly pointing to the non-existent Pantacombe. Nervously he tried to push aside the memory of the snarling dog which had twice barred his way at this spot.

He desperately wanted to press down his foot and speed past, but he could not. Some compulsion stronger than his own will forced him to brake hard and bring his car to a slightly screeching halt. He half expected to see the snarling dog still standing there, but the road was empty. It stretched before him, blankly inviting. Suddenly, and with an unreasoning surge of relief, he knew what he must do! Wrenching at the wheel, he sent his car leaping off down the lane, which was now even more overgrown and deeply rutted.

The thatched roof of the cottage soon came into sight, and Philip, curious to know if it was still occupied, slowed down almost to a stop. And there, sitting by the gate, was the dog – the same beautiful little golden cocker spaniel. It was gazing expectantly up the lane, as if it was waiting patiently just for Philip to appear. As soon as the car slowed, the dog trotted towards it and jumped up to look in through the side window. With some relief, Philip noticed that the scrape of its feet against the car door sounded reassuringly real.

For a long moment the dog gazed at Philip with eyes full of dumb appeal, then it jumped down and trotted back to the cottage. After a few steps, however, the dog stopped, looked back at the car and gave a short, sharp bark. There was no mistaking its meaning – the animal was asking Philip to follow.

Mystified, the young man allowed himself to be led up to the cottage door. It was not locked, and opened at his touch. Inside, the house was heavy with the scent of flowers and the fresh, clean smell of wax polish, but there was a hushed stillness which told Philip that the cottage was empty. Still mystified, he paused. It was embarrassing to find himself here as an uninvited stranger in a stranger's home. But the dog, it seemed, had no time for the niceties of human behaviour. He gave sharp, impatient barks and, in his own unmistakable way, demanded that Philip follow him to the back of the house and into the kitchen.

The light was burning in here, but at first glance this room, too, appeared to be empty. The dog now became frantic. It seized Philip's trouser leg and began to tug at it with all his strength. Philip was pulled further into the room, and it was then he saw the girl lying on the floor.

She was about his own age and very pretty except for the deathly pallor of her face. She was lying still – so still that it was impossible to see if she was breathing. One arm was flung out, and a little fountain of bright red blood was bubbling out from a long gash in her wrist.

Philip had a moment to notice the butcher's knife on the floor beside her and the piece of frozen meat on the table. The girl must have been trying to cut the meat when the knife slipped. He dropped to his knees beside her and his fingers probed her upper arm for the heavy, throbbing pulse which was pumping away her life's blood. With his other hand he ripped off his tie, and when he found the pulse he tied the tie tightly around her arm at that point. There was a spoon on the table, and he thrust it through the tie and used it as a handle to twist and tighten his improvised tourniquet.

To his relief, Philp saw the heavy drain of blood ease to a thin trickle, but there was still no time to lose. The girl was scarcely breathing, and in no more than fifteen minutes the tourniquet must be removed. Bending down he scooped her up in his arms; she was very slight and her weight scarcely hampered him at all as he raced back to his car and dumped her a trifle unceremoniously on to the back seat. The dog was plainly not going to be separated from his mistress; he scrambled into the car beside Philip and stood on the seat, gazing down at her with pathetic helplessness.

Philip's car was fast, and he knew how to push it to its limits. Thankfully, his memory served him well, for he remembered every twist and turn in the road as he raced across the moor and down the steep road to the nearest town, where he knew there was a hospital.

It was a hair-raising ride, but in little more than ten

minutes Philip was able to hand over his charge into the calm, efficient care of doctors and nurses. Now there was nothing more he could do except wait, and he waited a long time before someone came to tell him that the girl would live. She was very weak from loss of blood, but she was young and strong and would soon recover.

Philip had been in the hospital for so long that he had forgotten the dog, and it came as a surprise when he returned to the car and found the spaniel still patiently waiting. With a slight hesitancy, Philip put out his hand and for the first time touched the soft hair on the dog's head. He ran his hand over the spaniel's flanks and was almost surprised to feel the warm throb of life.

"Well, old boy, your mistress is going to be all right, but it looks as if I'm going to be stuck with you – at least until tomorrow."

The swift wagging of the short, stumpy tail seemed to indicate that the dog had no objection to this arrangement.

It was very early next morning when Philip returned to the cottage. Ostensibly he went to take the dog home, but, as he readily admitted to himself, his real interest was in the very pretty girl.

The cottage door was opened by a plump, middle-aged lady with a flat, country face. The dog hurled himself upon her, excitedly nibbling her apron and leaping up to lick her face.

"Well, bless me, if it isn't our Mufti! Then you must be the young gentleman as saved our girl. Well, do come in, sir. We just don't know how to thank you for what you did, nor give praise enough for the miracle which sent you down our lane last night. Why, yours must be the first car that's come down here for weeks. Then, to beat all, you stopped and came in – what blessed chance made you do that?"

"It was the dog – Mufti. He made me come into your cottage."

"Oh, you dear thing!" She bent down to give Mufti a bone-crushing hug. "So you helped to save your mistress . . . and to think we nearly took you with us. You see, sir – " She turned back to Philip. "Father and me were away to market yesterday, and we usually take Mufti with us to mind the van, only yesterday he wouldn't come. The little rascal ran off and hid somewhere, so we went without him. What a shock it was when we came back and found the police waiting to tell us what had happened. Lawd-a-mercy, my blood runs cold to think on it. There's no doubt our Lily would have been in her coffin be now if you hadn't come along."

Lily. The single white flower lying along the lid of that ghostly coffin – that had been a lily. Dimly, Philip began to understand. The coffin might have been for the girl, Lily, but it had not been a prophecy of inevitable doom, it had been a warning of a tragedy which could be averted.

"It's really uncanny," Lily's mother was saying, "the way that dog just would not come wi' us. It's as if he knew he'd be needed here."

It is even more uncanny than you know, Philip thought as he gazed down at the excited Mufti.

"Have you had Mufti long?" he asked on an impulse.

"No, not long. He's Lily's dog, really. We used to have another golden cocker, only he died, very sudden like, about three years ago. Lily was broken-hearted, and she gave us no peace until we got her another just like him."

So it was not this real, living dog, but the spirit of a dead dog which had lingered on, waiting for a stranger who would heed his warning and remember it.

When Lily was well enough to come home, Philip went to the cottage very often, and they became friends, but somehow he could never bring himself to tell her of the vision which, three years before, had warned him that one day he was to be the means of saving her life.

Years later, when Lily and Philip were comfortably married, they would sit before their fire with an ageing Mufti snoring at their feet. Sometimes they would talk of the accident which had brought them together, then Mufti would open one lazy eye to gaze up at Philip. There was a deep, indefinable expression in that one eye as the old dog slowly lifted his lip in a silent snarl – which was very odd, for Mufti never snarled at anyone – least of all his beloved master.

HOUSE OF GLASS

by Catherine Gleason

Kevin Brown and his sister Millie climbed out of the taxi
and sighed in unison as they surveyed the frontage of
number 68, Hollydene Avenue. It was a tall, Victorian,
terraced house in a large north-eastern town.

"Doesn't look much of a place to spend a holiday,"
grumbled Millie, as their mother paid the taxi-driver.

"It might be fun inside," said Kevin, without much
conviction.

"Come on, you two. It's only for a week," said Mrs
Brown encouragingly. "I'll be picking you up next
Saturday."

"A whole week," Millie said dismally, as she lugged her
case to the doorstep.

"Now then," said her mother quite sharply. "Northumberland's very interesting and historical. There's Hadri-
an's Wall, and . . . all sorts of Roman places and things,"
she finished vaguely. "You'll be able to write essays about
them when you go back to school."

"Whoopee," murmured Kevin, and Millie giggled.
Unfortunately, Mrs Brown heard.

"You must remember we're lucky to have a holiday at
all this summer, with Daddy working away so much," she
said, ringing the doorbell. "It's very good of Aunt Natalie
to put you up, or rather put up with you, until we can go
and join Daddy in Scotland."

"I bet Aunt Natalie is about seventy and smells of
lavender," whispered Millie.

The door was opened by Aunt Natalie herself. She was about seventy and smelled of lavender.

"Welcome! Janet, my dear!" cried the old lady, embracing their mother. "And the dear children. Come inside, please." Her voice carried strong traces of her original Russian tongue. She led them into the old-fashioned drawing-room, a slim, fragile little person with lively blue eyes and snowy hair piled into a neat chignon.

"It will be so good to have children in the house for a while – but I suppose I must not call you 'children', having grown so tall!"

"Well, Kevin's nearly thirteen and Millicent's eleven now, Natalie," said Mrs Brown, laughing, "so they – is anything wrong?"

Aunt Natalie had stopped short and was gazing earnestly at Millie.

"No . . . that is . . . Janet, who does Millicent most resemble?"

"Ah, I thought you'd notice that," said Mrs Brown. "She's very like Helena, isn't she?"

"To the life," said Aunt Natalie. Tears dimmed her eyes and there was a look of mingled pleasure and sorrow on her lined face.

The door opened and a plump, bustling woman came in. She was introduced to Millie and Kevin simply as Anna, Natalie's Veronik's companion. Anna had also been born in Russia, but thirty years of living in England had muted her accent so that it was barely noticeable. She was good-natured and friendly, and about twenty years younger than their aunt, who explained that Anna would be taking them out in the car to the seaside and places of interest during their stay. Millie and Kevin felt much brighter as they followed her upstairs to their rooms on the second floor to unpack.

"Perhaps it's not going to be as dull here as we thought," said Kevin, and Millie agreed.

After a cheerful dinner, Mrs Brown had to leave to catch the train home.

"Mummy," whispered Millie as they kissed her good-bye, "who's Helena?"

"Sssh." Their mother waved to Aunt Natalie and Anna, and led them out of earshot towards the taxi. "Helena Veronik was your aunt's daughter. She died young, and very tragically. You look very like her, Millie. Now, behave yourselves, both of you, and have a lovely holiday. Anna's really a lot of fun and she'll look after you very well. Oh, and Millie, try not to mention your ballet lessons. Helena was a dancer, you see."

Mrs Brown climbed into the taxi and waved as it whisked her away. Back inside the house, Millie and Kevin had a conference with Aunt Natalie and Anna. They decided on a trip to the country with a picnic lunch if the weather held the following day, to see the Wall and the site of a Roman camp which was being excavated. Before long they were yawning, tired out from their long journey, and Aunt Natalie suggested bed, which sounded a very good idea.

In his room, Kevin was annoyed to find his watch broken. He had left it on the bedside table after having a wash before dinner, and the glass had cracked across its face. He was wondering whether he had knocked or dropped it during the journey, when there was a knock at his door.

"Look at this mess, Kevin." Millie dumped her small vanity case on his bed. The mirror inside its lid had shattered, and slivers of glass glittered among the contents of the case.

"You must have bashed it on the train," said Kevin, helping her to take the pieces of glass out. "Hey, you've brought your ballet shoes along. I thought your teacher said you weren't to practise on your own at this stage?"

"Oh, a few *pliés* won't do any harm," said Millie, frowning as she picked bits of glass out of the case. "Mind your fingers, these pieces are very sharp. There, that's the lot. Thanks, Kevin. D'you think it's going to rain tomorrow?"

Kevin drew back his curtains and they peered anxiously out. The moon was riding serenely high in the clear night sky. Kevin turned to Millie with a grin.

"Not a chance," he said.

Sure enough, the next day dawned bright and beautiful. Aunt Natalie fussed happily over the picnic basket as they all piled into the car. They were all in a holiday mood as they headed for the country.

"Oh look!" cried Millie in astonishment as a sheep leapt from the grass verge and over a low hedge at their approach. "I didn't know sheep could jump!"

"Townie," teased Anna.

"They are quite agile, the sheep," their aunt told them.

Natalia Veronik was their mother's half-sister. Her father was a Russian who had moved with his family to Poland after the Russian Revolution. Natalie had married Serge Veronik, who had been killed, along with her mother, when the Nazis invaded Poland. She had managed to escape to England with her father and her little daughter Helena, and, of course, Anna. At first they settled in London, where her father had married again. He died shortly after Millie and Kevin's mother had been born, so the children had never known their grandfather. Natalie decided to live in Northumberland; she had never re-married.

All this the children gathered, in a rather sketchy way, from questioning their aunt as they drove along. She seemed quite pleased with their interest, and promised to tell them stories of her hair-raising escape from Poland through occupied Europe, thirty years ago.

They picnicked near the ancient Wall in the mild September sunshine. Probably because it was late in the year, there were no other tourists about, and the only thing that slightly marred their day was the return of Millie's hay fever which had troubled her during the hot summer months. She tried not to make a fuss about it, but was secretly rather glad to be away from the fields and back in the car that evening.

There was no television at 68, Hollydene Avenue. While Aunt Natalie was resting in her room and Anna was cooking supper, Kevin yawned and said:

"I wonder what the attic rooms are like in this house? We haven't been up to the third floor yet."

"We can go and see if you – atishoo! 'Scuse me – like," said Millie.

They went out on to the landing, tiptoeing past their aunt's room so as not to wake her. There was no light bulb for the top floor, and the white attic door at the top of the stairs gleamed pale and rather sinister through the evening gloom. For some reason he could not name, Kevin felt an odd reluctance to climb further.

"Achoo!" sneezed Millie behind him. "This wretched hay fever. Go on, Kevin."

Slowly he mounted another couple of steps.

"Millie! Kevin! What are you doing?" They froze in shock at their aunt's furious shout.

"Come down at once!"

Sheepishly, they turned back down the stairs. Their aunt was looking flushed, angry and somehow taller as they confronted her on the landing.

"We were just . . . just going to have a look at the attic, Aunt Natalie," stammered Millie.

"There is nothing of interest up there. You must avoid that part of the house, *especially after dark.*"

Was it imagination, or was there a trace of fear in her voice?

"Come to supper now, I am sure it must be ready." She turned and stalked downstairs.

Kevin shrugged. "Well, that's it then. Probably just an old lumber room."

Millie nodded, but her curiosity was aroused.

Aunt Natalie was frosty over supper, for which they had a delicious kind of Russian stew called goulash. She thawed over their game of Scrabble later, however, and things were back to normal by the time they went to bed.

Anna took them to a stables for an early ride the next morning. As they trotted down a woodland lane, Millie told Kevin of the peculiarly vivid dream she'd had during the night.

"There was a ballerina," she said. "I couldn't see her face, but she danced beautifully, and she kept beckoning for me to follow her. I must have sleep-walked, because I woke up standing in the middle of the room. I'd stubbed my toe on the wardrobe, you see, and that's what wakened me."

Kevin laughed. "You think about nothing but dancing these days. When you're a professional you'll have to change your name, you know – how about Millicenta Brownovich?"

"Sarcastic – achoo! – clot!" yelled Millie in mock rage as her brother cantered on down the path.

When they came back to Hollydene Avenue, Aunt Natalie was getting ready to go shopping with Anna.

"Are you sure you two won't come along?" she asked.

"No thanks, Aunt," said Kevin, repressing a shudder. Looking at ladies' hats was not his idea of fun.

287

When they had gone, Millie slipped out to the corner shop for a large bottle of lemonade. She left it on the coffee-table in the living room and went into the kitchen, where Kevin was piling biscuits on to a plate.

"Can you see any glasses anywhere?" she asked.

"There they are," said Kevin, reaching for a couple of Pyrex ones on a shelf. Suddenly there was a splintering crash from the next room. They rushed in to find the bottle in pieces on the floor, and lemonade soaking into the rug.

"You clumsy idiot, Millie! You must have left it on the edge!"

"I did not!" shouted Millie. "I put it right in the middle of the table. It must have fallen off by itself!"

"Oh, don't be so silly," said Kevin angrily. "It couldn't have!"

A row developed, and by lunchtime they were hardly speaking. Kevin had collected the broken glass and hidden it in the dustbin, and Millie managed to dry the rug fairly well in front of the fire.

They were meant to go to a football match that afternoon, but Millie's hay fever had worsened, so Anna took Kevin to the match and Millie sprawled sulking on a sofa, sneezing, with streaming eyes and a nagging headache. Aunt Natalie started a game of Monopoly with her, but nodded off after a few minutes. Millie fidgeted, bored, and tried to sneeze quietly. Then she had an idea. When she was sure her aunt was properly asleep, she crept noiselessly out of the room and up the stairs, towards the attic.

Kevin enjoyed his soccer. When they returned, he lingered in the back garden for a few practice kicks on his own. He dribbled the football up and down the path for a few minutes, then aimed a kick at the wall. Unfortunately the ball went wide and travelled straight for the kitchen window. Kevin closed his eyes and clapped his hands over his ears against the expected crash. The ball hit the window with a loud thud and bounced back harmlessly, the window intact. Kevin was astonished. Suddenly a disturbing thought struck him. He walked up to the kitchen window and began to examine it closely.

"Anna," said Aunt Natalie worriedly, "I found the children going up to to explore the attic yesterday."

"Oh no!" gasped Anna. "Did they see inside?"

The old lady shook her head. "I stopped them on the stairs."

"Thank goodness for that." Anna sank into a chair. "What did you say to them?"

"Simply that there is nothing to interest them. That they must not go to the third storey."

"But Natalia, hadn't we better tell them about the attic? Warn them?"

"No, Anna, I don't think so," she replied. "Why disturb their peace of mind?"

"But they may be curious," argued Anna, "and attempt another visit."

Natalia Veronik sighed wearily. "I think not," she said. "There is plenty to occupy them here, and there is no danger during the hours of daylight." Her lip trembled, and she turned away abruptly.

"My poor Helena . . ."

Millie and Kevin met up before supper that evening. Both were bursting to tell what they had found out that afternoon, but the morning's quarrel had left them standing on their dignity.

It was Kevin who spoke first.

"How's your hay fever?" he asked grudgingly.

"Much better, thanks."

There was a pause, then they both said together:

"I've got something to tell you!"

"You first," said Kevin with a grin.

"Well, I went up to the attic this afternoon when Aunt Natalie was asleep, and what do you think? – It's a ballet studio! It must have been Helena's. The floor's wooden, there's a practice bar, and one wall's covered by a huge mirror with a kind of house carved into the glass. It looks like a castle in a fairy tale. There are dozens of books about ballet, some cups and awards, and . . . a wheelchair."

"A wheelchair?"

"Yes. I suppose Helena must have had an accident or something. But, Kevin, it's a perfect place to practise. It's just like Mrs Carson's ballet school at home. I wonder why Aunt Natalie didn't tell us about it? Do you think she'd let me use it if I told her I'm learning to dance?"

Kevin shook his head. "Mum said not to mention it. Are you sure about the mirror in the attic? Because there's something queer about this house."

Millie looked bewildered. "How do you mean?" she asked.

"Well, nothing else here is made of glass."

"But there are mirrors, and windows . . ."

"Yes, but they're not ordinary glass. I can't be absolutely sure, of course, but I'm pretty certain that they're a kind of plastic substitute, or that special reinforced glass they use for car windscreens. All the drinking glasses are Pyrex, there are no glass ornaments, no television . . ."

"I see," said Millie slowly. "Whenever we've brought glass into the house – your watch, my mirror, that bottle this morning – they're smashed."

"Exactly," said Kevin excitedly. "We have to find out more about Helena Veronik, Millie, because I'm sure it all ties in with her – "

They were interrupted by Anna calling them down to supper.

Later in the evening, Aunt Natalie told them amazing stories of her escape to England. Millie and Kevin listened spellbound as she spoke of dangerous incidents, which sounded like television adventures to them, but which were common enough in those desperate years. She talked on, her strangely-accented voice making the tales compelling and real. Her last story was of hiding with Anna in a hayrick, holding their breaths as the tramp of jackboots came nearer, louder . . . then the tremendous relief as the patrol passed by, and the footsteps faded.

"It's just as well we didn't suffer from hay fever, Millie," said Anna, smiling.

"Yes, indeed," chuckled their aunt. "One sneeze and we surely should have been discovered! Well, all this talking has made me tired, and I must go to bed. Goodnight, my dears." She kissed them and left the room.

Kevin turned immediately to Anna. "You and Aunt Natalie have certainly had very exciting lives," he began.

"Too exciting, perhaps, and very sad sometimes," she replied.

"Will you tell us about Helena, Anna?" asked Millie, moving her chair closer. "She would have been our cousin if she had lived, wouldn't she?"

Anna stared at them for a few moments, then seemed to make up her mind.

"Very well. Helena Veronik was a dancer," she began. "The attic room was converted into a studio for her, and she used to spend nearly all her free time there, practising, when she wasn't having lessons. She had a kind of house etched into a mirror up there, and she often used to say that she wished it was real, so that she could live there and dance and dance forever. Well, she was a very gifted dancer, and at sixteen she seemed all set for a brilliant career. Then she fell in love with a worthless man." Anna frowned at the memory. "One day she missed a class to go out driving with him in the country, and he drove too recklessly and crashed the car. He was unharmed, but Helena hurt her back and could no longer walk. Her fiancé deserted her, and she lost everything."

"That's awful. What happened to her then?" Kevin prompted, as Anna paused.

"Helena used to spend hours in her wheelchair, just staring into the mirror. One day she died. It may have been the result of her spinal injury, or perhaps a broken heart. To Natalia, of course, her daughter's memory is sacred, and that is why she does not wish anyone, ever, to visit the studio. That is all you need to know about Helena, my dears."

Anna stood up briskly. "Heavens, look at the time – bed, both of you!"

"Do you think Anna told us everything?" asked Millie, half an hour later. She had crept into her brother's room for a whispered conference as soon as the house was silent. "Because what she said doesn't really explain the broken glass, does it? Unless . . ." She shuddered. "Unless there's some sort of spell on the glass in this house because of the mirror upstairs."

"Oh, it's probably just a coincidence." Kevin's attempted laugh sounded hollow.

"But, Kevin, what if Helena's still – I mean, if she's . . ."

"A ghost?" Kevin frowned. "No, that's impossible. Don't think about it. Even if the house *is* haunted, and I don't believe it is, it can't affect us as long as we don't go near the studio."

"I suppose not." Millie yawned. "Well, I'm going to bed now. Goodnight."

"Goodnight," said Kevin.

Both of them had quite forgotten Millie's dream of the previous evening.

Towards midnight, Kevin woke with a start, and the vague feeling that something was wrong. It was the same sense of unease that he had felt outside the attic door. He tried to ignore it, telling himself that he was imagining things.

Then, very distantly and sweetly, he heard music playing. Tchaikovsky, or some such . . .

Ballet music! In a second, Kevin was out of bed and padding to his sister's room. Millie's bed was empty. As quickly and quietly as he could, Kevin ran along the landing and up the stairs towards the attic. The white door was slightly open, and he could see a phosphorescent-like glow from inside.

Cautiously he pushed open the door and entered the studio. The scene before him rooted him to the ground with amazement. The source of the strange light was the mirror, and the turreted house which was carved upon it seemed lit from within by an unearthly glow. Millie, dressed in her tunic and ballet shoes, was standing motionless, her back to him, one hand resting on the practice bar. She seemed to be staring, hypnotized, at the slender, fragile figure of a ballerina, who was dancing slowly before her to the strains of the faint music.

Time seemed to have run down, like a slow-motion film, and Kevin could not tell if the dancer was outside the mirror or the mirror had become three-dimensional. The ballerina was deathly white, and lustreless as chalk. She drifted and swayed with the lazy grace of sea-ferns, her eyes blank and dark and fixed upon his sister.

As he watched, the dancer glided over to Millie and took her hands, and, stepping backwards, pulled her gently towards the eerie light. What would happen when they reached the house of glass? Would they vanish inside for ever?

Panic-stricken, Kevin tried to shout, but his throat was tight with fear. Millie was moving like a sleep-walker, ever closer to the haunted mirror. Kevin glanced wildly round, and suddenly noticed a crystal trophy on a table near his hand. Without pausing to think, he picked it up and hurled it with all his strength at the glass.

Instantly the glow faded, the music vanished and the mirror shattered silently, jagged fragments and splinters of glass scattering on to the floor soundlessly, as though they were autumn leaves. Then the studio was filled with the sound of a great peaceful sigh, and, dimly in the moonlight, the slight shade sped towards the open window and was gone.

Kevin ran to Millie, who was curled up on the floor, and shook her urgently. She opened her eyes and sat up, yawning and blinking.

"'Morning," she mumbled drowsily. "I had *such* a funny dream." She gazed around vaguely, then stared at Kevin in astonishment. "What are we doing in here? Who broke the mirror?"

"Ssh! Let's get out."

They crept away from the studio, down to Kevin's room, where he told Millie all that had happened.

"It sounds as if I had a narrow escape," said Millie gravely, when he had finished. "I dreamed that Helena was taking me to a kind of fairyland. I didn't know it was all really happening. Why didn't Aunt Natalie warn us?"

"I suppose she thought we were safe enough as long as we didn't go into the studio at night," said Kevin. "She didn't know about your ballet lessons, so she couldn't reckon on Helena feeling a kind of bond with you, and wanting to take you with her into the world that imprisoned her, before the house of glass and the spell that bound her were broken."

Millie shivered. "I suppose we'll have to tell Aunt Natalie in the morning," she said.

"Yes, we will," answered Kevin thoughtfully.

"But I think she will be glad to know that Helena Veronik is free now, and resting peacefully at last."

TEENY-TINY

Anonymous

Once upon a time there was a teeny-tiny woman lived in a teeny-tiny house in a teeny-tiny village. Now, one day this teeny-tiny woman put on her teeny-tiny bonnet, and went out of her teeny-tiny house to take a teeny-tiny walk. And when this teeny-tiny woman had gone a teeny-tiny way she came to a teeny-tiny gate; so the teeny-tiny woman opened the teeny-tiny gate, and went into a teeny-tiny churchyard. And when this teeny-tiny woman had got into the teeny-tiny churchyard she saw a teeny-tiny bone on a teeny-tiny grave, and the teeny-tiny woman said to her teeny-tiny self, "This teeny-tiny bone will make me some teeny-tiny soup for my teeny-tiny supper." So the teeny-tiny woman put the teeny-tiny bone into her teeny-tiny pocket, and went home to her teeny-tiny house.

Now when the teeny-tiny woman got home to her teeny-tiny house she was teeny-tiny tired; so she went up her teeny-tiny stairs to her teeny-tiny bed, and put the teeny-tiny bone into a teeny-tiny cupboard. And when this teeny-tiny woman had been to sleep a teeny-tiny time, she was awakened by a teeny-tiny voice from the teeny-tiny cupboard, which said:

"Give me my bone!"

And this teeny-tiny woman was a teeny-tiny frightened, so she hid her teeny-tiny head under the teeny-tiny clothes and went to sleep again. And when she had been to sleep

296

again a teeny-tiny time, the teeny-tiny voice again cried out from the teeny-tiny cupboard a teeny-tiny louder,

"Give me my bone!"

This made the teeny-tiny woman a teeny-tiny more frightened, so she hid her teeny-tiny head a teeny-tiny further under the teeny-tiny clothes. And when the teeny-tiny woman had been to sleep again a teeny-tiny time, the teeny-tiny voice from the teeny-tiny cupboard said again a teeny-tiny louder,

"GIVE ME MY BONE!"

And this teeny-tiny woman was a teeny-tiny bit more frightened, but she put her teeny-tiny head out of the teeny-tiny clothes, and said in her loudest teeny-tiny voice, "TAKE IT!"

STELLA

by Rosemary Timperley

Robert was used to the Underground journey between home and school. At first he had been rather nervous in the tube train, aware of a shut-in feeling, conscious of the weight of earth above his head; but custom had dulled such irrational fears and now, when he could get a seat, he settled down quite happily to read or catch up on homework which should have been done the night before.

On this particular morning, however, he felt jumpy. The roar of the train and darkness of the tunnels seemed sinister. He had that something-is-going-to happen sensation and couldn't concentrate on the chapter in his history text-book which he was trying to absorb.

He glanced at his fellow-passengers. A girl sitting opposite him caught his eye, leaned forward and asked softly: "Are you feeling all right?" She had a soft, Irish voice, musical.

"Yes," said Robert, feeling foolish. "Why?"

"You've gone so pale. I thought maybe you felt sick."

"No, I – I can't get this wretched history into my head, that's all, and we've got an exam this morning."

"Poor old you," said the girl. "That's enough to make anyone feel like death. I remember the state I got into when I took my nursing exams. Nervous! I was as tense as a fiddle-string."

"Did you pass the exams?" Robert asked.

"I did."

"So you're a nurse now."

"That's right. I'm just on my way to the hospital."

"Do you like nursing?"

"I like the work very much, but it's terribly tiring. Sometimes I feel too exhausted to go on." She was awfully thin, he thought, and she had dark shadows under her eyes.

"You're on your feet all the time, aren't you?" he said.

"That's the physical side of it, but it's emotionally wearing, too. I suppose I care too much about the patients. I've always cared too much about every suffering thing. It's as if I enter into their feelings, and it takes it out of you. A doctor has warned me that I may have to give it up, and then I don't know what I shall do with myself."

"Oh, what a shame!" said Robert, for she looked so sad. "Well, I think you're very brave to – "

He never completed his sentence, for there was a sudden tremendous noise: an explosion which seemed to pierce the ear-drums and deaden the brain. The lights went out. People screamed. There was a sound of glass breaking. Robert felt a stab of pain in his head. The screams around him turned weird, unearthly. Then they faded and all was silent darkness . . . His last thought was: I'm dying. So this is how it feels . . .

Later, he didn't know how much later, Robert opened his eyes. So he hadn't died after all. He was still in the Underground carriage and the girl who'd said she was a nurse was still there. The other passengers had gone and the train was rattling along as if nothing had occurred.

"What was that awful bang?" Robert asked dazedly.

"I don't know," the girl answered.

"I must have fainted or something," said Robert. "I didn't even see the other passengers get out."

"Nor did I," said the girl, and laughed. "Anyway, we've got the carriage to ourselves now, which is rather nice." She seemed more lively than before and quite unperturbed, but Robert was desperately uneasy. He had never known the morning train to empty out like this. Was it possible that the others had been told to get out, and he and the girl hadn't heard because they were unconscious and no one had bothered about them?

"I thought I heard the windows breaking, too," he said, "but they aren't even cracked. Anyway, the lights are on again – " He stopped. He was staring at the colour of the seats. Instead of being brownish with a dark pattern, they were plain green. A very fresh, lovely green. Like new grass. But he was in no mood to be consoled by a pretty colour.

"We're in a different train!" he cried.

The girl looked round. "So we are. A better one, too."

"Never mind about better – where's it taking us?"

They looked out of the windows but there was only the blackness of tunnel walls to be seen.

"Don't worry. We'll know where we are when we reach a station," said the girl. The stations on the line were not very far apart and they should reach the next one at any moment.

Except that they didn't. The train went on and on, into the dark, as if this were a line without stations.

"It's not only a different train, it's a different line," Robert pointed out.

"Then when we get to the end of the line, you can go back," the girl said soothingly. "Relax, my dear. When there's nothing you can do about a situation, accept it and conserve your strength. Don't get worked up."

"My head hurts!"

"Yes. Let me try to make it better. Look, there's a green carpet on the floor. It's a lovely train. You lie on the floor, and I'll sit down and lean against a seat, then you can put your head in my lap. Let's pretend you're one of my patients and I'm going to look after you till you're well again."

Robert felt so rotten that he obeyed her. Soon he was lying on the green carpet, his head in her lap, and he felt her hands on his forehead. He couldn't tell what she was doing, but the pain receded.

"Thank you," he said. "It's not throbbing so badly now. Are *you* feeling all right?"

"Me? I feel marvellous. All my tiredness has gone."

"Aren't you frightened? We don't know where we're going."

"No one ever really knows where he is going," she said. "People think they do sometimes, but they're usually wrong."

"What's your name?" he asked her now.

"Stella. And yours?"

"Robert. That's pretty – 'Stella'. It means 'star', doesn't it?" He looked up into her face as she smiled down at him. "You're a super nurse, Stella, and you're shining like a star. There's a sort of glow around you. Like an angel in a picture. Do you know, Stella, I think this must be a dream."

"No, because we're both in it."

"Maybe we're not – maybe you're part of my dream."

"Well! Talk about the arrogance of the male."

"Sorry." Robert chuckled and Stella laughed outright.

"Neither of us is dreaming," she said. "This is real and happening. The difference between us is that I accept without question and you're still struggling because your questions aren't answered."

"I wish we could reach a station, that's all," he sighed – and suddenly the train burst out of the tunnel and into the open. The scenery around them was breathtaking.

Purple mountains rose on either side of the track. Silver waterfalls glittered in bright sunshine. Emerald green fields lay at the foot of the hills. Birds were singing.

The train stopped against a green bank. The doors opened.

Robert forgot all about his headache and sprang to his feet.

"Oh, how beautiful!" he said. "I don't care where we are. I'm glad we came. Let's get out and walk right across the fields, and climb the tallest mountain – " He turned to Stella. She had gone.

Then he saw that she had already alighted from the train and was moving swiftly over the grass. "Hey, wait for me!" he called. She turned and waved, but didn't wait.

He rushed to the nearest door – but already it was beginning to close, in that inexorable way that tube train doors do close. He struggled to hold it open, but it was useless. He was trapped again. The train was already beginning to move back towards the tunnel, back into the dark . . .

He beat his fists against the glass. "Stella! Stella!" he cried. "Oh, Stella . . ."

"This one's coming round," said a voice. "A near thing. I thought he was a gonner when we found him."

"You ambulance men are so pessimistic," said a woman's voice.

And Robert found himself lying on a trolley with a red blanket draped over him. A woman in a nurse's cap was looking down at him. A nurse – but not *his* nurse. "Where's Stella gone?" he asked.

"Who's Stella? A friend you were travelling with?"

"Yes. She got out at the end of the line – she was going towards the hills – it was so beautiful – "

A man in a white coat replaced the nurse. "Let's have a look at that head. Hello, old boy. Lie still. I'm a doctor." Hands on his head. Gentle. But not like Stella's hands. "Mmm. Not as bad as it might be. I wonder what stopped the bleeding."

"Stella did, I expect," said Robert. "She said she'd make it better."

But the doctor wasn't listening. "Wheel him along to X-ray, please, Nurse. Now, who's next?"

The trolley moved. Robert lay staring at a series of different ceilings. And after that it was all go: X-ray room, being heaved on and off a couch, back on the trolley, operating theatre, the doctor again, an injection in his head so the wound could be sewn up without his feeling pain, conversation between the doctor and two nurses, all very casual – running down hospital food mostly: "The staff canteen gets worse and worse," and so on. Then there was another trolley-ride and he was put to bed in a ward, given a white tablet with a glass of water, and told to lie down and sleep. The white pill filled his head with fluffy white clouds. Robert slept.

He dreamed of the purple mountains at the end of the line. He dreamed that he saw Stella, tireless, happy, glowing, climbing the highest mountain, getting right to the top, and then stretching out her arms towards the sun and the sky – and taking off – like a bird in flight – soaring and singing – a white bird making a journey to a star – but she *was* a star – Stella –

He woke up. "Stella – "

"It's me, darling." His mother was there.

"Oh, Mum!" Arms around him. Tears on his cheeks. His mother's tears. He'd never seen her cry before. "Don't cry, I'm all right," he said. "Stella made me all right first, then the doctor sewed me up. I'm fine. And we went on the strangest journey. Through miles of dark tunnels, then into the open, and the mountains – "

"You've been dreaming," said his mother.

"Just now, I have, but before then, I wasn't. I didn't dream what happened in the train. You ask Stella, when she comes back."

"Darling, who is this Stella you keep talking about?"

"A nurse I met on the train. We stayed together after the big bang. Oh – what *was* that bang? What hit me on the head?"

"Time for another little pill," said a voice in uniform.

And his mother gave him a kiss and went away. He slept again.

Next day he was allowed to go home as long as he promised to take things easy. Only then did he find out, from his mother, what had happened in the train. Some maniac had planted a small bomb in the carriage. When it went off, there were moments of chaos. People had been injured by falling objects and flying glass. The train had stopped, officials had made their way to the damaged carriage and, as the explosion had occurred near a station, those who had only minor injuries had been able to walk the little way along the line and be taken straight to hospital. Robert had been knocked unconscious by something falling on his head, so he had been carried out by ambulance men.

"Quite a mercy that you were knocked out, really, darling," said his mother, "for the next thing you knew, after the big bang, was that you were safe in hospital, being looked after."

"But Stella looked after me first," said Robert, "and we went to the end of the line together – a different line – a different train."

"No, Robert. That was a dream you had when you were unconscious."

"It wasn't a dream," he insisted, "because Stella and I were both in it. She pointed that out to me. People don't have the same dream together. It's impossible. If a thing happens to two people at once, it's really happening. Stella went for a walk in the countryside at the end of the line. She'll have caught a train back by now, whatever that train was. I *did* have a dream in which she turned into a bird and flew away from the top of the mountain – that *was* a dream – and I knew it when I woke up. It was quite different from the real part."

"All right, darling," said his mother. "Forget about it now, anyway. It's over."

"Forget it? I'll never forget Stella! I'm going to find her again. I know her first name, and she's a nurse, so I'll be able to get in touch with her if I try. She was so tired and sad before the big bang, but afterwards she was lively and happy and – Oh, I loved her! And she looked after me. She may even have saved my life. The doctor wondered what had stopped the bleeding when he first examined me. Well, Stella did that."

His mother said nothing. She was looking evasive, half-guilty.

"You're keeping something from me," said Robert.

"No – "

"You are. What is it? Mum – did – did anyone die in the train?"

"Yes. One person. Oh, all right, Robert, I'll tell you. When the ambulance men picked you up, you were lying on the floor with your head in a girl's lap. And – darling, you mustn't let this upset you – but the girl was dead. She'd been killed outright in the explosion. Her name was Stella O'Brien. She was a nurse."

Robert stared ahead of him, speechless. His mother brought him a newspaper. "There's a full account of the incident here. Read it for yourself, love. Sorry I tried to hide it. Not very honest of me."

"That's all right," Robert murmured, and he read the paper.

What his mother had said was true.

"I know what happened now," he told her. "I must have almost died, too. I went part of the way with her.

305

Then she got out at the end of the line, but I came back. She *said* I'd be going back. She knew. It's true," he insisted. "Otherwise how could I possibly have known her name? She didn't tell me until long after the big bang that her name was Stella."

He swallowed tears. "I mustn't cry," he said. "She wasn't happy here – her work was too much for her. But she's happy now."

"'Whom the gods love, die young,'" his mother said unexpectedly.

"Yes," said Robert, and smiled.

GIBSON'S

by Ann Pilling

Our Aunt Mildred is the most practical person I know, and the least superstitious. She always walks under ladders, often wears green, and her city flat was number Thirteen. So the whole family was amused when she retired from teaching and bought a house on the end of a country village. The place she found had been up for sale for over a year, and she got it cheap, because nobody else would buy it.

"Well, I'm glad nobody *did*," she said, showing us the estate agent's details. "It's going to take every penny I've got as it is. Houses in those villages are always expensive. It's so convenient for Birmingham. Not that I'll want to go back there, once I've settled in."

She was delighted. My little sister Josie looked at some photographs of the cottage while I read the details. It was built of stone and was very small: two rooms downstairs and two above, with a tiny box-room Aunt Mildred was planning to "improve". There was quite a bit of land with it. She had never had a garden before.

We could just make out a date, 1620, carved over the door. The cottage had an odd name, too: *Gibson's*.

"I expect you and David think it should be called something like *Honeysuckle Cottage*," my aunt said, smiling at Josie. "No, I like *Gibson's*. There's no nonsense about it. Now, when are you coming to stay?"

She didn't need to ask twice. We'd never been able to stay in her small flat, though she'd often visited us. She is actually our great-aunt, and my godmother, and very

307

special. And she was as good as her word. Our phone rang before she'd been in her new house a week, and Aunt Mildred was soon arranging with my mother for Josie and me to stay with her during our October half-term holiday.

Gibson's was much better than the agent's description. Somehow, those typed leaflets never give you a sense of how a place *feels*. Perhaps it is because we have always lived in a modern house that I find old ones so fascinating, but the minute I walked into Aunt Mildred's I became very excited.

It smelt old. Every door, window, and floor-board creaked and rattled, and nothing was at right angles, or fitted properly. The beams in the living-room were black with age and spiked with rusty old hooks. There was even a well in the garden, and it worked. On our first night Aunt Mildred made a log fire in the old inglenook, and we sat around eating toast and staring into the flames.

"I'm never going back home, Auntie," my sister said dreamily. "I'm going to live here, with you."

We all laughed. Josie was always saying things like that.

"Think of all those silly people who decided not to buy it," Aunt Mildred said, buttering more toast. "Lucky old me. They must have been mad."

And I agreed with her; they must have been.

When we went outside after breakfast on our first morning, there was an old man digging near the well. He was called Joe Glover, and he was helping Aunt Mildred with the garden. It was a large plot, on three sides of the house, with grass and flowerbeds, and old fruit-trees straggling up a hill. Everything was very overgrown and weedy.

"It's been empty so long, y'see," the old man said. "Things've got a bit out of hand, like. But we'll soon sort

308

it out. Nice old place this is – it just needs a bit of paint. You interested in old things, are you?"

We nodded. "Well, you come down the village this afternoon. Vine Cottage I live in, next to the pub. I'll show you some old things, things I've dug up. You come this afternoon, after I've had me bit of dinner."

In Joe Glover's shed was a big wooden box. He opened it and began to arrange the contents carefully on his workbench. There were several large copper coins, as thick as three old pennies stuck together, two daggers without handles but with patterns delicately engraved along the blades, and a lump of black leather that looked as if it might once have been a shoe.

Just before he closed the box the old man reached down inside and drew something out very carefully. He blew the dust off, then put it on the bench very gently. It was a human skull.

"*Ugh*!" Josie said. "Did you dig that up in Aunt Mildred's garden?"

"Oh, *no*," he replied with a grin. "There's nothing like that round *Gibson's*. No, I found these years ago, on the hill, when I was a boy."

"Which hill?" asked Josie. I knew she was frightened. She didn't like the skull.

"Edgehill. There was a great battle there, hundreds of years ago. And people still find things now and then, in the fields, when the earth's been turned over: bits of armour and knife-heads, bones, too – the farmers, like, y'know. Most of it's in the museums now, but there's still finds."

Of *course*, I was thinking. *Edgehill*. It was the first big battle of the Civil War. I remembered the crossed swords sign on the map, when we were trying to locate Aunt Mildred's cottage, and Dad explaining to Josie about the Cavaliers and the Roundheads. We had driven up the hill yesterday, in Aunt Mildred's old Mini, along a steep lane that wound round and up, through the trees, on to a long ridge which we'd seen miles back, from the flat fields below. She'd stopped at the top so we could get out and look at the view.

"Your auntie'll tell you all about King Charles and the Battle of Edgehill. She's a school mistress, isn't she? I expect she'll know a bit about it."

She should do, I thought. She was a history teacher for nearly forty years.

Aunt Mildred's front door opened straight out on to a narrow road. If you turned right you walked down past the church and eventually reached the first cottages of the village. Left, the road climbed up a hill, petering out after a mile or so in a rough track. But if you carried on walking, along a kind of sunken lane, you came out on to Edgehill itself.

Aunt Mildred didn't waste time sitting down for meals, not when the sun was shining. "Come on," she said when we got back from Joe Glover's, "let's take our tea with us and go for a walk." We filled a bag with buns, apples and chocolate, and set off up the lane. The high, uncut hedges met over our heads, making a green, arched tunnel. Josie didn't like it much. It was too gloomy. She held on to Aunt Mildred's hand all the way.

From the top of Edgehill we could see for miles. The grassy slopes dropped sharply away under our feet, flattening out at last into a patchwork of fields which unfolded endlessly into the distance, becoming a green-gold blur, speared with the odd church tower. It was so quiet. There was only the buzz of a car on the main road down below, and the birdsong all around us, in the hedge.

"Hard to believe they all rushed together down there,

hacking one another to death," Aunt Mildred said, looking out over the lush Warwickshire plain. "Some of them were only boys, too."

"Who won?" I asked her. "The king's men, or the Roundheads?"

"They both claimed victory. Some of the dead are buried in the villages round here."

"Are there any in *your* village?" said Josie.

"I don't know. We must go and have a look."

As we walked back we told Aunt Mildred about Joe Glover's collection. She laughed. "I suppose he's told you all about his ghostly army, too? He bores the pants off everybody with that story."

"No, he hasn't. What army?"

"Well, on the anniversary of the battle people claim to have seen figures moving about on Edgehill, shadowy horsemen and foot-soldiers, fighting on the plain down there. They've heard noises, too."

"What sort of noises?"

"Oh, the sounds of battle, swords clashing together, cannons, people getting their arms and legs chopped off," she ended cheerfully.

"You don't really believe in it, do you Auntie?" Josie said, round-eyed.

"Not a word. It's just a load of rubbish. But it makes a good story."

After supper she found me sitting by the big bookcase on the landing.

"I know what you're looking for, David, and the answer's October 23rd, 1642. I read it all up the week I moved in."

"That's the date of the battle, is it?"

She nodded.

After a minute I said: 'But Aunt Mildred, that's this week! It's tomorrow, in fact."

311

"Oh, I know *that*. And there's just one thing. If you decide to go ghost-spotting put an extra vest on. I don't want your mother after me if you get flu."

But of course I didn't go. It was wet the next day, and by evening the drizzle had become a heavy downpour. I didn't fancy tramping up that sunken lane all on my own, in the dark. Anyway, I wasn't very interested in ghosts. As Aunt Mildred said, it was just a good story.

That night Josie woke up screaming. I opened my eyes and heard the clock downstairs strike two, then I heard her cry out. After the second cry her voice became a real shriek. By the time I got to the door of the box-room Aunt Mildred was there, sitting on the bed, with her arms round her.

"I can't *breathe*!" Josie was screaming. "I just can't *breathe*! Let me get to the window. Give me some air!"

There was no window in the room she'd been sleeping in. It was just a box-room off the landing. She'd chosen it because it had pretty wallpaper and a fairy-tale latch on the door. Aunt Mildred was waiting for the builders to come and knock a window in. There was only a tiny sky-light, and that wasn't made to open.

She held Josie very tight. "Just a nightmare," she was saying. "There's plenty of air, dear – look, the door's wide open. Now why don't you lie down again?" But Josie was still sobbing.

I switched the light on and looked at her. Her face was very white, and her hair was plastered to her head in damp curls. She was shaking violently.

"Let her stand by the landing window, Aunt Mildred. It's so stuffy in here," I said.

In seconds she was calmer. The cold night air flowed in over us, and we all shivered slightly. Josie's eyes were closing; she was falling back against Aunt Mildred and starting to breathe quite heavily.

"She's asleep again," my aunt said quietly. "Do you think, between us, we could carry her into my bedroom? She can sleep with me tonight."

Josie is quite small for eight. We lifted her quite easily and tucked her up in Aunt Mildred's bed. Five minutes later the house was quiet again. I whispered goodnight and shut my aunt's door. But I felt thoroughly awake now. What do you do, in the middle of the night, when you feel like running a hundred-metre sprint?

I could always read till I felt sleepy. I crept over to the landing bookcase, then noticed we'd left the window wide open. As I leaned out to shut it I glanced down into the garden. By the well there was a dark shape, standing out a foot or so from the old wall, in soft earth, where Joe Glover had pulled some bushes out the day before.

For a minute I thought it was a tree. Then it lifted its arms away from its sides. I wanted to shut the window, but my hand froze on the sill. A small wind sent leaves scurrying across the ragged grass, driving cloud off the moon's face, lighting up the garden. It plucked at the long cloak the figure was draped in, then moulded it round her.

I knew it was a woman because I heard her voice, a long, lamenting cry of great bitterness that echoed against the house. Surely I was dreaming? Ghosts do not cry out, nor do they communicate with those who see them. They live in another time from ours, in another world, and those worlds pass each other but never join.

I fastened the window and turned away from the garden, but the terrible crying went on, and as I looked out again, willing the woman to turn into an innocent tree, I saw that she was lifting up her arms to me and

313

tossing her draped head from side to side, voicing that deep wild cry of utter desolation.

I lay in bed with the light on, all night, and when I fell at last into a broken, uneasy sleep I dreamed about Aunt Mildred charging down Edgehill on a great black horse, and about Joe Glover, trying to sell that skull to an estate agent in Banbury.

THE DOLL

by Terry Tapp

About a hundred years ago, such a doll would have been quite commonplace; it would have been held in loving arms, cuddled and cherished. But Anna simply turned her nose up at it as she cautiously pulled back the faded dress between forefinger and thumb to examine the limbs and torso. The doll was filthy.

She decided to throw it away. After all, what was the use of a doll whose eyes had fallen back into her hollow, china head? The hair had been raggedly hacked short and the face of the doll was deathly waxen.

Yes, she would throw the doll away.

Rubbing her hands on her jeans, Anna delved into the cardboard box to see what other things were in there. When her father had bought the wardrobe at the house auction, he had not realized that the shabby cardboard box was inside it, and Anna was having a splendid time exploring the contents and sorting them out.

There were some lead soldiers, a book entitled "Nature's Window", and a carefully folded Union Jack. Some seed catalogues, a bundle of papers and letters and some faded, sepia photographs. One of the photographs was of a young girl, about Anna's age, holding a very pretty doll. Anna looked from the photograph to the twisted, broken doll which lay face down on the carpet beside her. There was no doubt about it, the girl was holding the same doll.

"One would never think that you used to look like that," Anna said to the doll, holding the photograph

315

closer to try to distinguish if the doll was still wearing the same dress. When she looked down at the doll again, it was lying on its back.

With a shrug, Anna turned her attention to the bundle of letters. Many of them were business letters, written on thick paper in a black, powdered ink which had long since faded. The writing was, on most of the letters, beautiful copperplate hand, and Anna resolved that she would pay more attention to her own writing in future. One of the letters had been torn into small pieces. Anna, who was very fond of jigsaw puzzles, idly pieced it together.

It proved to be an easy task and, before she realized it, she was reading the letter, her lips moving with each word.

> Fairlea Boarding School,
> Copper Beech Drive,
> Abbotsteignton,
> Devonshire.
> 27th February, 1898.

Dearest Mama,

I hate this place and live only for the day when I am allowed to return to you again.

Why did you send me away? I did nothing wrong, and it is not true what you say about the doll. Dearest Bess was my greatest companion, and I am so sad to be separated from her.

Mama, will you wrap her carefully for me and put her on the next coach to Abbotsteignton? I miss her so when I am alone at night, in my darkling bed. I cry for her.

Bess is not – could not possibly be – an evil doll, as you suggest. She did not set fire to my bedroom that night and neither did I. She is not an evil doll. How could she be?

This is a cruel and cold place to which you have sent me, and the teachers rule us by terror. They have been told that I purposely set fire to my own bedroom and they watch me day and night.

We are made to scrub the rough flagstones until our knuckles are raw, and the Matron beats us at breakfast without favour, even when our behaviour has been exemplary.

I will write again before the week is out. Please, if you have any affection left for me, believe me when I tell you that I would not do such a thing. I love my home, my dearest Bess and, above all you, Mama.

Ever your obedient and loving daughter,

Anna

"Same name as mine," Anna said aloud. "How strange."

She read the letter again and glanced over at the perpetual calendar which hung on her bedroom wall. It was February 27th.

"Same name and same date," she mused. "Curiouser and curiouser."

The girl in the photograph, although smiling, had a sad, rather resigned look about her, and she was holding the doll, examining the nape of her neck. Luxuriant hair fell around the shoulders of the doll.

"Why did she cut your hair, I wonder?" Anna said, gathering up the loose-jointed doll. "Maybe there was a squeaker, or something in the head."

She examined the nape of the doll's neck.

"*Heubach. Koppelsdorf. Three-twenty. Germany.*" Anna read aloud. There was no sign of a squeaker.

If Anna had sent that letter, she reasoned, her mother would have received it. And as the letter and the doll were in the same cardboard box, obviously her mother had not sent Bess. How sad. Why, anyway, would Anna's mother have blamed a doll for setting light to a room? It sounded very much as if it were the mother, and not the daughter, who deserved punishment.

"Anna? What are you doing up there?" Anna's mother called. The voice cut through the stillness of the bedroom, making Anna jump.

"Nothing, Mum," she called back, relieved that she, at least did not have such a cruel parent as the other Anna.

"Then come downstairs and do nothing," her mother replied. "It's cold up there without the heating on."

"I'm not cold," Anna said.

"Well come down anyway. I'm just making a hot drink."

"Coming," Anna called, snatching up the photograph and the doll. Mother was right – it was getting a bit chilly, and Anna certainly didn't want to catch a cold. Besides, she could show the letter and photograph to her mother.

Perhaps, she thought, Bess could be made to look pretty again. It seemed rather heartless to throw the doll away after reading that letter. Bess had meant a lot to the other Anna. She pushed the loose-limbed doll on to her toyshelf and stood back to look at it. A new wig, some pretty clothes and a lick of paint would make all the difference. And the eyes could be put back again. That would certainly improve her appearance. Anna did not like the way the dark, lifeless sockets seemed to stare at her. It gave the doll a menacing air . . .

She turned to leave the bedroom and, just as she was closing the door, she heard a loud thump. Something had fallen down.

"Oh, bother!" she sighed, going back into the room to see what it was that had fallen.

Lying in the firegrate, its head at a peculiar angle, the doll looked quite pathetic. Anna picked it up and noticed that the third finger on the left hand had snapped off. She picked up the plaster stump of finger and placed it beside the doll.

"Never mind, Bess," she said, grinning. "That's the least of your troubles. We can soon glue the finger on."

Making sure that, this time, Bess would not fall again, Anna carefully closed the bedroom door and ran downstairs to the kitchen.

It certainly was much warmer in the cosy kitchen, and on the table there was a steaming mug of hot chocolate.

"Thanks, Mum." Anna took the drink, sipped it and felt the warmth in her hands. How nice it was to live in modern times – not like the other Anna.

"Did you find anything interesting in the box?" Anna's mother asked as she expertly peeled some apples.

"Nothing much," Anna replied, helping herself to a custard cream biscuit from the tin. "I haven't finished exploring it yet."

"You shouldn't be eating so near to dinnertime," her mother said. "Mind you just have the one biscuit, or you'll be leaving your dinner."

Anna laughed. "I won't, you know. I'm famished."

The smell of peeled apples, spices and roasting meat filled the kitchen, making Anna feel almost guilty that she was enjoying herself. It didn't seem right, somehow, when one thought of the other Anna.

"What have you got there?" Anna's mother asked as she placed the slices of apple in a baking dish.

"Just an old photograph," Anna said, picking it up and casually looking at it.

"Oh, let me see. I love looking at old pictures."

Just as Anna was about to hand over the photograph, she noticed something very peculiar. The doll in the photograph had a finger missing. The third finger on the left hand . . .

"Let me see it, then." Anna's mother held out her hand impatiently.

Still Anna stared at the picture.

"Whatever is the matter with you, child? You've gone as pale as a sheet."

"The doll," Anna said weakly. "The doll in the picture has a finger missing."

"Much-loved dolls often do have bits missing," Anna's mother replied absently.

"But you don't understand, Mum!" Anna cried. "The doll in the picture is the same one I found in the cardboard box."

"There is nothing surprising about that," came the reply. "The doll and the photograph could well have been kept together, just like all the odds and ends we keep in our souvenirs case in the attic."

Anna's mother took the photograph and smiled. "My, she is a pretty girl. Not unlike you, Anna."

"You still don't understand!" said Anna impatiently. "I've just broken the finger off that doll. I did it just now, after you had called me. How could it be shown as broken in the photograph if I've only just broken it this minute?"

"Probably a different finger," her mother suggested. "Or, maybe it had been broken off before and was just held on by glue."

"No, it was a fresh break," Anna insisted. "The plaster was pure white and powdery."

"It stands to reason," Anna's mother said patiently, "that no matter what happens to the doll, the photograph will always remain the same. And if the finger was broken in the photograph, it certainly must have been broken before you did it."

Anna thought, perhaps, her mother must be right. She had not closely examined the photograph the first time, and it was possible that she had not noticed the fingers. Yes, that must be the answer.

"Is that all there is wrong with the doll?" Anna's mother asked. "Just a broken finger?"

"Good gracious no. The hair has been cut short, the legs and arms are all floppy and the eyes have fallen back into the head."

"Euh!" Anna's mother exclaimed.

"Do you think Dad could repair her?"

"If she's got all those things wrong with her, I doubt if it would be worthwhile, Anna. And talking about your father, look at the time. He'll be home soon and the dinner is way behind. Drink your chocolate up, dear, and then go and wash your hands."

"Do you think Dad could stick a new wig on Bess?"

"Bess?"

"The doll. She's called Bess. Do you think Dad could do it?"

"I expect he could, dear. Now do hurry up with that drink. When you've washed your hands, come down quickly and help me lay the table for dinner."

Sipping back the last frothy remains of her chocolate, Anna rinsed the mug under the tap and left it on the draining board.

"Take the photograph with you and bring down a fresh tea towel when you come," Anna's mother said as she placed the thin layer of pastry over the apple pie and sliced around the edges.

"Right," Anna said. "Can I pinch the pastry around the edge of the pie when I come down?"

"There won't be time for that. I'm late enough as it is."

321

Anna's mother used a fork to decorate the edges of the pie and quickly glazed the top with her pastry brush. "Don't stand there dreaming, now. Hurry up."

Taking the stairs two at a time, Anna dashed quickly into her bedroom and threw the photograph on to her bed. She was just about to leave again when something made her stop. Puzzled at first, she couldn't think what it was . . .

The room was colder, but maybe it was because she had just come from the warm kitchen. The doll was still on the shelf where Anna had left her. The finger was broken, and the plaster stump . . . the plaster stump of finger had a red tinge to it. Anna examined the doll's left hand.

It was bleeding!

Thinking, perhaps, she might have nicked her finger while handling the doll, she examined her own hands to see if there was any blood on them. Dolls don't bleed, she thought.

There was no blood, or marks of any kind, on Anna's hands.

She shivered as she stared at the doll and the thick, red liquid which had oozed from the stump of finger. And suddenly she was afraid.

Was it imagination, or had the hair grown an inch or two longer? She stepped closer to examine the curling locks of hair that now just touched the shoulders of the doll.

Bess sat on the shelf, her lifeless, cavernous sockets staring intensely at Anna. Almost hypnotized, Anna stared back at the horrific sight. An evil smile curled around the doll's mouth, and Anna felt that she was on the brink . . . the very brink . . .

"Anna! Do hurry up, child. I need your help down here."

"Coming, Mum!" Anna yelled back, almost in relief. Somehow, her mother's voice had cut through the menacing atmosphere and dragged her back to reality. Imagination. Of course it was imagination. Dad had always told her that she had too vivid an imagination, and he was right. The letter had started it all and she had frightened herself. After dinner, she would come back to the bedroom and try to work out how the end of Bess's finger had become red. There must be a sensible, logical answer.

One thing was certain. It wasn't blood. Dolls don't bleed. Anna grinned at the thought, thinking how silly she had been. But, all the same, she did make a mental note of the exact length of Bess's hair before she left the bedroom. It wouldn't be any longer, or shorter when she returned to the room, and she would laugh at her fears.

"Did you remember to wash your hands?" her mother asked as she burst into the kitchen.

"They're not dirty," Anna replied.

"Of course they're dirty after you've been handling all that rubbish from the auction," Anna's mother said. "What have you been doing up there? Now, for goodness' sake go up and wash your hands at once so that you can help me serve the dinner. I've had to lay the table by myself as it is."

"Sorry, Mum," Anna said.

"And don't forget the tea cloth."

"I won't," Anna called back. "What's for dinner?"

"Beef."

"Super!" Anna said, dashing from the kitchen.

The dinner was, indeed, 'super', and Anna hardly spoke a word to her father until her plate was clean.

"What's for sweet?' she asked eagerly. "Are we having that apple pie?"

"Yes, we are," Anna's mother replied. "And you can wait until we have all finished our meal. I don't know how you manage to wolf your food down so quickly. It isn't ladylike, you know."

"What have you been up to this morning?" Anna's father asked as he tackled the last potato on his plate.

"I've been sorting out that box of junk that came with the wardrobe."

"Find any fivers?"

"No, but there were some lead soldiers, an old-fashioned doll called Bess and some books," Anna told him.

"Keep the lead soldiers," her father advised. "They're becoming collectors' pieces now. What condition are they in?"

"I'll show you," Anna said.

"After dinner," her mother called.

But she was too late. Anna had jumped up from the table and was already halfway up the stairs. It had not been the thought of showing her father the lead soldiers which had made her run so eagerly to her room. It was the doll. All through dinner, the thought of the doll had intruded on her and, now that her father was home, she felt secure and confident. She would have another look at the doll and all her silly notions would disappear.

The room was still very cold, and Anna could not, at first, bring herself to look at the doll. She cast her eyes towards the bed, saw the photograph and picked it up. Slowly, she lifted her eyes to met the black, mysterious holes in the doll's head.

Bess was staring at her . . . a blind, penetrating stare.

How could the doll stare when it had no eyes? Anna went over slowly. The lips were curled in a leer, and the eyes were filled with black, deep malevolence. Suddenly, Anna wondered why she had picked up the photograph. She had come to her room to collect the lead soldiers, and somehow . . . somehow she had, instead, picked up the photograph. Bess seemed to be holding out her hand

– her bloodstained left hand – as if reaching for the photograph.

How ridiculous, Anna thought. Then, as she turned away, she noticed something out of the corner of her eye. A faint whisp of smoke was curling up from her bed. Instantly, she ran over to the bed and picked up the pile of letters. The fragments of the pieced-together letter fell out. And they were on fire!

Without thinking, Anna instantly dropped them on to the carpet and stamped out the flames. As she frantically stamped at the tongues of licking fire, the room seemed to fill with a bubbling laughter. She looked across at Bess.

Eyes! Bess had eyes! Laughing, leering eyes. An evil smile stretched across the doll's face, the lips stretched back over bared teeth. Chuckling and laughing . . . laughing . . . The room resonated with the sounds of hysterical laughter.

Smoke filled the tiny room and Anna choked as she ran to the window.

"Ha-ha-ha-ha!"

"You did it!" Anna screamed at the doll. "You set the letter on fire. You probably set the other Anna's bedroom on fire, too. It was you all the time!"

"Ha-ha-ha-ha!"

"Stop it!"

"Ha-ha-ha!" the doll roared with laughter.

"Stop it! Stop it!" Anna screamed helplessly.

"Hurry up, Anna. Your sweet is on the table and it's getting cold." Anna's father called up the stairs.

"Ha-ha-ha-ha!"

"Stop it. Daddy! Come up here quickly!"

"Anna?"

She could hear his footsteps pounding up the stairs.

"Anna? What's the matter? What's wrong?"

Jerkily, the doll raised its hands to reveal that all the

fingers were now intact again. The room vibrated with the dreadful sound of echoing laughter, and the eyes fell back into the hollow china head with a dull "clunk" just as the bedroom door burst open.

Anna screamed and screamed.

Her screams sliced through the air like the raw edge of sharp steel, freezing Anna with their intensity.

"Whatever is it?" Anna's father gripped her by the shoulders and shook her.

And Bess sat on the shelf.

"What is it, Anna?"

The doll sat on the shelf.

Innocently.

"Oh . . . Daddy," Anna choked.

"What on earth was all the screaming for?" Anna's mother came into the room.

"I don't know," her father said. "She hasn't told me yet."

"Look at her face. She's petrified."

"The . . . the doll . . ." Anna blurted out.

"The doll made you scream?" her father asked. "Well, I don't wonder at it. I must say, it looks pretty terrifying, just sitting there without any eyes. Gives me the shivers."

"It set light to the letter," Anna sobbed.

"Where?"

"There . . . on the carpet by the bed."

"Where? I can't see anything."

It was true. The carpet was quite clean, and there were no ash marks on it at all. When Anna looked around the room, she saw that the smoke had disappeared.

"What are you doing with your window wide open?" her mother asked. "No wonder it feels so cold in here."

Desperately, Anna wanted to tell them about Bess . . . how the doll had set light to the other Anna's bedroom all those years ago and how she had tried the same thing

326

in her own room. But she realized it would all sound too silly. They would think she was making it up. The finger was back on the doll. The ashes of the letter had disappeared and the room was no longer filled with smoke.

But the hair! The hair had grown even longer!

"Look at her hair," Anna said excitedly. At last she had positive proof that she could show. "The doll's hair has grown since I went down to dinner!"

"What is she saying?" her father asked.

"She says that the doll's hair has grown." Her mother smiled at the thought.

"Codswallop!" her father said, laughing. "You're trying to frighten yourself, child."

"I'm not!" Anna stamped her foot angrily. "The hair *has* grown longer, hasn't it, Mum?"

"How would I know?" Anna's mother replied pointedly. "This is the first time I've seen the doll."

Anna hadn't thought of that. Of course, her mother had only seen the photograph of Bess.

"The photograph!" Anna cried. "You do, at least, remember that the doll in the photograph had a finger broken off?"

"Yes."

"Then let's have a look at the photograph now," Anna said. She was certain that the photograph would have changed, to show a mended hand, and maybe that would convince everyone that she was telling the truth.

"Where is the photograph?" Anna's father said.

"On my bed. No . . . I picked it up when I came to get the toy soldiers. I picked it up and went over to Bess, and . . ." She paused. What had she done then? "I must have dropped it on the floor," she said desperately. "It must be somewhere around here."

"Look for it after dinner," Anna's mother said

impatiently. "Our sweets are on the table and they must be stone cold by now."

"But it was right here, Mum." Anna was almost in tears.

"After dinner," her father said firmly. "And you can have a jolly good sort out in here. Your bedroom is an absolute tip. I'm having a bonfire in the garden this afternoon, and you can bring down all your rubbish to burn."

"Nobody believes me," Anna said miserably. "I was telling the truth, Mum – honestly."

"I find that very hard to believe," her mother answered coldly. "You told me that the doll's hair had been hacked short, but look at her."

Long, flowing hair curled around Bess's shoulders, sweeping down, down, down to her waist.

"But I . . ."

"Now don't make things worse by arguing, Anna," her mother said. "You told me that a finger had broken off and it has not. You said that her hair had been cut and it certainly has not. And now you make up some story about the photograph."

"When I was your age," Anna's father said sternly, "I would have had my mouth washed out with soap and water if I told lies. Now let's go downstairs and finish our dinner."

There was nothing Anna could say. She could see that Bess had trapped her, and she knew exactly how exasperated the other Anna must have felt all those years ago.

Somehow, the apple pie did not taste very nice, and Anna had great difficulty in swallowing it. Her mother ate in silence, and she knew that the best thing she could do was remain absolutely quiet until after the meal was finished.

She finished the pie, refusing a second helping and waited until she was given permission to leave the table.

"Straight up to your bedroom, young lady," her father said. "Your cupboards are full of rubbish. I don't know why you keep it all."

Dutifully, Anna made her way up to her room.

"And don't make another mess while you're doing it," her mother called after her. "I know your tidy-ups, and they sometimes make a worse mess than before you started."

"I'll take care of it," she called back, her mouth set in a grim line. She now knew what she must do.

The hair, the cardboard body, the faded dress . . . they would all burn very nicely. She would burn Bess.

As her father had said, Anna's room was in a mess. Cupboards were crammed tight with things which "might come in useful one day" – but never seemed to. There were boxes, pretty pieces of wrapping paper which she had not the heart to throw away, comics and old magazines. Averting her eyes from the doll, she worked around the room, piling all the rubbish into the centre to be taken down to the bonfire. She did not want to look at Bess again, for she was afraid of what she might see. The fire in her room must have been an illusion, and the finger had not really fallen off. Anna kept telling herself that she had been very silly. Yes, it was all an illusion, brought on by reading that sad letter.

First thing would be to find a box big enough to stack all the rubbish in. The box from the auction filled that bill very nicely.

Comics, some magazines and layers of wrapping paper. She lined the box carefully.

A coffin. That's what she was making. A coffin for a doll.

Outside, she could hear the crackling of the newly-lit

329

bonfire, and the sounds of snapping twigs and hissing leaves made her work faster. Already the blue-grey smoke was curling up from the bonfire, and her heart pounded as she frantically stuffed more and more paper into the cardboard box.

Layer upon layer, she was almost afraid to stop. She wanted this box to burn . . . really burn. She wanted it to glow white hot and dissolve everything to a black, harmless ash.

Still not daring to look at Bess, she made her way over to the shelf and reached out her hand. Groping fingers felt the edge of the faded dress . . . a leg . . . body . . . shoulders . . . head.

"Ow!" Anna screamed, withdrawing her hand. "She bit me!"

Bess sat on the shelf, her red, stained teeth bared. Her eyes were back again, and she was almost restored to the condition she was in when new. Rosy cheeks, laughing eyes, ruby lips – and even the dress was no longer faded and shabby. Anna stared at the doll.

How could she have thought of burning it? My! It was so pretty.

Bess grinned her frozen grin as Anna walked woodenly towards her.

"You're not such a bad thing after all," Anna said, reaching out her hands to take the doll. "Maybe your teeth are a bit sharp, but it was my fault for not looking what I was doing. I'll have to be careful not to put my fingers near those teeth, though. Nowadays, they wouldn't allow such sharp cutting edges on toys – and that is what you are Bess . . . a toy."

Bess was in her arms, an innocent expression on her rosy face. She was beautiful, and Anna could not help but hug the doll tightly. Had anyone else been in the room at that time, they would have seen a much different picture.

They would have seen a girl holding a ragged doll with shorn hair and cavernous sockets for eyes. They would have wondered why such a revolting doll was treated with love and affection.

But Anna could only see the rosy-cheeked doll laughing up at her and she bent over to kiss it.

"I'm sorry," she said, "to have treated you like I did. It must have been my imagination. I really don't know what was wrong with me. Do you forgive me, Bess? Say you do."

Bringing the doll up to her face, Anna placed an affectionate kiss on the rosy cheek and hugged Bess tight.

Bess raised her arms jerkily and put them around Anna's neck . . . squeezing.

"You moved!" Anna cried.

Bess squeezed.

"You moved!"

Her mouth next to Anna's ear, the doll let out a low chuckle, squeezing tighter and tighter.

Frantically, Anna struggled to pull the doll away . . . but Bess was powerful.

Tighter . . . tighter . . . tighter!

"Let go!" Anna cried, her breath almost taken away with fear. The chuckling filled her ears, and Bess wriggled to get a better grip.

"Ha-ha-ha-ha!"

With all her strength, Anna wrenched the doll from her neck and threw her into the cardboard box. Paper! More and more paper was thrust into the box. Cardboard, comics, books and more paper. Anna was heedless as to what she was throwing into the box to cover the chuckling, evil doll.

Stamp it down! Stamp, stamp, stamp!

Quick as a flash, she scooped up the box and ran helter-skelter down the stairs.

"You shouldn't be carrying so much at a time, dear," her mother said, opening the back kitchen door to let Anna out into the yard.

Out . . . out into the garden where the bonfire crackled and roared. Over to the greedy, licking flames. Her eyes filled with tears and smoke, Anna hurled the box on to the fire, and the flames leaped upon it and started to devour it instantly.

"Burn! Burn! Burn!" Anna screamed.

"It will burn quite nicely without being shouted at," her father said, laughing as he watched her.

White-faced, she watched the orange flames slither over the cardboard coffin, seeking out the thinner paper first.

Page by page, the comics and magazines burned through and peeled back. Page after page, until Anna could see Bess's face through the roaring inferno.

One last scream of defiance, and the doll was engulfed in white hot fire.

"Don't scream so loud, Anna," her father called from the bottom of the garden. "You're not a child and you've seen a bonfire before."

"Sorry, Dad," Anna called back as she watched the black ashes of the fire soar up high into the sky. She couldn't tell him that it was Bess, not her, screaming. He wouldn't believe it anyway.

Up into the sky the black ashes flew . . . like birds.

"Free . . . like the birds," Anna breathed.

MR JONES

by Mary Danby

"If you children get under my feet once more I'll put you to scrubbing carrots along of Lizzie," threatened Mrs Porter, floury and hot, shooing Eddie and Eileen away from the kitchen table, where a vast pie-dish of beefsteak and oysters sat waiting for its cover of pastry. "There's guests for lunch today, and I can't be looking out for you two all morning. Go and see if you can help Polly." Polly was one of the housemaids, and not much older than the two Porter children.

She was out in the pantry, giving the silver a rub over with her polishing cloth and laying it on a tray, ready to be taken through to the dining-room. They chatted to her for a while – or rather, she did most of the talking, being a gossipy sort of girl – until she announced: "Well, this won't get us to Timbuctoo. How about you two laying up in the servants' hall for me, while I see to all this." And she straightened her apron, picked up the tray and went through the heavy swing door into "the house" which was what they called that part of Hartswell Manor occupied by its owners, Sir John and Lady Blane.

Eddie and Eileen spread a clean check cloth over the long table in the servants' hall and laid out knives and forks. This was where the servants ate together after the master and mistress had finished in the dining-room. They would not be eating steak and oyster pie – a chicken had been set to simmer on the range for the servants, and there was semolina to follow. The master and mistress were having raspberry ice-cream, churned by Lizzie in a wooden tub, with ratafia biscuits.

There were ten servants at Hartswell: Mrs Porter, the cook, who was married to the chauffeur, two parlour-maids, three housemaids. Arthur, the footman-valet, Lizzie, the kitchenmaid, and, in charge of all of them, Mr Jones the butler. Most employers didn't like their servants to be married, and few of them tolerated children about the place, but unlike the other servants, who lived in a wing of the main building, the Porters were allowed to rent a small cottage on the estate, and their children could come into the Manor as long as they kept to the servants' quarters.

Mr Jones peered around the door at them. "Good, good. Glad to see you making yourselves useful," he said in his grim, unsmiling way. He didn't like children, it was clear, and would have preferred to ban them from the Manor, but he had only recently come to Hartswell and had to accept, for the time being, whatever he found.

He was a forbidding man, cold in his manner and stern of feature. Across the top of his bald head he carefully combed a few strands of oily black hair, and his side-whiskers were kept neatly in line with the bottoms of his wax-white ears. In his formal wing collar and black coat he looked as much like an undertaker as a butler. To laugh in his presence was a bit like giggling at a funeral.

"You keep out of Mr Jones's way," the children's mother warned. "It wouldn't do to get on the wrong side of him."

In fact, they were only too pleased to obey her. There was a mustiness, a creepy greyness about the man, that gave them, in Eileen's words, "the grisly gruebugs".

"Why is he such a misery-stick?" she had asked Polly, soon after Mr Jones's arrival, and Polly had answered:

"Well now, duck, he's had a bit of a bad time. You

334

know he and his wife were cook and butler over at Stanton Place?" That was a big house whose land adjoined the Hartswell estate. "Well . . . suddenly his wife upped and left him, so he couldn't stay on there. They needed a married couple, see. Anyway . . ." Polly looked round, then lowered her voice. "The talk here about is that Mrs Jones found herself a fancy man because she couldn't stand her sourpuss of a husband any longer, and then she ran off with him. What d'you make of that, eh?"

Eileen gazed at her, round-eyed. "I bet it's true," she declared.

"We shall never know, I don't 'spect," Polly said darkly. Mr Jones was a private person, who kept his thin, pale lips tightly shut on matters of an intimate nature.

During the school holidays, Eddie and Eileen usually helped Polly with the servants' rooms. The more junior servants did their own cleaning, but Hilda, the head parlourmaid, and Mr Jones were considered too grand, so Polly was responsible for dusting their rooms and making their beds. The children hated going into Mr Jones's room, which smelt like he did – stale and stuffy.

"It's getting worse, you know," Eddie said one day, holding up a pillowcase by one corner. "The smell, I mean. Like something crawled in here to die."

Eileen peered under the bed, in case there could be a dear departed mouse. Straightening up, she said: "He does wash. His slop pail is always full of dirty water."

The slop pail stood under the washstand, with its big jug and basin. Dirty water was tipped from the basin into the pail and removed every morning by Polly.

"It doesn't do to be nosey about people's personal habits," she told the children. "Not when one's in service."

Before meals, Eddie and Eileen had to go to their mother to be inspected. Mr Jones had once caught Eddie with dirty hands at the lunch table and threatened to make him eat in the scullery. If Eileen's pinafore was dirty, or her stockings torn, she had to run home to change, and Eddie had to comb his curly brown hair and polish his boots with a duster.

"I don't see why we have to go to all this bother," he complained. "By the smell of him, Jonesey has worn the same clothes for a month."

"*Mr* Jones," admonished his mother, giving him a light cuff on the head. "And don't you give no disrespect. You'll get me sacked."

But Eddie and Eileen, who, like most children, were particularly sensitive to unpleasant smells, had to pinch their noses when they first entered his room, until they could get to the window and let in some fresh air. Mr Jones himself carried only a slight whiff of something nasty with him, but enough to make the children step back when he approached. Perhaps he thought they were making way for him out of respect.

"I wonder if the master and mistress have noticed," said Eddie.

"He doesn't get so close to them," replied Eileen, "except, I suppose, when he's serving the wine. But Polly says the mistress uses lots of that eau de cologne stuff, so perhaps that's all they can smell."

One morning, when they were helping Polly with the dusting, Eileen found something behind Mr Jones's bedroom door.

"Ugh!" she excalimed. "What's *that*?"

Eddie joined her. "One of Jones's rotting socks," he suggested.

Polly pushed past them. "Give over, you two," she

said. "It's only a bit of mud." She bent to sweep it up. Then she stopped and sniffed. "Coo, it's a bit strong."

"It's not as if he did any gardening," said Eddie, "and he doesn't go in for muddy walks."

"It smells of dead," Eileen remarked. "Like, you know – earth to earth . . ."

The next week, there were muddy marks on Mr Jones's sheets, and sprinklings of earth all over the floorboards of his room.

"Are you going to tell Hilda?" Eileen asked Polly. "I mean, you ought to tell *somebody*."

"Hilda'll just say to mind my own business," said Polly. "After all, who's she got to report it to except Mr Jones, and I dare say he knows all about it anyway."

The smell was now almost overpowering – a sharp, sweet smell of mouldiness and decay.

"For heaven's sake, open up that window," said Polly, "before we all suffocate."

That evening there was a big dinner party at the Manor. Eddie and Eileen had to sit quietly playing cards in a corner of the servants' hall while everyone else bustled here and there carrying trays, polishing glasses and preparing a six-course meal.

Mr Jones was in the pantry, uncorking the claret, when one of the housemaids came in backwards, pulling a trolley loaded with best china, and bumped into him.

"Really!" he exclaimed with disgust as a bottle flew out of his hands, spilling its deep red contents all over the pantry. "Stupid, clumsy girl!"

His green apron, which he wore to protect his smart black tailcoat and trousers, bore the brunt of the spillage, but there was wine on his starched white shirt-cuff, too.

Muttering furiously, he hurried up the back stairs to change, and Lizzie was summoned to clear up the mess.

"That won't help his mood, for sure," said Eileen, who

had noted a particular tetchiness in the butler's manner that day.

Bells from the house were ringing in the kitchen. The mistress needed Hilda to help her get dressed. Arthur had to put another log on the drawing-room fire. The master wanted to talk to Mr Jones about which brandy to serve to the gentlemen after dinner.

"What's keeping him?" Hilda was asking. "He only went up to change his shirt. Here, you children – run upstairs and tell Mr Jones the master wants him right away."

Eileen and Eddie clattered up the back stairs and along the dark passage until they reached Mr Jones's door. Here, they paused, Eddie's hand raised, ready to knock. They could hear Mr Jones inside the room. He seemed to be talking to someone.

"Leave me!" he was saying hoarsely. "For God's sake, go back! What do you want of me now? It's too late, I tell you. What's done is done!"

The only answer was a dreadful wheezy, rasping noise, like someone making a great effort to breathe, and a slow, soft dragging sound across the floorboards.

"I will *not* come with you! No!" said Mr Jones. "Go back to where you came from!"

Suddenly, the door opened, and Mr Jones came out quickly, shutting the door sharply behind him. He was white and shaking, and the smell was all about him. A look of fury, or perhaps it was fear, crossed his face.

"What do you want? How dare you wander about up here? Run along at once. I shall speak to your mother." And before the children could explain, he had hurried past them down the stairs.

"Who d'you think's in there, Eddie?" asked Eileen.

"Maybe nobody," answered her brother. "Maybe he talks to himself."

338

The following day, Polly was ill with a sick headache, and the children volunteered to change Mr Jones's sheets by themselves.

Actually, they had to dare each other, as they were none too sure what – or who – they might find in the room. Gingerly, they opened the door, but apart from the usual smell of rotting fungus there appeared to be nothing out of the ordinary except one or two dirty patches on the floor. They each took one side of the bed, and together began to strip it.

All of a sudden, Eileen gave a gasp of disgust. "*What* is that?" she asked, pointing a wobbly finger.

Nestling at the bottom of the bed was what looked like a damp and filthy white sheet.

"Who changed the sheets last time?" asked Eddie. "They don't seem to have made much of a job of it."

"No, no," said Eileen. "It doesn't belong anywhere here. Look, it's . . . it's all *grue-ey*."

The sheet was thick with old grime and mud. Smears of grey matter, thankfully unidentifiable, mingled with blotches of green slime. The smell was appalling, putrid, vile, and Eileen covered her nose and mouth with her hand and rushed out of the room. Eddie followed her.

"What now?" he asked breathlessly.

"We'd better tell, hadn't we?" suggested Eileen.

Eddie shrugged. "I dunno. But I'm not going back in there," he said firmly. "Whatever it is he's up to, he can cope with it himself from now on."

"What about Polly?" said Eileen. "She'll get into trouble if we just leave it."

"No she won't," replied Eddie. "Somehow I don't think Jonesey will mention it. It comes under the heading of 'intimate matters'."

That night, in the Porters' cottage on the Hartswell estate, Eddie crouched by his bedroom window in his

339

nightshirt, looking out at the full moon. Not far off, screened from him by a tall chest of drawers, Eileen slept quietly. Eddie was troubled. He had tried to go to sleep, but he had a strong feeling that something was about to happen, that Jones was up and about, and on the prowl. All day the butler had been twitchy and sharp with everyone, as if he knew what had been found in his room and was aware that he could carry on no longer without taking some action. Though what the cause of his problem was, and what action he might take, Eddie could not be sure. He had his suspicions, but they were so outrageous, so bizarre, that he couldn't take them seriously.

Suddenly he saw something, someone, moving through the trees. "Eileen!" he hissed. "Wake up! It's Jonesey!"

Silhouetted against the night sky, Mr Jones seemed to be making his way towards the open fields, where the Hartswell land adjoined that of Stanton Place. In one hand he held a bundle-like something at arm's length; across his shoulder was a spade.

Silently, Eddie and Eileen wrapped themselves up against the blustery night air and left he cottage. Eileen pulled her shawl about her shoulders as they slipped from tree trunk to tree trunk, following the eerie, trudging figure. Every now and then Mr Jones stopped, as if unsure whether to carry on, then re-shouldered his spade and continued. His destination appeared to be the edge of a large cornfield, an unsown area between the growing wheat and a high hedgerow. Here he laid down his bundle and began to dig. The children crept close, hidden behind a screen of blackthorn, and peered round it at him. They were near enough to hear him grunt with each thrust of the spade, and to see drops of sweat which glistened in the moonlight on his high-domed forehead. At last, he put down the spade and picked up the bundle.

As he did so, a strong rush of wind came up and almost

340

blew it out of his hand, revealing it as, not a bundle, but a sheet-like article. Eileen looked at Eddie. Was it the vile, odorous object they had seen in Mr Jones's room that morning?

Fighting against the wind, the butler gathered in the cloth and pushed it roughly into the hole he had dug, then, using the spade and the side of his boot, he shovelled the soil over it. When this was done, he stamped hard on the earth, as if demanding it should stay put.

Eileen grabbed hold of Eddie's hand and shivered. What on earth was the man up to? Was he insane? If he didn't want the sheet, couldn't he have burnt it? Why go to all this trouble to bury it?

The answer came very shortly.

Mr Jones picked up the spade and prepared to return to the house. The children waited, planning to follow at a reasonable distance before branching off in the direction of their cottage. They watched him, therefore, as he made his way back along the edge of the cornfield.

The moon slid behind a cloud, but, in the darkness, another kind of light could be seen. It arose from the patch of earth where Mr Jones had been digging.

"Look!" whispered Eileen, clutching her brother's arm. "Look behind him!"

The wind came up again and sang in the trees with a terrible moaning, and the butler quickened his step, but the light gathered itself into a tall, wispy column and moved after him. The air had turned icy cold, and gusts of wind whipped the tops of the corn. The column became a human figure, a thin, long-haired woman, wrapped in . . .

"The sheet – look – the sheet!" breathed Eileen in horror.

Draped in its loathsome shroud, the luminous, floating creature was gaining on Mr Jones. He turned round once, briefly, and gave a howl of terror, and then the thing was upon him, its talon-hands clinging murderously to his throat, pulling him down towards the cold, moist earth.

Eddie and Eileen, too petrified to scream, fled back to their cottage and the safety of their bedroom, where they lay for the rest of the night in a torment of trembling, unable to believe what they had seen, but knowing they must.

The following morning, Mr Jones was nowhere to be found. His bed had not been slept in – not touched since Eddie and Eileen had stripped it – and the dirty old sheet had vanished.

The two children had kept quiet about what they had seen the night before, thinking firstly that no one would believe them, and secondly that they would get into trouble for being out of their beds. But now Eddie decided: "It's no good. We'd better say."

When everyone had finished their "well I nevers", and telling the children what good imaginations they had, Polly said: "I knew it. She never went off with her fancy man. He murdered her. Strangle-ated her," she added, her eyes bright with the thrill of it.

Eventually, someone told the Blanes, and the police were called. Eddie and Eileen led a small party of people to the spot where they had last seen Mr Jones, and one of the under-gardeners was told to start digging. At a respectful distance, the other members of the household stood in a murmuring knot, watching.

Before long, two bodies were uncovered: one a few weeks old, and wrapped in a dirty sheet, and with its hands closed around the neck of the other body, which was very new, and which was Mr Jones.

THE GHOSTLY GARDENERS

by Ruth Cameron

Rain was drizzling down. Flatly, patteringly. He accepted it as fitting for today's general awfulness. Funny how sometimes the weather corresponded with one's mood. His mood this evening was wet and grey. School had been diabolical. He'd felt unwell, yet had tried to keep up. The result? At P. E. he'd made his usual flying leap over the "horse" – and landed with a plonk on the middle of its back. Everyone had laughed, including the teacher. He'd hated them all and wanted to die.

How did one die anyway? What *was* death? Was it just an escape, a nothingness, a refuge, like a sleep without dreams? Or did one have to go on in some after-life, which might be even worse than this one? Who was to know? Certainly not the headmaster, who read out religious bits every morning in a sanctimonious voice. He obviously knew nothing about anything. He even whacked you on your bottom with a slipper if you broke a rule. What a way to carry on!

And the rain drizzled down, soaking the shoulders of his jacket, seeping in between the soles and tops of his shoes, so that he plodded in sludgy socks. He walked now alongside the high wall, which went on for a long time and gave one an oppressed feeling, as it made the pavement seem narrower and the swishing traffic in the roadway more violent and threatening.

He drew closer to this long, blank wall, as if it might offer him protection.

And he saw the door.

What an extraordinary thing! He had walked past this wall hundreds of times, in all sorts of weathers and states of mind, and he had never noticed that door before. Yet it was quite a noticeable door. For it was black.

If you think about it, there aren't that many black doors around.

Why had he never noticed it before?

Was it new?

He stood in the rain, which he had forgotten for the moment, and studied the black door.

No, it wasn't new. It looked pretty ancient. He saw a keyhole, but no handle. Unhopefully, he gave it a little push.

And it opened.

For a second, he shrank back, fearing, like any child, a cry from some indignant adult: "Who are you? What are you doing here? Scarper!"

But there was no sound. The door stayed wide open, and, inside, he saw green: green grass – green trees – green leaves – and even the grey sky seemed to be of a sort of greeny-yellowy shade. It was a different world. And wasn't that just what he'd been wanting – a different world?

He went in. He left the black door open behind him and moved cautiously, timid as an animal on alien territory. He tiptoed.

His steps made no sound on the grass-green path which snaked across the vivid lawn. He could have taken short-cuts, but he didn't. He snaked with the path. After walking windingly for some time, he came to a black-and-green building.

It was as windowed as a greenhouse, but he couldn't see through the glass, which merely reflected the green-ness of the surroundings. Also, the glass was blurred with rain. Not that he could feel any wetness now. He was too absorbed with curiosity to have any physical feelings. He was all mind.

He found the door of the black-and-green glasshouse, with its invisible interior, and turned the handle. It opened. He peered round.

Before him was one of the strangest sights he had ever seen.

The place *was* a kind of greenhouse, but the plants were such as he had never imagined. They were potted plants, but not the ordinary stuff you see in shop-windows. There were some which looked like miniature willow trees . . . some with stems which twisted like bent wire and had round, petal-less flowers on top . . . some which grew like upside-down arrows . . . some which looked like little human figures. And there was no colour anywhere, except the green, and the black, if you can call black a colour.

Three gardeners – or so he supposed them – moved about in this black-and-green greenhouse. He could not see their faces, for hoods obscured their features; and they wore long black robes, like monks' habits, which made them figureless. Except that he could tell they were all thin. He was filled with wonder, and strangely, was unafraid. For there was a gentleness in the movements of the black-robed figures as they tended their plants which made him feel that they would never hurt anyone. They only wanted things to grow.

One of them held a big, black watering-can and was sprinkling with water a tiny little black plant shaped like a six-pointed star. It was turning its minute face up to the water, drinking it in. The spray of water was clearest silver. Silver droplets gleamed on black petals.

Enchanted, he gazed.

Another of the gardeners moved over to a desk and began to write, as if he were a doctor, writing up a record of this plant 'patient' or that. As he bent over his writing, his face was completely obscured by his big, black hood.

The third gardener was doing something at the far side of the greenhouse. Only his back could be seen: thin, with broad shoulders, and the dark robe flowing off them like an ebony waterfall.

The three took no notice whatsoever of the intruder. It was as if he didn't exist. Well – they must have seen him, so, if they didn't object to his presence, he might as well have a good look around . . .

And he did.

He walked among the strange, potted plants arrayed on the shelves and examined each one, marvelling at the exotic shapes, the uniqueness of each cluster of leaves and petals, the mystery of it all.

He wished he could help to look after the plants. Was there maybe some little job he could do to assist the black-robed gardeners?

Which one dared he approach?

The one with the watering-can? He was watering another plant now – one of the baby weeping-willows. And as he did so, tears seemed to be dropping from under the hood he wore – tears as silver as the water from the can. But was it ordinary water? Or was it – well, what? – distilled moonlight?

He went right up to the figure with the watering-can.

"Excuse me," he said.

The head turned slightly in his direction, but still he could not see the face.

"Can I do anything to help?" he asked.

The hooded head gave a small shake, resigned rather than impatient. Oh, well, there seemed to be only one watering-can anyway. He looked across to the figure which had its back to him and saw the gardener's hands training some black creepers around a stick. And those

346

hands paralysed him with sudden shock – for the fingers had no flesh on them. They were all bone. The hands then withdrew under the wide sleeves of the robe, and he wondered for a second if he'd imagined what he'd seen. Maybe the hands had merely been very thin, and the greenish light had given an illusion of fleshlessness.

Tentatively he moved towards the desk where the other figure was writing. Only the tips of the fingers showed. They were fleshless. That was no illusion. Who were these people? Lepers? Terribly sick men in some sort of hospital, and their gardening was a therapy? Fear was in him, yet it still wasn't strong because of the seeming gentleness of the creatures, and the utter quietness.

"What is this place? Who are you?" he asked. His voice sounded overloud, crude and intrusive. "Sorry. I didn't mean to shout," he said quickly, "but please don't ignore me any more. Please tell me who you are. Look at me, anyway!"

The figure at the desk looked up at him. The one with the watering-can looked down at him. The one on the other side of the place looked across at him. With their fleshless hands, they pushed aside the folds of their hoods.

Three sad-expressioned skulls regarded him.

A black curtain, like a great black hood descended upon him and there was nothing but spinning darkness . . .

"I think he's coming round. Hello, lad. You all right?"

He was lying on the wet pavement alongside the high wall. Two men were bending over him. One of them helped him to his feet. "What happened, then? Did you fall over and knock your head?"

"No. I – I don't remember falling . . . Oh, yes, I did, though – a black thing came over me – they must have put a hood on me and carried me out here . . . Where are they? Where's the black door?"

"What black door?" asked the other man.

"In the wall. I was here. I went in – "

"You've been dreaming, son," said the first man. "There's no door in this wall."

"That's right," agreed his companion. "Never been no door in this wall, not never."

"I'd never noticed it until today," the boy explained. "It must have been new. Except that it was old."

The two men exchanged glances. "You're not quite yourself, son. Where do you live?" asked one of them. He told them, and the man said: "That's not far from me. I'll see you safely back. At least it's stopped raining now."

So the kind stranger saw him home and told his mother: "Your boy had a bit of a turn in the street, missus, but he seems to be all right now."

His mother was worried and, after the man had departed, asked: "What happened? What did he mean by a 'bit of a turn'?"

"I don't know, Mum. I just sort of passed out. I've been feeling grotty all day."

During the walk back he had decided not to say a word about the greenhouse and the three robed skeletons. He couldn't get their sad skulls and fleshless fingers out of his mind's eye. The plants haunted him, too. The whole scene had stayed alive within him, yet common sense told him that none of it could really have happened. There had been no black door. He had passed out and had a dream.

Yet it had been so real!

"Straight to bed with you," said his mother. "People don't faint in the street for no reason." And she sent for the doctor, who declared that the flu bug had got him and that there was a lot of it around. He spent a restless night, tangled with nightmares of grinning skulls and weird vegetation, and in the morning his mother said he must spend the day in bed. He wasn't sorry to do so. He felt weak and strange.

In the afternoon, when she brought him a cup of tea, he asked her: "Mum, what's on the other side of that long wall? You know – the one I walk past on my way back from school."

"It's the back wall of St Dominic's, of course," she said. "Didn't you know? You've seen the front often enough."

It was true. He had. The front of St Dominic's, now a college for training teachers, was in a different street altogether. Somehow he had never connected those prim premises with the long, mysterious, high wall. A nightmare thought came to him: Who trained teachers? Black-robed skeletons? Was that why teachers were so diabolical . . .? No, no, no . . . What had happened to him had not happened . . . It couldn't have . . . He must hang on to that.

But it had happened. Even if it hadn't, it had. One day, when he was better, he must get into the grounds behind that college and find out what was there.

A week later, he was back at school, the flu bug conquered. He gave the high wall every chance first: he walked alongside it, looking for the door. No door. Right. Then he must enter by going round to the front. He'd be late home, but he could make some excuse – say he'd been 'kept in'.

He raced around the streets until he came to the front of the college. As he went in by the main entrance, he tried to look like a teacher-in-training. A dwarf teacher, maybe? He chuckled to himself. Then he remembered, reading something written by a burglar, who had said:

"Think yourself invisible. That's the trick. If you think yourself invisible, people won't see you."

Studiously thinking himself invisible, he walked up the front drive, then made his way across the grounds towards the back wall. He calculated where he was, where the greenhouse had been.

Now he was standing where the greenhouse should be. And there was no building there at all. But other things were the same – the greenness of everything, the trees, the grass, the leaves – and there was a sort of winding path, like the track of an invisible snake acrosss the grass. That was the path he'd tiptoed along when he'd come through the black door.

But there was no black door, and no greenhouse.

It hadn't happened. It had all been a dream, because he was ill and had a fever . . . He must settle for that . . .

"Hello."

He nearly jumped out of his skin. He turned towards the voice, half-expecting to see a skeleton in a black robe.

Not at all. A most ordinary, middle-aged man stood there, looking like anyone's father.

"Hello," he said nervously. He was going to be ticked off now, for being here.

Instead, the man said lightly: "Do you know you're standing in a haunted spot?"

"No. Am I?"

"Indeed you are. Want to hear about it?"

"Please."

The man spread out his arms. "Long, long ago, there was a building here, where three Dominican monks performed miracles. They shouldn't have been here at all. No one knew they were. The old monastery had been sacked, and most of the Black Friars had fled – but these three stayed, secretly. They brewed herbs, made potions – and they had a secret black door, a black door, there – "

He pointed to the blank wall. "People would come creeping through that door, to be healed by the three monks who weren't supposed to exist."

"If no one knew they were here, how did people know to come?"

"God knows," laughed the man. "Those who are sick, or falling sick, know where to come."

"I came," said the boy. "I met them. It was when I had flu."

"I remember," said the man. "Take my hand."

The boy held out his hand. The other took it. And, on the instant, the whole scene changed. They were in the greenhouse. The man who held his hand was black-robed, black-hooded, and, in his other hand, was holding a watering-can.

The formerly ordinary face looking down at him was no longer ordinary. It was a skull. Yet a gentle skull. It seemed to have a kindly expression. The hand which held his was that of a skeleton, quite fleshless – and yet he was not afraid.

"You were more ill than you knew," said the figure with the watering-can. "You were at Death's Door." He pointed. "See it?"

Yes, dimly through the glass of the greenhouse, he could see the black door in the wall.

"I left it open," the boy said, "when I came in before."

"Others have come in since and closed it behind them."

"What happened that other time? *Did* you fling something over my head and carry me outside?"

"Yes, but we gave you some medicine first, so that you'd recover quickly."

"A medicine made up from all these strange plants?"

"That's right. This is the Garden of Death. There are many such, all over the world. Only the sick see them. They come to us, and sometimes they stay, but most often we give them medicine and send them back, and nearly always they forget about us, or think that we were a dream. They forget us as a dream is forgotten."

"*I* thought you must be a dream."

"And you will think so again."

"Oh, no. This is so real." He looked at the figure at the desk, and the skull-face smiled at him; so did the more distant figure, tending climbing plants with his fleshless fingers.

"This explains," said the boy, "why some people get better quickly, even when they're very ill – miraculous cures and so forth. They're not 'miraculous' at all. You do it!"

The robed skeletons quivered with laughter, indeed, rattled a little as they chuckled. "That puts us in our places," said the one at the desk. "Not 'miraculous' at all – only us doing it."

"We thought you ought to know that the dead help the living, that we're not just a load of idle layabouts," said the one with the watering-can.

"But don't talk about it when you go back," said the one at the desk. "You won't be believed."

"I know that already," said the boy. "Don't worry. I won't give you away. Now – how do I get back?"

"Take my hand again," said the one with the watering-can.

As the boy did so, he found the fingers had become covered with flesh again, the skull-face had become the fleshed face of the man he had met in the grounds, and the black robes had changed into an ordinary suit. The greenhouse and the black door had gone. "Go out by the front, the way you came," said the man.

"Who *are* you?"

"The Gardener. Go along, off with you. Don't speak of us, but remember us. Next time you need us, you'll find us without seeking us. Each time you come, we'll help to cure your sickness, and when at last you stay, you will join us in our work and help those who have been left behind. Goodbye for the present."

"Goodbye. Thank you." He walked away for a few yards, then looked back. The man had vanished, yet there was nowhere to vanish to.

A voice behind him said: "Looking for someone, lad?"

He turned. A man, casually dressed in shirt and rough trousers, stood there. "I was looking for that – that person I was talking to."

"Well, I've been standing watching you for some time, and you were talking to yourself," said the man. "I'm the gardener here, and don't you come wandering round again."

"You're not the real Gardener," said the boy. "In this garden, there is another garden, and a greenhouse with – " He stopped. *Don't speak of us, but remember us*. The voice came through the sound of the wind in the trees.

"I'm sorry," he murmured to the voice.

"That's all right," said the man, thinking the apology was meant for him. "You don't look too well, actually."

"I've only just got over flu."

"Ah, well, they fill you up with funny drugs nowadays to get you better, then you can get nasty side-effects. My wife went on a 'trip' after some antibiotic stuff she took. Go along home, and no more trespassing on private grounds."

As the boy moved away, the gardener said: "Did *you* leave that thing there?" He pointed to the spot where the boy had been standing – the place where the greenhouse was invisible. What was not invisible, however, was the large black watering-can which stood proudly on the grass.

"It's not mine," said the boy. The gardener walked

over to it. Sunshine suddenly looked down through the clouds. The man's shadow was clear on the grass. But the watering-can cast no shadow. And when the gardener bent to pick it up, he grasped at nothingness, and the "thing" vanished. The boy burst out laughing and ran away, still laughing. He glanced behind once, to see the gardener standing there, staring in utter wonder at the nothingness on the grass.

And the wind in the trees chuckled like a rattle of friendly bones, and the boy ran all the way home, laughing in the sunshine, for the ghostly gardeners had done the one thing that would make him believe in them for ever, and never fear them again: they had done something funny. They had played such a lovely joke!

SOMEONE DROWNED

by Tony Richards

DANGER!

The sign was huge, the warning painted in large black letters on a white background. Fixed to a solid metal post, it stuck out of the water just downstream of the weir. The river widened and deepened there, where the powerful current had cut a weirpool out of the raw earth. Great care had been taken in placing the sign. Wherever you stood, it was the first thing which caught your eye. *Danger!*

It was evening, a long, hot, summer holiday evening, alive with the sounds of midges and moorhens. Jeff Hollis sat on the grassy bank of the weirpool, his fishing rod in his hand. As the light faded, the red tip of his float became harder to see. He strained his eyes trying to watch it. But, every so often, his gaze would wander to the sign, inspecting it guiltily. His parents and his teachers had warned him about coming here. A policeman had chased him off once. The weirpool was very deep and dangerously strong, and he knew that the adults were right to worry.

Someone – a young boy no older than Jeff – had drowned here last summer. The river had become a raging torrent after a heavy storm, and the boy had been sucked helplessly under.

But still Jeff, and his friends Tom and Leon, came to the weirpool each day through the hole under the tall wire fence. They got wet and tore their clothes, got told off

355

when they went home. It did not bother them. They were drawn here, to this secret and magical place. It beckoned them.

In the centre of the town, an adventure playground had been built to keep the children amused during the summer holidays. Jeff and Tom and Leon never used it, never even thought of using it. A dead thing, full of planks and ropes and big discarded tyres. No privacy there. It was everyone's. The weirpool was theirs alone. They could run splashing along the slippery shelf of the weir. They could fish in the pool. They could swim, fighting the current, braving the full might of the river. This spring, they had even built a raft out of boards and empty oil drums. It lay moored beneath an overhanging willow tree. Jeff could hear the muted thump of the steel drums against the bank as the raft wafted to and fro.

His thoughts were wandering. He realized that he had time for one more cast. Tom and Leon would be here soon to join him in a night swim. He reeled in his tackle, checked the bait, then cast out again for the deepest, darkest area of the pool.

Around the float, the water eddied and swirled. The teachers had said that it was twenty feet deep, and Jeff could well believe them. It looked black as oil, impenetrable to the gaze, and gave the impression of being bottomless. The surface glittered with wavelets and foam which formed beautiful, wild patterns. Of all the river, this place was unique.

The float was gone! A bite, at long last! Jeff lifted his rod and struck the hook home.

The rod immediately bent double.

His heart thumping, Jeff reeled in a couple of yards before realizing that the weight on the other end was lifeless and inert. A clump of weed, maybe, or a waterlogged branch. Disappointment welled up in him. He would not have a catch to show the others after all. Still, he had better get his line in.

He set to work, reeling in slowly, pointing the rod tip straight out so that it would not break. The obstruction was very large and heavy. And yet, Jeff noticed, the current was not affecting it. Whatever he had on his hook was coming directly, ponderously, at him. The angle of the line showed that it was almost in. Jeff gazed down into the ebony waters, trying to see what he had caught into. Something white and indefinable returned his gaze.

White? In this river?

He tugged the line, and part of the object surfaced. One part only. It had not been hooked, but was holding tightly on to the nylon line.

A hand.

Jeff yelled with fright and, dropping his rod, fell back on to the grass. He lay there, propped up on his elbows, wanting to close his eyes and finding he could not. He stared. The hand still protruded above the surface. It was small – a boy's, he guessed – and white as milk. Jeff immediately thought of the boy who had drowned last year. But the body had been found and removed. So what was this?

There was one answer to that question. An unbelievable, terrifying answer.

The line suddenly went slack. The hand had released its hold, and, as Jeff watched, it opened till the fingers were spread apart, straight. The palm gleamed ghostly pale against the dusk. Jeff wanted to scream, but his throat felt tight, his mouth dry.

The hand stayed there, above the water, for a moment longer. Then it vanished. It did not sink again, just . . . *went*.

* * *

357

"Caught anything?" asked Tom.

Jeff was huddled against a tree trunk, far away from the bank. He had been there for some time. Raising his head, he saw that his friends had arrived. Tom, slender as the willow near the pool. And beefy, bullying Leon.

"No, nothing," Jeff said feebly.

"He's caught a cold, if you ask me," said Leon in that too loud voice of his. "Look at the way he's shivering."

"On a night like this?" Tom bent down to have a closer look. "You're really pale, Jeff. Are you OK?"

"He's fine," Leon cut in. "Let's go swimming."

He began to strip down to his trunks. Tom, as always, copied him. They undressed in silence, leaving their clothes in an untidy pile on the grass. When, at last, they were ready, they turned to Jeff.

"Well?" asked Leon. "Are you coming in, or are you just going to sit there all night?"

"I don't think it's a good idea," Jeff replied. "It's dangerous. The sign says so."

Leon looked grim. "The sign's always been there. It's never bothered you before. So why now?"

"Come on, Leon," said Tom. "If he doesn't want to go, that's his business. Leave him."

"No," said Leon. "I think he's turned chicken."

Jeff considered telling them just what he had seen in the pool that had made him afraid to go in. But he knew that they would never believe him. They would think he was making it up because he was scared.

"All right," he said. "I'm coming. I'll show you who's chicken."

As he began to undress, the other boys dived in, splashing the sign as they went. They always splashed it. That was their way of defying it. Jeff watched them, and he realized what it really was that drew them to the pool. Not the beauty, nor the solitude, nor the secrecy. They went there because they were not supposed to, because the adults told them not to and the sign warned them off. The danger of the weirpool attracted them like moths to a flame.

Jeff knew that he could cope with almost anything the river threw at him. But the hand, rising pale and ghostly from the dark pool, presented more danger than he had bargained for.

Arriving home, he left his fishing rod in the shed and sneaked in through the back door. His mother was in the kitchen, standing by the oven, waiting for him. His father stood behind her. Their expressions were identical, wavering between anger and concern.

"Jeff," said his mother, "where have you been? Your supper's ruined."

Jeff stood still and tried to look ashamed. "Sorry. I've been playing with Tom and Leon. At the adventure playground."

Both of them stared at him disbelievingly. He became painfully aware of how transparent the lie was. His hair, he realized, was still damp. It was obvious where he had been.

Mr Hollis stepped forwards. "Come here," he said. Jeff walked to him, and his father took him gently but firmly by the shoulders. "You've been to the weirpool again, haven't you?"

Jeff nodded.

"You're stupid. Really stupid. We've warned you time after time not to go there. You'll get killed."

An answer trembled on Jeff's lips. He wanted to tell them how it felt to have a secret, private world, a haven of trees and water and solitude. How it felt to swim and ride the raft in fierce currents. How it felt actually to face danger. They would not understand. There was nothing to say. Jeff remained gloomily silent.

"I'm going to have to stop your allowance this week," his father said. "And send you to bed early, without supper."

There was a programme on the television Jeff had particularly wanted to see. He had been waiting for it all week. His lips went tight. Mr Hollis frowned.

"Cruel world, isn't it?" he said. "It would be even crueller if you'd got into trouble in that weirpool. This is for your own good."

"You know a boy drowned there last year?" his mother added. "Yes, of course you know. Doesn't that bother you?"

Jeff was about to reply when a thought occurred to him. He asked, "What was the boy's name?"

"What an odd question," said his father. "It was Alan Weeks, if you must know. Why do you ask?"

"Just curious," said Jeff.

Mr Hollis shook his head tiredly. "For a son of mine, you're a very strange boy," he said. "Now, upstairs. And say goodnight politely."

Jeff took his leave of them and went out into the hall. He reached the foot of the staircase, then turned and went back to listen at the door.

"I don't know what to do with him," Mrs Hollis was saying. "However much we warn him, he still goes back to that dreadful place. His friends are just as bad. Perhaps if I spoke to their parents . . ."

"That's worse than useless," Jeff's father replied. "The more fuss we make, the more the boys go there. They're fascinated by it. Anyway, tomorrow I'll give the council a ring. They should have blocked up that hole ages ago."

Then footsteps came towards the door and Jeff hurried before them, running to his bed.

* * *

He thought a little while about what his parents had said. They were right, he knew, but at the same time terribly wrong. Jeff lay back on his pillow, thinking of the gleaming water and what he had seen in it. He did not expect to sleep that night.

The swim, though, and the fright, had tired him more than he realized. He soon drowsed off and fell into a deep sleep. His dreams were black, and a thousand small white hands raised themselves up through the darkness.

The next morning, he awoke early. The sun was rising bright in a clear, cloudless sky. The day promised to be hot. Perfect. He ate his breakfast swiftly and was heading for the front door when he caught the look on his mother's face. It would be better, he decided, not to push his luck. He got his tennis racket and ball and went to play in the back garden.

"That's better," said his mother. "Don't break any windows."

By half past ten he was bored. The garden was large and nicely kept, but it held no mystery, no wildness. He longed to be with his friends. Finally, he could stand no more. He tiptoed back inside the house. From upstairs, he could hear the noise of the vacuum cleaner. It drowned out every other sound. His mother would not be able to hear a thing. Especially not the slamming of the front door.

The bank of the pool was deserted when Jeff arrived. It was odd. Tom and Leon should have been there hours ago. An unpleasant thought came to him. Perhaps they had gone swimming – and the hand in the pool had grabbed them. That was silly. Or was it? He began to panic.

He was just about to start calling their names when the boys appeared through the trees downriver. Both were red-faced and breathless, as if they had been running. Both looked miserable.

"The raft's gone." Tom explained. "It's floated down the river, and we'll never find it now. The rope must have come undone."

"It couldn't have," Leon burst in angrily. "I moored it with a special knot my brother in the Navy taught me. Someone must have untied it."

"That's crazy," Tom protested. "Who would do that?"

"Well *someone* did!" yelled Leon, his face turning from red to purple.

And Jeff had a funny idea who.

"Forget it, Leon," he said. "We can build another one."

"I suppose so," Leon replied bitterly.

They had been planning to ride the raft the whole day. Now it was gone, half way to the sea by now, and they were left to brood. It was Tom who finally broke the silence.

"I'm hot," he said. "And sticky. How about a good long swim?"

It was a way of taking their minds off the raft. All three of them agreed and quickly stripped down to their trunks. Leon and Tom dived in first, as usual. Jeff hung back a bit, hovering at the water's edge. He could not get over the hand he had seen last night. But then, perhaps he had imagined it. The darkness could have played tricks with his eyes, or he might have drowsed off and been dreaming. Yes, just his imagination, that was all. Steeling himself, he plunged in.

The water covered him, claimed him. Below the surface, everything was cool and dark. A stream of bubbles escaped his lips, quicksilver beads which sought the light. He followed them, broke through the surface and swam towards his friends. Before he knew what he was doing, he had swum over the deepest spot, the place where his float had gone down the night before.

Something brushed against his foot.

He froze and immediately began to sink. Only a weed, he reassured himself uncertainly. Gazing into the water revealed nothing. It was too dark, too black. Jeff wanted nothing more than to get away from this spot. He swam, reverting to a doggy-paddle in his fright.

Again, something touched his foot. This time it stayed and, moving up, grasped hold of his ankle.

Jeff opened his mouth to shout for help, only for it to be filled with water. The hand – he *knew* it was the hand – had dragged him under. It hauled him down, down, with incredible speed and strength. Jeff wriggled like an eel, but he could not get free. His lungs ached. He was running out of air.

The descent stopped.

Jeff found himself hovering a few feet above the mud. Through the underwater gloom, weeds loomed like octopuses, fish skittered. He should not have been able to see anything down here. The water around him was somehow filled with a strange pale light.

The grip on his ankle loosened slightly, allowing him to turn round. For the first time, he saw the owner of the hand. It was a boy of roughly his age, and it had to be Alan Weeks. Or at least, his ghost. The spectre seemed at one with the water, part of it. The body, clad in tee-shirt and short trousers, wavered with the current. The fair hair flowed like weed. The boy's skin was completely white, his eyes a startling blue-green. And he glowed.

Jeff kicked at first, then became calm. The drowned boy was staring at him carefully. There was no malice in his eyes, only anger and concern, the same expression Jeff had seen on his own parents' faces. This was no more than a warning. A very grim warning.

363

Jeff understood.

The spectre of Alan Weeks vanished, and so did the grip on Jeff's ankle. He shot back to the surface like a cork, came out coughing and spluttering. As soon as his breath was back he struck out for the bank.

"Hey!" his friends shouted. "Where are you going?"

They caught up with him on the bank, as he was getting dressed. Jeff told them what he had seen, what he knew. Leon did not believe him.

"You liar," he said. "You're just making this up because you're scared of the pool. Chicken, just like I said."

"I'm not," Jeff protested. "I really did see the ghost of Alan Weeks. He was warning us away."

"Why now? Why wait the whole year? We've been all right all summer, danger sign or not."

"I – I don't know," Jeff mumbled. "Perhaps he knows something that we don't. Perhaps he can see that something bad is going to happen to us."

Leon snorted and began to turn away. It was Tom who caught him by the arm and stopped him.

"Leon," he said, "maybe it's true."

Leon shrugged his hand off with contempt. "Don't you start now," he snapped. "There's no such thing as ghosts, right? He's just a coward, and if you start believing him then you're no friend of mine, ever again. Now, are you coming back in the water or not?"

The look of worry on Tom's face was intense. He was obviously not sure who to believe. But in the end he would do what Leon said. He always did.

Jeff walked home alone.

That night, the sultry weather broke. Huge, rolling clouds filled the sky towards evening, and later on a thunderstorm shook the town to its foundations. The pouring rain went on until the early morning, flooding everything.

The next day, when Jeff awoke, he was filled with an uneasy feeling. He crossed to his bedroom window and gazed out. The bright sun was slowly drying out the ground, but huge puddles still lingered here and there. The rain had been torrential. And the river, Jeff knew, would be in full flood.

Just as it had been a year ago when Alan Weeks had drowned.

That was it! Now he knew what the ghost had been trying to warn him. Only a fool would go near the weirpool today, only a madman. *Leon!* He was just brash, just stupid enough to try swimming in these conditions. Glancing at the alarm clock by his bed, Jeff saw that his friends would be at the pool by now.

He got dressed quickly and rushed for the door.

Jeff could hear the weirpool even before he saw it. The roar of water tumbling over the ledge was deafening. As he drew closer, he could faintly hear another noise. A voice, Tom's voice, shouting for help. Jeff burst through the trees to see Tom standing on the bank, teetering to and fro. He was in a state of extreme panic. Fearing the worst, Jeff ran to his side and stared out across the water.

He could not see Leon at first. The weirpool was the worst he had ever seen it. The water had turned brown and was alive with foam and flotsam. It thundered, rushing past the bank, carrying everything in its wake. The trunk of a dead tree sailed by, and then Jeff caught a glimpse of a tiny black object further out. He only just recognized it as the top of Leon's head.

Jeff turned to Tom.

"Get help!" he shouted. "Move!"

As Tom broke out of his stupor and ran back for the fence, Jeff kicked off both his shoes and, without even thinking, dived in. He battered his way to the surface, took in a deep gulp of air, then fought outwards against the mighty current. The air trapped in his clothing helped at first by buoying him up, but as it seeped out the material became waterlogged. Feeling as heavy as lead, Jeff battled on. Every other stroke, the water would break over his head, threatening to carry him under. But he made it.

Wild with terror, Leon was in no state to help in his own rescue. Jeff tried to swim around behind him to get hold of his shoulders when suddenly Leon grabbed hold of him.

"No, wait!" Jeff yelled. "Let go!"

Leon was too frightened to hear. He clasped hold of Jeff, pinning his arms to his sides. They both sank like stones.

Below the surface, Jeff could still hear the noise of the water. It was louder now, filling his head, drowning him in fury. The harder he tried to free himself, the tighter Leon's grasp became. They were sinking further. Jeff knew that they would never come up again.

From behind, a strong pair of hands suddenly took hold of his shoulders. It wasn't Leon, and Tom had gone to fetch help.

The murky water was filled with a peculiar glow.

Jeff felt himself and Leon being drawn towards the surface. Then he passed out.

He came to not long afterwards. Opening his eyes, he saw that he was lying on the bank. Tom was standing over him, and, with Tom, a policeman. Other people were rushing towards them with blankets. Beside him, Leon was coughing out water.

"You saved his life," the policeman said. "Brave lad. You'll get some kind of reward for this, I'm sure."

"No," said Jeff weakly. "Not me."

* * *

The last time Jeff visited the weirpool was after the award ceremony. He was still wearing his suit. It had got dirtied from the crawl under the fence, but nobody would mind now.

Walking through the trees, he went right up to the edge of the bank. The pool was still the same. The midges, the ripples, the never-ending blackness of the water. It would never change.

Jeff gazed at his own reflection. It was he who had changed. He had become a little more grown up, and in exchange had given up his secret, private world. For the rest of his life, he would never return. He felt he owed that to the pool's inhabitant.

And there was something else he owed.

He fished in his trouser pocket and drew out a black, leather-bound box. A gleam of gold escaped as he opened it. Cushioned on red satin inside was the medal the mayor had presented to him an hour ago. He took it out and turned it over in his hand, reading the inscription. It bore his name. That was a mistake, and only he could put it right.

"It belongs to you, not me," Jeff whispered across the pool. "Thank you."

He threw the medal out towards the deepest area of the pool. It splashed, glimmered once, and then was gone. Into darkness.

THE THIRD EYE

by R. Chetwynd-Hayes

It all began when Uncle George gave Michael a lecture on keen observation.

"Everyone can see," he stated, "but few observe."

"Same thing," Michael protested. "If you can see something, you must observe it. Stands to reason."

Uncle George wagged his finger pontifically. "That's where you're wrong. Read the Sherlock Holmes stories and you'll know what I mean. For example – you must have seen the steps leading up to your front door. How many are there?"

Michael made a quick guess. "Ten."

"Wrong. There are thirteen. You saw the steps, but didn't observe them." He got up and walked over to the window, which, being on the first floor, commanded a clear view of the street. "Come here and I'll give you a practical demonstration of E. O. P."

"E. O. P.?" queried Michael.

"Extra Ocular Perception. You've heard of E. S. P., perhaps – Extra Sensory Perception – telepathy, and that kind of thing? Well, E. O. P. concerns your powers of observation. 'Ocular', from the Latin *oculis* – 'eye'."

To be honest, Michael thought his uncle was an old show-off, who had only the slightest idea of what he was talking about but was good for the odd pound note if treated with respect. So the boy joined the tall, grey-haired man at the window, prepared to express admiring astonishment, no matter how mundane the performance.

Uncle George pointed to a plump lady who was trudging along the far pavement.

"What can you tell me about her?"

Michael creased his forehead into a thoughtful frown. "She's quite old – sixty, at least. Is fat. Wearing a blue dress. And – oh, yes – she's been shopping. Carrying a full shopping bag. I think that's about all."

His uncle emitted a vast sigh.

"You must be half blind, boy. Even without using E. O. P. it must be obvious that the lady is a grandmother, has recently returned from abroad, was once quite well-off and is prudent by nature. For heaven's sake, use your eyes."

Michael stared at his uncle with unfeigned astonishment before asking: "How on earth did you work all that out?"

"Elementary," Uncle George replied with irritating complacency. "Let us take each point in turn. You should have noticed that a toy rifle is poking out of the shopping bag. This suggests the lady has a young male relative, who will not be more than ten years of age. As she is too old to have a son of that age, it is reasonable to assume the little wretch is her grandson. Her arms and face are deeply sun-tanned, and as there is nowhere in Great Britain where the sun shines that strongly at this time of year, she must have acquired it abroad. Had she been back in this country for any length of time, the tan would have started to fade. It hasn't. So – she recently returned. Are you with me so far?"

Michael nodded, albeit reluctantly, then scratched his head.

"Yes, I suppose you're right. But what about her once being well-off and being prudent by nature? I can't see how you know that."

Uncle George narrowed his eyes. "Wait a minute – she's stopping to have a rest. Respiratory trouble, I wouldn't wonder. Too much weight. Now she's sitting down on that low wall and we'll be able to *observe* her more closely. Don't fiddle with the curtain, you little idiot. We don't want her to know she's being watched. Look at that dress. I'm willing to bet that when new that cost all of two hundred pounds, but now it's worn and faded, suggesting she no longer has the money to replace it. Not even with a cheaper model.

"Now, observe that she has with her an umbrella. Is there a cloud in the sky? No, there is not. Never have I seen a day with less promise of rain. Therefore, the lady is prudence itself – and no doubt a pessimist as well, if she considers it might rain. You see, boy? It's a simple deductive process that comes easily to a man who has developed his sense of E. O. P."

The fat lady clambered laboriously to her feet, took up the shopping bag and continued her slow progress along the pavement.

"Well, young fellow," Uncle George went on, "I trust that I have lit a tiny spark of enquiry in your brain. Start developing your sense of E. O. P. and there'll soon be a blazing fire of knowledge."

Michael wandered back across the room and flopped into a chair, where for a while he sat staring blankly at the artificial-log electric fire. Presently he said: "It all sounds most convincing, but you could be wrong about some of it. I mean, she could have bought that toy rifle for a nephew or a neighbour's child."

Uncle George helped himself to a drink from the sideboard.

"Maybe. But surely she's far too old to have a ten-year-old nephew and most certainly too poor to buy presents for neighbours' children. The trouble is, I started to develop my powers of E. O. P. too late in life. My eyes aren't what they used to be. Mind you, I could still spot

that her hair was tinted. It was almost white at the roots
. . . But at your age! My word, if you work hard at it,
you'll achieve wonders. Be very useful in later life."

"I'll certainly try," Michael promised. "Gosh, it'll be
like having a third eye."

Uncle George went to America the following week, and
although Michael never saw him again, he most certainly
had reason not to forget him.

Developing a sense of E. O. P. is not easy – at least,
not at first. Michael found that the mere fact that a man
has mud-caked trousers does not automatically mean he
has been trudging across fields just after a rainstorm. He
more than likely has slipped into a water-logged hole that
a road worker has left inadequately lit, or been splashed
by a passing vehicle. Neither could one assume that a lady
with a black eye has an unkind husband. She might have
walked into a lamp post.

But after several months spent in watching, taking
elaborate notes and learning to spot that little *extra
something* that non-observant people never see, Michael
began to achieve some remarkable results. For example,
he soon realized that the burly man in the grey suit that
was much too small for him, who had a blister on the
index finger of his right hand, walked with a pronounced
limp and kept looking back over one shoulder, could be
none other than the convict whose escape from Marston
Prison had been reported in the national press a few days
earlier.

"Blister on finger – sawing through cell bars. Limp –
rope broke when climbing down wall. Stole suit much too
small for him. Looking back over one shoulder – afraid of
being followed." Michael explained the results of his E.
O. P. in a brisk, professional style to a passing policeman,

who merely smiled and said: "Mustn't let your imagination run away with you, lad," while the escaped convict disappeared round a corner.

Michael would have voiced his indignation, had not the little two-way radio that policemen carry in their top pocket suddenly erupted into rasping life. "Escaped prisoner James Bradley seen in Plumstead Road area. Description – five feet ten inches high, heavy build, wearing over-tight grey suit. Walks with a pronounced limp . . ."

"He went round that corner," Michael said gently. "If you run you should catch him."

The policeman gave him one startled glance, said: "Strewth!" and lumbered off in the indicated direction, blowing his whistle furiously as he went.

That incident was really the turning point in Michael's career as a professional practitioner of E. O. P. As time passed he all but developed X-ray eyes. A smile, a frown, the flick of an eyelid, when coupled with such irregularities as odd socks, a missing coat button, a frayed shirt collar, told him where a person worked, lived, the size of their income, if they were married or single and what they had been up to during the past twenty-four hours.

Practice makes perfect – too much practice can result in over-perfection. Or, to put it another way – over-perception. Michael suddenly observed something he would rather not have seen.

Mr Manfield was a commercial gentleman.

He had a nice glossy car that was owned by his company and spent five days a week travelling across the country, selling a very superior brand of kitchen hardware: gleaming aluminium saucepans, non-stick frying pans, glazed oven dishes of every size and description, and rather terrifying pressure cookers.

When not travelling, Mr Manfield was a lodger in Michael's house. He slept in the spare room and took his meals with Michael and his widowed mother, Mrs Carrington. Of course Michael's E. O. P. told him a lot about Mr Manfield that was not apparent to those who had not developed this extraordinary gift. He knew a blonde lady occasionally replaced missing buttons; a left-handed barber cut his hair: a careless person (most likely the blonde lady) scraped mud from his shoes; he had a weakness for brown ale and pickled onions; he threw away his socks when they acquired their first hole.

He also had a ghost that walked behind him.

Michael suspected the ghost had been following Mr Manfield for some time, but due to his previous lack of E. O. P. he had not seen it. When the commercial gentleman had first entered the dining-room, accompanied by what appeared to be a little old lady with white hair and a large curved nose, and attired in a shabby green dress, he all but fainted. His mother asked: "Aren't you well? Why are you staring like that?"

Michael just could not tear his horrified gaze from the apparition, which seemed solid enough at first glance, but revealed a hint of transparency when subjected to prolonged inspection. But the really frightening aspect was the ferocious expression on the old lady's face and the futile efforts she made to punch Mr Manfield in the ribs. Michael watched her clench tiny fists, drive them with considerable force in the direction of the tall man's ribs, then do a little dance of rage when he appeared to feel no effects.

"Michael, I'll not tell you again," Mrs Carrington protested. "Really, I will think there's something radically wrong with you if you keep staring at Mr Manfield in that fashion."

"What's the matter, son?" Mr Manfield enquired. "Have I got egg on my tie?"

Michael gasped: "No," and ran from the room, quite unable to watch the antics of that grim spectre any longer.

Having reached the reasonable security of his own bedroom, he sat down by the window, and after giving the matter his full consideration, came to the conclusion that in developing his sense of E. O. P. he had also given life to another inborn gift: the ability to see ghosts. Or, at least, one ghost.

Michael spoke his thoughts aloud. "Why couldn't Uncle George keep his big mouth shut? I was quite happy not observing anything. Now I've got to watch that old woman following Mr Manfield and trying to punch him in the ribs. Which means I must find out why. A thirst for knowledge is a dreadful thing."

Then he stopped and jerked his head forward, for Mr Manfield has just come out of the front door and was walking sedately down the garden path. And behind him trotted the old woman, her white head bobbing up and down while she unsuccessfully tried to aim a punch at the bottom of his spine. He opened the front gate and closed it carefully behind him – not, however, before the old woman had slipped through and taken up a position by the near door of his car. When he climbed in behind the steering wheel, she somehow seemed to flow on to the seat beside him, where she swung a really wicked right hook in the direction of his protruding stomach. Michael was unable to see if it made contact.

He decided that here was a problem that might well have baffled Sherlock Holmes, although that rather irritating gentleman would doubtlessly have tried to find a rational explanation for it. Uncle George would have stopped drinking whisky and taken to his heels. But

Michael knew he must find out "Why" and "How" if he were ever again to know peace of mind.

"What do you know about Mr Manfield?" Michael asked, while watching his mother peel potatoes in the kitchen sink. She frowned and shot her young son a suspicious glance.

"All I need to know. He's quiet and well-behaved and pays his rent regular as clockwork on the first of every month. Why are you so interested in Mr Manfield, all of a sudden?"

Michael shrugged and considered a possibility of telling his mother the truth, but quickly dismissed the idea as impracticable. She was not a lady who would accept the presence of a ghost in the house with anything like equanimity. He would most likely be dosed with something vile and made to stay in bed for several days. So he said quietly: "I'm just interested in people. Like to know what makes them tick. Do you suppose Mr Manfield was ever married?"

Mrs Carrington prised two eyes from a large potato, cut it in half, then popped both portions into a saucepan.

"He may have been. In fact, now you mention it, I believe he did say he was a widower. That means he was married, but his wife died."

Michael exclaimed: "Ah!" and followed it with an equally expressive: "Oh!" before realizing that the shade that followed Mr Manfield around did not look much like a defunct wife. He asked another question: "Do you suppose Mr Manfield would have married someone much older?"

His mother laughed softly. "I wouldn't think so. He can't be more than forty-five, and I can't see him tied to an old woman. More likely one younger than himself. Your poor father was ten years older than me."

Michael sighed deeply and once again wished he had never developed his sense of E. O. P. The entire business was becoming much too complicated and required more courage and judgement than he could manage. Michael knew nothing at all about ghosts, but clearly Mr Manfield must have done something dreadful for that old woman to be continually trying to punch him in the ribs. Michael shook his head, thereby causing Mrs Carrington to ask:

"What's wrong with you now? I must say you're acting very strange lately."

"I'll have to watch some more." Michael answered thoughtlessly.

"Watch what?"

"Oh, what's going on around me."

"Sometimes," Mrs Carrington remarked caustically, "I think you're not quite right in the head."

Mr Manfield did not arrive back until the end of the week, and then only a little before midnight, so Michael did not see him before breakfast time the next morning. On entering the dining-room Michael experienced a feeling of relief, blended with disappointment, on realizing that there was no apparition standing behind Mr Manfield's chair. The commercial gentleman looked up as Michael entered and gave him a wan smile.

"Good morning, Michael. I trust you are well."

The boy seated himself opposite and endured his mother's kiss when she placed a bowl of Shredded Wheat before him. He gave Mr Manfield a conventional reply. "I'm quite well, thank you. Did you have a successful trip?"

The man sighed gently and brushed back a lock of grey hair with a not over-steady hand. "Mustn't grumble. Managed to nail one or two respectable orders." He looked up at Michael's mother. "Mrs Carrington, I don't think I can tackle your excellent breakfast this morning. To be honest, I feel a wee bit under the weather."

Mrs Carrington at once expressed grave concern. "I am sorry to hear that, Mr Manfield. I do hope you're not sickening for something."

Mr Manfield shook his head. "No, I don't think so. But lately I've had a kind of dull ache in my left side. Around the kidney. Anyway, that's where it seems to be. Probably a touch of wind. But I don't feel much like eating."

"I've got some milk of magnesia in the kitchen," Mrs Carrington stated. "A spoonful will work wonders. Let me fetch it."

Mr Manfield smiled bleakly. "You are too kind, but I'm beginning to feel a little better. I've probably been over-doing things lately. Tension, you know, upsets the old tummy."

It was then that Michael realized that the old woman had not been so far away at all. He suddenly saw her standing in the gap which separated the sideboard from the left hand wall, an almost imperceptible figure that lurked in the shadows, for the early morning sunlight did not reach that part of the room. When Mr Manfield had finished speaking, and Mrs Carrington was insisting he have a fresh cup of coffee, the old woman left her hiding place and walked with terrifying slowness towards the table. Michael trembled when Mr Manfield said:

"No need to look so frightened, son. I'm not going to die."

Her face creased into a grimace of pure hate, the old woman took up a position behind her victim and drove a clenched fist into the small of his back. Mr Manfield emitted a hoarse cry and jerked forward, until his nose was only five centimetres from the butter dish, an action that had Mrs Carrington shouting instructions to a petrified Michael.

"Don't sit there staring. Help me get the poor man up to his room. If he's not better soon, I'm calling in the doctor."

Together they managed to raise the groaning man from his chair and guide him towards the door, while Michael did his utmost not to look at the apparition, which was now standing to one side, apparently well content with its handiwork. Mr Manfield seemed to have partially recovered by the time they had propelled him up the stairs, and kept muttering: "No need to worry . . . over-work . . . only a pain in my back."

They got him on to the large bed, and Mrs Carrington removed his shoes and loosened his tie, then gave Michael some unpalatable instructions.

"Now, you stay here and keep an eye on him. If he has another turn, call me. Then I'll ring the doctor."

Michael looked anxiously around the room. There was no sign of the old woman, and he could only suppose she had remained behind in the dining-room. He expressed grave concern.

"You mean – I'm to stay here – all by myself?"

"Of course you won't be by yourself. Mr Manfield's here, isn't he? Don't be so silly."

And she left the room, leaving the door wide open so as to hear Michael, should he have occasion to call out. The boy sat down on the very edge of the bedside chair and ejected a muffled cry when a cloud passed over the sun, causing a shadow to go racing across the far wall. He managed to produce a pale smile when Mr Manfield stirred on the bed and opened his eyes.

"No need for you to stay, son. I'm feeling much better."

"Mother said I was to sit by you," Michael said, "so I'd better do that. How long have you been – well – feeling these pains?"

"Three or four weeks," Mr Manfield replied. "They

were only little twinges at first. Scarcely felt them. But lately they've been getting worse."

Michael jerked his head round and stared wide-eyed at the open doorway, for there had been the suggestion of a figure flitting across the landing. He smothered a cry and asked in a tremulous voice: "Mr Manfield, do you know an old woman with a big nose, wearing a shabby green dress – someone who doesn't like you?"

For a while it seemed as if Mr Manfield had not heard the question, for he lay completely motionless and stared up at the boy with unnaturally bright eyes. Michael laid a hand on his arm and shook it gently. "Mr Manfield, are you all right? Did you hear what I said?"

The man's thin lips parted, and a hoarse voice, so unlike his normal gentle tone, manufactured fear-tinted words.

"What are you talking about, son? How can you know anything about that old hag? Who have you been talking to?"

Michael was not far from tears, what with Mr Manfield speaking with such a strange voice and the prospect of that dreadful phantom appearing in the doorway at any moment. His next words did not appear to reassure the man on the bed.

"I've developed Extra Ocular Perception – I can see her. She's punching you – that's why you have those pains. And I think she may have something to do with that nice, but not very bright lady, who sews your missing buttons on with the wrong coloured cotton, leaves blonde hair on your coat collar, and scrapes mud from your shoes with a blunt knife."

His voice died away as the man gripped his arm and vainly tried to speak. Michael felt a rising wave of pity drive the fear from his mind, for no matter what he had done, no one deserved to look so terrified as Mr Manfield

379

did now. He tried to think of something to say that would at least create an illusion of normality, but before he could speak, Mr Manfield collapsed back on to the bed. Michael was about to call his mother, when the old woman entered the room and walked round to the far side of the bed, where she stood looking down upon the motionless man.

Michael whispered: "Why? Why?" But the apparition did not spare him so much as a single glance, merely turned and moved slowly towards the dressing-table. Michael thought he saw the mirror gleam brightly just before she disappeared.

The doctor said Mr Manfield's illness was due to overwork and nervous exhaustion, and only complete rest and quiet would ensure his recovery. Michael took him at his word and kept well away from the sick-room while he tried to solve the bizarre riddle. Then, on the third day after Mr Manfield's collapse, the unexpected happened.

When the door bell sent its melodious chimes through the house, Mrs Carrington called out from above the stairs: "Answer that, Michael. I'm making Mr Manfield comfortable."

The woman who stood on the front doorstep was possibly thirty-five to forty years of age, had well-groomed blonde hair and a round, unlined face, enhanced by large blue eyes. She wore a bright red coat and carried an over-large handbag. She spoke with a voice that was tinged with the suggestion of a Northern accent.

"Hello, love, I do hope I've come to the right house, but Gerald is a shocking writer, and I couldn't be sure if the number was thirty-two or fifty-two."

"Gerald?" Michael asked.

"Yes, dear, Gerald Manfield. He rings me up regular every Monday and Friday, and I haven't heard a dickybird from him for the past three weeks. I thought I'd pop down and see if everything was all right."

Michael stood to one side. "You'd better come in. Mr Manfield is ill."

The woman exclaimed: "Oh, dear! I knew something was wrong," and all but ran into the hall, where she laid the large bag on a chair, then removed her coat and hung it on the hat-stand. Mrs Carrington's voice demanded information.

"Who is it, Michael?"

"A friend of Mr Manfield."

Michael could see that his mother was not all that taken by the visitor, for she gave the floral-patterned dress and bright blonde hair a disapproving look, while she said quietly: "You'd better come into the sitting-room. Can I offer you some refreshment?"

The stranger bared her perfect teeth in a polite smile. "Thank you, love, but I had a cuppa at the station." She preceded Mrs Carrington into the sitting-room, where, without waiting to be invited, she flopped down into an armchair. "That's better. I couldn't wait to get the weight off me feet. Well, now . . . I'm Nora Sugden. And you must be Mrs Carrington. Gerald often speaks about you and how well you look after him."

Mrs Carrington eased herself down on the sofa. "He most certainly has never mentioned you. I was under the impression he was alone in the world. Am I to understand that you are a close friend?"

Nora Sugden giggled. "You could say so, dear. I'm his intended."

"Intended!"

"Yes, dear. We intend to get married as soon as he's cleared up some business matters. Lawyers, you understand. Never hurry themselves. I told him not to worry. I said: 'I've got enough for both of us, until your first wife's estate is sorted out.' But he wouldn't hear of it."

Mrs Carrington frowned. "But I understand that his wife died years ago. Surely by now . . ."

"Oh no, love. She only passed away last year. Mind you, I gather they hadn't got on together for some time." She leaned forward and lowered her voice to a confidential whisper. "Mother-in-law trouble, I believe. Some old hen who kept making trouble."

Mrs Carrington said: "Really!" and Michael felt his pulse quicken with rising excitement. Nora Sugden relaxed back in her chair, then looked enquiringly at the door. "Do you suppose I could see Gerald now? I'm sure the sight of me will cheer him up no end."

Before his mother could answer, Michael fired a question that just had to be answered. "Excuse me, but do you know what his wife died of?"

Mrs Carrington exclaimed: "Michael, really!" while the blonde woman patted her hair and appeared to give the question some thought. "I'm not all that certain, love. Something to do with her stomach, I believe. Gastro-something. I remember Gerald saying it was very painful."

Michael ignored his mother's forbidding frown and asked his second important question. "And what happened to her mother?"

Nora Sugden began to display signs of some impatience. "My, he is an inquisitive little lad, isn't he? If you must know, love, she died. Quite recently. Fell down some stairs, I believe. Broke her back, at any rate. Gerald said she was no great loss. Now, if I could . . ."

Mrs Carrington rose and moved towards the door. "Yes, indeed. But you mustn't excite him. The doctor said he must have rest and quiet and no visitors. But seeing that you're his fiancée, I suppose it'll be all right. I must say I didn't expect to have a sick man on my hands."

The two women left the room, and Michael waited until they had mounted the stairs before hurrying over to the bookcase and taking out a bulky encyclopaedia. He turned the pages until he found the entry he was looking for.

Gastro-Enteritis: Inflammation of the mucous membrane (lining) of the intestine. Unripe fruit, decomposing meat, irritant poisons (e.g. arsenic, mercury) will cause it. Abdominal pains are symptomatic . . .

Michael closed the book. There was no need to read any more. He knew with a dreadful certainty that Mr Manfield had poisoned his wife, and the doctors had probably assumed she had eaten bad meat or unripe fruit. Possibly she had always suffered from some form of stomach trouble. Then her mother had become suspicious, and Mr Manfield had pushed her down the stairs. He whispered the awful truth aloud.

"Now she's in this house, making him suffer in the same way her daughter did. And I am the only one who can see her."

His deliberations were interrupted by a loud scream that came from the top of the stairs, followed by Mr Manfield's voice shouting: "Go away! She don't want you near me! Go . . . o . . . o . . . o away!"

Footsteps came running down the stairs, and Nora Sugden burst into the room, her face transformed by an expression of sheer terror. She slumped into a chair and sat trembling so violently that Michael half expected her string of glass beads to rattle. Mrs Carrington came in a few moments later and, after giving her visitor a quick glance, went over to the sideboard and quarter-filled a tumbler with neat whisky. She thrust it into the woman's shaking hand and said abruptly:

"Here, drink this. It will steady your nerves."

Nora Sugden emptied the glass in a single gulp and gave the impression she would not object to a refill. But Mrs Carrington sank down into a chair and wiped her moist forehead with a lace handkerchief, while waiting for the woman to recover. Presently she said: "Well, you can see what kind of a state he's in. I don't think I can stand much more of it, not with a young boy in the house. I'd be obliged if you would arrange for him to be taken somewhere. After all, he's more your responsibility than mine."

Nora Sugden shook her head violently. "No, I couldn't. I just want to go home and forget that I ever saw him. There's something wrong. Dreadfully wrong."

Mrs Carrington raised her voice. "But you can't expect me to look after him, not now he's in that state. Shaking like a leaf, continually staring at the dressing-table, then screaming like that. If you don't . . ."

The old woman was standing in the hall, looking in through the open doorway, her face wearing an expression that suggested complete satisfaction – even triumph. Then she turned to the left and moved in the direction of the front door. Presently Michael – now oblivious to the women's arguing voices – rose and crept from the room. The hall was empty. Impelled by a burning curiosity that was stronger than fear, he slowly mounted the stairs and pushed open the door of Mr Manfield's room. He was propped up in bed, his face frozen into a mask of abject horror. Michael knew he was dead.

The boy turned his head away and whispered: "I guess, in the end, Mr Manfield must have developed his own sense of E.O.P."

Then he went back downstairs to inform his mother that she need no longer worry about who was to look after Mr Manfield. He had been well and truly taken care of.

THE SERVANT

by Alison Prince

Ginny ran down the path. Her mother shouted after her
from the back door, "When you've got a house of your
own, my girl, you can make as much mess as you like.
But you're not having your pocket money until you've
tidied your bedroom!"

Ginny snatched her bike out of the shed, kicked the
side gate open and set off down the lane. Her mother was
waving her arms frantically and shouting something, but
Ginny took no notice. Summer holidays were *awful*, she
fumed, pedalling fast. Just because there was no school to
go to, people treated you as if you were nothing at all –
just a meek little figure who had to fit in with the rest of
the household and not be noticed. A handy person to
boss about. Run round to the shops, Ginny, dry the
dishes, Ginny, tidy your room, Ginny. It was like being a
servant.

Ginny came to the top of Bunkers Hill and let the bike
freewheel down the long slope. The wind blew her hair
back and made the hot morning cooler. Below her the
green landscape spread out like a toy farmyard. Further
down, Bunkers Hill crossed the busy main road and
became Nebbutts Lane, leading through the distant fields
to Cuckoo Wood where the bluebells grew so thickly in
the spring. Much nearer, just before the cross-roads, a
disused track wandered off to the right. Ginny touched
her brakes to check the bike's speed as she approached
the junction. Nothing happened.

Panic clutched at Ginny's heart like a cold hand. The

385

sunny day was whistling past her with a speed which made her eyes run. She grabbed repeatedly at the useless brakes, remembering now that she had told her father when he came home from work last night that they needed adjusting. The brakes had been slack yesterday, but now they had completely gone. And she was hurtling towards the busy highway. To go out there at this speed meant almost certain death.

There was only one escape. The track. A milk float was coming up the hill towards her, threatening to block the entry to Ginny's haven unless she got there first. She crouched over the handlebars to increase the bike's break-neck speed and banked the bike hard to her right. She missed the oncoming milk float by inches and caught a glimpse of the driver's startled face as she shot down the stony, disused lane.

The bicycle jumped and rattled over the rough surface but, to Ginny's relief, the track began to level out as it narrowed to an overgrown path between dark trees and straggling banks of brambles. Impeded by the long grass, the bike slowed down and at last stopped. Ginny got off shakily. Her knees and elbows felt as if they had turned to water. After a few minutes she bent down and looked at the bike's brakes. They had been disconnected and the blocks removed. Her father must have been intending to buy some new ones for her today. But why hadn't he *said*? True, she had been out at a disco last night, but he could have left a note or told her mother . , . Ginny had an uneasy memory of her mother shouting something after her as she rode off this morning, but she thrust the thought away. Her parents simply didn't *care*, she told herself with a new burst of anger after being so frightened.

And now what? She had come out with every intention of staying out until lunchtime and she didn't want to go crawling home again so soon, no doubt to be bossed about and scolded for not stopping to listen to what her mother had been saying. Ginny propped the bike against the ivy-clad trunk of a tree and stared round her. It was very, very quiet. The trees seemed almost to meet overhead, shutting out the sunshine. Ginny gave a little shiver. And then she heard the bell.

It was a faint, tinkling bell, very distant. It rang with a peremptory rapidness as if shaken by an impatient hand. Somebody wanted something, and quickly. Ginny pushed her hands into her jeans pockets and set off along the path, leaving the bike where it was. Since she had nothing to do, she might as well go and find out where the sound of the bell had come from.

The path went on between its high banks in such deep shade that it was almost like being in a tunnel. Daylight glowed at its far end as if promising a clearing, and Ginny walked towards it quickly. The bell rang again, sounding closer this time. Ginny emerged from the trees to find that she had come out further along the hillside. The path ended in a field of ripening barley. Butterflies danced in the sun.

On the sloping ground beside the field, slate-roofed behind a flint wall with a gate in the middle, stood a house. Heavy lace curtains were tied in loops at its windows, and its doorstep was spotlessly white. A plume of smoke ascended from its chimney straight into the windless sky. As Ginny stared at the house, the bell sounded again, a longer, rattling tinkle. A looped curtain twitched back in the ground-floor window to the left of the front door and a face looked out. White hair, a high-necked blouse and two black eyes which stared accusingly.

"Violet! Come along in at once!" snapped a dry voice, and a finger tapped on the pane.

Ginny glanced over her shoulder in case somebody

called Violet was standing behind her, but she was alone. The butterflies danced above the motionless barley.

The bell tinkled again, and this time Ginny's hand reached for the latch of the gate and she found herself running up the path. The untrodden whiteness of the front doorstep warned her not to enter this way, and she darted round the side of the house to where blue-flowered periwinkles fringed a paved yard. The back door stood open.

The large, dim kitchen had a red tiled floor, and a huge wooden plate rack stood above the stone sink like an ominous, complicated cage. Ginny found that she was listening intently, in a kind of dread. She was waiting for the bell to ring. In a few moments its jangling tinkle sounded, so close that it was almost inside her head. She ran through the shadowed hall, where patches of red and blue light gleamed from a panel of stained glass in the front door, and tapped on the white-painted door to her right.

"Come *in*," said the dry voice impatiently.

Ginny opened the sitting-room door. The fingers which gripped the small brass bell by its ebony handle were thin and bony, the hand blue-veined, veiled by a ruffle of lace from the tight silk sleeve. Tiny jet buttons ran up the narrow bodice to the cameo at the high neck, and then there was the white face, the mouth thin and pinched and the nose as craggy as a parrot's beak, the eyes astonishingly black under the elaborate pile of white hair.

"You are not to go outside, Violet," said the woman. "You belong in here, with me."

Ginny found that she was standing with her hands behind her and her feet together, and almost smiled at her own sudden politeness. "My name's Ginny," she said.

"Not suitable," said the woman heavily. The black eyes travelled slowly down Ginny's figure until they reached her plimsolls, then travelled up again. Vertical lines appeared above the lips as the mouth tightened a little more.

"Violet," said the woman, "you will wear your uniform at all times in this house, do you understand?"

"But I'm not – " began Ginny. Her voice petered out as the tight lips smiled grimly.

"Oh, yes, you are, my dear," said the woman. "My servants have always been called Violet. So much more convenient. I am Mrs Rackham, but you will call me madam, of course."

Ginny shook her head in confusion. This could not be happening. But she looked at the little brass bell with the ebony handle, and stared into Mrs Rackham's black, unblinking eyes, and knew that it was true.

"I have been *waiting* for my breakfast," said Mrs Rackham.

Ginny stared guiltily into the black eyes, struggling to hold on to the idea that Mrs Rackham's breakfast had nothing to do with her, Ginny Thompson.

Mrs Rackham leaned forward a little. "Light the spirit lamp," she instructed impatiently, "then go to the kitchen and get my breakfast." The blue-veined hand gestured towards the table which stood by the window, draped with a lace cloth over heavy red chenille. On it stood eggshell-thin cups and saucers, a silver teapot and sugar bowl and a thin-spouted brass kettle which, supported on a brass stand, stood over a small burner. Ginny moved towards it. At any rate, she thought, it was better than hanging about at home. If she was treated like a servant there, she might just as well play at being a servant here.

A box of matches lay beside the brass kettle. Ginny struck one and turned up the wick in its holder. It burned with a steady blue flame. The old woman was mad, of course, Ginny told herself. It wasn't unusual in old people. Her own granny had been very absent-minded, always calling Ginny by the name of a long-dead aunt, Flora, which was even worse than Violet.

"That's better," said Mrs Rackham, darting a black-eyed glance at the spirit lamp. "Now get along to the kitchen, quickly. When you bring my breakfast, you will be properly dressed."

Ginny smiled and said, "All right."

Mrs Rackham looked outraged. "That is not the way to answer," she snapped. "Say, 'yes, madam.' And curtsey."

Ginny held out imaginary skirts and curtsied deeply as she had been taught at her ballet class.

Mrs Rackham seemed even more angry. "Just a small bob, you stupid creature!" she hissed. "Do you girls know *nothing* these days?"

Ginny expected to feel amused as she gave an obedient little bob, but as Mrs Rackham growled, "That's better," and the black eyes bored into Ginny's mind, the hidden smile shrivelled and died.

Ginny left the room with quick, neat footsteps, closing the door quietly behind her. As she made her way back to the kitchen the voice of reason in her mind urged her to walk out of the door and back along the lane to her brakeless bicycle, and start pushing it home. On the other hand . . . Mrs Rackham had to have her breakfast. Perhaps whoever looked after her had gone out for a while. No doubt they would be back.

The kitchen was cool and quiet. Greenish light filtered through a small, ivy-covered window, and a few flies circled aimlessly under the high ceiling. Gazing up at them, Ginny saw that a black dress and several white aprons hung from a wooden airer, and a starched white cap dangled from the end of one of its bars. She unhitched the airer's rope from its hook on the wall and released it hand over hand, lowering the airer so that she could reach the clothes. If she was going to humour the old lady's delusions, she might as well do the job properly.

But as Ginny peeled off her tee shirt and jeans she found that she was listening in a kind of terror for Mrs Rackham's bell; as if its demanding tinkle had dominated her whole life. She struggled into the black dress and did up the rows of buttons down the front and on each sleeve. She pulled on the thick black stockings which she also found on the airer, sliding up the pair of elastic garters which were looped round the airer's end beside the cap. Then she tied on a white, lace-edged apron and pulled the starched cap over her curly hair. She looked round for something more suitable than her plimsolls and found, neatly placed beside the wooden mangle, a pair of highly-polished black shoes, fastened by a single button.

The shoes fitted as if Ginny had always worn them. She pulled up the airer then stared round the kitchen with increasing anxiety. What did madam have for breakfast? Plates of all sizes stood in the cage-like wooden plate rack, but there seemed to be no fridge and the pantry contained no muesli or cornflakes.

Mrs Rackham's bell rang.

Ginny jumped round, a hand to the high-buttoned neck of her dress. The voice of reason seemed to have deserted her, and she could only think that madam was waiting for her breakfast and that she, Violet, had failed to get it yet. She ran to the front room.

"Do I have to wait all day?" demanded Mrs Rackham. A vigorous spurt of steam was hissing from the brass kettle over its burner.

"I – I'm sorry, madam," stammered Ginny. "I didn't know what you wanted."

"Two lightly boiled eggs, brown bread and butter cut in fingers, toast and marmalade," said Mrs Rackham. "Stupid girl. You can make the tea now you are here."

Ginny went across to the table. She found an ornate tea caddy and put two spoonfuls of tea into the silver teapot. Then she picked up the brass kettle – and let it fall back into its stand with a gasp of pain. The handle was almost red hot. Tears sprang to Ginny's eyes as she nursed her stinging pain, but Mrs Rackham threw herself back in her chair, convulsed with cruel laughter. "They all burn their hands!" she cackled delightedly. "It's always the same – again and again!" Then, just as suddenly, she was angry. "Turn the burner down, you idiot," she snapped. "The room is full of steam. And fetch a kettle holder."

In the pale light of the kitchen, Ginny looked at her hand and saw the long red weal across the palm, and wanted to sit down and cry. But Mrs Rackham's bell was ringing, and she snatched the kettle holder from its hook beside the great black range and ran back to the sitting room. She made the tea and said, "I'll go and boil the eggs."

"*When* you have moved the table within my reach," said Mrs Rackham. "And where is the milk?"

Ginny pushed the heavy table across to the old lady's chair, hampered by the stinging pain in her hand. Then she ran back to the kitchen for the milk, which she found by some kind of instinct in a small lidded churn on the pantry shelf. She snatched a blue jug from its hook and ladled some milk into it. The bell was ringing.

"That is a *kitchen* jug!" screamed Mrs Rackham as Ginny proffered the milk, and lace ruffles flew as a hand flashed out, sweeping the jug from Ginny's hand to smash against the sideboard. "Clear all that mess up," Mrs Rackham commanded, her face tight with fury, "then bring my milk in the proper jug. Where are my eggs? Don't you dare boil them for more than three minutes!"

Ginny ran sobbing to the kitchen, found a small glass

jug and filled it with milk then carried it back to Mrs Rackham, who said nothing. Milk dripped from the polished edge of the mahogany sideboard.

As Ginny went in search of a cloth she tried to recall the reasonable voice which told her that she did not belong here; but there was nothing in her mind except worry and guilt and the stinging of her burned hand. She found a rather smelly piece of rag and cleaned up the spilt milk as best she could, and picked up the pieces of the broken jug.

"Violet, *where* are my eggs?" enquired Mrs Rackham.

"Coming," said Ginny desperately.

"Coming, *madam*!" shouted Mrs Rackham.

"Coming, madam," Ginny repeated, and went out with a little curtsey, wiping her eyes on her sleeve. The bell tinkled and she turned back.

The black eyes were fixed upon her with a new energy as the tea was sipped, the cup returned with neat precision to its saucer. "Have you done the fires?" asked Mrs Rackham. "Black-leaded the grates, washed the hearths, swept the carpets, dusted? Cleaned the knives, whitened the doorstep, done the washing, scrubbed the kitchen floor? And what about the bedrooms? Are the beds clean and aired?"

"I don't know," said Ginny helplessly. Tears overwhelmed her.

"I don't know, *madam*!" screamed Mrs Rackham.

Ginny fled to the safety of the kitchen, shaking. She found eggs in a large bowl, and an egg timer with red sand in the lower half of its double-bulged shape. She took a saucepan from the shelf, still crying a little, and filled it with hot water from the huge black kettle which steamed on the range.

Ginny found that her burned hand was beginning to blister. Like a remembered dream, a voice in her head told her that she did not have to stay here. There was a memory, too, of wearing different clothes. Trousers, a shirt made of soft stuff which left her arms bare . . . Ginny wiped her eyes on her black sleeve again, with a gesture so familiar that it seemed as if she had done it many times before. She gazed round the kitchen as if seeking those other garments, but the wooden chairs with a pattern of pierced holes in the seats were bare in the dim light, and the flies circled endlessly against the high ceiling.

The water in the saucepan began to bubble, and Ginny lowered in two eggs with a spoon, then turned over the egg timer. As the trickle of red sand began to run through the narrow neck, she got a brown loaf out of the earthenware bread crock and cut two slices, biting her lip because of the pain in her hand. Then she buttered the slices and cut them neatly into fingers.

When the eggs were done she assembled a tray and carried it through the hall to Mrs Rackham. The sitting-room was dazzling after the dim kitchen, for sunlight poured in through the long window. Outside, the barley shimmered in the sun and the butterflies danced. Tears suddenly brimmed again in Ginny's eyes. She would never be free to walk through the fields, to come so fast down a steep hill that her eyes ran, but not with tears.

"Don't stand there gawping, Violet," said Mrs Rackham. "Put the things down here."

Ginny obediently slid the tray on to the lace cloth.

"Where is my toast?" demanded Mrs Rackham.

"I – I didn't know how to make it," Ginny faltered. Remotely, she remembered making toast by putting slices of bread into little slits in the top of – of what? She shook her head, confused. She had always been here. She would never leave. She would die here.

"With a toasting fork, you stupid girl, in front of the

range," said Mrs Rackham. She decapitated an egg then added, "The spirit lamp has gone out. Light it."

Ginny held a burning match to the wick, but no flame sprang up.

"Refill it," snapped Mrs Rackham, waving an irritable hand towards the corner cupboard.

Ginny opened the tall, panelled door and took out the bottle of spirit. Violet, she thought as she gazed at its wonderful purple colour. Violet. Like me.

With the kettle holder she gingerly removed the top of the burner and filled up its reservoir with spirit. Her burned hand made her clumsy and the spirit spilled over and ran down on to the lace cloth, soaking through into the red chenille below it. Ginny shot a fearful glance at Mrs Rackham, but madam was probing an egg with the delicate silver spoon, and did not look up. Ginny fed the wick carefully back into the reservoir and fitted the top into place again. Once more she struck a match and applied it to the wick.

A blue flame leapt up, not only from the wick but from the whole top of the burner, following the spilt spirit down the brass stand and on the soaked cloth under it. Ginny shrieked with terror and jumped back, brushing against the uncorked bottle of spirit with her sleeve as she did so and knocking it over. More spirit gushed out, and sheets of flame sprang up, engulfing the kettle and its stand, the teapot, the cups, the table. Mrs Rackham began to scream, her mouth wide open in the white face, her blue-veined hands upraised. The red chenille cloth was ablaze, and the varnish on the heavy mahogany table legs was wrinkling as it caught fire. Flames began to leap up the side of the chintz arm chair where Mrs Rackham sat, still screaming. The skirt of her silk dress shrivelled as the flames licked across the chair, and Ginny saw that

Mrs Rackham's legs were as twisted and useless as a rag doll's, encased in heavy contraptions of iron and leather.

Outside, the dancing butterflies shivered behind a screen of heat as the looped curtains burned. The room filled with smoke, and Ginny began to gasp for breath. Suddenly she realized that she must get out. She could not help Mrs Rackham. The hem of her long black dress was beginning to smoulder as she ran from the room. She grappled with the bolt on the front door. Her dress was burning. The house was full of fire, and the red and blue stained glass windows in the front door were dimmed with the choking smoke.

As Ginny wrenched the door open and daylight burst upon her like an explosion it seemed that Mrs Rackham was screaming a single word, senselessly and repeatedly. "Again!" she shrieked, and it was like a mad song of agony and triumph. "Again! Again! Again!" And Ginny knew what the terrible word meant. Like a recurring nightmare whose end only leads to the next beginning, she was condemned to repeat this experience over and over again. Even now, as the air fanned her burning dress into greedy flames and the screams were swallowed up in the inferno which had been a house; even in the agony of burning alive, Ginny was listening for the tinkle of Mrs Rackham's bell. It would all begin again.

Somebody was shaking her. "Ginny!" a voice was saying urgently. "Are you all right? What are you doing here?"

Mrs Thompson stared down at her daughter, who lay huddled by the rusted gate in the flint wall, an arm flung protectively across her face. She appeared to be asleep.

"Again," said Ginny, and trembled.

"Are you all right?" Mrs Thompson repeated. "I was frantic when you went off like that – your dad said to tell you about the bike, that he'd get new brake blocks. He'll murder me. Then the milkman said you nearly crashed into him tearing down Bunkers Hill – well, I got the car out straight away and came down here looking for you."

Ginny's eyes were open but she was not seeing her mother. Her gaze searched the sky with a kind of despair. "Butterflies," she murmured. Tears welled up and she rubbed her eyes on the back of her wrist wearily.

"Darling, don't cry," said her mother. "It's all right – I'm not cross or anything. I mean, it was partly my fault." After a pause she went on, "I found your bike along the lane. But why did you come here? I hate ruined houses, they're so creepy." Rose bay willow herb, the fire weed, stood tall among the blackened heaps of stone. It really was a horrible place, Mrs Thompson thought. Some distance away the remains of a brass kettle lay dented and squashed in the sun.

Ginny stood up and brushed fussily at her bare arms, fiddling at her wrists as though buttoning tight cuffs. Her mother watched with dawning concern as the girl straightened an apron, smoothed out a long skirt, her anxious hands not touching the surface of her jeans. "I must go," she said.

"You're not going anywhere," said Ginny's mother. "You're coming home with me. You must have had a nasty shock. We can put your bike in the back of the car."

Ginny gave a sudden start. "I must go," she said again with worried alertness. "Mrs Rackham wants her breakfast. That's her bell. What am I doing out here?"

Her mother stared. "Mrs Rackham? This house is known as Rackham's, yes, but there's nobody here now. Some old crippled woman owned it, they say, but she died in the fire when it was burnt down, along with some poor little servant girl."

"Violet," agreed Ginny. She dropped a small curtsey, not looking at her mother, and called, "Coming, madam!"

Then she set off with oddly neat little footsteps through the weed-grown rubble, trotting parallel to the garden wall until she turned at a right angle and ran on to where some blue-flowered periwinkle bloomed among the stone. Her mother intercepted her and caught the girl by the hand. Ginny flinched violently. A long, red, blistered weal lay across her palm.

"How on earth did you do that?" demanded her mother. "There's nothing hot on a bicycle. Unless – you didn't put your hand on the tyre, did you, to try to stop?"

But Ginny did not hear. She was staring into the black eyes again, watching the thin mouth in the white face as the orders were snapped out, hearing the cruel laughter as she burned her hand again. Outside the tall window, the barley shimmered in the summer sun and the butterflies danced. But Ginny would never be free to walk among them again. She was Mrs Rackham's servant, and madam wanted her breakfast. Again – and again – and again.

THE THING THAT WENT BUMP
IN THE NIGHT

by Rosemary Timperley

Bump . . . bump . . . bump . . .

The sound was clear as clear. Something was rolling down the stairs; rather as a ball might roll, yet more heavily, more thuddingly, and with less resilience than, say, a football.

Tom lay petrified in bed and listened. He had been warned about this noise in the night, but his uncle had said that whether you heard it or not probably depended upon whether you were psychic.

"Well, I'm not physic." Tom had responded jauntily, deliberately making mock of the word, and his uncle told him: "If you've never been in a supposedly haunted house before, you're unlikely to know whether you are or not. Anyway, lad, if you do hear any bumps on the stairs at midnight, just ignore them. They're unexplained but they do no harm. I've never heard them myself, but I got this house cheaply because of its reputation."

Tom's Uncle Bob, retired grocer, widower with no offspring of his own, had invited his nephew to spend a week of the summer holidays with him in his house in the country, where he lived alone. A village woman, Mrs Miller, came in daily to do the chores, and it was from her that Tom's uncle had first heard about the "bumps in the night". He'd told Tom about it today because he was afraid the boy might be bored, just staying with his old uncle, and he had added, almost apologetically: "Not much of a haunting. No clanking chains or black monks or sceptres dripping gore or what-have-you. Just a series of silly old bumps at midnight, and you probably won't hear them any more than I have."

But Tom had heard them all right, and he felt his hair creep on his scalp as if suddenly possessed of an independent life of its own.

The bumping sound was growing fainter now, and then there was a final distant thud, and silence. Whatever the rolling-downstairs-thing was, it had landed in the hall.

And suddenly Tom felt suspicious of Uncle Bob. He'd always been one for practical jokes, at family parties and such. This was one of his tricks – so Tom "wouldn't be bored"!

No longer afraid, the boy got out of bed, opened his door and looked down the stairs. Nothing was lying at the foot. But then Uncle Bob would have had plenty of time to nip out of his ground floor bedroom and retrieve the object, whatever it was.

Now his uncle's door opened and the grey-haired, stocky little man stood there in his blue-striped pyjamas. "Tom? I heard you moving about. You all right?"

Tom laughed. "You're a wicked old man. Did you think I wouldn't guess what you were up to?"

"I've not been up to anything."

"Go on! You crept up these stairs, let a ball or something roll down, trying to scare the pyjama-legs off me, and then retrieved it before I had time to come out and look."

"You mean," said Bob, "you heard the bumps?"

"Well, I'm not deaf – "

"But I heard nothing, Tom, and I haven't moved since I went to bed."

Tom said: "Will you swear, cut-your-throat-and-hope-to-die, that you didn't roll anything down those stairs to fool me?"

"Cut-my-throat-and-hope-to-die, I swear it," said Bob, and as that had been a kind of password between them since Tom's early childhood, the boy believed him.

"Cripes," he said, feeling suddenly very cold.

"Come on down and we'll have a cuppa," Bob suggested.

They went into the kitchen, Tom looking warily at the stairs as he descended, and especially at the place at the foot of the stairs where the "thing" had landed. The "thing" which wasn't there. Which didn't exist. Yet did. Because he had *heard* it.

Bob made a pot of strong tea, poured cups for the two of them, with plenty of milk and sugar, brought out a tin of biscuits and said: "Little midnight feast to calm you down, so you can go to sleep again. You do look pale, lad. Would you rather not stay on here with me after this?"

"Not stay!" Tom exclaimed. "Wild horses wouldn't get me to leave! I shall listen again at midnight tomorrow and, if I hear those bumps, I hope to have the guts to get up and look out of my room as soon as the noise starts, instead of lying there like coward. Wouldn't it be great if, while I'm here, I could solve the mystery of the haunted house!"

His uncle said: "Mrs Miller says that the people who lived here before did look at the stairs when they heard the noise. They went on hearing it, but saw nothing. Two retired schoolmarms. They were so unnerved that they left. That's right, Tom, drink your tea. You've got a bit of colour coming back into your face. But what your mother would say if she knew – "

"Don't you dare tell her," Tom interrupted. "She *is* psychic. She believes in anything to do with spooks and spirits and apparitions. She'd be wanting me to come home. No, Uncle, we won't let on. We'll be ghost-investigators. As you're here, I shan't be too scared – I hope," he added, as a precaution.

For now he seemed to hear again in his mind's ear those queer bumping sounds, and recollected the shuddery feeling that had come over him, and how his hair had "crept".

"My hair stood on end, I think," he said wonderingly. "Wish I could have seen it. Never happened to me before."

The tea finished and a quantity of biscuits consumed, the boy returned to bed and slept, but on the following night, after a day of rambling about the countryside on his own, he lay alert, waiting for midnight, listening – and – sure enough – BUMP . . . BUMP . . . BUMP . . .

"I will be brave. I will," he muttered. "All right, silly old bumpety-bump, I'm coming!" And before he had time to think and funk, he sprang out of bed and opened the door.

Eyes wide, heart banging, he gazed at the staircase. He could still hear the sound of the "thing" rolling down, but could see nothing. His spine felt as if it had turned to ice.

Bob must have been listening and waiting, for his door opened immediately. At the same moment, the bumpings stopped, as the "thing" landed. Tom called: "I heard it again, but there's nothing to see. Those two old women were right. What can it *be*?"

He came running down the stairs, paused at the bottom, bent over, and groped with his hands to discover if he could feel the invisible "thing". He felt nothing, but then, to his horror, he saw that his hands had turned red. "There's blood on my hands!" he cried, and dashed into the kitchen. He turned on the tap, but before he had placed his hands under the water's flow, the redness had vanished, as if it had never been.

402

"You saw the blood on my hands, didn't you?" he asked his uncle, who had followed him.

"No," said the other. "You didn't give me time."

"It was there, and now it's gone."

"You imagined it."

"I did not!" Still rather tremulous, he washed his hands, drying them on the towel, which bore no stain afterwards.

"That does it," said Bob. "If you're getting into such a state that you start hallucinating bloodstains, you mustn't stay here another day."

"But I am staying," said Tom. "I'll not run away. I'll sort out this bloody mystery – I mean it literally – if it kills me. Cut-my-throat-and-hope-to-die, I will!"

Cut-my-throat-and-hope-to-die. The words suddenly seemed to have an added significance, and Tom was afraid, but he repeated: "I'll not run away."

Bob gave in. At least the boy wasn't bored, and he seemed so determined that maybe he would solve the mystery one day.

Once again a pot of tea was brewed, out came the biscuit tin, and they discussed the phenomenon.

"My guess is," said Tom, "that murder was done here. Perhaps the 'thing' which bumps down the stairs is the ghost of a sack with a dead body in it, and some of the blood seeped through the fabric on to my fingers."

"There was nothing on your fingers, Tom."

"Ghost blood *is* nothing when you stop seeing it. When you see it, it's something. It's a clue." He paused, then added: "The 'thing' doesn't really sound like a sack full of body, but I can't decide what it does sound like."

Next morning, after his uncle had gone into town for the day, Tom wandered into the kitchen where Mrs Miller was washing the breakfast dishes.

"Like some help, Mrs Miller?"

"I wouldn't say no. You can dry and put away."

Tom picked up the tea-towel and set to work with a will, although normally he detested household chores.

"Did you work here before my uncle came?" he asked casually.

"No, dear. There were two retired lady schoolteachers here before. They did their own housework, cooking, gardening and even wood-cutting."

"But you knew them quite well, living so near."

"Quite well."

"Uncle was telling me about the bumps they heard in the night. I suppose they were scared."

"Wouldn't you be? They were scared all right. They'd been here for some years before they heard a thing, then one night at midnight there was this noise like something bumping down the stairs, but nothing to be seen. They heard it every night after that. They stuck it out for a month or so, then packed their bags and went to live at Maple Cottage on the other side of the village. Then – "

"What's their names?" Tom interrupted.

"Miss Upward and Miss Downley." She laughed a little. "I nicknamed them the Upsy-Downs."

Tom put away the last of the dishes and hung up the towel. "I think I'll go for a walk now," he said.

He walked across the village, past the church and the few shops. Right on the outskirts he saw a cosy little cottage shadowed by a large maple tree. "Maple Cottage," said the sign on the gate. He went up the path and knocked on the door.

It was opened by a tall, broad-shouldered, white-haired woman in sweater and slacks. She didn't, Tom thought, look as if she'd scare easy.

"Good morning," he said. "Please may I see Miss Upward and Miss Downley?"

"You're seeing Miss Upward now." Her voice was high-pitched. "What's your name?"

"Tom."

"Why have you come? No one sees us nowadays."

She sounded rather reproving, so Tom said, in his most grown-up tone: "I am investigating the mysterious bumpings in the haunted house where you and Miss Downley used to live. You see, I've heard them, too."

"Who is it?" a deep voice called.

"A ghost-hunter," Miss Upward called back. "Come in, Tom."

She took him into the living-room, where another white-haired woman, short and thickset, also in trousers, sat knitting a pullover.

"This is Miss Downley, Tom, so now you've got both the Upsy-Downs, as the village people used to call us. What did you want to ask?"

"First, what do you think the bumpety-bump-thing is, or was?"

To his astonishment, the two women answered together: "A head."

A head! Why hadn't he thought of that himself? That was just what it did sound like – not exactly a ball – a head.

"And why do you consider," Tom continued, "a rolling-downstairs-head is haunting my uncle's house?"

"Because," replied Miss Upward, "ghosts, or even parts of ghosts, have no sense of human beings' property. As far as the head is concerned it's his (or should I say 'its'?) house."

"We believe," boomed Miss Downley, starting another row of knitting, "that the head can't rest until it finds its body."

"You take it all very calmly," said Tom.

"We were nervous at the time. We admit it," said Miss Upward. "That's why we left. But now we just feel sorry for the poor old head."

"And even the body, that lost its head," said Miss Downley.

"A body doesn't lose its head, dear," said Miss Upward. "Its head is taken away from it, often as punishment. In the French Revolution, when the rich virtually robbed the poor, the poor punished the rich by taking their heads. Those were gruesome times, but I can see the justice of it. It's very wicked to rob the poor."

Tom thought: trust a schoolteacher to start moralizing and bringing in a history lesson!

"Did you ever touch the ghost head?" he enquired.

"No," they answered in unison, Miss Upward's voice a tinkle, Miss Downley's a boom. "There was nothing to touch."

"I touched that nothing last night and got blood on me which then vanished," said Tom.

"But how fascinating," said Miss Downley. Then she added with a note of mischief, "has it crossed your mind, Tom, that this might be a ghost of things to come – that it might even be your own future head rolling down those stairs – "

They both broke into cackles of laughter, like witches. And suddenly Tom didn't like them one little bit. On the surface, they were so conventional and respectable, but there was something – something sinister.

"Oh, you're frightening the child," said Miss Upward. "We don't think that at all, Tom. As a matter of fact, we know more about the mystery of the haunted house than we ever let on. It's no mystery to us. Shall we tell him, dear?"

"Yes, let's," said Miss Downley. "He's the first ghost-investigator we've met and shall have his reward. You see, Tom, *we* did it."

"Did what?" Tom had risen to his feet and drawn away a little.

Miss Upward said: "It was one midnight when we heard a sound on the landing. I came out of my room and saw a burglar, a very well-dressed burglar too, a decent suit and rings on his fingers – so vulgar. He made a rush at me, then Miss Downley crept up behind him and bashed him on the head with a big vase. He fell unconscious."

"So we went to the shed," continued Miss Downley, "and fetched the axe we used for wood-cutting. Honestly, we meant to threaten him with it when he came to – that was all – but when he did come too, he behaved so savagely that it was a case of us or him. We wielded the axe together and – and executed him. Why not? A rich burglar robbing us poor old pensioners!"

"And the head went rolling down the stairs – bumpety-bump," said Miss Upward animatedly, her voice rising higher and higher.

"And then it rolled away, across the shadows of the hall, away into the timeless dark – and although we hunted, we couldn't find it," said Miss Downley deeply. "So we had to make do with driving the headless body in our car – "

" – and burying it in a wood some miles away – "

" – at the dead of night – "

" – and no one ever knew that we'd rid the earth of that villain – "

" – but every midnight after that – "

" – we heard the head!"

Their voices reached a climax, then there was silence.

Now they were both smiling at him.

"You shall have another reward tonight," said Miss Upward.

"Yes, we will call up a storm," said Miss Downley.

"We are witches, Tom," they said, together.

And Tom fled.

Back at his uncle's house, Mrs Miller asked: "Where did you go for your walk?"

Faintly, he answered, "I went to see Miss Upward and Miss Downley at Maple Cottage."

She looked at him in dismay. "There, you never did! What a disappointment. I never told you, because you didn't give me time, but Maple Cottage was burned down six months ago, and both the ladies were burned to death. Poor souls, they had their hell-fire on earth. All there is to see now is derelict ground and the old maple tree. Tom! Tom, where are you going now?"

Tom ran back to the cottage.

He saw nothing but a patch of dark, empty ground, shadowed by the maple tree. The tree was beautiful. It had not burned. The innocent tree. Distantly, the merest shadow of a sound, he seemed to hear laughter: the laughter of two females, some notes shrill, others deep. Ghosts – ghosts –

But had they been truth-telling ghosts? Or had they been pulling his leg? Could you trust the word of a ghost any more than the word of a living person?

That evening, his uncle asked: "What sort of day did you have?"

"Interesting," said Tom, feeling appallingly tired.

"How's the ghost-investigation?"

"I'm giving it up. Waste of time."

"I agree," said Bob. "Long walks and plenty of fresh air, that's what you need. You're so pale."

That night at midnight, Tom lay listening – and – BUMP . . . BUMP . . . BUMP . . .

And then – a blaze of fiery light and a tremendous crash.

The boy shot up in bed, hair rising. Then, almost laughing at himself, he realized it was only an ordinary thunderstorm. He went to the mirror to look at his hair, but it had lain down again. He returned to bed, lay down himself, watched the lightning and listened to the thunder. He fell asleep with the last low, distant rumble, like a deep Downley chuckle.

On local radio next day, it was announced that during the storm a tree in a wood some miles away had been struck by lightning and had crashed to the ground, uprooted, disturbing the soil thereabouts. A dead body was revealed – little more than a skeleton – with rings on the fingers. It was mysterious, unidentified. And the strangest thing about it was that its head, instead of being attached to its shoulders, was nestling under its arm, like a creature come home to rest.

On the following midnight, Tom lay and listened –

To the silence.

SIR HARRY MORTLAKE'S CLOCK

by Joyce Marsh

The low, grey stone building sprawled rather untidily a few yards from the cliff edge. The Rowan family's battered old car had barely come to a halt on the gravel drive when its doors were flung open and the children, Anthony and Gillian, tumbled out, squealing and shouting in excited merriment. This was the moment they had longed for with such impatient eagerness, but now the waiting days were over. The long journey from London to Devon was done and they had finally arrived at Pontepelly House, which was to be their home for the whole of the long school holidays.

Anthony, the elder of the two, led the way as the children raced to the cliff edge, where they flung themselves down on the short, springy turf to gaze at the beach below. A steep flight of steps led down the cliff face to a tiny, sandy cove curving between two long arms of high rocks, which enclosed it so completely that even at low tide the beach could only be reached from the sea or from the cliff top.

The late sun, hanging low over the sea, darkened the yellow sand to a deep, glowing orange. Here and there rock pools glittered with the rosy reflection of the sunset. It was a quiet, secluded playground, promising hours of exploration and delight. Both children were tempted to begin at once, but their father's voice called from the house.

"Tony, Gill, the beach can wait. Come in now and help your mother with the unpacking."

Fortunately the house itself was a rival attraction. Not only was it large and rambling, but it was very old and had a long, interesting history. It had once been a farmhouse, a fact which was evidenced by its sprawling, irregular shape where the outbuildings had, over the years, been altered and incorporated into the main house.

In the eighteenth century, Pontepelly House had been acquired by a certain Sir Harry Mortlake, and it had remained in the Mortlake family until the present day. Unfortunately, the family resources had been severely depleted by high taxation and poor management, and the present Sir Peter Mortlake was forced to lease out his ancestral home to summer visitors.

Tony and Gill's parents had already begun to carry the suitcases inside, and the children followed them through the thick oak door which led directly into a wide, panelled hall. The polished wooden floor gleamed and threw back the reflections of the brasses and pictures lining the walls, but the children's attention was immediately riveted upon a huge clock which stood against the wall at the foot of the stairs.

The door of the pendulum case was large enough for a man to pass through, and the intricately carved decoration above the brass face reached to the ceiling. The engraved figures on the dial were faded and difficult to read. No sound came from the clock and, although it was late afternoon, the long gilded hands stood at ten minutes to twelve.

A little jumble of luggage stood neglected in the hall as Dick and Marjory Rowan stood gazing up at the monumental clock.

"Gosh, Dad, what's that? Big Ben's little brother?"

"Well, Tony, it's called a great-great-grandfather clock, but I feel more inclined to call it a super great-great-grandfather clock. It's certainly the largest clock I've ever seen inside a house."

"You can say that again."

Tony had planted himself squarely before the clock and was dwarfed by its great size.

"It's not going, though, Dad. Does it want winding?"

"I'm afraid not, young man. That clock stopped nearly two hundred years ago, and it has never gone since – not properly, that is."

All the Rowans turned as they were joined in the hall by a pleasant-faced, middle-aged lady, who had spoken with a slight, but unmistakable, Devonshire accent.

"I am Mrs Trevellan," the newcomer went on. "I am housekeeper here, and I hope that I shall be able to make your stay at Pontepelly House both happy and comfortable."

The Rowans introduced themselves, but Tony could hardly wait for these introductions to be completed before returning eagerly to the subject of the clock.

"Do you mean to say that this clock is more than two hundred years old, Mrs Trevellan?"

"Yes, it is indeed. It is known as the Mortlake clock, and is quite famous, I believe. The first Sir Harry Mortlake built it himself in seventeen hundred and something. His hobby was clock-making. He made dozens of them, but this was his masterpiece. It's one of the largest clocks of its kind in the country. If you look carefully, you will see that it is actually built into the wall; that is because of its great size."

The Rowans obediently peered at the back of the clock and saw that it did appear to be part of the wall.

"Once upon a time," Mrs Trevellan continued, "it is supposed to have been so accurate that it lost only one minute in ten years, but it stopped the night old Sir Harry disappeared and has never gone since, although any number of experts have been down here to examine it."

Tony, who dearly loved a mystery, could barely wait

for Mrs Trevellan to finish speaking before he burst in with his eager question.

"How did Sir Harry disappear? Was he lost at sea or something?"

"No, my dear, nothing as simple as that. According to the old story, Sir Harry went into that parlour over there, and – " She waved her hand in the direction of one of the doors leading off the hall. "The footman served him his brandy, bade him goodnight, locked all the doors and windows and went to bed. That was the last that anyone ever saw of Sir Harry, for next morning it was discovered that his bed had not been slept in and he was nowhere in the house, although all the doors were still bolted from the inside. The whole place was searched and the panelling examined for secret passages, but nothing was found. Everything was exactly as it should be, except that the clock had stopped at ten to twelve and it has never gone since."

"But you said just now that the clock doesn't go *properly*. Does that mean that it still works after a fashion?"

It was Dick's turn to question Mrs Trevellan, and it was apparent that his interest was almost as great as his son's.

"Well, no. It is a very peculiar thing, but sometimes the clock will start up of its own accord – always at exactly ten to twelve. It keeps perfect time for a day, and then at ten minutes before midnight it stops again."

"Gosh, that *is* odd. Do you think it will start up while we're here?"

"'Tis not likely, I fancy. It has only happened four or five times in two hundred years, and the last time was long before I was even born."

Tony looked crestfallen, but was still inclined to pursue the subject of the Mortlake clock, until a sudden, sharp exclamation from his mother interrupted him.

"Gill, whatever is the matter? Are you ill?"

For the first time they all noticed that Gillian had taken no part in the conversation, and now she was leaning against the wall. Her face, which only a short time ago had been pink and rosy with excitement, was now pale and drawn. Her arms were folded tightly across her chest and she was trembling violently. Her blue eyes, which were nearly always sparkling with gaiety, were flung wide and they seemed dark with fear as she gazed fixedly at the clock looming above her.

"Gill, what is the matter?" Marjory Rowan asked again anxiously.

"I don't know, Mummy, but I don't like it here. I want to go home. I want to go home now. I'm frightened."

The little girl's voice rose to a scream, and the unnaturally dark eyes brimmed over with tears. Immediately the centuries-old mystery of Sir Harry Mortlake's disappearance was driven from their minds as they hastened to comfort and calm the distraught child.

Gill would not, or could not, tell them of what she was afraid, and eventually they assumed that she was overwrought by the excitement and the long journey; so she was put to bed, where she fell asleep holding tightly to her mother's hand.

The hot sun hung in a cloudless sky and painted sparkling silvery splashes on the blue-green sea. The children were on the beach, as they had been every day for the past week. Tony, his body already browned by the sun and sea, was endeavouring for the fiftieth time to balance upright on his makeshift wooden surf-board, which was being continually snatched from beneath his feet by the frothing, seething waves.

Gillian, sitting on the hot sand, watched her brother with listless, uninterested eyes. Then Tony temporarily abandoned his strenuous sport and raced across the sand to fling himself down beside his sister.

"The water's lovely today. Aren't you coming in, Gilly?"

"No – and don't call me Gilly."

She snapped back irritably and, at that, Tony's patience was exhausted.

Since her inexplicable outburst on the day they had arrived at Pontepelly House, Gill had not indulged in any more hysterical demands to be taken home. She had, however, been strangely unlike her usual self. Her little face was pale and pinched; she was as quiet as a mouse and crept about nervously as if every corner, every lurking shadow held some fear for her. Like his parents, Tony had hoped that this strange mood would soon pass, but plainly it was not going to, and the time had come for different methods.

He planted himself before his sister and spoke firmly.

"Now look here, Gill, what is the matter with you? You say you aren't ill, and yet you moon around as if you're afraid of your own shadow. Mum and Dad are worried sick about you. They are even talking of packing in the holiday and taking you home. You are making everyone miserable. It's too bad of you."

Suddenly his voice softened and he dropped down on to the sand beside his sister.

"Come on, kid. We've always talked things out – tell me what's the trouble."

"I don't know, Tony. It sounds so silly."

"Never mind how it sounds, Gill. Just tell me."

"Well . . ." She hesitated for a long while and her lips trembled. "When I am in that house I have the oddest feeling, as if there is something that I must do. I don't know what it is, or why, but I can almost hear someone calling to me: 'Gilly . . . Gilly'. It goes on and on running through my head, pleading for help. There you are, it does sound silly, but it frightens me."

She looked at her brother anxiously as if she expected him to laugh at her, but Tony had no inclination to scoff. One look at her woebegone face was enough to convince him that the strange fears she felt at Pontepelly House were very real to her.

"The voice calls you 'Gilly'," he said thoughtfully. "That's odd, because no one calls you that – at least, only once in a blue moon."

She nodded. "It's always the same – 'Gilly'. Oh, and there's another thing: sometimes a silly little rhyme keeps popping into my head. I don't know where I read it, or heard it, but it goes . . .

> *My beloved son, O pity me,*
> *For I have naught to bequeath to thee,*
> *Save a hazardous wealth from over the sea."*

Tony looked at his sister very sharply.

"I know where that rhyme comes from – it's engraved around the face of the clock, but you couldn't have read it because the letters are too worn to be seen properly. Mrs Trevellan told me about it. Perhaps she told you, too?"

Gill shook her head vigorously. "No, no one told me. I just hear it – mostly at night, as if someone was whispering it in my ear while I'm asleep. What does it mean, Tony?"

"I don't know. Apparently, when he disappeared, old Sir Henry left no other will except those few words written on the clock face. His son searched in almost every country but could never find the 'hazardous wealth from over the sea', and his father's fortune had disappeared, too, for the son was left penniless."

"Oh, Tony, I'm fed up with Pontepelly House, with old Sir Harry and his horrid clock. I wish we could go home."

Thick tears ran down Gill's cheeks and, despite the hot sun, she began to shiver violently. Tony placed a protective arm about her shoulders as he gazed thoughtfully out at the sparkling sea. When his sister was more calm, he spoke gently. "I don't think going home now is the answer, Gill. It's just running away, and that never solved anything. No, we must find out who or what and why you are being . . . well, haunted – that's the only word I can think of to describe it."

"But I'm frightened," she said in a small voice.

"I know you are, kid, but you have just got to face up to it; find out what you are being asked to do."

"I can't, Tony. I really can't. When I hear something calling me I say my 'time's tables' over and over until it goes away."

"But that's the trouble – it only goes away for a short while. Next time you must answer the voice. I don't mean you should go around shouting 'What do you want?' as if you were batty. Just concentrate your mind and try to find out what the voice wants of you. Will you try?"

She looked at him pathetically, but after a while nodded slowly and a trifle uncertainly.

"Good girl, but whatever happens you are not to go anywhere or do anything until you have told me first – promise?"

She nodded again and her short dark hair bobbed and gleamed in the bright sun. She smiled, and for the first time in days the smile upon her lips was reflected by a soft gleam in her eyes.

"I feel better now."

"'Course you do. Telling me was half the battle. You have been dotty keeping it to yourself all this time. Now come and have a go on the surf-board. I've taken enough tumbles – it's your turn now."

For the rest of that day everyone noticed, with some relief, that Gill had at last begun to recover some of her usual high spirits. She went off, quite eagerly, to accompany her parents on a 'courtesy visit' to Sir Peter Mortlake, who, unable to afford to live at Pontepelly House, occupied a small cottage in the village.

With the rest of the family out, and Mrs Trevellan busily engaged in the kitchen, Tony was alone in the vast and rambling old house. Generations of Mortlakes had altered it, added to it, left their mark upon it, and now, in the shadowy silence, even the practical Tony sensed some of the mystery which seemed to lurk in its dim recesses and odd corners.

Rather glumly he gazed up at the monumental timepiece towering above him and peered at the faint, indecipherable letters engraved around the face. With probing fingers he explored the carved moulding, searching for the hidden spring which, Mrs Trevellan had told him, was the only way to open the door of the pendulum case. He could not find it, and with a faint shrug he abandoned the search, deciding somewhat apprehensively that his frail, frightened little sister was the only one likely to discover the haunting secret of the Mortlakes and their great clock.

Gillian lay in her bed wide-eyed and sleepless. It was a time which, of late, she had come to dread, for she was alone in her room. All around her the silence of the sleeping house was thick and absolute. The dark shadows, criss-crossed by silvery shafts of moonlight, seemed to hover over her, enfolding her and forming a seemingly impenetrable barrier between herself and the comforting presence of the other people in the house.

Suddenly there was a loud rap on the wall, and at the

sound the threatening shadows receded a little, for it was a pre-arranged signal; it told her that Tony, in the next room, was still awake and would come running at her call.

It was reassuring to know that her brother was so close at hand. Gill closed her eyes determinedly, resolving that until she fell asleep she would fill her mind with busy thoughts to keep at bay the strange voice with its insidious calling and pleading.

For a while she thought of Sir Peter Mortlake, whom she had visited with her parents that afternoon. From the very first moment, Gill had liked Sir Peter. A fine network of little lines at the corners of his eyes gave his face a jolly expression, but the eyes themselves were dark with a look of deep sadness – which was not surprising, for Sir Peter would soon have to part with Pontepelly House. She had heard him tell her father that all his efforts to keep the house had failed, and before the year was out the old Mortlake home would pass out of the family, probably for ever.

A picture of Sir Peter seemed to form before her; she saw him quite clearly with his greying hair tumbling over his forehead and his old tweed jacket flecked with the little pieces of ash which fell unheeded from his pipe.

Her body felt light and free, as if she were floating, and the mental picture of Sir Peter became blurred over with a bright mist. Then from the centre of this mistiness another figure formed. The face was Sir Peter's – but now the hair was drawn tightly back and the tweed jacket had become an elegant blue coat made of shiny fabric, with frothy white frills at the neck and wrists. Bright blue eyes were fixed upon her with a desperate urgency. The lips moved . . .

> "Gilly, Gilly, . . .
> O, pity me,
> For I have naught . . ."

Gill sat up sharply, abruptly cutting off the words which were running through her mind.

"Once two is two, two two's are four . . ." Desperately she pushed out the frightening voice which filled her head. Then she remembered her promise to Tony. The strange dream-like figure had faded now, but, with an effort, she conquered her fear. Closing her eyes again she recalled every detail of the man who, but a moment before, had seemed so real.

"What do you want of me?" She whispered the words into the still darkness.

"Come. I will show you. Be not afraid, Gilly."

The answer was not spoken aloud, but came as if from her own mind.

Suddenly unafraid, Gill left her bed and slipped out on to the landing. The bright moon could not reach in through the high windows, and it was very dark as Gill's bare feet padded across the polished floor to the head of the stairs.

In the hall below a shaft of light struck across the clock face, and it gleamed in the darkness like beaten gold. The great clock glowed with a misty light, shot through with rainbow colours. The colours streamed and blended together until they became a pair of bright blue eyes. Gill looked down into those eyes and read in them the answer – she knew now what she must do.

She remembered her second promise to Tony and, turning quickly, she ran to his room. The boy was not asleep and he sat up as his sister burst into the bedroom.

"Tony, come quickly. I know now what I must do, and there is not much time. What does your watch say?"

Tony opened his mouth to speak, but she cut him off. "Please, no questions now – I must hurry."

Her brother obediently rolled over and consulted his

watch. "It's exactly quarter to twelve," he said. "And I know that's right. I checked my watch with the radio."

Gill barely waited for him to finish speaking before she ran out, and the bewildered boy quickly joined her on the landing.

"Come on," she said. "I have to start up the clock – and it must be done at exactly ten to twelve."

Tony followed as her small white-clad figure sped down the wide, shallow stairs.

"Hang on a minute, Gill. You don't know *how* to start the clock. You don't know even how to open the case."

She did not bother to answer; she had already reached the clock and her fingers went out unerringly to a carved leaf in the decorative moulding. There was a sharp click and the door of the pendulum case sprang open a few inches. Long years of disuse had stiffened the hinges, and both children pulled hard at the door until, with a loud creak, it opened wide.

Inside the weights were pulled high and the great pendulum hung straight and still.

"Tell me when it's ten to twelve exactly."

Moving slightly so that a patch of moonlight shone upon his watch, Tony carefully counted off the seconds.

"Five, four, three, two, one . . . now!" he said.

Gill's finger barely touched the pendulum before it began to swing, and suddenly the whole house seemed to echo with the deep ticking of the clock.

"That's it," Gill said with a little sigh of satisfaction. "Now there is nothing else to be done for the moment."

Tony was agog with curiosity, but by now Gill's eyes were almost closing with weariness, and he tactfully postponed his questions until the morning.

The next day the household had awakened to the unaccustomed sound of the Mortlake clock as it ticked off the seconds, sending the sound of their passing echoing through the house.

Sir Peter was sent for immediately, and he came post-haste to see his clock, which, as he told them excitedly, had not started up since his great-grandfather's time. From then on the house saw a constant stream of visitors; for it seemed that the entire village must come to see for themselves. Little groups of them gazed up at the clock as it once more measured out the time, and they wondered what strange circumstances had set it going. But the two children who knew the answer held the knowledge to themselves.

Gill had not been able to explain her actions on the night before very satisfactorily.

"It came to me in a sort of dream," was all she could tell her brother. "But you wait until tonight," she added, and it was these words which filled Tony with a sense of nervous apprehension.

The glowing sunset had faded and the purple velvet of the night sky was spangled with a host of tiny stars. The last of the visitors had finally left, and the household slept. All, that is, except Tony. So anxious was he for his sister that he had crept from his own room to sit watching by her bed. She appeared to be sleeping peacefully, but suddenly her eyes flew open and she sat up abruptly.

"It's almost time," she said, without expressing any surprise at finding her brother sitting by her side.

She slipped out of bed, and together the children crossed the landing to the head of the stairs.

Only the ticking of the clock disturbed the silence and, in the moonlight, the hands could be seen standing at a quarter to twelve. Quietly, Gill sat down on the top stair, resting her head against the carved banisters, and Tony dropped down beside her.

Abruptly came the sharp sound of a door opening,

422

cutting across the regular ticking of the clock. Gill turned to her brother and her eyes glittered with excitement. Soundlessly she put a finger to her lips and then pointed down the stairs.

The door of the parlour swung slowly open, a blue radiance streamed out, and then, framed in the doorway, the children saw the bright figure of a man. For a moment he paused there, motionless. He was very tall, with long powdered hair tied into the nape of his neck with a broad black ribbon; the shiny fabric of his blue coat gleamed softly. He yawned slightly and held one pale hand before his mouth in an elegant gesture. From his wrists, white lace hung in a cascade of billowing frills.

Effortlessly, seeming to glide rather than walk, the glowing apparition began to cross the hall. At the foot of the stairs he glanced upwards and his eyes looked straight into Gill's. He seemed to smile, and then one elegant hand reached out to the clock. There was a faint click and the pendulum case sprang open. The hands showed exactly ten to twelve as the figure, still shining with an unnatural brightness, leaned inside and grasped the pendulum.

The ticking stopped and, by contrast, the ensuing silence seemed more absolute. With one last glance up the stairs to where the children were sitting, the man stepped inside the clock and the door slowly closed behind him. The ethereal radiance which had lit the hall faded away, and Gill moved swiftly. She would have sped on down the stairs had not her brother held her back.

"Gill, you can't go down there."

Their positions had been reversed – now it was Tony who was nervous while Gill was confident and excited.

"There's nothing to be afraid of, Tony. That was old Sir Harry Mortlake. He wants me to follow him. He wants me to know where he disappeared to, and that's why he's been calling to me and why he came last night and told me to start up the clock."

"I don't understand."

"Neither do I, exactly, but I know that Sir Harry must have stopped the clock the night he vanished, and he wanted me to start it up again so that everything would be the same as it was that night. Then he could come back and show me – whatever it is he wants to show me or wants me to know."

It was a very involved explanation, but it made some sort of sense. Gill believed so, anyway, for she was already half way downstairs, and by the time Tony had joined her in the hall she had already swung open the door of the clock. Her slender figure gleamed whitely in the moonlight as she bent forward into the clock. Her fingers quickly found what they sought. There was a sharp sound, then, creaking slightly, the whole back of the clock slid away and the two children found themselves looking into a black, yawning opening. A dank, musty odour wafted out, and far away they could hear a faint rushing sound.

"There you are!" Gill said triumphantly. "That's how Sir Harry Mortlake left the house. And, of course, that's why the clock stopped – for he couldn't pass through the opening while the pendulum was still swinging."

Impulsively, she stepped into the clock case, and would have passed through the opening, but once again Tony held her back.

"Hang on a minute. Just cool it, Gill. I'm going to fetch a torch and something warmer for you to wear, then we can go and find out why Sir Harry Mortlake had a secret passage leading out of his house – and why he went through it and never came back."

Fortunately there was a torch in the cupboard where they hung their outdoor clothes, and Tony shone the beam into the opening while Gill struggled into the coat he had brought for her.

The strong beam showed them a rough passage carved out of the living rock. It descended steeply and was so lengthy that the torch could not penetrate the end.

Carefully they picked their way along the damp, evil-smelling passage. Tony led the way and, as they went on downwards, the rushing sound grew louder and more distinct.

"Gill, I believe we're going towards the sea."

A few minutes later, Tony's guess proved correct, as the thick, foul atmosphere gave way to draughts of fresh air carrying the unmistakable smell of the sea. The passage widened and finally opened out into a cave. Through the tiny entrance they could see the star-spangled sky and her the rattling, rushing music of the waves as they hurled themselves against the beach.

Following the sides of the cave, they made for the opening and looked out. Below them the cliff dropped sheer and straight down to the beach – their own beach.

For a moment the children crouched on their knees, pondering this odd circumstance.

"Well, we had better look around," Tony said at last, and turned the torch to flood the cave with light.

The beam fell upon something which gleamed a hideous, yellowish-white, and Gill gave a little scream. In the far corner was a large iron-bound chest, and lying across it was the skeleton of a human. Here and there a few tattered remnants of blue and white cloth still clung to the bones, and an old pistol dangled from one bony finger.

With a shudder, Tony jerked the beam away from the gruesome sight, only to see the thin pencil of light fall upon yet another pile of human bones – with a gaping skull which seemed to be staring at them from wide, empty sockets.

Gill's courage seemed to have deserted her, for she shrank back against the damp wall and covered her face with her hands. Tony swung the torch, again sending the beam into the furthest corner of the cave.

"Here, Gill, look at this," he called suddenly.

"I can't, it's horrible," she answered.

"No, look over there, those little barrels – I think they're brandy kegs. I believe this was a smuggler's cave."

"Of course! The 'hazardous wealth from over the sea'. That's it, Tony! Old Sir Harry Mortlake made his fortune smuggling. This place was perfect for it. The boats could pull on to the beach without being seen, then the goods were hauled up here until Sir Harry could carry them through the secret passage to his house."

"Well, it looks as if his smuggling brought him to a sticky end. He must have come down here one night, quarrelled with that other man, and in the fight they killed each other. No wonder Sir Harry vanished so mysteriously."

"Poor man," Gill said with soft pity. "For two hundred years he has haunted this place, waiting to show someone how to restore to the Mortlakes the only treasure he had to bequeath to his descendants."

"I think you're right. Come on, we mustn't touch anything – let's go and tell Mum and Dad everything."

The wavering torchlight bobbed and faded as the children hurried back along the passage, and behind them the cave receded once more into the darkness which had shrouded it for two centuries.

For some days following the children's discovery, Ponte-pelly House was a veritable hive of activity. Police, officials and other experts came and went, but at last the examinations were complete and a sad little procession headed by Sir Peter left the house bearing the remnants of Sir Harry Mortlake to his last and final resting-place in the nearby churchyard.

Expert opinion had confirmed the children's guess. The cave was indeed a storehouse for smuggled goods, most of it mouldering and decayed. The chest which Sir Harry had apparently given his life to protect was found to be full of old coins, which by present-day values represented a small fortune, quite sufficient to keep Pontepelly House in the Mortlake family for ever.

"Well, it's all over now," Gill said. "We can enjoy the rest of our holiday in peace."

"No more funny voices in the night, eh, Gill?"

"No. But there is still one thing that puzzles me – why *me*? I mean, why did Sir Harry's ghost pick on me?"

"I think I can answer that." Tony and Gill turned as Sir Peter came into the room.

"I have been studying the old papers in the attic, and I have come across something rather interesting. I told you that the last time the clock started up was in my great-grandfather's time; well, apparently there was a little girl staying here then, and this child was taken home hurriedly because she began wandering in her sleep."

"Perhaps she was told to start up the clock, just like me."

"Yes, I believe so. And the odd thing was that her name was Jill."

"It rather looks as if Sir Harry had a weakness for that name."

Sir Peter laughed. "Yes, and I suppose that now we shall never know why."

"Well, I'm not going to ask him," Gill said. "I'm not going through all that again."

The rest of their happy holiday passed in an endless succession of glorious, sunlit days. Only one other odd circumstance occurred to puzzle them.

The great Mortlake clock began once more to measure out the passing hours, but this time it did not stop again, and as the Rowans finally closed the door of Pontepelly House at the end of their holiday, its long, slow, regular beat was the last sound they heard.

THE HAUNTED CIRCUS

by Sydney J. Bounds

Dianne lost her balance and fell to the padded mat – again.

"Are you hurt, dear?" her mother asked anxiously.

"Of course she isn't hurt," her father said testily. "Now, Dianne, you must try again, and keep trying. It's practice that counts in our business."

Dianne sighed as she climbed the steps to the small platform leading to the wire stretched across the circus ring. It was only six feet above the ground, and how to fall was the first thing she had been taught.

Being the daughter of a pair of circus acrobats was sometimes a hard thing to live up to. "Dianne on the Silver Wire" . . . some hope! She wasn't very good, and she knew it. The height didn't worry her, or falling; it was being laughed at she couldn't stand. Imagine, the daughter of acrobats who couldn't even balance on a wire! And not just any old acrobats. Her father and mother were the Red Devils, the star attraction of Ringwall's circus.

Her father turned away. "There's something new I want to try."

Dianne watched her parents climb a swaying ladder to the high trapeze. Forgotten already . . . the story of my life, she thought sadly.

She wandered slowly across the ring, a thin figure in patched tights, and made for the menagerie. Since Charley had died, the only real friends she had were the animals. Charley the Clown had always found time to talk to her, even though circus people were constantly busy. Dianne, at fourteen, had never known loneliness before.

Maxine, the bareback rider, was brushing her horse for the evening show and Dianne helped her. Besides the horses, the circus had a lion act, and performing dogs.

"I wish I could work with animals all the time," Dianne said wistfully.

Maxine smiled. "I don't think your parents would like that."

"I suppose not."

When the horses were groomed, Dianne returned to the Big Top. She climbed the steps and started across the wire. Practice, practice, practice, she thought. She was half way across when she realized there was someone beside her, and froze. There couldn't be, not six feet off the ground.

She balanced carefully, watching the figure from the corner of her eye. It looked like Charley, in his spangled clown's costume, his face whitened for the ring. The figure floated in the air beside the wire.

A voice whispered, "Come on, Di, I know you can do it. Do it for Charley."

She knew that voice; no one else called her "Di", ever . . .

Suddenly frightened, she jumped down to the mat.

Carl, the lion-tamer, was passing and saw her pale face. He stopped. "Are you all right, Dianne?"

She glanced up at the wire, but there was no one there now. "Did you see anybody? Or hear anything?"

"No." Carl was mystified. "What is it?"

"Oh, nothing."

Dianne hurried away. Charley had come back; no, that wasn't right. His ghost had come back. She didn't have to be frightened, Charley wouldn't hurt her – but it was still a shock, even if he only whispered encouragement.

Outside the Big Top, a queue was forming, and soon she was caught up in the preparations for the show. Ringwall's circus was a small one, which meant that the performers doubled up; everyone had two, or even three jobs to do. Every piece of equipment had to be in its exact place, and it was Dianne's job to retrieve small items as they were no longer needed.

The seats were filling, the band played "The Entry of the Gladiators", and the clowns ran into the ring.

Dianne was with Maxine, helping to hold the horses. She had quite recovered now and was beginning to think she had only imagined that she'd seen Charley when she heard his voice at her side.

"Don't worry, Di, you'll do it one day."

She turned, startled, but there was nobody there.

The horses snorted and broke free, galloping into the ring and running wild. The clowns scrambled over the barrier to join the audience, and it took Maxine a long time to get them under control again. Her act was ruined.

"I don't know what got into them," she fretted. "It was just as if something spooked them."

Tom Ringwall, the circus owner, looked worried. "We can't afford to let that happen again," he said. "It's the sort of thing that could ruin our reputation."

Dianne thought she could have told them what had frightened the horses, but decided to say nothing. She knew the circus was moving to another town when the performance ended and she didn't think Charley's ghost would be following them.

But in that she was wrong . . .

When the Big Top was erected in Wexley, Dianne started to practise her wire-walk. Charley's ghost bobbed along beside her, making encouraging remarks.

"There's nothing to worry about, Di. Keep at it."

Dianne overbalanced and fell. She was more frightened

than she wanted to admit; suppose the ghost never stopped haunting her?

"Oh, leave me alone!" she burst out hysterically.

Her mother overheard and looked startled. "What was that, dear? Is someone bothering you?"

Dianne shook her head and ran away. No one else saw the ghostly clown, so who would believe her?

As the time drew near for the evening performance, the lions became restless. They prowled up and down their cage, roaring, their tails lashing angrily.

Tom Ringwall hurried up to see what was wrong.

Carl stared gloomily at his cats through the bars of the cage.

"They can't perform like this, Mr Ringwall. It would be too dangerous. Something's upset them."

The circus owner looked unhappy. "The audience is going to feel cheated if they don't see a lion act – but I have to agree, we can't send them into the ring in this state."

The news that the lions would not be appearing spread fast – and attendance dropped. Tom Ringwall was worried.

"This is a disaster! The circus may have to close if we have any more trouble with the animals."

Only Dianne knew what was wrong. The animals were sensitive; they knew a ghost was around and didn't like it.

The show went on as usual, to a small audience. Dianne was retrieving some props from the ring when Charley whispered in her ear:

"It'll soon be your turn, Di. Just keep trying."

She looked round, startled, and hissed: "You've got to leave me alone, Charley. I'll be all right. You're frightening the animals and spoiling the show."

She didn't know whether he heard her or not, and

432

wondered if she should stop practising altogether. Would the dead clown stop haunting her then?

Next morning, before practice, she tried to tell her father. He looked stern and cut in before she could explain properly.

"No, Dianne, you can't give up – that wouldn't be professional. You know we want you to train for our trapeze act as soon as you've mastered the wire. It's only a question of time, so keep practising."

Dianne sighed, climbed the steps to her wire and started to walk. Below, in another part of the ring, Maxine was putting her performing dogs through a new routine.

Dianne was halfway across when Charley appeared beside her, whispering encouragement.

"That's it, Di. Try, try, try again . . ."

Dianne paused, balancing carefully. She looked down to see if Maxine had seen or heard anything. Obviously not. But her dogs had. Scenting the ghost, they howled and ran with their tails between their legs.

Tom Ringwall stared in dismay. "What the deuce is going on? All our animal acts seem to have a jinx on them."

Maxine was close to tears. "I don't understand it, Mr Ringwall. The dogs were doing so well – they were nearly ready to go into the ring."

Charley still floated in the air beside Dianne. No one else saw him and he, obviously, was unaware that the dogs had bolted.

Suddenly, Dianne started to listen intently to what he had to say. It seemed almost as if he could read her mind. And what Charley had to say made Dianne think furiously.

Is that how you exorcized the ghost of a clown? she wondered. She blamed herself for the failure of the circus and felt desperate enough to try anything.

She hurried back to her parents' caravan and sat down with pencil and paper to work out the idea Charley had given her. She'd need a wig, and a cane, and –

There was a knock at the door and Tom Ringwall's voice: "Dianne?"

"Yes, I'm here."

When she opened the door, the circus boss was looking very unhappy.

"It's the dogs," he said. "They're still misbehaving and will have to be left out of tonight's show. We need an act to fill ten minutes. Do you think you're ready to step in?"

Dianne gasped with pleasure; this was the chance she needed. "Oh yes, Mr Ringwall – I'm sure I can manage it!"

"That's fine, then."

At the evening performance, it wasn't only the audience who got a surprise. The circus folk had assumed that Dianne would be doing the act she had practised for weeks.

Instead, she ran into the ring wearing the spangled costume of a clown, with her face whitened. And a trampoline had been placed under the wire. At first, Dianne hesitated on the platform, pretending to be afraid of the wire. She essayed a few steps like a complete beginner; her cane caught in her wig and tore it off. Swaying wildly, she tried to get the wig off the cane, lost her balance and fell . . . she rebounded from the trampoline and swung like a monkey, one-handed, from the wire. Then she was up again and performing more of Charley's tricks she had adapted for use on the wire. She was so caught up in her new act that she was, at first, only distantly aware of people laughing. The audience and the other circus performers roared at her antics, and now she began to appreciate laughter as only a clown can. It gave her a warm feeling and she worked harder for more laughs.

Dancing in the air beside her, unseen by anyone else, the ghost of Charley the Clown laughed loudest of all. As her act came to a climax, he chuckled: "I knew you could do it, Di. Good luck . . ."

His voice faded away, lost in a barrage of applause.

Her parents were proud of her first-time success, and the animals behaved perfectly again. Sometimes, though, as she capered on the wire and the audience nearly died of laughing, Dianne felt a little sad inside, because she longed to see Charley's ghost bobbing along beside her. But she knew, now, he would never come back.

THE POST ROOM

by Catherine Gleason

The school trip to Austria sounded great, but I knew I wouldn't be able to go because we couldn't afford it. There are just the two of us, and, although Mum has a full-time job, there isn't usually enough money for holidays and things like that. So I didn't even mention the trip to Mum, but of course she found out about it, from the gossip of the other mothers at the office where she works.

"I want you to go on this trip, Joey," she told me one tea-time, about a week after they'd given us all the details at school. "It'll be educational, and all your friends are going, aren't they?"

"Well, yes," I said, feeling a bit stunned. "But it costs eighty pounds, you know, and I can't save up anything like that much out of my paper round money."

"H'mm. Well, I've been doing some sums, and I think we might just manage it." She's very determined, my mum, when she sets her mind on anything. "The trip's in September, isn't it? You could get a job in the summer holidays for a few hours a week, and the money would help pay for it."

This was even more surprising. Mum isn't even keen on my doing an evening paper round in case it interferes with my homework, and for her to suggest a job was something right out of the blue. I said I was all for it, and what sort of a job could I get? "Leave that to me," Mum said. "I'll fix it." And she did.

A couple of weeks after the school holidays started I

went for an interview at Harmon and Co. Ltd, and arranged to begin work the following Monday. Mr Johnson hired me – he was in charge of all the staff. There were quite a lot of them, because Harmon's is a huge old place, with offices and a factory for making protective clothes, asbestos suits, bullet-proof vests and that kind of thing.

On my first day I was pretty excited and a bit scared. Mr Johnson took me to the office where I was to work, helping Fred.

"He's been on his own since Charlie died a couple of weeks ago," Mr Johnson explained. "That's why he needs an assistant. Charlie and Fred worked together here for years, then poor old Charlie had a heart-attack when he was sorting out the mail one morning. Ah, here's Fred now. Fred, this is Joey, who'll be working with you for a few weeks."

"Hello," I said nervously, and shook his hand.

Fred was small and thin and friendly, with blue eyes and grey hair. He was past retiring age but, he told me later, having worked for the firm for thirty years, they'd let him stay on in the post room, because he was still very active and got bored at home. He had no one belonging to him, and his best friend had been Charlie, now deceased.

"Come and have a cup of tea, sonny," was the first thing Fred said to me. "Not nervous, are you? Well, there's no need to be. I remember my first job – dithering like a leaf, I was. 'Course, things were different in those days."

He chuckled and poured out the tea. "There, you just drink that and then I'll show you the ropes. You'll find your feet in no time, don't you worry."

"It's a nice office," I said. And it was: rather small but cosy somehow.

"Oh, we made it comfortable over the years, Charlie and me." Fred's eyes dimmed as he mentioned his friend, and I suddenly felt very sorry for him.

"What's that?" I asked, to change the subject, and I pointed to a big machine under a plastic cover in the corner of the room.

"That's the telex. It's a kind of cross between a telephone and a typewriter. Most firms have got one. Come over and I'll show you how it works."

You've probably seen teleprinters on TV – they use them for football results in the sports programmes. There's a typewriter keyboard with a roll of paper fixed above it and a separate box for the telephone dial. What you do is to switch it on and type on to the paper, while a tape runs out punched with the message you've typed. Then you tear off the paper and dial the number of the telex in the firm you want to contact, and when they answer you run the tape through the machine and it types your message very fast on to the other firm's telex. It's cheaper than telephoning, Fred told me, and quicker than sending letters.

Harmon's machine was big and old-fashioned, but it fascinated me because it reminded me of a simple computer, and at the time I wanted to work with computers when I grew up.

While Fred was explaining how it worked, a red light came on and the machine hummed and chattered into life. It was a message from Japan for the factory manager.

"Oh good, he's been waiting to hear from them," said Fred, tearing the message off the roll. "Just pop across to the factory with this, would you, Joey?"

A big part of my job was doing errands like that. Every morning I'd help Fred sort out the mail, and then take the letters up to the different departments in the offices upstairs. I soon got to know my way around, and everyone

438

was very friendly. Sometimes I went out on my bike to buy string and sellotape, or take a parcel to some other firm on the industrial estate. Other times I'd help Fred stamp the letters or wrap packages ready for the post office in the evening, but my favourite job was using the telex machine.

I soon learned where the letters were on the keyboard, and it gave me quite a thrill to send messages all over the world and wait for the replies. I really enjoyed working the teleprinter then, though now I don't think I could touch one ever again.

People were always popping in to the post room to ask Fred or me to do little jobs, or just to have a few minutes' chat over a cup of tea, and I began to see why Fred didn't want to give up work just yet. He was very popular and had a lot of friends at Harmon's. They used to tease him about his gambling, because he bet a few shillings nearly every day on the horses, and we always celebrated with a bar of chocolate when he won.

I liked Fred a lot. Well, you couldn't help liking him really, he was so cheerful and easy-going. He was a good story-teller too, and told funny stories about his life and how things used to be years ago, except he would never talk about the War. I think it's because his wife got killed in the Blitz.

Anyhow, I settled into Harmon's routine quite easily. It was such a comfortable, normal sort of place that the last thing I ever expected was the appearance of anything supernatural.

After the first week I used to race Fred into the post room to see if I could get the kettle going before he arrived. The first real job of the day was always to separate the messages on the telex that had come in during the night. It used to give me a strange feeling to think of the clumsy old machine suddenly lighting up in the dark, the electricity flowing through its wires, and chattering out its messages. Then shutting off with a click when it was finished, all by itself, until someone in, say, California – where it's mid-day when we are getting ready for bed – would decide to contact Harmon's, and the old machine would hum with life again in the deserted post room.

One day I gobbled my breakfast and pedalled like mad to Harmon's because Fred had beaten me to it two days running. It was a quarter past eight when I arrived, and I dashed into the post room without turning on the light. I felt very disappointed when I realized I wasn't alone – there was somebody there, bending over the desk in the corner.

"Fred?" I said, but the man never moved, and suddenly I felt very cold and frightened because I knew the figure at the desk wasn't Fred. It wasn't anybody, anybody human that is. It was like a bulky stiff shadow, and it raised its head mechanically to look at me.

The fading face was sad and white and old. It vanished quite slowly, mingling with the shadows of the room.

I don't know how long I stood there, just staring.

"'Morning, Joey, you're early – why, what's the matter, lad? What is it? Here, sit down."

I was glad to do that, because I suddenly realized my knees were shaking, my heart was thumping and my hands were all clammy.

Fred came to the rescue with a cup of tea, which was his medicine for almost everything.

"You've seen him, haven't you?" he said slowly, stirring sugar into the cup.

I just nodded.

"It's Charlie, you know. He gave me quite a shock when he first turned up, a couple of days after the funeral."

"The place is haunted, then?" My voice came out in a high-pitched squeak.

"I'm afraid so. Charlie, well, I'm afraid he's a bit lonely since he, er . . . passed on." Fred drummed his fingers nervously on the desk. "He doesn't mean any harm, you know, Joey. He just kind of drifts around sometimes, because he didn't have any close friends except for me, and he worked here almost as long as I have."

"Does he talk to you?" I asked. I was much less scared now. I wasn't shaking so much.

"No, that's the worst thing." Fred shook his head sadly. "I think he wants to, but he's only a shade now, you see, so he can't. I suppose . . . I expect you'll want to be leaving, son, now that you know we've got a ghost?"

Well, I wasn't going to run away from a shadow, however frightening it was, and anyway, I hated the idea of leaving Fred on his own in the haunted post room. So I swallowed my tea and forced a smile.

"Not on your life," I said. "I've never met a real ghost before, and Charlie might like a bit of extra company, don't you think, Fred?"

Fred beamed.

I never quite got used to seeing Charlie. He made only a very few appearances over the weeks that followed, mostly early in the morning or towards the evening, but catching odd glimpses of the ghost never failed to make the hair at the back of my neck prickle like a cat's. What made it worse was that Charlie always looked so pathetic, drifting hopelessly over the mail sacks or hovering by the kettle, as if he really wanted to help but couldn't.

Then Charlie went to ground for a couple of days.

"Do you think he's gone for good?" I asked Fred, glancing round to see that no one was about. If anyone had heard us talking about Charlie they'd have thought we were crazy.

"Maybe," said Fred doubtfully. "But I don't think so, somehow."

He was right. A couple of days later it was Fred's birthday. I bought him a scarf for the winter, and when I got to work that morning I found him puzzling over a message on the telex.

"Joey, did you write this?" he asked, showing me the paper. On it was written:

HAPY BIRTDAY FRED.

I laughed. "I can spell better than that. Anyhow, it must have come in during the night – look, there's a message to Mr Johnson from Los Angeles just above it, and one from New York underneath, and they certainly weren't there when we went home last night."

"That's right," agreed Fred, peering at the greeting. "Queer, that is. Nobody in America would know about my birthday, so perhaps someone's playing a joke."

He was pleased with his scarf, and we forgot about the peculiar telex message during the morning. People kept coming in with little gifts and good wishes for Fred, and the morning flew by until at eleven o'clock we stopped to have a cup of tea and some biscuits for our break.

As we sat there, alone in the little office, the telex suddenly whined into life. Someone was trying to get through, and we both jumped at the noise – I don't know why, because we were well used to messages coming through at all times of the day.

We rushed over to the telex to watch. This message wasn't on tape, it came through in a series of slow clicks, as if someone unfamiliar with typewriters were laboriously picking out the letters, one-fingered. It said:

MENY HAPY RETUNS FRED.

A pause. Fred quickly typed:

THANK YOU. WHO IS THAT?

He was as fast as a secretary on the keyboard. No reply came, so he pressed the "Who are you?" button, which automatically makes the machine sending the message type its own number for identification. Nothing happened, which should have been impossible. Then the slow typing began again.

BIRTDAY PREZENT FRED, GREES LITNIN.

Then the machine shut off abruptly as someone came in through the door. It was a security guard, with his dog, who had been hired as a watchman after one of the firm's lorries had been wrecked by vandals a couple of nights before.

"'Morning," said the man. "I was told I could get a cup of tea here. There's nothing doing in the canteen just now."

He never did get his tea, because suddenly the Alsatian started acting strangely. It sniffed around the post room warily, flattened its ears and snarled savagely. Then it began a flurry of vicious barking and strained at its chain lead. The man shouted at it, but the dog wouldn't be quiet, though it changed to whining and cringing, eventually setting up a pitiful howl and scratching with its paws at the door.

"Don't know what's got into him," said the puzzled guard. "Well, never mind the tea, Granddad. We'll be off duty in another hour or so."

"I bet that dog sensed Charlie's presence," I told Fred when the guard had gone. "I've read about animals being able to sense ghosts."

"Yes, I've heard that too, sonny. I wonder what this message is all about?"

We didn't have long to wonder, because right after that we were busy again, and the mystery wasn't solved until Fred turned on the radio that afternoon to find out what had won the three-thirty. He hadn't had time to glance at his *Daily Mirror* all day, much less slip out to place a bet.

" . . . And at Chepstow today the Cup was won by the outsider Greased Lightning at 100 to 6. Second was – "

Fred dropped a cup and I choked on my tea, and we both raced to the telex. There it was, mis-spelled but accurate.

"Grees Litnin – Greased Lightning," I said, and we both stared at each other, struck by the same thought.

"Charlie never could spell," murmured Fred at last. "Couldn't read very well, come to that. And he wants to talk, to communicate with us, doesn't he? So – if he could somehow get inside of that telex – "

He jumped to his feet, all excited, and peered into the machine.

"*Charlie*!" he yelled. "Are you in there?"

At that moment the door opened and Mr Johnson came in. From the look on his face he thought Fred had gone clean off his rocker, and poor Fred, caught talking to a machine, simply froze. I was the first to move.

"Hello, Mr Johnson!" I shouted, sounding a bit theatrical even to my own ears. "We're just – just fooling around with the telex, you know."

"Oh, I see." Slowly Mr Johnson relaxed, and then he burst out laughing. "Always having a joke, aren't you, Fred? Now, don't let him tell you there are little green men inside that machine, Joey – it's really all worked by electricity!"

Still chuckling, Mr Johnson turned and walked out of the post room, having quite forgotten what he came in for.

Fred gave a long, slow sigh of relief. "Quick thinking, Robin . . . ?"

"Oh, it was nothing, Batman," I said, and we both collapsed, laughing like a couple of idiots.

"Now look," said Fred, pulling himself together. "This is serious." And he plugged in the kettle for more tea. I can tell you, whenever there was anything the slightest bit unusual going on, he would gravitate to that kettle like iron filings to a magnet. Perhaps it was something to do with the War.

"I think it's great," I said. "I mean, Charlie must be a lot happier now he's in touch with you."

"H'mm. Well, *I'd* feel a lot happier if he was at peace, instead of wandering around," said Fred, frowning. "Catch me haunting anybody when *I* go! Charlie never could do anything right on his own – he was always useless by himself. I expect," he added thoughtfully, stirring his tea, "he's waiting for me to join him."

I felt a cold shiver when Fred said that, but I tried to sound cheerful. "You're not thinking of popping off just yet, are you, Fred? Because I couldn't manage here on my own, for one thing!"

He laughed. "No, don't worry. Hello, here we go again."

The telex machine had lit up and begun its phantom typing:

```
-
x
-
-
x
-
x
-
-
-
x
```

all down the roll of paper.

"It's gibberish," said Fred, when it stopped. "Can you

445

make anything of it, Joey? I wonder what he's trying to say?"

"Perhaps he's just sort of doodling," I suggested.

That was a Thursday, and we heard nothing more from Charlie for the rest of the week. It wasn't till Saturday afternoon, as I watched the sport on television, that I realized what Charlie had meant.

Football results.

The x's represented the drawn games, and the lines were the home and away results on that day's football pools coupon. If we had understood in time, and Fred had done the pools that week according to Charlie's message, he would have won a fortune.

"Oh well, what would I do with a fortune at my time of life, anyway?" said Fred when I told him on Monday morning. "I'd like to know how he does it, though."

"Now's your chance to ask him," I replied, as the telex hummed into life.

"Oh dear, he's cross," said Fred as the machine typed accusingly:

YOO DIDDENT GAMBLE FRED.

NO. SORRY. HOW DO YOU KNOW THE WINNERS? Fred typed back.

This question gave Charlie some difficulty. Laboriously he typed:

I IVESDROPP EEVSDROOP XXXXX LISSEN IN TO OTHER TELEXS TORK TO THEM ENWAY NONE OF YOUR BISNUSS TRY FED FLAGG IN THE 2.30.

The machine shut off with a dignified click.

"So that's it!" I cried. "He can eavesdrop on, or listen in to, the telexes in the big bookmaking firms. That explains the racing tips – but what about the football results?"

Fred shrugged. "Maybe he talks to the Football League Association, or perhaps a Higher Authority, even, than that," he added reverently, glancing upwards. "Anyway, as he says, it's none of our business. I think I'll have 10p each way on Red Flag."

He did, and it won.

Nearly every day after that, Charlie sent a tip through for Fred. The horses were nearly always successful, but Fred never gambled more than a few pence. He said it was unfair to the bookmakers; Fred was like that. Charlie appeared very rarely now, but when he did he looked much more cheerful. Fred said it was because Charlie was feeling useful at last. He told me that when Charlie was alive, he used to say that he felt he had never done anything really important in his life, and hadn't done a great deal to help other people, though he had always been a kind-hearted sort of character, if he did get a bit crusty at times.

"I think he's trying to make up, now, for what he didn't do during his lifetime," Fred reckoned, and, as it turned out, he was right.

The weeks flew by, and before I knew it the time came to leave and go back to school. Mum was very pleased that I had managed to save up quite a lot for my holiday, and she was almost as excited about the trip as I was. I arranged to see Fred again during the half-term holidays, when I came back from Austria, to tell him about it. Harmon's were re-organizing things so he wouldn't have so much to do after I left, because he said he didn't want another assistant – well, he couldn't, with Charlie around.

The trip was super. I didn't see a single ghost the whole fortnight. On the first day of the half-term holidays, a Monday it was, I pedalled over to Harmon's for eight-thirty in the morning.

As soon as I walked into the post room I knew something was wrong. I'd braced myself, you see, in case I caught a glimpse of Charlie vanishing into the shadows, but the atmosphere of the office was different: calm and peaceful. I sensed at once that Charlie was gone. But where was Fred?

From habit, I walked over to the telex machine. There was just one message on the roll, and my heart sank as I read it. I tore off the message, stuffed it into my pocket, and raced up to Mr Johnson's office.

"Hello, Joey. Nice to see you again – "

"Mr Johnson," I interrupted urgently, "Fred's not here. He's never late – I think something might have happened to him!"

"Well, we'll soon find out." Mr Johnson tried to telephone Fred's home. There was no reply; I had known, somehow, that there wouldn't be. I was so worried that Mr Johnson started feeling concerned, and he decided to go round to Fred's house himself to see if anything was wrong.

He came back an hour later with the news that Fred had had an accident. He'd fallen downstairs and cut his arm very badly on a glass vase he'd been carrying. Mr Johnson saw him through a window, lying unconscious at the foot of the stairs, and called an ambulance. The doctors said it was just as well he'd been found so soon. I think it saved his life.

As it was, Fred was back in the post room within a few weeks, and I went to see him.

"Well, Joey, Mr Johnson tells me I've got you to thank for having me rescued so quickly," he said, clapping me on the shoulder.

"It wasn't only me, Fred," I told him, "it was Charlie as well."

"Charlie? How do you mean? – He's gone, you know,"

448

Fred added, glancing round. "And the telex doesn't work any more. We're getting a new one."

"It was working the morning you had your accident," I said. "Look at this." And I handed him the last message that Charlie had sent through the old machine.

Slowly Fred unfolded the bit of paper. On it was typed simply:

HELP FRED. HE S IN TRUBBLE.

Fred stared at the message for a long time. Then he raised his head and smiled.

"So that's why Charlie disappeared," he said. "Remember I told you that he'd always regretted not having done more good in the world when he had the chance? Well, now he's helped to save my life, so maybe he feels he can rest at last."

"I hope so," I replied. "I expect you'll miss him sometimes, Fred."

"Yes, in a way – no more racing tips!" said Fred, grinning, and he gave the old telex machine an affectionate pat.

"One thing's for sure," I said. "Ghosts can turn up in the most unexpected places!"

"That's true. But I rather think we've had our turn to be haunted, and things are going to be fairly peaceful for all of us from now on." Fred settled back in his chair and glanced round the quiet post room with a contented sigh.

I hope Fred's right. You never can tell with ghosts, though, can you?

THE DAY I DIED

by Terry Tapp

It really was the most inconvenient time to die. Not that there is, I suppose, a truly convenient time for such things. But when I died, last Tuesday morning, I could have hoped for a sign, or some sort of warning. After all, I usually take my washing to the launderette on a Tuesday evening. But then, I would not be needing clean clothes, so perhaps it was better to save the money. (Although, having saved the money by *not* having to launder my clothes was frustrating too, for I never had the chance to spend the money I had just saved!)

Yes, dying can be a vexing affair, but I do realize that, for everyone, there is a time to live and a time to die. Given the choice (which I was not), I would have preferred to have finished my beef tea, and the fact that I had suddenly become unable to drink more than half a cupful of it was, to say the least of it, very disappointing.

One minute I was seated comfortably in my favourite chair in the staff room; the next minute I was dead. I felt rather as one does when the film breaks at a cinema – sort of switched off and empty.

However, dying does have its good side, too. I was most fortunate in being spared the indignity of expiring whilst teaching Form 2C. It is not difficult to imagine the delight such a spectacular occasion would have caused the boys and girls of that class! Come to think of it, I had spent a considerable time during that last lesson bending over the aquarium, and it would have been a very messy business had I fallen head first into it! Young Andrew

Smart would undoubtedly have come up with one of his usual witticisms. Come to that, had I been a few seconds later in completing my leave of this world, I am certain that the thick, ash cane which was gripped in the trembling hand of Mr Bassett would have fallen upon the posterior of young Mainwearing with devastating effect. So, I suppose, looking back on it, I rather timed everything quite well! But I digress, for I am describing my end before the story begins.

A few minutes before I died, I had been making my way along the corridor to the staff room, ordering the children to "walk, not run" whilst inside the school building, as was my habit. Not that the running children ever took much notice of my orders, anyway, but they did at least slow down somewhat. Once inside the staff room (a blessed oasis in the desert, away from noisy children!), I had seated myself in my favourite chair to wait for Mrs Simpkins (Domestic Science) to make my usual cup of hot beef tea. Mrs Simpkins makes an extraordinarily good cup of beef tea and I always looked forward to it enormously.

For a few minutes I enjoyed some friendly banter with my fellow teachers, and Mr Evans (History) asked me when I was thinking of retiring *again*. This caused much amusement, for, as they knew, I had already retired from teaching some five years ago, but each year I received a letter from our headmaster inviting me to apply for a position again. I must admit that having received a handsome clock and a cheque as a retiring present from the staff and pupils, I did feel rather fraudulent turning up for work each day! Mr Roper (Integrated Studies) was full of good humour that morning, and he suggested that I should retire every year and thus receive a clock and cheque each time.

As we chatted amiably, the door suddenly burst open

and Mr Bassett, a red-faced young teacher with an unruly temper, came charging into the room, his fingers pinched, crablike, to the ear of young Mainwearing, whose face was contorted with pain. "I'll teach you!" Bassett cried. "I'll teach you not to be rude to me in my classroom!" Bassett (Mathematics, by the way) dragged the child into the centre of the room and gave the ear an extra pinch for luck.

For myself, there is nothing I like better than a good book and a bag of clear mints at my side. Mr Evans plays golf, and Mr Roper is, I believe, a keen philatelist; Mrs Simpkins is, so I am told, an excellent knitter. Mr Bassett has no such outside interests and loves nothing better than to whisk his cane before the terrified eyes of an ashen-faced child before beating him thoroughly and without pity. A strange fellow is Mr Bassett, and one whom I have not the slightest desire to befriend – not that I would now be capable of doing such a thing, anyway!

We must not, however, leave the poor child in suspense whilst I tell you about my likes and dislikes. The child, in this particular instance, was young Freddy Mainwearing, and I found it most surprising that this inoffensive little fellow should have fallen foul of Bassett, for the boy was usually well-mannered and, I would have thought, almost incapable of being rude. But then, when Mr Bassett was on the prowl, he was like a lion seeking for prey. And Mr Bassett usually managed to feed at least one child a day to the insatiable appetite of his brutal cane.

"Bend over that chair, you young hooligan!" Bassett roared. "I'm going to flog the living daylights out of you!" He selected his thickest cane from the staff cupboard and flexed it menacingly, bending it expertly until it was almost doubled over. (I had made a habit, in the past, of stealing a cane now and then from the cupboard, but Mr Bassett replenished his stock regularly).

Freddy Mainwearing, having heard dreadful tales of the force with which Mr Bassett caned his victims, broke down at the sight of Bassett standing there. "I didn't mean to be rude, sir," he sobbed. "Honestly I didn't." He blinked his moist eyes owlishly behind his thick-lensed spectacles.

My heart went out to the lad, and had it been myself in charge of the matter I would have let him off with a severe caution. However, the matter was not in my hands, and Bassett took advantage of the situation to fuel his temper so that he could, when the cane fell, muster all the force in his body. "What?" he cried. "Are you being rude again? Who told you to speak, lad? Eh? Can't take your punishment like a man, eh? Is that it Main-Wear-ing?" He deliberately mis-pronounced the boy's name, spitting out the syllables with venom. "Well, we shall soon see what stuff you are made of. Bend over." Bassett removed his coat and checked that everyone in the staff room was watching him. He loved nothing better than to make an exhibition of his brutality.

"Mannering," I said.

"Eh?" Bassett turned to face me. "What did you say?"

"The boy's name is pronounced 'Mannering', not 'Main-Wearing', Mr Bassett," I told him.

"That's what I was telling Mr Bassett, sir," said young Freddy tearfully. "I wasn't trying to be rude to him."

"Shut up!" Bassett yelled. "Heaven help us when you *are* trying to be rude, Main-Wearing! For a person who was *not* trying you have managed to be very rude indeed. I refuse to be corrected by a mere child!"

"Even when you are wrong, Mr Bassett?" I enquired mildly.

"What?" Bassett had lifted the cane above his head and stood there, poised, yet uncertain. "What are you talking about, Morgan?"

"If you have been guilty of making an error, and a child has pointed out that error to you, I do not think the child should be punished for doing so," I said. "Surely young Mainwearing is best qualified to know how to pronounce his own name."

The cane wavered. Other masters were nodding their heads, and Mrs Simpkins, appalled by the sight of violence, had turned away, her hands over her eyes.

"He corrected me!" Bassett shouted. "Whether he is right or wrong is not the question. I will not be corrected in front of my class. It makes me look such a fool."

"And surely you would look even more foolish if you punished a child who was simply speaking the truth?" I asked. "May I ask you to postpone this boy's punishment whilst we discuss the matter over a cup of tea, in private?"

"Very sensible," said Mr Evans (History, if you remember). "You need to cool down, Bassett, old chap."

"Wait outside," snarled Bassett. "When we have had our discussion I will be out there to beat the daylights out of you, Main-Wearing!"

Young Freddy left the room, an expression of terror and misery on his stricken face, and I was determined to intercede most strongly on his behalf. I was not, however, allowed the opportunity of doing so, for it was at that precise moment that I died.

It had been a peculiarity of my life that I am always the last person to know about important things which affect me. Why, only last week I was heartily congratulated on winning "The Neatest Garden in Brastonbury Award" at least two hours before I had been officially informed by the judges! Everyone had been aware of the award except me. The same situation existed when I died: I was the last one to learn of it.

Bassett had slammed the door hard behind young Mainwearing, then wheeled to face me, his expression menacing and hard. "I will not have you criticize my teaching methods before a child, Ernest Morgan!" he yelled. "What do you mean by interfering?"

"I mean to see that justice prevails," I told him quietly.

Evidently Bassett was not to be intimidated with such grand words. He stared at me, his mouth thin and cruel. "Well? Answer me, Morgan!"

"I have just this minute answered you," I replied. "But, if you wish me to particularize, then I am bound to say that I find you a brutal, uncaring fellow and – "

"Answer me!" Bassett screamed. "Don't just sit there like a statue." He bent over me, staring intently into my eyes. "Have you suddenly gone deaf?"

"I can hear you perfectly," I replied, although I must admit that a strange feeling of warmth was now pervading my body. Bassett leaned closer, still staring, then was joined by Mr Evans and Mr Roper. They were all staring at me in a most peculiar manner.

"Is he deaf?" Bassett asked, his eyes still fixed upon my face.

"Of course I'm not!" I shouted.

Mr Evans shook his head. "No, he's not deaf. He's dead."

"Dead!" Bassett stepped smartly backwards.

"Deader than a door post," said Mr Evans.

"A door nail," I corrected. "The expression is 'dead as a door nail'."

They appeared not to be able to hear me, and Mr Roper, always a practical man, lifted my wrist and felt for my pulse. It was an extremely unsettling experience to have one's wrist lifted, yet not feel anything.

"He's gone, all right," said Mr Roper, ignoring the fact that I was still there. He let my wrist drop into my lap, and I just sat there, watching it fall, unable to control it.

"Has he – passed over?" asked Mrs Simpkins tearfully.

"I am not an aeroplane," I interrupted, "and I certainly have not passed over."

"Yes," said Mr Roper. "Poor old Ernest is dead." And he made the statement with such authority that I was half inclined to believe him. Mr Roper has an authoritative way about him.

Mrs Simpkins stood before me, dewy-eyed, clutching an invisible bunch of flowers in her nervous, fluttering hands. A thin tearlet welled up into her left eye and she assisted its passage by squeezing it out on to her cheeks with a series of furious blinks.

It would, I think, have been regarded by her as a sin not to shed at least one tear on such an occasion, and she demonstrated her achievement noisily by searching in the sleeve of her voluminous cardigan and producing an immense paper tissue into which she trumpeted like an elephant. "A lovely man," she said, lapsing into her Welsh accent (a habit she was prone to when distressed). "An' him never finishing his tea, look you."

To confound their suspicions, I decided to demonstrate that I was alive, and well, by finishing off that delicious beef tea. Reaching out to take hold of the mug, I was amazed to see my hand pass straight through it! Come to that, my hand had a rather watery look about it – so watery in fact that I could see right through it! This phenomenon caused me so much surprise that I leaped from my chair with a cry. Yet no one appeared to be at all interested in my gymnastics, for they were still staring at the chair which I had just vacated. And no wonder – I had not vacated it! I was standing some four feet behind them, and they were staring at my lifeless body in awe. Now I know exactly what is meant by the expression 'jumping out of one's skin', for that is precisely what I did!

My first thought was that I had no business leaving my

body without permission and that I ought to jolly well thread myself back in again before I caught cold! But getting inside one's insides is rather more difficult than you can imagine. I sat on my own lap and pressed down as hard as I could, sinking through the still frame of my body, but it was not easy. Imagine trying to put on a stiff, one-piece suit of armour and you will have some idea of the problem.

As soon as I had comfortably threaded myself into my arms, my feet popped out through my knees, or my calves! Some moments of panic passed before I realized that I was exiled from my body and that I was, as everyone else had agreed, perfectly dead.

So what was I? Or, to be correct, what am I?

Mr Bassett soon accustomed himself to the situation and shrugged indifferently. He passed off my passing on and told everyone that he had better get back to his class.

Mrs Simpkins, afraid that she might be left alone in the staff room with my lifeless body, made some excuse and rushed away. It was Mr Roper who decided that the undertaker should be telephoned and that I should be removed as quickly as possible so that the children would be unaware of what had happened until the headmaster could announce it in a dignified manner at the morning assembly. Gosh! It would be fun to turn up at the assembly and watch the expressions on their faces!

As they made arrangements for the discreet disposal of my remains, I came to terms with the fact that, apart from being unable to communicate with anyone, I was still the same Ernest Morgan. No – to tell the truth, I had become a new, improved Ernest Morgan, for my aches and pains had entirely disappeared and I felt young and frisky as a lamb. When Mr Roper walked right through me, I was delighted with my new state. Invisible! Now I could see without being seen, and listen, too! Death is not at all the miserable experience it is presumed to be. On the contrary – I was enjoying it.

But I had not yet discovered the full extent of my powers. I started to hear voices, like whisperings in the mind (rather similar to tuning in a radio set). Soon I learned to tune into voices and could hear them quite clearly. The "voices" I heard were the innermost thoughts of people in the school buildings.

Travel presented no problems at all, for I merely had to think of a place, and I was there! For me, time, distance and all physical considerations had ceased to exist. For a while I remained with my body out of a sense of loyalty. Having lived within its narrow confines for so many years, I felt rather like a traitor deserting it now, although it was no use to me.

The undertakers came within minutes, sombre-faced, and set about their task, lifting my body into a polythene sack and placing it on a stretcher to take it out to the large, black car which had been parked discreetly by the door. Fortunately the children were not in the playground and no one, save the headmaster, witnessed my departure. I stood beside the headmaster as he waved a last farewell to the departing car. "Goodbye, Ernest, old fellow," he said under his breath. "We will all miss you most sadly."

I patted him on the shoulder, but my hand went through his clothes and his bones, and he did not hear me try to comfort him. "Cheer up, Headmaster," I said. "Dying is rather fun, once you get used to the idea!"

Then I heard an insistent voice in my mind, loud and brutal. It was Bassett, shouting at his pupils. "You blithering idiots!" he was yelling. "I am going to drum this into your minds if it is the last thing I do."

Thinking of Bassett was enough to cause me to appear

in his classroom instantly. He was standing by the black-board, his face as red as an Indian sunset, his eyes wild with anger. Two girls sitting near the front of the class were shedding tears, and everyone was sitting upright, startled, waiting to see what would happen next. Young Freddy Mainwearing had been made to stand on his chair in front of the class (a mild punishment for Bassett!) and he sobbed fitfully, waiting to be flogged, as Bassett glowered at the class.

"Stop that snivelling, Main-Wearing!" Bassett yelled.

Well, I must admit that I completely lost my temper at that! In fact, to be perfectly honest, I resorted to physical violence – or tried to. My hand came up behind Bassett's ear with all the strength I could muster, then passed straight through his head! (I always knew that the man had little between his ears, but I had not suspected that it was *so* little!) It was, of course, the fact that I was dead.

How frustrating it was to swipe out at someone and miss! I tried again in the vain hope that this time it would work, but it did not. My hand sailed through Bassett's thick head and appeared not to affect him in the least. I glanced down at the cane which lay across the desk in a prominent position. If only I could hold that cane – if only I could grip it in my hand and – and –

As I thought about it, the cane slowly began to rise from the desk and sail towards me! Gracious! Another Great Power had revealed itself!

I tried the same experiment with a piece of chalk, completely forgetting that the cane was now suspended in mid air. As my attention was diverted from the cane to the chalk, the cane fell to the floor with a loud clatter which made everyone, including Bassett, jump. He bent down, picked it up gently, then replaced it on the desk, evidently thinking that it had rolled to the floor by accident. Meanwhile, the chalk I was concentrating upon had floated up from the battered tobacco tin in which it was kept and was making its way towards me.

My next experiment was with a ruler which lay on the desk of young Andrew Smart. This was a most satisfactory experiment. Andrew noticed his ruler move, then, as it rose before his face he stood up, his eyes rounder than tea plates. "Look at that!" he yelled. "My ruler is floating!"

His reaction to my experiment attracted the attention of Mr Bassett, who was still glowering at the class. Naturally my concentration drifted, probably because I had not expected such a reaction, and the ruler fell to the desk with a loud report.

"Smart!" yelled Mr Bassett. "What are you doing, lad? Eh? Playing the fool again, are you?" Bassett now appeared to be extremely happy to have secured a victim without having to make up an excuse.

"It was my ruler, sir!" Andrew cried. "It just floated up from my desk!"

Bassett grinned, displaying his yellow teeth. This would be a "six of the best" case at least.

"Your ruler floated up off your desk?" Bassett asked.

"Yes, sir," said Andrew. "It just took off."

"Amazing," said Bassett. "I never cease to wonder at the marvels of nature. One thing is for sure, Smart . . ."

"What's that, sir?" asked young Andrew innocently.

"That you were mis-named!" Bassett shouted. "Smart by name and stupid by nature," he went on. "If you think you can stand there, in my class, and make an exhibition of yourself without expecting punishment . . ."

"But it did!" Andrew replied.

"Ten of the best," said Bassett slowly. "Ten of the best, Smart, that's what you deserve."

"I saw it!" Andrew said. "Honest, sir!"

"That makes it fifteen," Bassett said evenly. "I can't abide liars."

Realizing that he was making matters worse, yet still exasperated by the unexplained incident, Andrew held his tongue. But Bassett now seemed intent on exacting revenge. "Have you anything to add to your statement?" he asked.

Fearing to utter even one word, Andrew blushed furiously.

"Dumb insolence!" Bassett screeched. "When I was in the army you could be put on a charge for that! Don't just stand there, boy – say something!"

As I had been the culprit in getting Andrew into such trouble, I decided that I ought to do my best to help him. Using my newfound powers of concentration I managed to get the ruler to lift itself from the desk.

"Look, sir!" Andrew cried. "It's doing it again!"

At first Bassett refused to look where the boy was pointing. "You don't catch me out with childish pranks like that," he said. "Twenty of the best, my boy!"

With some difficulty I managed to steer the ruler towards Bassett so that it hovered at his eye-level. He stared at it, then blinked twice as if to remove the image from his eyes. It was, of course, all a trick (he thought).

"Make it go down," Bassett snarled. "I will not have these cheap joke-shop tricks brought into my classroom. We are here to study."

"I can't make it go down," Andrew said.

"You made it float," Bassett replied evenly. "Now stop it from doing so before I increase your punishment to thirty of the best."

Thirty! I was astonished at the man's brutality. How could he ever dream of caning a child thirty times? It was disgusting.

But Bassett was now impatient to enjoy punishing the boy. Too impatient to waste time. He lunged at the floating ruler, but not before I had foreseen what he was about to do. His hand grasped around fresh air and he looked at his empty fingers in amazement. Thinking that young Andrew Smart was playing games with him, he cried out in anger: "Stop this nonsense, boy! Let me have that ruler!"

Again he lunged at the ruler, which I had whisked away from him so quickly. This time he succeeded in grasping it, and I concentrated my full energies so that it twisted out of his hand and floated up towards the ceiling. "Get that ruler down here, Smart!" he yelled. "I will not be made a fool of in front of the whole class!"

By this time I was enjoying my new powers enormously. So I obliged Mr Bassett by bringing the ruler down slowly, slowly, so that it came within inches of his outstretched hand. He reached up for it, standing on tip-toe, his fingers almost touching it. "More," he said. "Just a bit more and I can reach it – "

I teased him by holding the ruler just out of reach, then Bassett pulled a chair forward and stood on it. Imagine the fury on his face when I allowed the ruler to float up, just out of reach again.

"Andrew Smart!" he screamed. "Bring that ruler down!"

The children, although they did not understand how the ruler was managing to float by itself, were thoroughly enjoying the pantomime. Bassett was now making tiny leaps from the chair in an effort to reach the ruler, and I must admit that I did something rather naughty just as his feet left the seat of the wooden chair.

I made the chair move. Samantha Cooper screamed – but too late!

Now, Bassett knew as well as anyone that what goes up must come down again. He also thought that if he jumped *up* six inches, he would then *fall* six inches before reaching the chair once more. When he jumped up eight inches and fell twenty-four, the look of surprise on his face was wonderful to behold! In the short space of time it took him to fall to the floor, his arms and legs splayed out like those of a newborn lamb. He landed most untidily, his arms waving wildly in the air. Instantly he was on his feet, his right hand automatically reaching out for the cane. "You moved that chair!" he yelled at Andrew.

Rather than make matters worse, I decided that it was, indeed, time to bring the ruler down to Mr Bassett, and, if I may be permitted a moment of unashamed boastfulness, I think my aim was superb!

Mr Bassett is possessed of an enormous rounded bottom which appears to be straining continuously to tear his trousers asunder. His tailor, I hear, lives in mortal fear that his workmanship is perpetually on trial. When the ruler came sailing down and connected with that bottom, it gave out a very satisfactory report (far better than any report Bassett ever gave a child!), and the brutal teacher straightened up, his eyes bulging with the exquisite agony of it all.

"One!" I cried – although no one could hear me. Then I caused the ruler to strike again, but with more force this time. "Two!"

I had not expected Mr Bassett to possess the qualities of an athlete, but he demonstrated admirably that he was a superb high-jumper and could sprint respectably. His high-jump took him over the first desk, his feet just missing the head of young Alison Thomas.

"Three!" I followed him with the ruler, bringing it down with all the mental force under my control. Rather than leave matters to chance, I decided to devote some of my energies to lifting a stick of chalk from the tin on his desk so that I could keep count on the blackboard; but the children were too engrossed in the action to be aware of the phantom chalk steadily noting the punishment.

"Yipes!" screamed Bassett. "Wowee!" The ruler descended again and again as Bassett leaped and ran with remarkable agility. His mind was throwing out powerful thought waves as I made the ruler chase him, and I gathered that he was genuinely surprised at the fearfulness of the pain which the ruler was inflicting. But he was learning now, very quickly indeed!

"Twenty-eight, twenty-nine, thirty!" The ruler came down triumphantly, and Bassett, now too weak to run, lay exhausted over a chair (a position he had often demanded of pupils about to be caned).

The chalk squeaked the last number on the board, and I resisted the temptation to give him one for luck, and made the ruler float slowly upwards until it touched the ceiling and stayed there as if held by glue. Bassett looked up at it, his bottom now stinging as if he had sat in a bed of thistles. He rubbed his eyes, unable to believe what he had experienced, and the children, equally dumbfounded, giggled aloud at him. Angrily he made to reach out for the nearest child, but I willed the ruler to float down threateningly in front of him and he withdrew his hand immediately, his eyes wide with fear.

Now that Bassett had learned to respect the hovering ruler, I decided to leave it up there, on the ceiling, where it would constantly remind him of his brutal ways. Willing a small tube of glue up to the ceiling was quite easy, but unscrewing the cap and squeezing a little out was more difficult to my unpractised mind. However, I managed it, and soon the ruler was stuck securely to the ceiling.

After all the excitement, I decided to have some fun. Firstly, I thought it would be wise for the children to be sent home so that they could recover from their experience. A couple of days' holiday would soon wipe the memory clear from their young minds.

Another thought which had been on my mind was to

cause just a tiny bit of havoc in Mrs Simpkins's class. (The reason for this whim was that Mrs Simpkins is very well-ordered and precise, and I wanted to see what would happen if her cakes burned, or if her jellies refused to set!)

I floated down through the floor to the basement where the central-heating boiler gurgled and bubbled contentedly. Naturally I did not simply use my powers to turn the control knob to the "Off" position, because someone would have noticed that almost immediately. What I did was to concentrate upon the thermostat so that the contacts bent away from each other at right-angles. It would, I knew, take quite some time to repair.

Whilst waiting for the temperature of the school to reach an uncomfortably cool degree, I amused myself by visiting the classes.

Mr Evans was most surprised, when he turned to face his blackboard, to see that he appeared to have written "The Battle of Hastings – 1966", and he hastily rubbed it out before the children could comment upon it. Mrs Simpkins was equally dumbfounded when a ring of the cooker kept switching itself on and off. In the chemistry laboratory I managed to make an evil-smelling gas which drove the pupils and the master into the playground, coughing and spluttering; and I finished my performance in the Integrated Studies class by making the globe of the world spin so fast that it fell from the table and whizzed around Mr Roper's feet like a spinning top!

By this time the temperature had dropped considerably, and Mr Bassett had adjourned to the staff room for the next lesson. It was his free period, when he could mark exercise books and test papers.

Soon the headmaster was making his rounds to tell everyone that the central heating had broken down and that it would be wise for the children to go home. This, of course, delighted them.

As the head made his way towards the staff room, I decided to play a trick on him which none of his pupils had so far dared to do. It was a simple matter to use my powers to raise a heavy mathematics book from the table behind Mr Bassett, and I carefully floated it around the walls of the room until it hovered over the staff room door. When the headmaster opened the door, I was ready.

The book fell upon the round, bald patch with a resounding thudding noise, and Bassett looked up from his exercise books with a startled expression on his face.

"Mr Bassett!" roared the headmaster. "I am surprised at you!"

"Wha – ?" Bassett was puzzled to see his headmaster sitting on the floor. "Did you fall?" he asked.

"I most certainly did not fall," came the reply. "If you must play childish tricks, kindly do so after school hours. Placing a book over the door is not a very intelligent thing for a teacher to do."

"But I didn't!" Bassett cried.

"Please do not compound matters by lying," the headmaster said crossly. He stood up, rubbing the egg-shaped lump which was rising from his domed head. "You are the only person in the room, aren't you?"

Bassett agreed that this was so.

"And the book could not have been put up there before you came in, otherwise it would have fallen on your head."

The logic was faultless.

"And the book is yours," said the headmaster. "I think perhaps you had better see me in my study in the morning. We shall discuss your future at this school."

"My future?" Bassett asked.

"*If* you have a future here," came the retort.

Well, Mr Bassett did have a future with the school, and still has. You see, after the headmaster had left the room, Bassett went back to his work, shaking his head. He sat down, gazing dismally at the exercise book before him, then, as he was about to pick up his red pen, I caused it to move.

"Mighty mackerel!" Bassett cried, leaping from his chair. He watched, fascinated, as I made the pen skip and dance over the page of the exercise book, then, when I had finished writing, he cautiously picked up the book and began to read aloud.

"Dear Mr Bassett," he said, his voice becoming a whisper as his eyes scanned the page. "I am sorry to have surprised you by writing in such a flamboyant manner, but I feel that your cruelty to the children deserves a comment from me. As you know, I have now passed on and I live beyond the restrictions of my old body. I shall be watching your behaviour very closely in the future, and you may rest assured that I will not hesitate to punish you should you raise your cane to the children ever again. I am sorry that this has to be such a severe letter, but I feel very strongly about all this. Yours sincerely, Ernest Morgan."

He stared at the page for some minutes, read the letter again, then suddenly grabbed at the page and shouted: "But this is fantastic! I have proof of life after death! Ghosts exist!"

And that is when I moved faster than I ever have done in all my death! I whisked the page from the book and floated it up, up, then out through the window (which, fortunately, was not quite closed), then on, across the playground towards the smoke of a bonfire which was crackling merrily at the bottom of the school garden.

Bassett watched the paper float away, then, without a

word, he opened the cupboard door, selected an armful of canes and set off across the playground after the paper. When he reached the bonfire he threw the canes into the flames and stood there for some minutes, his face illuminated by the bright fire. It took two more journeys for him to dispose of all his stock, and when he had finished the task he returned to the staff room, made himself a cup of tea and drank it thoughtfully.

Mr Bassett was a changed man.

I understand, from conversations I have overheard in the staff room, that he even went so far as to attend my funeral (something which even I could not bring myself to do, for I do so hate those miserable gatherings).

Of course, I expect you think this story is a complete fabrication, but I intend to prove to you that this is not the case. The name of the author at the beginning of the story should, of course, be Ernest Morgan, but I was forced to use this fellow, Tapp, to write it on his typewriter. I am certain that he would be quite upset if my name, and not his, appeared beneath the title, for the poor, deluded man is convinced that he has hit upon a brilliant idea in telling this story to you, and he has no notion that I am using his mind. Perhaps, sometime in the future, I may use him again!

Note from Editor to Printer:

Please delete the last paragraph from this story as I feel that it might frighten our readers if they suspect that Ernest Morgan is still floating around. I have had permission to delete from the author, who swears he did not write it anyway!

Note from Ernest Morgan to the Reader:

The printer did as he was told and did *not* make up the

print for the last paragraph, so I had to spend all night in the printing works finding the right letters and laying it out neatly. I *told* you I have special powers, didn't I? Actually, I thoroughly enjoyed searching through all those boxes of printing letters to make this up, and I am happy to say that I have managed to do a good job, without a single misdake . . . I hope we meet again, soon!

CAN'T HELP LAUGHING

by Alison Prince

Outside the Maths Hut, a bird was tugging a worm out of the earth, leaning backwards with the worm stretched like tight elastic. Sophie watched through the window. It'll go ping in a minute, she thought, and the bird will fall on its bum. She giggled.

"Sophie Mayhew, get on with your work," snapped Miss Webb. Sophie looked at her and thought what a peevish little mouth the teacher had, its corners running down into the sagging lines of her cheeks. It was the first time they had been taught by Miss Webb. Last term Mr Thompson had taken them for Maths. He was young and cheerful – not a bit like Miss Webb, who looked like a bad-tempered Pekinese. A grin crept across Spohie's face at this thought, and she glanced out of the window again to try and hide it. Outside, the worm came out of the earth with an almost audible plop and the bird fell over backwards. Sophie burst into fits of giggles.

"Sophie!" Miss Webb's jowls shook with anger. "What, may I ask, is so funny?"

"Nothing," said Sophie, trying to pull her face straight.

"I can hardly see that you have anything to smirk about," spat Miss Webb. "Your attainment in this subject would do no credit to a backward five-year-old. You will report to me after school. Perhaps when you are working on your own you will find it a little less – *funny*." She pronounced the last word with extreme dislike.

"Yes, miss," said Sophie. It was not the first time she had been in trouble for giggling, but she could never help laughing when something struck her as funny. Her friends made sympathetic faces, and one of the boys muttered, "Who's a naughty girl, then?" Miss Webb glared at him but said nothing. Everyone knew that she was never quite so nasty to the boys, probably because she had taught in the Girls' Grammar School all her life – that is, until it became part of the Comprehensive. Rather like a cavalry officer having to drive a tank, Sophie thought. She very nearly giggled again.

Being in detention was particularly dreadful on a summer afternoon. The Maths Hut smelt frowsty and, now that everyone had gone home, the school was silent except for the cheerful whirr of the mower as Mr Atkins, the caretaker, rode round and round the field and the wide cutters tossed up a cloud of grassy dust behind the machine.

"I am going to the staff room for a few minutes," Miss Webb announced tightly. "I shall want to see your work when I return."

Sophie watched her go out. She hated Miss Webb. She hated the solid, tweed-encased body, the plump fingers, the high carriage of the sagging chin which somehow implied that life was full of nasty smells. When the door closed behind the teacher, Sophie put her pen down and leaned back in her chair, stretching her arms above her head. The very air of the Maths Hut seemed to relax in Miss Webb's absence. Sophie opened the window and leaned out. The sweet, delicious scent of the mown grass poured in. "M'm," said Sophie aloud. "Lovely." I wonder what the old bat's gone down to the staffroom for, she added to herself.

"Needs a wee, I expect." The comment came in a confidential whisper, just behind Sophie's shoulder, and was followed by a raucous cackle.

471

Sophie jumped round and stared into the empty room. She looked suspiciously up at the fanlight above the door. There was nobody to be seen.

"Only human, aren't they?" said the voice. It was as intimate as though the owner stood at Sophie's elbow, nudging her. The hair rose on the back of Sophie's neck. Trying to ignore the fact that the voice was so close, she told herself that she must be overhearing a conversation outside. She got up and went to the door.

"No use looking out there," said the voice, still close beside her. "I'm here, silly."

Sophie felt embarrassed as well as scared. This sort of thing did not happen. There must be a reasonable explanation. She looked around the room again, thinking suspiciously of tape recorders or radios.

"Oh, do sit down, dear," said the voice. "It makes my feet tired, you walking about like this. I used to have terrible trouble with my feet. 'Course, I'm lighter now, you might say. Ha-ha-ha-ha-ha!" Sophie nearly laughed as well, although she was breathless with alarm. And what was so funny about being lighter now?

"I knew you was my sort this morning, when you got the giggles," the voice went on. "That's why I've chosen you to talk to. Madam got proper upset, didn't she?"

Sophie glanced round, still very alarmed and half-convinced that the whole thing was some kind of trick. To say something would be to admit that she could hear the voice – but she could think of no other way to find out what was going on. "Who are you?" she whispered aloud.

"They call me Lil," said the voice cheerfully. "No, you can't help laughing, can you, the fuss some of these teachers make."

Sophie gave a scared, breathless laugh, then blushed, still afraid that she was the victim of some practical joke.

"Now, look, dear," said Lil in a matter-of-fact tone, as

472

close to Sophie's ear as though she had her arm around the girl's shoulders, "there's no need to panic. People are so silly about ghosts. We don't all go moaning around in a grey mist, you know. Ha-ha-ha!"

"You're a – ghost?" said Sophie, her voice rising to a squeak.

"Well, what do you *think* I am?" said Lil impatiently. "And don't pretend you're scared – you're not the scary sort, otherwise you wouldn't be here. You're only in detention because you weren't frightened of the old battle-axe – so why be frightened of me? I wouldn't hurt a fly."

"Wouldn't you?" Though half reassured, Sophie still sounded rather shaky.

"'Course not," said Lil. "Ha! I don't say I wouldn't like to, but I just don't have the weight for it. Ha-ha! A ghost is no blooming good as a fly swat!"

Sophie could not help joining in with Lil's roar of laughter. The door was flung open and Miss Webb stood there. Sophie at once tried to put on a suitably grave expression, but Miss Webb swelled like an angry bluebottle.

"Here we go," muttered Lil as the teacher advanced. "Fuss."

Sophie put her hand to her mouth, trying to smother a further giggle. She had suddenly seen what Lil meant about being lighter now. You couldn't have anything much lighter than a ghost. Her diaphragm shook with amusement.

Miss Webb gave no sign of having heard Lil. "You are either extremely stupid or just plain insolent," she said to Sophie. "Shut that window at once. I did not give you permission to open it."

Sophie got up, trying to control her face. The sensation of having an unseen person in the room made her feel quite hysterical.

"Got on her high horse now," observed Lil cheerfully.

"Shut up!" muttered Sophie.

Miss Webb heard her. "I *beg* your pardon!" she shouted, outraged.

"I didn't mean you, miss," said Sophie. "I'm sorry, I sort of – "

"Put me foot in it," finished Lil. "Ha-ha-ha!"

Sophie collapsed into giggles.

"You appear to have taken leave of your senses," said Miss Webb icily. "You are perhaps an object of pity rather than contempt, but don't imagine you can get away with such behaviour. I shall expect an apology from you tomorrow, when you have recovered some semblance of mental stability."

"Nasty," said Lil.

"Meanwhile," Miss Webb continued, oblivious, "I shall waste no further time with you. You may go."

"Yes, miss," said Sophie. Still shaking with horrified amusement, she pushed her books into her bag and fled. "Goodnight," she said over her shoulder.

"Bye-bye, love," said Lil comfortably.

Miss Webb said nothing.

Sophie told Sharon, her closest friend, about Lil the next morning. Sharon looked at her with wide eyes and said, "You mean the Maths Hut is *haunted*?"

"No," said Sophie. "Not exactly. But – well, yes, I suppose it is."

"Get off," said Sharon contemptuously. "You don't get ghosts in modern buildings like this, only in old castles and things. You just imagined it."

Sophie looked at her friend and decided not to pursue the point. If Sharon didn't believe it, nobody would. "I suppose I must have done," she said. "You won't tell

474

anyone, will you? I'll get sent up rotten if the boys find out."

"'Course I won't," said Sharon. "I don't want people saying my friend is a nut case, do I?"

"No," agreed Sophie meekly. Sharon's words echoed disturbingly in her mind. *Was* she a nut case? She pushed the thought away firmly. A nut case would never have invented a ghost that *laughed*.

Maths was the last lesson of the afternoon. When Miss Webb came in she beckoned to Sophie with a plump, imperious finger and, when the girl stood in front of her, said, "Well?"

Thus prompted, Sophie said, "I'm sorry about yesterday."

"I should think so," said Miss Webb. "If there is any repetition of such behaviour, you will go straight to the Headmaster, do you understand?"

Among ironic groans and sighs from the boys, Sophie said obediently, "Yes, miss."

"Three bags full, miss," chipped in Lil loudly. "Ha-ha-ha!" There was a shout of amusement from the boys and everyone craned their necks to see where the voice came from.

Sophie gave a gasp of horror. There had been no sound from Lil that day, and she had begun to feel sure that whatever had happened during her detention last night had been an isolated incident, never to be repeated. But now – what?

Miss Webb glared at her suspiciously, and Sophie quickly turned the gasp into a cough. "Sorry," she said, scuttling back to her place. Sharon was scribbling on a scrap of paper which she pushed over to Sophie's desk. On it she had written, "THREE BAGS FULL???!"

So Sharon could hear Lil's voice. Everyone could hear it. Sophie's skin prickled as she looked at her friend and nodded. Who was the nut case now? The boys were still laughing and the girls were staring round the room and giggling. Miss Webb, ignoring the noise, was writing an equation on the board, her back to the class. Still looking at Sharon, Sophie touched her own ears, pointed at the teacher and shook her head. Sharon shrugged hugely, spreading her hands. No, Miss Webb couldn't hear the voice.

"Tell you the truth," said Lil, loudly but confidentially, "I never took to Big Fat Spider Webb. Ha-ha!"

Amid the shrieks of amusement, Sophie reflected with some relief that Lil no longer sounded as if she was standing at Sophie's side, whispering into her ear. She was speaking to the whole class. Miss Webb's hand paused when the laughter broke out. She checked her figures quickly to see that she had not made a mistake which might have caused the amusement, then swung round to face the class. Among all the excited faces, Sophie Mayhew's was the only one which was struggling to look innocent. "Stand up!" she snapped at the girl. Sophie, pinkfaced, did as she was told.

"You will go to prison for twenty years," said Lil gloomily. "Ha-ha-ha!" The class exploded into a gale of laughter, and even Sophie could not repress a panic-stricken giggle. Miss Webb's cheeks turned a dull crimson. "No doubt you think you are very clever," she snarled at Sophie. "I have no idea how you are managing to induce this disorder in the class, but I doubt if Mr Craig will share your inflated opinion of yourself. Go to his office at once. And the rest of you, get on with your work."

"Now you done it," said Lil. Her laughter and that of the class faded as Sophie closed the door of the hut behind her, but renewed shouts of amusement were clearly audible as she set off for the Head's office.

Sophie knocked on the door and heard the bell on Mr

476

Craig's desk ping as a signal to enter. With a lurch of the heart, she went in. Mr Craig's bushy hair was white, his glasses as thick as bottle-bottoms. He sat behind his large desk and said nothing.

"Er – Miss Webb sent me," said Sophie.

"Yes?" Mr Craig said unhelpfully.

"I – well – everyone was laughing."

"At what?"

Sophie blushed. "I know it sounds silly," she said, "but there was a voice. Saying funny things."

Mr Craig's glasses glinted as he tilted his head at a sarcastic angle. "Like Joan of Arc?" he enquired.

"No," said Sophie. Joan of Arc could never have heard anything like Lil.

Mr Craig's glasses looked at Sophie for a moment. She wondered what his eyes were like behind them. Then he said, "Do you really expect me to believe this story?"

"No," said Sophie honestly. "But it's true."

There was a pause. "Can the others hear this – voice?" asked Mr Craig.

"Yes," said Sophie. "That's why they're laughing. But Miss Webb can't."

The headmaster sat back in his chair, tapping a pencil inconsequentially on his desk. "I think this voice is something to do with you," he said.

Sophie watched the pencil tapping, and shook her head. "I don't want it to be," she told him.

"So I shall hold you responsible for it," continued Mr Craig, ignoring her. He put the pencil into a glass tray with several others, snapping it down with a sharp click. Sophie transferred her gaze unwillingly to his glasses.

"Go back to your lesson," said Mr Craig, "and let me hear no more of this nonsense."

"But – " began Sophie.

Mr Craig leaned forward. "Don't push your luck," he said with menace.

"No, sir," said Sophie, and crept out.

Mr Atkins, the caretaker, was walking down the corridor studying the list of jobs on his clipboard. "Hello," he said at the sight of Sophie's downcast face. "Been in trouble?"

"It's not my fault," protested Sophie. "Someone keeps laughing in the Maths Hut." She knew Mr Atkins quite well because he and Sophie's father flew racing pigeons together.

"One of your class, d'you mean?" asked Mr Atkins.

"No." Sophie frowned. Although the others thought it was so funny, there was something about Lil which she found upsetting. "It's a voice. Someone called Lil. The others can hear it but Miss Webb can't, and everyone thinks it's my fault."

"Lil?" Mr Atkins was staring at her. "Are you sure?"

"That's what she said." Sophie gulped. "She sounds ever so funny and sort of nice, but I wish in a way it hadn't happened. I feel as if I'm – well – nuts."

"The Maths Hut," repeated Mr Atkins. "Well, I'm blowed. Lily Barnum." He rubbed his forehead in perplexity.

"What do you mean?" asked Sophie.

The caretaker looked at her consideringly, as if trying to decide whether to tell her something.

"Oh, go on," Sophie begged. "Please!"

"Lily Barnum was one of our cleaners," said Mr Atkins, making up his mind. "The others called her Laughing Lil. Funny woman. She couldn't read or write – lived in a caravan on the edge of the Common. I think she hated schools, really, but she needed the money from the cleaning job. She used to laugh at the teachers, and some

478

of them got really cross with her. You couldn't be cross with Lil for long, though. Not the way she laughed."

Sophie nodded. She knew. "What happened to her?" she asked.

"Well – " Mr Atkins hesitated again. "You won't be upset, will you? The fact is, she was found dead in the Maths Hut. Face down, with her mop in her hand. It turned out she'd had a heart condition for years, and the other cleaners said she'd had some sort of disagreement with Miss Webb. Maybe they got really angry with each other and it was too much for her heart. I never really got to the bottom of it – but we all missed old Lil." He stared at Sophie curiously. "And you say you heard her talking to you?"

"I don't know." Somehow Sophie wanted time to think about what Mr Atkins had said. She regretted confiding in him so impulsively. Although Mr Atkins was very nice, his concern made Sophie feel self-conscious. Mr Craig had simply not believed her, but Mr Atkins did, and Sophie realized afresh that what she had told him was very, very odd. "I certainly heard something," she said lightly. "Perhaps it was the record player next door." She gave what she hoped was a cheery smile.

"The Maths Hut doesn't have a next door," said Mr Atkins. Sophie wished he would stop looking at her in that worried sort of way.

"Oh. No, of course it doesn't." She smiled again, rather wildly. "How silly. Gosh, I must go or I'll get into more trouble." She fled, leaving Mr Atkins where he stood, frowning after her.

She dived through the swing doors into the safe haven of the toilets and leaned her hands on the cold edge of one of the wash basins, staring unseeingly at her reflection in the mirror. Lil could not read or write. No wonder the sight of people studying books all day seemed so funny to her. She must have said something cheeky to Miss Webb. Sophie could imagine the response all too clearly. "Oh, yes, Mrs Barnum? I suppose your fluent command of written English gives you the right to be insolent, does it?" The sarcastic voice rang in her ears.

She made her way back to the Maths Hut as slowly as she dared. She was beginning to dread meeting Lil again. There was something nightmarish about the constant laughter. As she approached the hut she could hear screams of amusement. Girls were shrieking and boys were shouting and banging the desk tops. It sounded as if the whole class was in complete hysterics. Sophie ran up the wooden steps and pushed open the door.

"Well, I told her," Lil was saying conversationally, "it's no use you coming the lah-di-dah with *me*. You may be very natty with your blooming books, I says, but who needs them? Not me, for a start-off. Ha-ha-ha! Poor old bird. She looked that took aback, I had to smile." The class collapsed in fresh fits of laughter. Miss Webb, who was clearly unable to hear a word that Lil was saying, stood leaning her knuckles on the edge of her desk, fighting for control of the class. "Be quiet at once!" she shouted. "I have had quite enough of this nonsense!"

Nobody took the slightest notice. Suddenly Sophie felt sorry for Miss Webb. It had gone too far. The laughter was horrible. "Lil," she said aloud, "do stop it."

There was too much noise in the room for anyone to notice what Sophie had said, but she was standing right beside Miss Webb, who heard her. She glared at Sophie and said in a voice choking with fury, "When I want you to take over the control of this class, Miss Mayhew, I will ask you. Sit down at once."

"Ha! Charming!" said Lil in the slight lull caused by Miss Webb's words.

There was a renewed explosion from the class, who

were by now in such a hysterical state that the slightest thing precipitated a fresh outburst. Miss Webb stood back from her desk and Sophie saw that her hands were trembling. She sat down in her chair. Her mouth twitched, and for a moment Sophie thought that at last Miss Webb was going to join in the infectious laughter. The teacher put her hands over her face. Her shoulders heaved. Gradually, the class became quiet. Miss Webb, unable to laugh, was weeping.

"Oh, Lor'," said Lil in the sudden quiet. "That's done it. Gone too far." To Sophie's horror, the voice was close to her ear again, a husky whisper which only she could hear. "I better stick to you in future, dear. Shouldn't have bothered with those others. But we're the same sort, aren't we, you and me? We understand each other. If you get a chance, you can tell the old bag I'm sorry. Still – can't help laughing, can you? Ha-ha-ha!" Sophie shuddered.

Miss Webb got up, a handkerchief pressed to her face, and bolted out of the door. Standing up to stare furtively out, they saw her stumbling blindly along the concrete path which led to the staffroom.

"We'll have old Craig over in a minute," said one of the boys.

"Wasn't our fault, was it?" said another, sounding injured.

Books were retrieved from the floor and hurled back to their owners, and a rather breathless silence descended.

When the Headmaster came into the Maths Hut to find out the cause of Miss Webb's extraordinary breakdown, the class was working industriously, every face innocent and busy. Sophie Mayhew, however, sat bolt upright in her seat by the window, with her hands pressed over her ears and her elbows sticking out sideways. Her eyes were staring.

"Sophie, what is the matter?" asked Mr Craig. For a moment the girl did not appear to have heard him. Then her face contorted in a horrified laugh. "Shut up!" she shouted. "Shut up, shut up, shut up!"

Mr Craig opened his mouth to protest, then closed it again. A sweat broke out on his face, which caused his glasses to mist over. Sophie Mayhew, he realized, was talking to somebody else. The bell rang for the end of afternoon school.

"You may go," said Mr Craig unnecessarily, for books were already being stuffed into bags. He cast an uneasy glance at Sophie, who was surrounded by urgently chattering friends, and went back to his office to ring the Educational Psychologist.

Sophie could not wait to get out of the Maths Hut and away from the voice in her ear, which had become as maddening as a buzzing insect. She did not even want to talk to Sharon. Lil's intimacy was horrifying, like a parasite lodged in her mind.

Sophie's house was within walking distance of the school, and so she set out along the road, glad that she did not have to wait with a Bus Group.

It was a tremendous relief to be alone and in silence. Sophie turned off the road to follow the footpath which led across the Common to her house. There was no sound except the wind in the silver birch trees and the faint swish of Sophie's feet as she walked across the dry grass. She wondered idly where Lil's caravan had been – not that it mattered. It was long gone by now, anyway. Tomorrow, she told herself, she would ask Mr Craig if she could be transfered to a lower maths group. She was quite bad enough at maths for the request to seem natural. That way, she never need go into the Maths Hut again, for the lower group worked in a room in the main building. She could avoid any further contact with the awful Laughing Lil, who had died in the Maths Hut. That is where she was found, face down with her mop in her hand, and that is where her spirit had to stay. So there, you old baggage, thought Sophie happily. That's fixed you.

"Don't kid yourself, love," said Lil. "We're going to be good mates, you and me. I don't mind you telling me to shut up occasionally, like you did this afternoon – I ain't easy offended. Ha-ha-ha! Can't help laughing, can you? Ha-ha-ha-ha-ha!"

Standing alone on the Common with her hands over her ears, Sophie screamed and screamed.

THE RETURN OF THE LORELEI

by Ken Burke

Four Winds Cottage stood high on the clifftops. Two hundred years and more it had gazed defiantly down at the restless, angry sea as it battered itself against the rocks far below. The four winds rushed endlessly around its casement windows and gable ends.

Below the eaves was one large window with many small panes which looked out across the cliffs and over the sea. It kept out the wind, the muffled cries of the seagulls and the roar of the breakers. It was Davy's bedroom window. Four Winds Cottage was where he lived with his mother and father.

To the side of his room, and oval window had a view of the path which wound down over the clifftops to the small fishing village. He could see way below the white walls of the houses, their grey-tiled roofs and the winding cobbled streets. And from that window, Davy could see any visitors, who were few, as they toiled up the path from the village.

The most frequent user of the path was his own father, who left Four Winds Cottage late at night and descended to the secluded cove, where the fishing boats lay at anchor, bobbing on the tide. Late at night, Davy would gaze from his many-paned window and watch the fishing smacks upon the dark sea, wondering which one was his father's, and whether his catch would be big – or pitifully small. He would return when it was barely light, and many times Davy had seen him wearily climbing the path after a night's fishing, as the first grey fingers of dawn spread across the sky.

Long ago Davy had realized that life was a struggle against the wildness of Nature. It was an ancient struggle, one which he could understand, one which he could accept.

But the day the stranger came over the clifftop path portended the beginning of another, older conflict. The one between Good and Evil.

It was a blustery day. Davy was looking out of the oval window at the clouds which scudded across the windy sky, and at the foam-crested waves breaking in the bay. It seemed to Davy that one minute he wasn't there; next minute he was – a tall figure in black, staring up at Four Winds Cottage. Then he saw Davy at the window, and Davy ducked down below the ledge. He sat against the wall, his mind whirling. He could hardly have mistaken the look on the man's face. It was a look of hate.

His father was asleep after a hard night's fishing. His mother had gone down to the village for the shopping. He waited, his heart thumping faster and faster. If the man knocked at the door, he wouldn't open it.

Thud! Thud!

Davy jumped. The crash of the doorknocker echoed throughout the cottage. Fighting his fear, he heaved himself up and out of his bedroom. He crept down to the bottom of the stairs.

"Who is it?" he whispered, his head against the hard wood of the door.

There was a moment of silence.

"A friend of your father." The voice was cold, like the rasp of an iron file. "Open the door, lad, there's a good boy. It's your father I've come to see."

Suddenly unable to think clearly, Davy pulled back the

big iron bolt and opened the door. A blast of chilly wind blew into the cottage.

Davy looked up. The man was very tall. He wore a black peaked cap and seaman's jacket with brass buttons. He had a black patch over one eye, and below it was a deep groove in his cheek, running down to the jawbone. His one eye was crimson, and blazed like the setting sun. It pierced Davy with a cold stare.

His thin, cruel lips hardly moved as he said, "Now fetch your father, boy."

Davy spun round and ran up to his parents' bedroom. He burst in the door, saying, "Dad, Dad! There's a man come to see you!"

He saw his father's tousled head rising from the bedclothes, and his bleary eyes coming suddenly wide awake as they looked over Davy's shoulder.

"Hullo, shipmate," came a quiet voice. The man with the patch was standing in the doorway.

Davy's father looked alarmed for a second. Then he said, "It's OK, Davy. Leave us now."

Davy needed no second bidding. He squeezed timidly past the stranger and sped off along the landing into his own room. He heard a long, chilling laugh, a laugh that had no humour in it, abruptly shut off by the closing of his father's door. For a long time he sat on his bed, looking out of the window with unseeing eyes, hearing only the muttering of low voices in the next bedroom.

Then there was somebody shouting – a voice he barely recognized as his father's.

"Get the hell out of my house! Take your evil carcass out of here! And don't you ever come threatening me again, or I'll – "

The bedroom door opened.

" – You'll what, shipmate?" came the quiet, menacing tones. "What can *you* do?"

There were footsteps down the stairs. Davy peeped round the doorpost. His father stood at the head of the stairs, his face like thunder. The stranger had reached the hallway. He turned and looked up the stairs, putting one hand casually on the banister rail. His black eye-patch seemed even blacker, the groove even deeper in his cheek.

"Don't forget what I've said, shipmate," he sneered. "*Tomorrow*. It's coming for you tomorrow. Just a friendly warning, that's all." He smiled, showing blackened, rotted teeth. Then he turned, opened the front door, and went out, slamming it against the force of the wind. A couple of dead leaves blew across the floor of the hall.

Davy followed his father into his parents' bedroom. His father sat in his pyjamas on the edge of the bed, looking dejectedly at the rug.

"Did you see him go, Davy?"

"Yes, Dad," Davy replied. "Dad, why did that man come here? There's no place for him here. He's – " He shivered.

"I know, Davy. Cruel, wicked. Look, when I was younger, I – " He sat Davy next to him on the bed. " – I did a lot of foolish things, son. But the most foolish thing I ever did was to get mixed up with that man."

He sighed. "We met in a bar in Naples, on the waterfront. It was the lowest place on God's earth. Foul, dirty – the refuge of the most desperate villains who ever drew breath. Why I ever went there I'll never know. I regret it to this day. That was where I met him. Called himself Black Patch. We got to talking about various things, and he said he was looking for a man for a special trip – one which was very dangerous, but which would reap a lot of money. I fell for it, Davy! Hook, line and sinker!" He bowed his head in his hands and groaned.

"We took a voyage out to a sunken wreck which had

been cast up on a sandbank by the tide. One slight movement of the waves could have sent it down to the sea. But I was reckless, Davy! The though of that money! I did what Black Patch said. I climbed into the water from our boat, with a rope tied round my waist. He held the other end. I swam to the wreck, and then I saw the name 'Lorelei' on the bows – after the beautiful siren who lured sailors to their deaths. In its time, it must have been a fine, three-masted schooner, one of the fastest sailing ships afloat. But now she was just a wreck. I clambered aboard and went down to the captain's cabin, which was flooded. The seawater was up over my knees. There was barely enough light to see, but there was a safe in the corner, and I opened it up – Davy, there were enough bars of gold in there to make a man rich for life." He stared into the distance. "But Black Patch wanted only one thing – a black tin box, which I was to take back to him at all costs. Then I could come back for the gold.

"I went up on deck with the black box. All the time I was below, the tide had been rising. And I could feel the scrapings of the hull as the *Lorelei* shifted on that sandbank. I dived in the water just in time. Black Patch pulled me back to the boat. When I looked round, the wreck suddenly lurched and heaved over sideways in showers of spray. She went down, Davy, down into fifty fathoms, down amongst the weeds. The waters closed and rolled over her forever."

Davy's father stood up and went to the window, staring out at the sea, in his mind still seeing the wreck go under the waves. "I never saw that box again. I honoured my part of the bargain and gave it to Black Patch. I came away penniless. I met your mother and we settled down here, at Four Winds Cottage. That was a long time ago."

Davy frowned. "What was in the box, Dad?"

"I don't know for sure, son. Some said that on her last

voyage the *Lorelei* was carrying a fabulous diamond, that there was a curse on it, and that was why the ship was wrecked, and all aboard were drowned."

"How many were there?" asked Davy.

"Twelve, son. All drowned. All battened down and trapped in the hold by the thirteenth man. He got away when the ship sank. Some said that they were all evil men, and that they deserved to die. They committed all sorts of crimes and used the ship's sails to run far and fast at night, without noisy engines to give themselves away."

Davy said, "But why has Black Patch come back after all this time?"

"The curse brought him," his father replied over his shoulder. "He says that the *Lorelei* has become a ghost ship, crewed by spectres. Somehow it's returned, to claim the soul of the thirteenth man. And since I was the one who took the tin box, it's come back for me. Tomorrow night, he says."

"No, Dad, no!" cried Davy. He leapt up and flung his arms around his father, choking back the tears.

At last, his father took him downstairs. When his mother came home with the shopping, they had tea, but Davy couldn't eat much.

That night, Davy had troubled dreams in which he was floundering through the flooded hold of a ship, forever chased by a shadowy figure wearing a patch over one eye.

He awoke shivering. It was midnight. The wind had dropped, and all was quiet outside his window. On the far wall flickered the silvery reflections of the moon on the sea, from time to time obscured by clouds. He sat up and stepped on to the floor. He felt the coldness of it against his feet as he moved, drawn irresistibly to the window.

He looked out over the cliffs. A sudden chill, cold as steel, gripped his heart. Upon the sea floated a ghostly ship. The sails were unfurled on its three masts, rippling in the motion of a phantom wind. And on the deck swayed a crew of evil-looking men, who heaved on the ropes, cursing and screaming against the crash of the breakers.

Davy felt his heart begin to thump in his chest. He gripped the window ledge to stop himself from falling. He watched in horror as the ghostly ship swung slowly round, and he caught a glimpse of the name on the side. In gold lettering on the black hull he saw the one word: "Lorelei". It had returned. It would come tomorrow night as Black Patch had said, to take his father's soul. As he watched, a sea mist drifted across, and the ship with its terrible crew vanished.

He fell back into bed and knew no more until he awoke with the sunlight streaming in through his windows. He started as his mother came into his room.

"Where's Dad?" he asked her, suddenly wide awake.

His mother sat on the bed and ruffled his tousled hair. "Your father stayed out last night, and he'll be out tonight, too, Davy, on a long fishing trip," she told him. "There's a big shoal of fish lying close to shore, and he has a chance of a big haul. We won't see him again until tomorrow morning."

Davy's heart sank. Now he could not tell his father what he had seen the night before. And by tomorrow it would be too late. His father couldn't have told his mother about Black Patch. Neither would he tell her. She would remain oblivious of the tragedy which was about to strike and tear their peaceful lives apart.

All day Davy moped about the house, hoping against hope that his father would return early from the fishing trip. Evening came, and it was time for Davy to go to bed. In vain he pleaded with his mother to let him stay up a little while longer; eventually she marched him up the stairs and into bed.

Davy was unable to sleep. He stood at the window, waiting in vain for his father to return. As it came closer to midnight, a squall started up. It soon grew into a storm which started the whole house shaking. Down in the bay, the waves hurled themselves unceasingly against the rocks, their white foam spitting fury at the raging sky. The clouds raced across the face of the moon as the tempest howled about Four Winds Cottage.

It was no ordinary storm, of that Davy was quite sure. It was a supernatural storm, and any God-fearing people were safest in the warmth of their own homes. The greatest danger was to fishermen out on the sea – like his own father, he suddenly realized.

And while he stood at the window, cold fear clutched like a steel band around his chest. Sailing out of the storm over the sea came the ghostly schooner, the *Lorelei*, with its sails flapping in the wind, its evil crew straining at the ropes. In that moment Davy saw that there was no one at the helm, and he knew that the thirteenth man would stand there, to steer the ghost ship across eternity. It would be the voyage of the damned – damned to roam the seven seas, forever hauling on the phantom ropes and heaving up the sails, forever riding the restless tide until the end of time.

Then Davy looked down, below his window. With a shock, he realized that somebody was standing on the edge of the cliffs, with his back to the house. In the gloom, Davy could make out the man's peaked cap and seaman's jacket which was blown about by the wind. It was Black Patch. He had his arms raised and was staring down towards the *Lorelei* like a being with the power of life and death. He was shouting something, but Davy couldn't make out the words. He dressed quickly and ran downstairs.

The wind almost blew the front door from his grasp, as

he opened it and hid in the shadows of the porch. He could see the silhouette of Black Patch several yards away on the edge of the cliffs. He was shouting to the crew of the *Lorelei*, and now Davy caught snatches of his words, whipped back to him in the force of the gale.

"Here I am, shipmates!" he cried. "'Tis me you'll be wanting, I fancy! But look there, there on the water!"

Davy held his hand against the biting wind which lashed into his eyes, and tried to see out over the cliffs. Far out to sea was a solitary fishing boat, being tossed up on the crest of the waves and then down into the trough, moving closer and closer to the rocks. It was his father's boat, of that Davy had no doubt.

Black Patch flung out one bony finger and pointed at the boat. "Look, shipmates!" he howled like the wind. "There's your prey! He's the one who stole your diamond, not me! He's the one you want!"

With a gasp of horror, Davy saw the ghost ship begin to keel round in the direction of his father's boat. The phantom sailors were cackling with evil pleasure, holding fast to the ropes as she came about. In the darkness, Davy could barely make out the lone figure of his father in the wheelhouse of the fishing boat as it battled through the high seas. And he knew that his father must be straining to the limit to get every last ounce of power from the old engines of his little boat. But it was hopeless against the dreadful might of the *Lorelei*, speeding through the waves towards it.

Giving a cry of desperation, Davy flung himself forward at the twisting shape of Black Patch and hammered with his small fists on the man's back.

"You're the one!" Davy shouted in anger. "You're the one they're after! How can you let them take my dad!"

Black Patch half-turned, with a sneer on his lips, and caught Davy's hands. "Well, well! What have we here?

The young whelp has come to save the dog! But you're right, my friend, more than you know. I was captain of that ship! And I was the one who scuppered her, to get my hands on that diamond. But before I could take it, the ship sank, drowning everyone aboard." Black Patch laughed evilly, revealing his blackened teeth. "I was the one who sent them all to a watery grave! And they deserved it, every last one of the miserable curs! Now they've come back for me. But they won't catch me now. Yesterday I tricked your fool of a father into thinking they're after *him*. And when he sacrifices himself, they'll take him instead of me!"

He pointed down into the bay, where the ghost ship was already bearing down on the tiny fishing boat. Meanwhile, the sound of the storm had risen to a shriek.

"No!" screamed Davy. He hurled himself up at the leering man and tore at his face. He felt the eyepatch give, then come away in his hands. Black Patch howled with pain, flinging a hand up over his missing eye.

"My patch, you cur! My patch! Give it to me! Aah – !"

With one sudden movement, Black Patch stumbled sideways on a slippery hump of grass. Unable to save himself, he plunged headfirst over the edge of the cliff.

Davy ran forward and peered over the side. Just out of reach, hanging by one hand on a single tuft of grass, was Black Patch. His body dangled precariously in mid-air. The fitful light of the storm-ridden moon lit up his face, which glistened with spray cast up by the wind. His eyepatch was gone, and now Davy could see the groove running up his cheek, and the hideous, livid flesh of the hollow eyesocket.

His mouth started to tremble.

"Save me, shipmate!" he begged in a hoarse whisper. "Save me! I'll see to it your father gets away!"

All his swagger was gone. And there was something in

493

his manner, an abject terror in his one eye that made Davy hesitate. No man should die in this way, not even an evil person like Black Patch.

"You promise?" said Davy.

"Yes! Yes, shipmate!" wept Black Patch.

Davy lay down across the grass and reached over the cliff. Black Patch's other hand came up, slowly, painfully. Davy leaned out as far as he could. He almost reached the outstretched hand. Next moment, the tuft of grass Black Patch was holding gave way. His other hand was poised, white and crooked, clawing the air for a second like a wounded vulture. Then it was gone, and there was only the sound of the wind rushing over the clifftops and the crash of the sea against the rocks far below.

Black Patch had hurtled to his doom.

Davy lay there, his face buried in the grass. In one swift, cruel stroke, the chance of saving his father had gone. Gradually he looked up, tears stinging his eyes.

The storm had stopped, as suddenly as it had started. He looked down, into the cove. To his joy, the fishing boat had gained the shore. His father was safe. From his position on the windswept cliff Davy could see his father climbing down from his boat on to the sand.

Davy looked back towards the sea. Out on the waves still floated the ghost ship. He watched it, mesmerized, knowing that never again would he or his father fear the curse of the *Lorelei*.

The thirteenth man now stood at the helm of the ghostly schooner. It was Black Patch. His broken body lay at the foot of the cliffs, but his ghost was on board the *Lorelei*. Davy saw for one moment his tortured figure at the helm, his mouth torn open in anguish. Then he heaved the tiller over, and the ship swung round across the swell of the sea and vanished into the sweeping mist.

THE GHOST WRITER

by Mary Danby

Vernon Prewett always began with the title. He found it easier to think of a plot once he had some kind of peg to hang the story on. He wound a sheet of paper into the typewriter.

"The Phantom of Craggy Creek," he typed. No, that was too similar to last month's title: "The Spectre of Misty Mountain". "The Haunted Forest" . . . "Fear at Midnight" . . . "The Moaning Maiden" . . . nothing seemed quite right today. He had been a regular contributor to *Creepy Tales* ever since the magazine's first issue, five years ago, and he had written about sixty stories in that time. He knew from the letters he received from the young readers that his tales were very popular. "Dear Mr Darke," they wrote – he called himself Damon Darke, which he felt gave him a certain supernatural something – "we read your stories every month. They're ever so good. It must be exciting to know so much about ghosts. You've probably seen quite a few." He hadn't, but he was always at the ready. With a small notebook in his pocket wherever he went, he was at all times prepared to record in exact detail the smallest sighting, the merest whiff of ectoplasm.

"Tomb of Evil." That was better. He could use as a setting the old cemetery on the far side of the town, the one with the railings and wrought iron gates, where the older graves were left untended and smothered with weeds and ivy. Yes, very spooky. He'd make this a real chiller, a proper hair-raiser. He knew how children loved a good, shivery read. He'd have a child as the central character, so that the readers would be able to see themselves in that same situation, feel their blood running cold as the tomb of evil yielded up its ghastly contents . . .

He flexed his fingers, and began.

"Will you go and see Gran on your way back from school?" Mrs Bowman asked her son Chris as he scooped up the last spoonful of cornflakes and stood up from the table. "She's in Princess Margaret Ward, just to the right of the main hospital entrance."

"OK," said Chris, pulling on his blazer. "Will they let me in all right?"

"Say you're sixteen but your great-grandfather was a pygmy," suggested his father from the hall. "Come on, I'll give you a lift to school."

"Be home before it gets dark, Chris," Mrs Bowman called, "and tell Gran I'll be in to see her tomorrow." Chris's grandmother was recovering from an operation, and it was quite a trek across town to visit her. Mrs Bowman had been to see her every day, but now Chris could take his turn. The hospital was not too far from his school, and he and his grandmother had always enjoyed each other's company.

Princess Margaret Ward was painted green and white, with bright orange curtain screens for the patients to be private behind. Chris's grandmother was in the second bed on the left, propped up on a hill of white pillows and dressed in a fluffy yellow bedjacket.

"Hello, Gran." Chris bent forward to give her a quick peck and caught the reassuring smell of her face powder. Gran always liked to look her best, even in hospital. Chris sometimes wondered if she hoped to find another husband. She was still quite young – at least, you couldn't say

496

she was *old* – and she had had to live on her own since Grandad had died.

"How are you feeling?" he asked, pulling a chair up beside the bed.

"Getting a few twinges from the stitches," she replied, wincing as she shifted her position, "but I'll soon be right as ninepence."

They chatted for quite a while, then Chris told her he had to go. "I told Mum I'd be back before dark."

"I suppose . . ." his grandmother began, then she paused.

"What, Gran?" Chris waited.

"Well, you wouldn't do something for me, would you? It'd only take you another ten minutes, and it won't be dark quite a while yet." They both looked over to the big window at the end of the ward, through which the sky was a dull grey behind the concrete walls of the physio-therapy block.

"Today's the twentieth. October the twentieth," she went on. "Your grandfather's birthday. He would have been sixty-three."

Chris pictured the broad, almost bald-headed man who smoked a pipe and watched Westerns on the television. After four years, the memory was a little hazy, but Chris could remember the feel of the rough tweed jacket he always wore, and the voice that came rumbling up from the depths somewhere behind his winter waistcoat. "Good boy. Good boy, Chris," he used to say, as if Chris were a dog.

"I've always taken him flowers for his birthday," Chris's grandmother was saying.

"Have you? That's nice," said Chris, then he realized what she was asking. "You want *me* to take them this time, do you?" He felt a pang of unease. He had never been alone in a churchyard before, and his grandfather's grave was right down at the far end of the old cemetery by the river. He didn't like going past the place, let alone into it.

"Oh, Chris, love, would you?" She pointed to a vase of chrysanthemums on her bedside locker. "Your aunt Mavis brought those in today. I'm sure she wouldn't mind . . . Here, wrap them in this paper."

A few minutes later, as he approached the gates of the cemetery, Chris found his tremors of fear were tinged with a spark of excitement. Alone in a graveyard, alone among the dead. It would be a fair old tale to tell his friends. He'd make it sound good, tell them how the wind moaned through the low branches of the trees, how he fancied he heard footsteps behind him on the gravel path . . .

On either side of him, the grass was mown and the edges were well trimmed, but deeper into the cemetery grass and ivy pushed up against the grey headstones and marble memorials. The trees had begun to drop their leaves, and Chris could feel the chill of autumn in the air. He made straight for the plot against the far wall where he knew his grandfather was buried. His mother had brought him here before, and he knew the inscription off by heart. "Graham Hodgkins, 1919–1978, beloved husband and father." There was a space alongside, which was reserved for Chris's grandmother. He wondered vaguely what would happen if she ever married again – which husband would she be buried next to?

A green metal vase stood on the pinkish-grey chippings which covered the grave. Chris took it over to the water tap nearby and filled it, then arranged the flowers as well as he could. As he replaced the vase, he muttered, "Happy Birthday, Grandad," and felt rather silly on hearing the words out loud.

There didn't seem much point in hanging around the

grave, but, despite the uneasiness that made his heart beat slightly faster than usual, he couldn't resist exploring a little deeper into the cemetery before he left. The track branched off to his right, and he could see a stone angel, reading a book, and beyond that a bust of a stern-looking man in a wing collar. When he himself died, Chris thought he'd like something exciting to mark his grave, like a dragon, perhaps, or a lion. To ward off the evil spirits, he told himself. But the idea of dying didn't seem very real. He couldn't imagine it happening to him.

He began to read the words on the tombstones. Some of the carving was very dirty and worn, but he came across some interesting quotes. This one was gloomy:

> *There is a Reaper, whose name is Death,*
> *And with his sickle keen,*
> *He reaps the bearded grain at a breath,*
> *And the flowers that grow between.*

He much preferred:

> *Better by far you should forget and smile,*
> *Than that you should remember and be sad.*

And there were a few verses that were rather more homely. One he liked was:

> *Dearest Alfred*
> *Laid below*
> *Never more*
> *To say Hello*
> *Never more*
> *To say Goodbye*
> *Now you're with*
> *The saints on high.*

The older graves were covered with grass, labelled only by their headstones, and the more recent ones were marked out with a stone border filled with granite or marble chips. Very new graves were high mounds of turf and flowers – sprays and wreaths with cards attached, saying things like: "*Cherished memories of a wonderful wife and mother.*" They made Chris feel sad. Further down the path he came upon some very old headstones, leaning at crazy angles, this way and that, as if they had been pushed up from beneath. Chris shuddered at the thought. There were tombs, too. Huge grey stone coffins with words and pictures carved around the sides. Some were fenced in, as if the occupants were too grand to allow common people near them.

It was beginning to get dark, and Chris knew he should set out for home. He continued along the track, hoping it would lead back to the main path. Every now and then he paused, as something caught his eye. First it was a child's grave, tiny, with a carved cherub at one end: "*Martha Abernethy, aged 6. A bud that never came to blossom.*" Then there was a newly-dug grave, a brown, gaping hole, surrounded by a cloth of fake grass, like greengrocers display their fruit on, to hide the mud. Probably there would be a burial tomorrow.

Then Chris saw a most amazing tomb. It was made of some kind of blackish stone, shiny, with all kinds of strange creatures, half man, half beast, carved on the sides. He leaned over the slab on the top and read the inscription: "*Here lieth the remains of Lord Sebastian Slade, who died in the year 1847. May he rest in peace. Take care if he do not.*" Chris thought this last statement a little odd, almost like something out of "Dracula". Not that he believed in vampires, of course. Witchcraft, now, that was something else. He was always reading about it

in the Sunday papers. Perhaps Lord Sebastian had practised black magic. That would account for the weird
pictures on his tomb. They seemed to Chris very sinister
– a far cry from all the angels and crosses and open books
which adorned the other graves.

Chris opened the tomb. Well, if Lord Sebastian felt like
rising from it he'd have a pretty tough job. The stone slab
looked as though it was heavy as concrete. He put his
hands under the edge and tried to lift it, just to test the
weight.

At the time, he could have sworn he felt a pressure
from underneath, helping him lift the slab, though afterwards he put it all down to his imagination. But however
it happened, the slab suddenly moved sideways. The
pressure caused a crack to appear in the side of the tomb,
and, as the edge began to crumble, the slab toppled off.
Foolishly, Chris tried to hold on to it, but it was much too
heavy, and it fell on top of him, pinning his legs to the
ground. There was a moment of sharp and terrifying pain,
then he lost consciousness.

The daylight waned; a breeze came up and blew the
fallen leaves along the paths; the air grew cold and damp
as a slight fog from the river settled over the cemetery. A
man with a bell had walked up and down, ringing it, to
warn mourners that they must leave before the gates were
locked, but he had not noticed the boy, fallen and still
beneath the grim black slab. In the distance there were
lights, and people going home from work, and appetizing
smells from restaurants, but here in the graveyard there
was darkness, and silence, and the smell of dead leaves,
and dampness.

Chris regained consciousness just as the moon broke
free of the cloud and began to peer through the trees like
a night watchman's lantern. As he gradually remembered,
with a feeling of sick dread, where he was, he became

sharply aware of an agonizing pain in his legs, which made him groan out loud. He closed his eyes, hoping for release once more, but he remained stubbornly awake. He tried to shout, "Help me! Is anybody here? I'm trapped! Help me!" But the only answer was the rumble of buses down the distant high street. "Help me!" His voice was feeble. His arms, when he tried to lift the slab from his legs, were totally without strength. A sudden panic hit him. "Somebody, please!" he called urgently, as loudly as he could, but there was no answer.

Unless . . . yes, there *was* somebody, or something. He could hear them – it – quite near. A kind of snuffling noise, like a dog. Even a dog would be a help, could keep him company. "I'm here," he said hopefully into the darkness.

A low chuckle came from the tomb, and Chris froze. Slowly, slowly, out of the open sepulchre there rose a curl of mist, which became thicker and thicker until it began to form a definite shape. It seemed at first to be a snake, then a dog, then a goat . . . then it grew taller and stronger, and its face was a gaunt white skull. A shadow passed over it, and then it was clearly a man who stood there beside the tomb. He wore black kneebreeches and a white shirt under a black velvet cloak, and his eyes gleamed greenish-yellow in the moonlight. His mouth was open in a wolf-like smile, and Chris could see his teeth glinting white. The boy tried desperately to pull away, but the stone slab held his legs fast, and a red-hot fire of pain forced him to lie back again. "Wh-who are you?" he said bravely.

The figure just smiled even more nastily and stared at him, taunting. Chris could see the outline of the tomb through him. "You're a phantom, you're not real, you can't hurt me!" he cried desperately, but the figure smiled on.

All about him, Chris could hear rustlings and chatterings. The ground beneath him trembled, as if the earth all around were being shaken up. There was a stench of decay in his nostrils. From all over the cemetery, wisps of feathery whiteness arose from the ground and formed themselves into shapes. The wind danced among the dry leaves overhead, and they hissed and whispered. "Ssss . . . Sssss . . . Chrisssss . . . Chrisssss." A pale, bony old lady, dressed in mouldy grey, came around the other side of the tomb, a fearsome shadow, with sharp, cold fingers that pointed at Chris. He could feel the malevolence streaming from her, as her small, hate-filled eyes fastened on to his petrified features. "No . . . No!" Her feet never moved, but he could feel her coming closer and closer.

A youth was there, a sneering apparition in jeans and a torn leather jacket, his coarse face mocking as he lounged against the tomb, and a great laughing giant of a man, red-cheeked and beery, roaring with silent laughter at Chris's predicament. A pretty young wraith-woman came near, leering at him, her lip curled superciliously. She lowered a white, transparent hand to his head, and he felt his hair rise at her icy touch. The air was filled with evil; the spirits had come to claim him as their own, their plaything, and there was no one to save him. "Let me alone. For pity's sake, leave me," he begged, groaning in pain and terror.

All at once, the phantom's eyes left him and were directed at a point behind his shoulder. Slowly, as if yielding to an overpowering force, they began to shrink away, to become wispy. The light in their terrible eyes grew dimmer and dimmer. Soon, they were far away; then they were gone. All except for one. The man in the black cloak had not moved. He still smiled his wolfish smile, but his yellow-green eyes were now filled with fear. In an agony of effort, Chris turned his head to see what or who had come to his aid. A man stood there on the track. He was tall and broad, and his bald head shone in the light of the moon. He wore a thick tweed jacket, and on his face was a look of such strength and fury that Chris cowered from it.

There was a battle of minds, a battle of beings, almost, going on between the two spirits, and Lord Sebastian – if that was, indeed, the identity of the black-cloaked man – was losing. Gradually, with his smile twisted into a snarl, he was retreating. The flesh seemed to melt from his face, revealing once more that awful skull. Then his image grew fainter and fainter, eventually dissolving into a light grey mist that slipped back into the tomb.

The sense of relief was immense. Chris turned to the figure behind him, only to find no one there, but as the cold wind subsided and the smell of autumn returned, he heard a voice in the distance. "Good boy, Chris," it said. "Good boy." Rather as if he were a dog.

He slipped back into unconsciousness, and when next he awoke it was to find his father beside him. The moon was still high, but there was no fear of anything but pain.

"All right, Chris," said his father. "The ambulance is on its way. Just keep still and it won't hurt so much." He felt a cool, rough hand pass across his forehead and the comfort of a warm sweater placed across his chest.

"The tomb, Dad," he muttered. "Something came out of it. Awful. A ghost and that woman, and the boy in the leather jacket . . ."

"Sure, Chris."

"Look in the tomb. Go on. You'll see."

"See what?"

"Lord Sebastian. He's got a black cloak, and someone – it was Grandad – came and sent him back."

"It's the pain," said his father. "The shock. It's probably made you see all sorts of funny things."

Chris shook his head. "Please, Dad. Look in the tomb."

With a sigh, his father got up and peered into the black depths. "Absolutely empty, old son. Not a bone, not an eyelash, not a speck. Probably been empty for years. Oh, listen, here comes the rescue squad. I think they're bringing something to lift this stone off your legs. The ambulance'll be along soon, too. Hurt a bit, when they move you, I expect, but you'll soon be comfy. Be a brave chap, eh?"

A sudden vision of his grandfather crossed Chris's mind. The good, strong spirit that put paid to evil.

"Grandad was brave," he told his father.

"Go on, you were too young to remember," was the reply. "But he was quite a hero in the war, I believe."

The next few minutes were a nightmare of pain. Chris slipped in and out of consciousness as firemen moved the stone slab and ambulancemen lifted him on to a stretcher and carried him through the cemetery. His father kept up a cheerful commentary, to take his mind off it all, and when they reached Chris's grandfather's grave, said: "Next time you put flowers on a grave, you might do it more tidily."

Chris, from his position on the stretcher, couldn't see. "What?" he said, trying to concentrate through a cloud of pain.

"They're tipped out all over the place," his father went on. "Anyone would think Grandad has been turning in his grave."

Chris managed a weak smile. "Perhaps," he murmured, "perhaps he has."

Vernon Prewett sat back from the typewriter and drained the mug of tea that his wife had placed on his desk while he worked. There, that would do nicely. He'd go over it tomorrow and tidy up a few commas and so on, then he'd

505

take it in to the office of *Creepy Tales*. Another story under his belt. Quite a good one, he thought complacently. Ought to give the kids a right old scare this time.

He leant back in his chair and stretched, then he called his dog, which lay curled up in a corner of the room. "Like a walk, Bones?" The dog, instantly awake, fussed around his ankles as he got ready to go out. "I'll be an hour or so, Beryl," he told his wife. "I thought I'd just go by the old cemetery, do a bit of research, as it were." He wanted to look at some of the graves, copy down a few inscriptions. He could add these to his story, and it would seem all the more authentic.

It was beginning to get dark as he approached the wrought iron gates. Better hurry up, he told himself, or the gatekeeper would be coming to lock up. He strode down the main path, then branched off to the left. Bones busied himself inspecting the stonework, while Vernon took out his notebook and began to jot down one or two phrases. "*I am the resurrection and the life*." That was from St John, of course. "*He travels the fastest who travels alone*." Kipling – such a jolly poet.

Ahead of them was a big, dark tomb. Funny, thought Vernon. That's quite like the one I imagined for Lord Sebastian. He made his way towards it.

The dusk was closing in, now, and the night air blew chill around him, making him glad of his overcoat. An owl, waking to the darkness, hooted in the far corner of the cemetery. Owls, thought Vernon. I forgot owls. "Owls," he wrote in his notebook.

Suddenly, Bones uttered a deep, quiet growl. Vernon stiffened. Ahead of them there arose from the black tomb a dark shape, swirling its cloak around itself. He heard a dreadful moaning sound, and Bones began to bark wildly.

"Ah!" shrieked Vernon, dropping his notebook. As he ran back along the path, his dog at his heels, he fancied

506

he could hear feet crunching behind him, and he didn't pause until he reached the pavement outside the railings. He hurried off in the direction of the high street, his face drained of blood and his heart thudding against his ribs.

Back in the cemetery, Smelly Harry, as the old tramp was known, picked up his plastic carrier bag from the bench behind the tomb. It was all very well, sleeping on graveyard benches, but they threw you out at dusk, and with his rheumatism . . . He moaned again and drew his old blanket more tightly around him as he set off down the path.

By the time he'd reached the bright lights of the high street, Vernon Prewett felt calmer. It just goes to show, he said to himself, that supernatural matters should be taken seriously. After all, he'd just had the proof. He'd seen his first ghost. And actually, he prided himself, he'd dealt quite calmly with the situation, recognized the phantasm for what it really was – a spirit creature, a picture on the air.

Still, he could see how a child might have been quite terrified. Perhaps he should tone down that story. It *was* rather strong stuff, and children are so easily scared . . .

The Pit

ANN CHEETHAM

The summer has hardly begun when Oliver Wright is plunged into a terrifying darkness. Gripped by fear when workman Ted Hoskins is reduced to a quivering child at a demolition site, Oliver believes something of immense power has been disturbed. But what?

Caught between two worlds – the confused present and the tragic past – Oliver is forced to let events take over.

£1.95 ☐

Nightmare Park

LINDA HOY

A highly original and atmospheric thriller set around a huge modern theme park, a theme park where teenagers suddenly start to disappear . . .

£1.95 ☐

ARMADA

Barmy Jeffers

J. H. BRENNAN

When schoolboy Barmy Jeffers stumbles through a Möbius Warp into a crazy fantasy world, his main concern is how to get home. He enlists the help of Ben, a dwarf, Bong, a mad cleric, Facecrusher, an awesome fighter, and many other colourful characters. His adventures bring him into contact with many gruesome and devilish creatures, before he finds the one man who can help him return home.

Fast moving and highly amusing adventures.

The
Counter Force
Series

GEORGE ERSKINE & IAN CAMERON

The Counter Force comprises the four Melville children and their friends whom they invited to join forces against an alien force of intelligent electronic cells which live in computers and whose aim is to dominate the world.

ARMADA

Run With the Hare

LINDA NEWBERY

A sensitive and authentic novel exploring the workings of an animal rights group, through the eyes of Elaine, a sixth-form pupil. Elaine becomes involved with the group through her more forceful friend Kate, and soon becomes involved with Mark, an Adult Education student and one of the more sophisticated members of the group. Elaine finds herself painting slogans and sabotaging a fox hunt. Then she and her friends uncover a dog fighting ring – and things turn very nasty.

£1.95 □

Hairline Cracks

JOHN ROBERT TAYLOR

A gritty, tense and fast-paced story of kidnapping, fraud and cover ups. Sam Lydney's mother knows too much. She's realized that a public inquiry into the safety of a nuclear power station has been rigged. Now she's disappeared and Sam's sure she has been kidnapped, he can trust no one except his resourceful friend Mo, and together they are determined to uncover the crooks' operation and, more importantly, find Sam's mother.

£1.95 □

ARMADA

Nancy Drew Mystery Stories

Nancy Drew is the best-known and most-loved girl detective ever. Join her and her best friends, George Fayne and Bess Marvin, in her many thrilling adventures available in Armada.

ARMADA

All these books are available at your local bookshop or newsagent, or can be ordered from the publisher. To order direct from the publishers just tick the title you want and fill in the form below:

Name _____

Address _____

_____

Send to: Collins Childrens Cash Sales
PO Box 11
Falmouth
Cornwall
TR10 9EN

Please enclose a cheque or postal order or debit my Visa/ Access –

Credit card no:

Expiry date:

Signature:

– to the value of the cover price plus:

UK: 60p for the first book, 25p for the second book, plus 15p per copy for each additional book ordered to a maximum charge of £1.90.

BFPO: 60p for the first book, 25p for the second book plus 15p per copy for the next 7 books, thereafter 9p per book.

Overseas and Eire: £1.25 for the first book, 75p for the second book. Thereafter 28p per book.

ARMADA